IMMORTAL

Immortal

Traci L. Slatton

DELTA TRADE PAPERBACKS

IMMORTAL

A Delta Trade Paperback / February 2008

Published by Bantam Dell
A Division of Random House, Inc.
New York, New York

Cover design by Min Choi
Cover images: *St. John the Baptist* (detail) by del Sarto, Andrea (1486–1530),
Palazzo Pitti, Florence, Italy, and *The Arno in Florence with the Ponte Vecchio* (detail)
c. 1745 (oil on canvas) by Bellotto, Bernardo (1770–1780)/Fitzwilliam
Museum, University of Cambridge, UK/Bridgeman Art Library

Book design by Glen M. Edelstein

Library of Congress Cataloging-in-Publication Data
Slatton, Traci L.
Immortal / Traci L. Slatton.
p. cm.
ISBN: 978-0-385-33974-2 (trade pbk.)
1. Orphans—Fiction. 2. Renaissance—Italy—Florence—Fiction. I. Title.
PS3619.L376I46 2008
813'.6—dc22
2007043737

Printed in the United States of America
Published simultaneously in Canada

www.bantamdell.com

BVG 10 9 8 7 6 5 4 3 2 1

FOR

Jessica
Naomi
Madeleine
Julia
and
Sabin

Jesus said, "If you bring forth what is within you,
what you have will save you.
If you do not have that within you,
what you do not have within you will kill you."

Saying 70, The Gospel of Thomas

IMMORTAL

11 June, 1324

Your Grace, I pray you will excuse me for bringing to your
attention a matter which may seem, at first, of little import. But I
am compelled by conscience and by the order of my Confessor,
and by virtue of a promise made in the long-ago days of my youth
to the Holy Father himself, to relate to you an experience in the
very marketplace of Florence. Whilst I shopped for certain fruits of
the season, I was accosted by a weeping woman. She had a heavenly
beauty and hair the color of ripe apricots, that is, golden and blush,
who implored of me if I had seen her son. He was barely more
than a babe, lost from our home, said the lady, weeping. Her
tongue seemed quaint with accent and she wore fine costly garb,
which assured me of some foreign nobility. I answered that I had
not seen such a child, and she was quickly ensconced within a
protective throng of people. These people spoke with an accent I
had heard as a boy, when I had traveled with the Arch-Bishop
Pierre Amiel himself to oversee the righteous crusade of His
Holiness Pope Innocent against the heretics of the Languedoc and
bring down the Synagogue of Satan at Montségur.

   I was compelled to affect a cordial air with a young man, and
by virtue of pleasant conversation, inquired about the lady and her
husband. The young man admitted that he and his fellows espoused
that belief in direct knowing into the nature of God, beginning

with the self, because to know oneself as the spark of light entrapped within matter is to know human nature and human destiny. I knew I was listening to perilous and profane material, in which no right thinking Christian soul could partake without compromising his soul, a diabolical heresy designed to seduce well-meaning folk, and denounced by long-ago church fathers who sought to protect us. But I affected no surprise, as I desired to know the extent of the vileness at hand. The young man whispered that the noble couple was elect and unusual, born of an incorruptible blood.

I have reached this advanced age of ninety years bearing a secret entrusted to me when I was a boy at Montségur. I have long since reached the age when I expect to be called to the feet of Our Lord at any moment, and have no wish to bear the burden of this secret any longer. This lost boy child must, I beseech you, be found and sequestered until manhood, however long that takes, when his body will give him away with signs both subtle and demonical. His breast will bear the very mark of blood heresy, indicting him. It is my most terrible fear that he is one of those whose fleshly being calls into question our Holy Mother Church, threatening even her very existence as the sole source of Our only begotten Lord's will upon the earth. He will instigate beliefs in the minds of men that will damn souls for generations. Indeed, the four corners of the world will founder and split apart if this abomination is allowed to roam unfettered, engendering plagues and scourges that will kill the greater part of mankind. He must be stopped.

My most cordial and humble respects, as always,
Fr. John

PART 1

Chapter 1

MY NAME IS LUCA AND I AM DYING. It's true that every man dies, that cities fade and principalities ebb and whole brilliant civilizations are snuffed out into thin scrims of gray smoke. But I have been different—the blessing and the curse of a Laughing God. These last one hundred eighty years, I have been Luca *Bastardo,* Luca the Bastard, and if I knew little about my origins, I knew about myself that I was exempt from death's call. It was not my doing; my life simply flowed on through the shining city of Florence like the volatile river Arno. The great Leonardo da Vinci once told me that capricious nature took pleasure in creating a man with my lasting youthfulness, to watch the spirit imprisoned within my body struggle with its longing to return to its Source. I don't have the Maestro's brilliance, but in my small opinion, my life has amused the Lord. And if it weren't for the hand of the Inquisitor claiming to do His work, life would use me still.

But now the burns and broken bones, the gangrene

putrefying my leg and nauseating me with its odor, curtail
my time. It's just as well. I have no wish to ramble on like a
braggart, boasting about the great men he befriended, the
beautiful women he touched, the battles he fought, the marvels he witnessed, and his one incomparable love. Those
things are true, and they mark my life, as have wealth and
hunger, sickness and war, victory and shame, magic and
prophecy. But they are not the reason for my story. My story
must be told for other purposes. I offer it to those whose
souls long to know the soul of the world. From almost two
centuries of living may be learned what matters in life, what
is truly valuable upon this earth, and in what music the voice
of the Laughing God leaves behind irony and becomes immortal song.

I NEVER KNEW WHERE I CAME FROM. It was as if I
woke up on the streets of Florence in 1330, a boy already
grown nine years. I was smaller than most physically, perhaps because I never had enough to eat, but alert, of brutal
necessity. In those days I slept in alcoves and under bridges
and scrounged for dropped soldi during the day. I begged
alms from rich women and slid my fingers into the pockets
of well-dressed men. I spread a rag at the feet of elders
alighting from their carriages on rainy days. I emptied chamber pots into the Arno and cleaned brushes for grooms and
chimney sweeps. I climbed up onto high roofs and repaired
terra-cotta tiles. I ran errands for a peddler who knew me to
be quick and dependable. Sometimes I followed a priest
around, chanting Hail Marys and long sections of the Mass
in Latin, because I was a natural mimic who could repeat
whatever I heard, and it amused the priest into rare
Christian charity. I even let some of the older men pull me

under the bridge and stroke me, holding my breath while their greedy hands roamed over my back and buttocks. Anything for a coin for a meal. I was always hungry.

One of my favorite activities was scouring the ground at the market for fruit that rolled off carts and stands. Usually it was abandoned as bruised, dirty, and worthless, but I was never that finicky; I always thought a few dark spots made anything more interesting. Sometimes I found dropped coins, and once a pearl-studded bracelet that, sold, kept me in bread and salted meat for a month. I couldn't visit the same market often, because the *ufficiale della guardia* were always on the lookout for ragamuffins like me and would beat us, or worse, if they caught us. But every week or so I would go early to one of the dozens of markets that served the hundred thousand inhabitants of Florence and let myself be dazzled by the wares. The markets were voluptuous in both scent and appearance: sweet-smelling red apples and piquant speckled apricots, golden rows of thick-crusted breads exuding the warm fragrance of yeast, herb-cured haunches of pig and pink ribs of beef and pale, soft cuts of lamb that smelled like field lavender, thick aromatic wedges of cheese, and clots of yellow-white butter. I glutted my gaze and my nose, promising myself I would one day feast until sated in all of my being. I also calculated how to score precious morsels immediately. Even a few crumbs would stave off the restless night of a groaning belly. Every bite mattered.

My family in those days consisted of two other street urchins of whom I was fond, Massimo and Paolo. Massimo had a clubfoot, droopy ears, and a milky eye that spun off in all directions, and Paolo had the dark cast of a gypsy, reason enough for them to be cast out onto the street. Florence never tolerated imperfection. I myself never knew why I'd been abandoned. Massimo, who was clever, claimed I must be the son of a nobleman's wife by the family friar, a not un-common mishap. It was he who laughingly dubbed me "Luca Bastardo."

"At least they didn't suffocate you!" he teased me, and we had seen enough dead infants tossed into the gutters to know the truth of his words. Whatever my history, I was lucky to live. Physically, there was nothing wrong with me, other than being small and scrawny. I was perfectly formed in all my parts. My appearance was even pleasing. I'd been told many times that my yellow-red hair and peach skin were beautiful, that their contrast with my dark eyes was com-pelling. It was not the kind of thing I listened to when the old men were stroking me. I kept myself occupied dreaming about food, then I took their soldi and bought warm rolls and chunks of cured fish to salve my hunger and my unease.

Those early days were filled with simple intentions: to feed myself, to stay warm and dry, to laugh and to play whenever the opportunity arose. There was a purity to my life that I would experience only one other time, more than a century later, and I would prize those later years fiercely because I knew how life could be despoiled.

I often diverted myself by playing board games with clever Massimo and wrestling with strong Paolo, who had a fierce temperament that matched his gypsy heritage. I al-ways lost to my adopted brothers, until one day when the three of us were playing in the grassy Piazza Santa Maria Novella in the western end of the city. It was a fine spring day, with a faint breeze puffing beneath an endless blue sky and playing in ripples across the silvery-blue Arno, the after-noon before the festival of the Annunciation. The powerful and zealous Dominicans liked to preach there, but that day the piazza had been taken over by throngs of people: boys running and playing; mercenary soldiers called *condottieri* gambling and catcalling; groups of women gossiping, with their girlchildren hanging on their full brocade skirts; wool-workers and shopkeepers strolling out for the midday meal; notaries and bankers manufacturing errands just so they, too, could enjoy the rare day of warmth and high sunshine during *Marzo pazzo,* crazy March. A group of noblemen's sons raced about, practicing swordplay with the sure prerogative of their station. I couldn't help but envy them, they had what every Florentine wanted: good food and well-made clothes, skill with swords and horses, and the certainty of a fine marriage to strengthen their position in society.

The boys wore fine woolen *mantelli* and were thrusting and feinting with blunt wooden swords under the watchful eye of their master, who was famed in Florence for his strategic swordplay. I scooted around to better hear his instructions—I had a thirst for learning, and I remembered whatever I heard. Paolo had other ideas. He picked up a stick from the grass and charged at me, chortling wildly and mimicking the boys.

"Bastardo, defend yourself!" Massimo called from a short distance away, tossing a stick to me. I caught it and spun around just in time to deflect Paolo's thrust. It was a lucky save; Paolo hadn't meant to hurt me, but he was slow in the head and often left bruises. He grinned and I gathered he meant to have some fun at the rich boys' expense, so I bowed, and he bowed back. We lofted our fake swords and danced around each other, pretending to be noblemen's sons, mocking them with exaggerated flourishes and foppish prancing. A nearby group of condottieri laughed, a coarse sound full of derision, and the noble boys bristled.

"Let's teach these street bastards a lesson!" the tallest boy cried, charging. Instantly Paolo and I were surrounded by five wooden swords chopping at our sticks. The condottieri cheered. Paolo had a bull's strength and he knocked down two of the boys. I didn't have his brawn, so I ducked under the blows, leaping out of reach. Paolo fell, blood spurting from his nose, and anger flared through me. I swung my stick at the boys in front of me, hacking futilely, and the stick broke in half. Taunting laughter rose up. Now the condottieri were laughing at me. It made me angrier and I lashed out wildly with what was left of my stick. It was a stupid move. Two boys cut sideways at me at the same time. I was thrown onto my back, ribs sore on both sides and the breath frozen in my chest. The condottieri guffawed.

"Boy, you're going to get yourself killed," said an old man, bending over me. By then a sizable crowd had gathered. Florentines relished nothing more than a lopsided brawl.

"Those boys hurt my friend!" I cried. "And they're laughing at me!" I pointed at the condottieri.

The old man was short and stout and homely, but had lively eyes that seemed to take in everything at once and to understand it all instantly. "Men laugh because God laughs, and right now, God is laughing at you," he said, with a clear-eyed look of empathy. It was a look I'd never before received, a look that made me almost feel like a real person, and his words were graven on my heart. *God laughs,* I thought with wonder. *Yes, that makes sense of what I've seen on the streets.* Those long-ago words have, in fact, made sense of my entire life.

"I don't like when anyone laughs," I sniffled, "and I want to make them stop hurting me and my friend!"

"That broken stick of yours is pitiful." The old man shrugged.

"It's all I've got!"

He shook his head and squatted beside me. "Boy, the solid things you can hold in your hands are never all you've got. They're the least of what belong to you. The qualities inside you, those are what you've really got to defend yourself with."

"All I've got inside me is the street!"

"If that's true, it's a Florentine street! We Florentines have great souls. We're imaginative, creative, spirited; we make the best artists and merchants. That's why we're famous for our sharp wit and intelligence, our *ingegno*. You have it, too, or you wouldn't survive on the streets!" His eyes twinkled, taking in without judgment my rags and filth. "When you're faced with superior strength and numbers, when you're faced with a challenge, you must go inside yourself, find that ingegno, and use it."

"How?" I asked suspiciously, wrapping my arms around my aching rib cage.

"I saw you listening to the sword master before this fracas started. You're clever, if you pay attention to people who know more than you do. You can come up with a sideways strategy, something unexpected, to defend yourself. Surprise, strategy, and subterfuge, those are your weapons!" He gripped my shoulder in warm encouragement.

"Come on, bastarda girl," sneered one of the noble boys who'd knocked me down. "Let's see you wield your broken stick!"

"Against three of them?" I said sotto voce to the man. Fear rippled in my gut and I had to fight to still the quiver in my chin. "They're big and well fed!"

"Ingegno." He shrugged. I nodded and lurched to my feet. He patted my shoulder.

"Here you go, girlie!" One of the boys kicked the broken stick to me. I eyed it and instead of picking it up, I mimicked panic. It wasn't a stretch; I was terrified. The three boys would thrash me to gore if they caught me. A crowd of onlookers circled us, with the ragged line of condottieri standing to the side. Shrieking like a girl, I ran around the boys and behind the condottieri as if fleeing. The crowd railed with hilarity to see me running away, and I took the opportunity to relieve an unheeding condottiere of his dagger. It was a quick, practiced lift out of his belt. Then I charged out from behind the soldiers with the dagger raised high.

"Look, the little bastard's got a tiny bastard sword," quipped one of the condottieri. The dagger I held was kin to the mighty *spada da una mano e mezzo,* the longsword also known as the bastard sword. The other mercenaries howled with laughter at his wit.

The three noble boys simply stared at the dagger, while I ran over to stand beside blood-spattered Paolo, who still lay on the ground, moaning. "Come on!" I challenged, gesturing with the sharp point of the blade. "Who wants to feel my broken stick now? Wary and suddenly unsure, the boys stood frozen and mute. None of them wanted to feel the dagger's prick. It was a standoff.

"Come, boys, you've had enough fun; your master will want to school you," the old man called dryly, allowing the boys to stand down with dignity. They muttered sullenly but dropped their swords and knelt to help their comrades. The sword master, a big, bearded man with hulking arms and thighs, walked by and thumped my chest so hard that I rocked back on my feet.

"Clever." He smiled. "You can come watch whenever I'm training these dunderheads. From a distance, though." He bowed his head to the old man and murmured, "Master." The old man inclined his head, and then turned to me.

"What's inside you is the gate to everything." The old man smiled. "Remember that."

"Maybe God won't laugh at me so much if I use my ingegno," I said shyly, awed at the attention from this stranger who commanded even a famous sword master's respect.

"God just laughs, boy, it's not about you. It has something to do with how life is a divine comedy." He stroked his beard. "Now give the dagger back to the soldier, or your ingegno will win you some fine blows to the head." I laughed and ran over to the hapless condottiere, who hadn't even felt me lift his dagger. I offered it to him hilt first, and he took it with an elaborate bow to me, hand over his heart and head swept low. I bowed back, copying him, and the condottieri laughed again, this time with approval. Almost dizzy with pride, I ran back to help Paolo, who was struggling to sit up. I gave him my hand and he rose to his feet grinning.

"Bastard sword, that's funny," he said, having only just understood the joke. I exchanged a glance with Massimo, who, until now, had been standing off to the side, well out of the fray.

"Let's go by the river and play at dice," Massimo said. "I lifted some off one of the condottieri while they were watching you. He won't miss them for a long time!"

"Oh no." Paolo groaned. "I hate playing against you, Massimo, I never win!" His lower lip pushed out in a pout and his dark brow furrowed.

"Yes, but you always win at wrestling." Massimo smirked. It was true, and I thought that Paolo's victories would be harder won now that I had in my thoughts the old man's advice about ingegno. Then I realized I could use the old man's advice against Massimo, too; ingegno was a tool fit for many occasions. I looked around to thank the man, but he was distant, having passed along the beautiful green-and-white marquetry arches of the unfinished Santa Maria Novella. He must have felt my gaze, because he twisted around and raised a hand in farewell. I waved back, and he disappeared into the church.

Massimo leaned forward, his ears waggling. "I also lifted a few soldi, so we can buy food to eat while we play!"

"Sure, since you're buying," I said slyly, and Paolo laughed again.

"Sure, today I'll buy!" Massimo agreed. He was generous when the mood struck him, though he would hoard his take when it didn't. Today he would share, as long as we were playing one of the board games he loved. He had rummaged his chess board and various pieces of Alquerque and chess from the garbage piles behind *palazzi,* and he had taught us to play, though Paolo didn't have the wit for them and I pre-ferred to work to earn money for food. Massimo himself had learned the games from gypsies, who were amused by the combination of his contorted physiognomy and his clever mind. They took him up as an object of fascination one season, and then they moved on, as gypsies do, leaving him behind. Massimo liked to tell stories about his time with them, and he persisted in their habits. He and I would squat down outside a silk *bottega* on nice days and set up for a few hours of play. After taking in the old man's advice that day on the piazza, I grew to be a worthy opponent, cagey in strategy. I would play in slow moves followed by sudden bold turns that threw Massimo off and left him grumbling about his loss. Massimo, clever as he was, never quite caught on to the value of the unexpected. It was the same with Paolo's penchant for wrestling. He would lock me into a tight hold, but I would shout, *"Ecco, ufficiale!"* His grip would loosen as he turned to see, and I would wriggle out and trip him. Then I'd run like a dog from a surly master with heavy boots. Like Massimo, Paolo wanted to win, but unlike Massimo, Paolo would rain blows on me when he didn't.

When winter came, the three of us shared food and rags and huddled together for warmth. When we grew especially hungry and, therefore, daring in our pursuit of food, we worked together to acquire it. I would engage some well-dressed old woman in conversation, inventing a story to keep her occupied, while Massimo, with his smooth, quick fingers, would empty her money purse of a few coins. Or Paolo would dart out under a carriage's wheels and pretend to have been hit, and Massimo and I would threaten the

driver, insisting that we would set up an outcry to attract ufficiali, priests, and spectators unless he gave us a few soldi.
We had many such schemes for securing a meal, and time,
like a swift-moving river, rolled on in these ingenuous pursuits until the day that caprice struck and the direction of my
life was altered forever.

On that decisive autumn day, I was more ravenous than
usual. It was after a stormy week of stinging rain and lightning that shrieked through cold air. We had spent the week
huddled under the Guelf coat of arms on the church of San
Barnaba in the teeming San Giovanni quarter in the heart of
Florence. I went alone to the Mercato Vecchio late in the
day, when the ufficiali were usually holed up in the *tavernas*
drinking wine. I didn't even stop to covet the *mercato*'s wares;
I had no head for dreaming that afternoon, just a belly that
hadn't been fed in four days. I circled the central butchers'
pavilion, throwing wary glances over my shoulder for any
sign of the police, but I was made bold by the dizzying min-
gled scents of food, fruit, wines, and oils. A good olive oil
gives off a piquant aroma with bitter nutty undertones, and
dried figs smell like honeyed meat. I prowled through stalls,
my eyes sweeping the muddy ground for anything that had
been dropped. At the same time, I looked for an easy mark
amid the bustle of patrons cloaked against the changeable
autumn weather. I soon spied a jittery old woman and her
young granddaughter, plainly but not poorly dressed, with
no maidservant following them to carry their purchases.
They would be absorbed in each other and in the wares, too
busy shopping, squeezing vegetables, sniffing melons, and
counting *dinari* to notice a hand slipping away with a *paniota*.

I followed them, keeping my distance, then stealing closer.
The girl was about my age, nine years, though plumper and
much more innocent. She had wavy chestnut hair tied back
in a red ribbon and a face shaped in a long oval just like her

grandmother. They even moved alike, with the same tilt of their heads and similar hand gestures. For a moment I envied them their obvious closeness. It was a longing of mine to have a family. The closest I had were Massimo and Paolo, who would beat my pickings from me in an instant if they caught me with something desirable. Then I saw the grandmother haggling for some pastries, and the sentiment abandoned me like a discarded husk. There's nothing like hunger to focus the mind.

I was trained entirely on them when someone bumped my shoulder. It was Massimo swiping past, and I groaned. He would want the old woman and girl. I wasn't ready to relinquish them and turned to face my friend. He gave me a quizzical, apologetic look, his crazy blue eye tipping upward and his loose ears waggling. Then he pointed at me and bellowed, "Thief! This boy is a thief!"

My feet were well schooled in fleeing, that being the education I'd had until then, but I was so shocked by Massimo's accusation that I froze. The little girl turned and looked at me, her pink lips dropping open in surprise. I waved my hands to placate Massimo, whose cries were attracting attention. "Thief, thief!" he yelled louder. I stumbled backward—right into the arms of a waiting ufficiale della guardia.

"I've got you, dirty thief!" the ufficiale growled.

"I'm not a thief!" I cried.

"Check his shirt," Massimo urged. "I saw him stuff it in there!"

"There's nothing on me," I argued. But there was a subtle brush against my rib as Massimo leaned into me, pointing and jabbing, and my heart grew cold and quiet. There was something there now. The ufficiale thrust his hand into the tattered sash that bound my shirt.

"A signet ring!" the ufficiale cried. He waved it aloft, gold glinting between his thick fingers. "Where did you get this, scoundrel?"

"I didn't take it!"

"It's mine," a cool voice said, tones of scorn ringing out. The crowd around me settled into a quiet that reeked of distaste. The grandmother pulled the little girl behind her. People pressed back as from a viper as a lean, well-dressed man made his way toward us. "It was in my purse just a short while ago. This young thief picked my pocket."

"I never saw you, sir," I protested, but the ufficiale slapped my ear, hard, so that it popped. Pain and an insistent buzzing swallowed my head. The man who claimed I had stolen his ring stepped closer to me, and I recoiled in fear. Wafting perfume, he bent his face down close to mine, so that I saw the acne pits on his lean cheeks and the brush-strokes in his coiffed dark beard. He had a pointy, protruding chin and a sharp, whittled nose like a blade. I turned my face away, gagging, and struggled in the ufficiale's grip.

"Look at me, thief," he breathed. I slanted my eyes upward. One side of his mouth lifted in a smirk. "You'll do nicely, my fine lost boy." He nodded, then straightened.

"He stole something from me that is more valuable than his miserable life," Bernardo Silvano said. "He belongs to me now. He can work off his debt. That will be fitting punishment for the likes of him." The crowd melted back silently, and Silvano dug his fingers into my shoulders. "Bind him," he instructed the ufficiale, who produced coarse rope with which he jerked my wrists together behind my back. I protested and the ufficiale boxed my ears again. A trickle of blood warmed the pinna of my right ear. I looked, unbelieving and horrified, at Massimo, whom I'd considered a brother. He refused to raise his mismatched eyes to me. The rest of the onlookers turned away, the matter resolved, if unpalatably, in their minds. Silvano leaned over and took Massimo's hand in his own. With his other hand, almost in a caress, Silvano dropped something into Massimo's palm. Metal gleamed, and Massimo quickly clutched the florin to his chest. A whole florin; that would feed him for a month. Was that what I was worth, a month's meals?

"No, Massimo!" I pleaded.

Massimo looked up at me and whispered, "I win!" Then he fled.

The ufficiale shoved me at Silvano. "Take him!" he growled. "Just so he stays out of trouble."

"Trouble doesn't interest me. I have other plans for him," Silvano said coolly. Bile washed up on my tongue. I had never felt so alone and afraid. I jerked wildly away from Silvano, but his long silky fingers hid an uncanny strength, and he held me by the ropes around my wrists. He twisted them upward, forcing my arms into an unnatural position. Pain sliced through my shoulders and I groaned, falling to my knees. I looked around for an escape, for help, but there was none. Everyone had returned to their business. There was an old woman begging alms in a whiny voice, and I knew her from under the Ponte Vecchio, had even shared some scraps with her. Now she wouldn't look at me. Massimo was gone, Paolo nowhere in sight. I thought bitterly that the old man from Piazza Santa Maria Novella was right, that God laughed. And His laughter was cruel and filled with the worst kind of mockery.

Silvano lifted me by my wrists, compelling me forward. "It's not a far walk," he said. "Just by the city walls. I'm sure you know where my beautiful establishment is. Everyone does."

I thought of the discarded bodies, some cut up, always young, that drifted down the Arno from his establishment. "Beautiful isn't what people call your establishment."

"What do people know? Beauty is everywhere, in all things, and comes in many forms," he replied cheerfully. He took up whistling a hymn as we moved through the streets. Twice I wrenched violently to escape him, and twice he caught me by the ropes around my wrists and yanked my arms viciously until I thought they would come out of their sockets. Once I threw myself on the ground, and he boxed my hurt ear so that the blood ran onto my neck. I stumbled forward. The Ponte Vecchio, with its little houses clustered like so many nests, barred the evening sky like a black ribbon stretched across an expanse of yellow silk. The city spread around us in harmonies of gray and ocher, and the hills of Fiesole beyond were already shrouded in the indigo shades of night. Its beauty made exquisite agony of the fate I knew lay ahead. My stomach bucked and heaved with terror, and despite the pain, I stumbled and flopped as much as I dared, desperate to prolong the walk. Silvano was patient, expertly twisting the rope to torture my wrists and hands, and then pressing me forward when I cried out. After some short time we arrived at the city walls, at a palazzo whose immaculate plastered facade belied everything that happened within it. I didn't know the details exactly, and had never wanted to. I had, of course, witnessed all manner of fornication on the streets, but this place represented a darker, deeper level of fleshly sin. I knew from whispered conversations with Paolo and Massimo that the door that was now opening to swallow me belonged to the most famously depraved brothel in all of Tuscany.

Chapter 2

SILENCE GREETED US. It was thick and clotted and overwhelmed me. It scared me as much as Silvano did, made me want to shrink into myself and hide. I wasn't used to silence. The streets of Florence were never quiet. There were always sounds: drunken laughter, whinnying horses, dogs baying, bells ringing in the tower of the Badia Fiorentina, whores calling out, carriage wheels rattling on cobblestone streets, hammers clanging on anvils, boats clanking on the Arno, garbage from windows slopping wetly onto the flagstone street, stone-workers buzzing as they labored on the huge new church of Santa Maria del Fiore that everyone said would one day crown the city. . . . Even at night the streets vibrated with noise. I expected it. More, the babel had become part of me, like threads woven into a cloak make up the pattern of the fabric. This silence that seeped around me when I entered Silvano's brothel was unnatural, poisonous. It was alien to me, alien thing that I was, with no family or name.

Silvano shoved me at two stout women who waited in the foyer. "Feed him and clean him, he smells like sewerage. Put him in Donato's old room. He'll work tonight."

The women nodded and one took my shoulder. She had a moonshaped face, dark brown hair, and slack eyes shot through with red veins. The other woman, younger and paler, with a strange red mark across her cheek, reached around my back, and my wrists popped free. I cradled them to my chest as I watched her pick up the cuttings. Through her filmy white shirt, I saw that her back was crisscrossed with red welts.

"Get rid of the lice," Silvano said, disappearing down the foyer. "He's meant for a fine class. And tend to his ear. Damaged goods fetch a lower price."

Neither woman spoke as they led me through the palazzo. It seemed shrouded in shadows, with windows swathed in heavy fabrics and tall candles flickering, but even in the dark I could see that it was sumptuously furnished. Ornate tapestries decorated the walls and gorgeous carved furniture and painted chests adorned the corners. Despite my dread, I couldn't help but ogle. I had often peeked in windows to sate my curiosity about the way other people, real people, lived, but I'd never actually been inside a palazzo. I gaped at the heavy candelabra and plush carpets, and once I caught a glimpse of someone small slipping behind a door. The women gave me no opportunity to dawdle, but took me straight to an atrium lit brightly with torches and lanterns. A large tub filled with steaming water awaited us. The moonfaced woman untied the sash around my shirt. I wasn't used to such intimacies and I jerked back. Blank-faced and mute, she persisted, and the sash and shirt came off, followed by my breeches. Everything I owned in the world was, after all, a small, filthy pile of rags; even I could see it moving with insects. Shamed, I covered myself with my hands. The paler woman disappeared and returned with a small bottle and some cloth. I grabbed the bottle and took a deep swig of the green olive oil. It was thick and almost sweet on my palate, and I grunted.

"No, not yet," she whispered, taking the bottle back gently but firmly. She motioned to the other woman, who grasped my head and tilted it. Then the paler woman poured a few drops into my injured ear. The oil slid slowly through the canal, and the burning inside my head eased. She tore off a small piece of the cloth, wadded it, and plugged my ear. Then she gestured for me to get into the tub.

"What is this?" I asked, touching the mark on her cheek. A few curls from her blond braid wisped against my fingers.

"A birthmark. Don't worry, it's not one of those that are the devil's kiss," she said.

"I don't believe in the devil," I confided. "A man once told me that God laughs, and I think God's laughter is so cruel that there doesn't need to be a devil."

"Hush, now, boy, don't speak such things, even in this place." She pointed at the tub.

"What's your name?" I asked as I climbed in. I sat and warm water lapped out around me in rings. It was my first bath. On summer days I had swum in the Arno, but that was about relief from the scalding heat. Cleanliness wasn't the goal when I was dodging offal and excrement.

"I'm Simonetta, she's Maria." She smiled a little as she took up a boar-bristle brush from a tray beside the tub, as did the moonfaced Maria. Each also took up cakes of lye soap and set to work lathering me and scrubbing me with the brushes. I yelped and swatted the soap away, because it stung the rashes on my skin and the abrasions on my wrists. Maria rapped my knuckles with the back of the brush and I stopped resisting. The water turned muddy and cool. They soaped up my head, taking care to keep my damaged ear dry. Finally they pulled me out of the tub, still covered in soap, and used pails of water to rinse me. Something made the hair frizzle on the back of my neck. Someone was watching me. I peered into the shadowed corners of the atrium until I saw a young man under a trellis covered with grapevines.

"Hey!" I exclaimed, covering myself with my hands.

"Don't be afraid," he said. "I'm Marco. I always welcome the new children." The women glanced around nervously but then went back to work on me, brushing and rinsing. Marco stepped out of the shadows. He was several years older than me, tall and slim-hipped, with an elegant gait and black hair and black eyes framed by absurdly long lashes. He was quite beautiful, with a face like the porcelain dolls I'd seen in the bags of peddlers. He held something in his hand. "You're the boy from the street?"

"Luca," I said. "Luca Bastardo."

"Don't feel bad about that, we're all bastards here"—he chuckled—"and worse. You hungry?" He tossed the thing in his hand to me. It was a small pastry and I snatched it gratefully from the air and gobbled it. Marco sighed. "He's been planning to take you for a long time, you know. Silvano was waiting until he had use for you, and then last week he got rid of a boy who didn't work well."

"Why me?" I asked, intrigued.

Marco shrugged. "I heard him speak about a beautiful noble woman with hair like yours. She came through Florence looking for her son, and she wept as she asked people if they'd seen him. Silvano always laughed about it."

"I had a mother who looked for me," I said, wonderingly.

"You're lucky, she wanted you. I was left here by my parents. They got three florins for me. That's the most Silvano's ever paid for one of us."

I swallowed the last crumb and licked my fingers. "My friend Massimo only got one florin for me."

"I was worth more than you because I wasn't covered

with dirt and lice," Marco teased, wagging his black eye-brows playfully. I scowled and he shrugged. "Good friend, that Massimo."

It was my turn to shrug. People do what they must to survive. The streets of Florence had taught me that. I shouldn't have been surprised, except perhaps that Massimo hadn't sold me sooner. Trust was not to be indulged in by such as me. Maybe I had once had parents, but for as long as I could remember, I had been alone in a way that other people weren't. "At least it wasn't my parents who sold me!" I said.

"At least I knew my parents," Marco returned, grinning. "Did you ever try to find yours?"

"I never really thought about them," I admitted. "I was just glad they didn't strangle or drown me."

"Sometimes I think it would be better if my parents had killed me, instead of selling me to Silvano. Maybe if I hadn't been so beautiful." Marco's face shuttered with despair, as if it really were made of porcelain, as if he weren't a living thing. It was a look I would see often on the faces of the children at this establishment.

I ventured softly, "Is it bad here?"

"Very bad, but they feed you well," he said flatly. "You can't work if you're not well fed. He's going to beat you soon. Whatever you do, don't resist! And don't scream. He likes that and it'll make him hit you more."

"I've been beaten before and I never screamed," I said, with some pride. I was no doughy girl to shriek at a little pain. Many times I had withstood Paolo's fists when he knew I had bread or meat and he wanted it. I often hid myself when I acquired something. The burnt-out walls of the old granary market at Orto San Michele, or the wooden supports of the Ponte Santa Trinita, those were good hiding places. I would have given anything to be squatting there now. I knew all the hiding places in Florence, all the secret passages and shortcuts. Some of my faith in ingegno trickled back into me and I lifted my chin. "I won't let him beat me! Even if he does, I won't be here long. I'll find a way to get out."

"There's no escape from Silvano!"

"I'll think of something. I'll use ingegno," I said with certainty. "I'll run away."

"He'll find you and bring you back."

"If Silvano knows who my parents are, I'll find them, and they'll protect me," I said vehemently. "Or I'll hide. I know everywhere there is to hide in Florence!"

"No one can protect you from Silvano." Marco looked at me with pity. "There's no leaving this place. You'll see. You have to learn that if you don't do what he wants you to, it will go hard on you. You'll be hurt. You could be killed. He enjoys killing."

"In the Arno, the bodies—" I started. Maria and Simonetta were pouring some flowery scented potion on me and rubbing it into my skin with coarse mitts. They had left lye soap caked in my hair to kill the lice, and my scalp tingled with heat, but I shivered. I remembered the corpse of a young woman, little more than a girl, that I'd seen floating out in the water. She had been famous, a beautiful and desirable courtesan. Everyone knew she had lived here. The ebbing water had exposed her slashed face, ribbons of skin floating out with her hair, and her horribly burnt hands with her arms reaching up out of the water to end in blackened nubs.

"When someone's displeased him, he makes a demonstration. It's always bloody. Don't displease him. Please, Luca Bastardo, take my advice. You seem like someone I could talk to, someone like me who could survive in here. Don't make it worse for yourself."

I stared at Marco. His face was serious. With the single exception of the old man at the Piazza Santa Maria Novella telling me to use ingegno, no one had ever before told me to take care of myself. Now here was Marco pleading with me to do so. Massimo, my brother from the streets, hadn't felt this way. I asked, with some suspicion, "Why do you care what happens to me?"

"Because I care about myself," Marco said, turning away and pacing. "I've been here for eight years. I've learned how to stay alive. Most children break into pieces; they wither and die. I stay alive by protecting what's good inside me. That's all we have in here, and if we're not careful, what we're forced to do makes it go away."

"I don't think people have much goodness inside them," I said, biting off the words.

"Some people do. Not the patrons. That's one of the reasons I'm nice to the other children. It makes me different from the patrons. It gives me something to live for." He lifted his head as if he'd heard something. "Take care of yourself, Luca!" He waved and vanished back into the shadows.

"Shush, we work," Simonetta breathed. A frisson of fear coursed up the back of my neck, but when I looked around, I didn't see anything. Her eyes flicked toward a window and I glanced there. Perhaps I sensed movement out of the corner of my eye, but the window was empty, like a mirror with no one behind it. The suggestive absence terrified me more than if Silvano had stood in front of me. I fought the urge to cover myself. If he knew that I knew he was watching, perhaps it wouldn't please him.

THE LAST PLUM CLOUDS HAD VANISHED into the stars when Simonetta and Maria finally stepped back to survey me. My hair fell in a straight red-blond sheet down my back to my shoulder blades, my skin was scrubbed pink and shiny all over, and a soft musky scent wafted out from me. I held the crook of my arm to my nose and sniffed, smelling myself, feeling myself. Was I still me? I'd never imagined I could look or smell this way. Simonetta licked her thumb and brushed it across my left eyebrow. The inner hairs of that brow bristled straight up; I'd seen that before, on a windless morning when the capricious Arno was flat and silver and showed my face to me. Simonetta scowled at my eyebrow, then shrugged. Maria held out a gauzy yellow *camicia* and I slipped it on, relieved not to be naked. They led me back through the palazzo.

We took a different hall, just as opulent as the first, and came to a dining room. On the table was set a roast boar with an apple in its mouth, a plate of roast fowl, a bowl of steaming bean soup, a small round of bread, and a basket of figs and grapes. The savory smell of rosemary and crispy fat perfumed the air. I ran to the table and grabbed up the soup, gulping it down in loud slurps. It must have been delicious, because the food in that place always was, but all I cared about was assuaging the ache that beat in my blood and stomach. Then I tore into the fowl, ripping off a drumstick with one hand and a hunk of breast meat with the other. I was reaching for the second drumstick when Silvano spoke behind me.

"You eat like a starving dog."

I froze, my fingers still locked into the soft hot meat of the succulent bird. Slowly I drew my hand back and then turned to face Silvano. He stood in the threshold, holding a long, weighted silk sack that swung back and forth like a pendulum. He stepped closer, scrutinizing me. With his free hand he lifted up a lock of my newly clean hair, then let it fall. A quiver started in my spine, but I stilled it before it could grow into a shudder.

"You clean up well," he said, with a satisfied smirk. "I knew you would." He moved his hand in a slow circle so that the lumpy sack swung in a wider arc.

"There are rules in this establishment," Silvano said, his pointy chin quivering with venomous pleasure. "Rules that must be followed at all times." His hand moved faster and the sack picked up speed. "You will be clean and quiet," he said. And then he flicked his wrist, a tiny, expert motion, and the bag blurred toward me. It snapped into my ribs with a force that rocked me on my feet.

I opened my mouth to scream and Marco's words rang in my brain: *"And don't scream. . . . It'll make him hit you more."* So I exhaled slowly through my open mouth. The sack was still circling. Silvano wasn't done; he was going to hit me again. I couldn't help myself. Despite Marco's warnings, I darted around to the other side of the table. Panic like lightning flickered in every limb, every vein. There was nothing but fear of the pain. Silvano tittered and followed me, herding me against the wall.

"You will please the men who come to you." Silvano's wrist shook, and the sack slammed into my gut. I fell to my knees, retching. "Do as you are told, or I will kill you!" He struck me again and again. Water filled up my eyes, but I never uttered a sound. After a while his admonishments took on a disappointed tone. He whipped the sack at me in frustration and then left the room. I lay curled up on my side, clutching my stomach. Tears plopped past my nose, the food I'd just eaten was disgorged on me, and, yes, a pool of urine was spread out around my legs. I had respect for pain ever afterward. It can deprive even the strongest man of his dignity.

When I could see through my bleary eyes, Marco was kneeling over me. "A patron left my room and I saw Silvano going out, so I came to check on you. I was worried about you; some children don't make it through the first beating. But you did well. You didn't scream."

"I wet myself like a little girl and puked like a dog," I said, groaning as he helped me up.

"But you didn't cry out, and it was your first time," Marco consoled me. "Even I cry out sometimes, and I'm the best at taking pain." He handed me a silver cup filled with wine. I took it with a shaking hand, grateful for his kindness. "Drink it all, Luca," he urged me. "Simonetta will clean you and take you to your room. Rest. Silvano will send a patron to you later. Just lie there. That's all they want, in the beginning. Lie there and breathe." I bowed my head over the wine cup, hoping Marco wouldn't see the tears stuttering the purple surface of the wine.

"What's the bag filled with?" I asked.

"Gold florins," Marco said. "They hurt but they don't cut. Come now, drink. It will ease the pain. It will make you stronger."

I managed a deep swallow. "It would have been better if I'd died on the street."

"You can't think that way. You get used to it. Time goes on," Marco said softly. "Come on, you're the bastardo who uses ingegno, that's what you told me."

"What good is ingegno here, now?" I sniffled.

"Use your ingegno to imagine things that will help you survive, like finding your parents." He rose. "I have to go. I have special privileges because I've been here so long, but if I'm late, Silvano beats me. And he doesn't go easy on me, like he did with you." He left quickly, and Simonetta and Maria entered the room, holding rags, brushes, and a clean shirt.

THERE WAS BARELY TIME for me to look around and take in the bed and the little chest. The bed was covered with a red silk coverlet which lay over sheets of yellow cloth. I lifted the sheets to see an unimaginable luxury: a mattress. It was thin and a rip in the corner revealed it to be stuffed with horsehair, but I'd never before slept on one. There was a tall window, but it was heavily draped, like all the other windows in this palazzo. A few tallow candles shed a graceless, wan light. This was my room. I'd never had a room before. Then the door opened and I jumped away from the bed as a barrel-chested man with long curling hair and silver in his beard strode in. He was expensively dressed and shod in calf-leather boots. He was the well-known head of the armorers' guild, and I'd seen him at the market. Or rather, I'd seen him watching me there.

He smiled at me greedily and I thought of how the roast fowl must have felt when I spied it on the table. Terror and humiliation overwhelmed me, and I backed up against the wall. Out on the streets, I could run away when one of the men who paid me a soldi to touch me grew too insistent; here there was no escape. My heart scrambled. I looked around desperately, but there was nowhere to go. The armorer strode over and his hands shook as he reached toward me. I pushed his hands away, but he was strong and wrapped one thick arm around me, pinioning my arms to my sides, and ripped off my shirt. I struggled, but he didn't notice.

"So soft, so beautiful," he murmured, his breath gurgling in his throat. "So young." He fumbled at his breeches and then pushed me facedown onto the bed. It was worse than dying. I screamed and screamed, kept screaming at full volume even when the breath left me. I resisted even though Silvano had made it clear that he would kill me if I did. I would have preferred to be killed, in that moment. I was too shamed to weep and could only close my eyes and pray for death. I realized that God was laughing at me again, and that He was too cruel and uncaring to let me die as I asked.

It was then that I learned that God's mockery sometimes contains shards of kindness, for He threw me a mote of grace. Suddenly, miraculously, I was no longer in Silvano's. All of Florence beyond the palazzo was laid out in front of me, as if I could simply step down into the city streets. But it wasn't just my mind that went there, it was my whole self. The boundaries between physical and imaginary dissolved, and reality seeped into both realms. There was a supernatural vaulting, first of my imagination, then of my senses, and, finally, upon seeing the pigments in the frescoes and hearing the soft voices of the choir, of my entire being into the monumental church of Santa Croce. The *Raising of Drusiana* in the Evangelist's life was spread out before me. I had once crouched down in the pews near a priest telling the story to a Catechism class, telling how Drusiana had so loved St. John and kept his commandments that the saint had resurrected her in the name of the Lord. It thrilled me that devotion like that could result in salvation, and I resolved that one day I, too, would demonstrate that kind of love. Perhaps not for a saint, because saints would have nothing to do with trash like me; perhaps not for a person, though I'd longed to be of noble station and belong to a family and wife of my own; perhaps only for the painting itself.

The painting before me deserved my veneration. Every detail was vibrant and beautiful, from the varied emotions on the faces to the blue sky arching over them. If I put my finger to a cheek or brow, I would feel warm skin. It was as if the artist had painted real people thronged around St. John, and I was one of them, watching faith rewarded with renewed life. The artist must have leapt to that marvelous moment in order to paint it thus, just as I leapt there now.

The door closed and the guildsman departed. I slipped bonelessly to the floor. Tears crusted my face, bile soured my mouth, and whitened blood was smeared on my buttocks. I scooted along the floor to wipe it off. Then I just lay there, hurting, staring at the plastered ceiling. I knew that the guildsman was just the first. There would be others. I'd never think well of myself again. The best I could hope for was simply to live on.

After a while—I never knew how long, because time had changed for me, and would never again be the same— Simonetta came in with a towel and water. She pulled me up and cleaned me with brisk, practiced motions. Then, with sad eyes, she gently kissed my forehead.

"Marco?" I whispered. I didn't quite trust him, though I wanted to, but he had ingegno about this place. He would know what to tell me so I could live with what had just happened to me. Simonetta shook her head.

"I'll bring food," she whispered back. At least I wouldn't starve here.

The many days following that first awful night fell into a rhythm of eating, bathing, working, and sleeping. I felt so disembodied that the rhythm was present but the passage of time wasn't. While I was working, I traveled. Mostly to Santa Croce, where I spent much time examining the frescoes. I discovered details about them that I'd overlooked when I'd seen them physically: the graceful pose of one pair of praying hands, the rapture in a devoted face, stars twinkling in a blue sky so expansive that I almost fell up into it. The paintings were always there for me, the way a family was for another person. I could belong to them, and they to me, in a way that sustained me. What the old man at Santa Maria Novella had told me was wondrously true: the gate was within me. When beauty called me, the gate opened, and I could travel anywhere. I felt lucky.

Sometimes I saw twilight figures on the stairs or darting behind doors, but other than the patrons, whose faces I tried not to look at, and Simonetta and Maria, I didn't see anyone.

Silvano kept us mostly locked alone in our rooms. I sneaked a look out my door whenever it was unlocked and spied condottieri at the end of the corridor. When I was taken from my room for a bath, I noted other condottieri patrolling the brothel grounds; the only way out was past them. There was simply no way to escape. With the silence and the isolation and the oppressive sense of being trapped, I was sad, lonely, and often bored. I was used to plentiful noise and to the boisterous company of Paolo and Massimo. I was used to the freedom of the streets.

One dusk, after about a fortnight, Marco finally ventured out to the atrium. I was glad to see him.

"How's it going, Luca? Found your parents yet?" he asked, his jovial tone belying the black-and-yellow bruise on his cheek.

"Yeah, they're coming for me tomorrow in a gold carriage with twelve white horses."

"Give me a ride?" Marco returned with his ready smile. "I'm so handsome I'll make the carriage look good." I gave him a sardonic look. "I brought you a sweet," he said, tossing it to me. "Though you're getting plump now."

"The patrons wouldn't like it if I looked like I was made out of sticks. They like it that I'm an innocent boy," I noted, sucking on the sweet.

"I thought you were Luca Bastardo from the street, not so innocent." Marco grinned.

"It doesn't matter who I am to them."

"You're right, you don't matter. Realizing that is the start of surviving. So just keep getting fat. You'll keep Silvano happy. Me, I'm going for a walk in the Piazza Santa Croce."

"You're going out?" I asked, astonished, rising partly in the tub.

"Silvano gives me privileges. Because I've been here for so long, and I work good. And because boys look better when they're active outside. They look like, you know, real boys. Regular boys. Patrons like that."

"I didn't know it was possible for one of us to leave this place! You could run away from Florence, escape forever!"

"I have to come back."

"I wouldn't," I said in a quiet voice. Simonetta lifted her big, tired face and stared at me.

"I tried to leave once," she said. Her voice was soft but compelling, because she rarely spoke. "Before this place, I was saving to open a tailoring shop with my cousins. I was a seamstress, I was good at it. My cousins sold me to Silvano for money to open the shop. The patrons didn't like me because I'm not pretty. But I was good at taking care of the children and sewing things, so Silvano kept me. One day the condottieri at the door got drunk and fell asleep, so I snuck out. Silvano caught me at the gate and beat me. I couldn't walk back inside. He left me out there bleeding overnight, then had me dragged in."

I was horrified to think of big, soft Simonetta hurt so badly. "You're pretty to me," I said fiercely, touching her hand. She took my palm and rubbed it gently across her cheek.

"No one's prettier than me," Marco said, with an exaggerated sniff and lift of his nose, which made Simonetta and me smile. Marco ruffled my hair. "Don't worry, Luca, you're almost as handsome as me. But it's your ingegno that makes me like you!" Then he sobered. "Simonetta is lucky. Those bodies in the river, that's how he usually handles escape attempts."

"There must be a way," I argued. "There are places to hide, and people go out into the *contado;* you could get a ride out on a peddler's cart. I used to think about that, but I decided to stay in Florence, where I knew how to take care of myself. How stupid was I? You could dress so you look different. You could disguise yourself. It wouldn't be easy to find you outside the city!"

For a few beats Marco's black eyes were trained on me like a diving falcon's. He came and stood close to me, trailing one of his long, elegant fingers in the bathwater. In a low voice, he asked, "How would I dress differently? I have no money to buy clothes."

"That's easy!" I laughed. "Any beggar will exchange clothes with you. Look in the garbage, or steal from a washerwoman's line. Even some of the churches have clothes. There are a hundred ways to score a camicia and a mantello. No one on the street has to go naked!"

"I could get clothes from the garbage," he mused. "I wouldn't want anyone to know what I was doing, or a report could get back to Silvano. He has a lot of spies."

"Not just paid spies. People owe him favors, so they tell him things," Simonetta warned. "Silvano hears everything that goes on in Florence. He knows everything. It's too dangerous."

"It's more dangerous to stay. Here, death is the only way out! If Marco gets away from Florence, he has a chance," I argued. "Look in the alleys behind the palazzi for clothes. The nobles toss their garbage there. You'll find what's left after the servants have picked through it."

"And after disguising myself, I should go to . . ."

"The Ponte alla Carraia. There are lots of carts there, people coming in from the contado with their wares and going back to the countryside with empty carts," I said.

"There must be a way to free you," he said softly. "You've given me this plan; I can't leave you. I want you to come with me. Neither of us has to be alone in exile from Florence!"

I wanted to believe that Marco could be my family, that he could care about me as I'd once imagined Massimo and Paolo did. Massimo's betrayal made it hard for me to trust anyone, but Marco was kind. He seemed genuine. I nodded with all the earnestness in my being. "How can I convince Silvano to let me go outside, as you do?"

Marco shook his head. "He has to offer it and tell the condottieri to let you pass. For a long time, I wanted to die. So I stopped eating. That's when Silvano let me go out, as if giving me some small freedom would make me grateful to him and I could work better."

"So I won't eat," I said. "I'll starve and look sickly." Even after all the excruciating time I'd spent hungry, it was better than what I faced now.

"That might do it," Marco said slowly. "Patrons won't pay for a sick-looking boy, and he doesn't like to lose money. He'll want you to regain your color. When he lets you go outside, I'll come back to the Ponte alla Carraia. We can go together to Siena or Lucca, start over!"

"Roma," I said. "I always wanted to go there. I can look for my parents there!"

"Why not?" Marco smiled. "I'll make the escape in three days. Today I'll scout around for someone to take me out to the contado. I'll wait two weeks, that'll give you time to fast—"

"I'll start today!"

"Good. Then I'll come back to the city. I won't be able to get word to you, but I'll wait for you at the Ponte alla Carraia. You'll meet me there."

"Bring food," I said anxiously. "After a few weeks of not eating, I won't just look sick, I'll be sick!" I knew that from my years on the street. A week without food made the limbs sluggish, the mind foggy, the will weak. I did not underestimate the power of hunger.

"I'll have food and clothes for you," Marco said, looking determined. "Since you helped me make a plan. I always take care of my friends!"

"We made a plan together with our ingegno," I said, eager for him to feel the bond that I was starting to feel.

"Silvano has more ingegno than anyone," Simonetta whispered. "And his is deadly!"

"It's true," Marco admitted. "No one has ever escaped here. He finds everyone. Always."

"But we'll try," I pressed him. "We have to try!"

"It's worth trying. Maybe it'll work. I'm the lucky sort, it goes with my good looks. Look how lucky I am to meet you, and you have the ingegno to help me escape!" Marco grinned. He flipped me a jaunty salute and spun off. I was left smiling and dreaming that he and I would win freedom together. Perhaps he and I would be real friends, even brothers, as I'd imagined Massimo and I were.

DAYS PASSED THAT I DRANK WATER but ate nothing. It was easy because, after all, I knew how to be hungry; I'd practiced it often enough. But Silvano didn't seem to notice that I was wasting away, and after Marco's fortnight had come and gone, I grew desperate. Sixteen days had passed since I'd taken anything other than water and a few mouthfuls of wine. I was on the verge of being too incapacitated to make it to the Ponte alla Carraia. I cast about for a way to come to Silvano's notice without being beaten, so he would see that I was ailing and needed to be let outdoors. Massimo had betrayed me, but I didn't think Marco was like that, so I trusted that Marco would be waiting with food for me at the bridge.

That night, after the final patron left, while I was still reveling in the graceful rise of St. John soaring to heaven in his ascension, I took action. This patron had taken longer than most. It made me impatient but also permitted me to bask longer in the frescoes. Starvation had enhanced the clarity of my vision and taken my attention away from the humiliation and despair. The colors of the paintings had never seemed so bright, the flesh of the figures so warm and alive. They were truly my brothers and sisters, and their intimacy lent strength to my weakened limbs, so I could pull on my camicia and hose and stumble out the door of my room. I was surprised and encouraged to see no condottieri about. Perhaps it amused a baleful God for my plan to succeed, I thought, as I tottered through the halls of the shrouded palazzo. I was determined to encounter Silvano and wrest from him the privilege of going out. I leaned against the wall to gather my strength.

"Luca, I was coming for you," Simonetta said, appearing in front of me. She stroked my hair gently. "What are you doing out of your room? Be careful, you'll call Silvano's attention to yourself!" She motioned. "Come," she said, taking a candle out of the sconce on the wall. She led me through the long hall. As we passed other doors, she knocked, and motioned the occupants to join us. It was so unusual a happening that, despite the lassitude in my body, I eyed them with unabashed curiosity. Mostly they were children like me, boys and girls in assorted ages, shapes, and sizes. There were pale blonds, redheads, dark gypsies, and even a few Africans with glossy ebony skin over rolling round muscles. There was a slender red-eyed boy whose skin and hair lacked color, like white linen, and a dwarf child who stood barely to my waist. We were all silent, most so demure they didn't even raise their eyes. I wondered how they'd arrived here, if they'd been plucked off the streets like me or sold by their parents, like Marco. Women joined us, mostly young, all beautiful, except for two enormously fat women. Two grown men couldn't have circled the fat women's waists with their arms. I tried to imagine how much they had to eat to grow so huge, and had to stop when I felt weak visualizing a breakfast of sweets with butter and cream and lunch with a pot of soup and an entire haunch of spit-roasted beef. Simonetta turned another corner and brought us to a large door. She threw the sash and led us downstairs.

Torches set in sconces lit our way down worn stone stairs. A little blond, beribboned girl behind me started to cry. I slowed until I was beside her. She seized my hand in a spastic gesture and squeezed. It was the first time anyone had ever turned to me for comfort, and I was unaccountably moved. My chest puffed out with courage. Despite my light-headedness, I squeezed back gently and smiled. She gave me a terrified look out of blue eyes as big as milk bowls and clung to my hand as if it comforted her.

We entered a large cold cellar lit with torches. Flames threw malignant shadows on gray stone walls, and Silvano stood in the center with a group of burly men who had the hardened look of condottieri, the hired soldiers who defended Florence from those old rival cities Pisa and Torino. Silvano's face, with its bladelike nose, looked relaxed and ruddy in the torchlight. He turned abruptly so that he stood in profile to us, and the play of light and shadow on his hair and beard gave the appearance of another face on the side of his head, where his cheek and ear should be. He motioned and two tall, coarse men stepped forward, holding Marco limply between them. Marco looked pale and dazed. His porcelain face was dirty and scraped, his lower lip was split, and his clothes were torn. I gasped, then covered my mouth with my hand.

"This is Marco. You know him," Silvano announced, with a wave of his hand. "He had privileges here, didn't you, beautiful Marco? But you abused my trust." Silvano clucked his tongue in mock disappointment. He circled Marco, who kept his eyes trained on the floor, and I felt fear gripping my chest. Something gleamed white in Silvano's hand. At first I thought he had a giant tooth growing out of that hand, but then he tossed it into the air and caught it in his other hand, and I saw that it was a long, thin knife.

"By my supreme grace, Marco was granted the privilege of going outside," Silvano said. "But he thought he would stay out. He thought he would never come back!" With that Silvano pounced on Marco, slashing. Blood spurted from the flexion fold in the back of Marco's right knee. Marco screamed then, his chin lifting toward the ceiling as he howled in anguish. His leg went limp and he folded over on that side. The children and women around me fell to sobbing, mutely. Something inside me ripped apart. *Don't scream, Marco,* I prayed, *that will incite him.* Marco had been kind to me. Had I repaid him with a fantasy of escape that had ripened into this violence? Then, sickened by my own selfishness, I could not help trembling with a worse question: had Marco told Silvano about my part in his actions? My chest felt like old, charred leaves crumbling into dust.

"Foolish boy." Silvano slashed again. Blood sprayed out, drenching his rich vestments. The men holding Marco guffawed. They released him and Marco collapsed onto the ground, still shrieking and weeping. I held my breath as he fell silent, his dazed eyes searching through the crowd until they found mine. I felt sick, and, though I am still ashamed to admit it, I was silently begging him not to inform on me. I knew that in my heart I was betraying Marco, and I thought that perhaps this is the way Massimo had felt when he sold me. Part of me remembered telling Marco that there wasn't much kindness in people; that included me, I knew now. Perhaps people would be kinder if God were. Then Marco closed his eyes and rolled over onto his face, weeping and moaning into the floor. I felt a relief so potent that it dizzied me. He would not tell on me.

"Bind the wounds." Silvano jerked his chin at Simonetta, and she leapt forward to do his bidding. Silvano's eyes swept the crowd of children and women. "Marco can have his wish. He will live outside my beautiful establishment. He can live anywhere, but he will never walk again." He stepped over Marco's limp form and approached the stairs. We all moved to the side to let him pass. Silvano paused on the second stair. "There is no escape. Anyone who tries to escape will suffer this, and worse! You, come." He pointed at me.

The little blue-eyed girl smothered a sob and released my hand. I shook all over, but I moved quickly to obey Silvano. He said nothing as we ascended the stairs. I followed him back into the dining room where I'd been led on my first evening at the palazzo. This time the table was laden even more profusely with roast meats, pungent cheeses, breads, fat green olives, and wine. I wondered if I was going to be beaten again, if, after all, Marco had told Silvano about my part in his escape plan. I looked around for the weighted silk sack.

Silvano sat at the table, wiped the bloody knife on his shirtfront, and speared a lamb rib. He dropped it on his plate, laid the knife down, and picked up the rib with fastidious fingers. He began to eat with great delicacy. I stood frozen, barely breathing, waiting.

"Would you like something to eat, Bastardo?" he asked. "You aren't really a bastardo, but the name suits you. Some wine? You look pale. Wine will fortify you."

"No, sir," I said.

"Are you sure? Are you ill?"

"I don't think so, sir."

"Is there another food you prefer?" he queried. I shook my head. He frowned. "More sweets?" I shook my head again. "My patrons are pleased with you, except that you look ill. Are you certain you're not ill, boy?" he asked as he dropped the denuded rib onto his plate. "I remember how you stood in this room with your fingers dug into a roast capon, a hungry little animal, clean for the first time since your smug, proud mother lost you." He chuckled almost fondly and the sound sent a shiver up my spine.

"I'm not hungry, sir."

"We can't have you getting thin, Luca. Part of your appeal is your sweet round ass. That's what they tell me." Silvano chuckled again. I looked away. "You're no use if you die of starvation. I will lose profit. Do you think going out into the city would stimulate your appetite?"

"Outside?" I breathed the word, caught in torment. Marco and I had planned for me to be released. But now he was crippled, probably dying. Even if I went outside, neither of us would have our freedom. Silvano truly did have more ingegno than anyone. He was all-seeing and all-knowing. There was a deep ripping in my belly as all the hope I had left in the world dissolved.

"I would like to go out," I whispered. Oh yes, I would like it very much, to have some relief from this rich, mute, lonely prison. I hated myself for the gratitude that surged in me at the prospect of even a small portion of freedom, for I knew I would more willingly let myself be used because of it.

"There are rules." He gave me a meaningful look.

"Yes, sir." I nodded vigorously. "I understand rules. I will follow them exactly."

"You wouldn't want to end up like Marco, would you?"

"No, sir," I squeaked.

"He didn't end up so badly." Silvano shrugged and scratched his narrow, protruding chin under his coiffed beard. "I've sent others out of here into the cool arms of the river. Once she has you in her embrace, you don't last long. He will live on the street. People out there are generous to cripples. Isn't that so, boy?" He didn't really seem to want an

answer and I didn't want to give him one because it would
entail lying, and I neither wanted to lie nor to displease him.
People out there weren't generous. I had worked hard to
collect alms, and still often went hungry.

"The women will give you coins to buy food at the market. You'll like that. I used to watch you there, coveting
everything. You have a lustful and acquisitive nature. Feeding
it will make you plump again." He motioned for Simonetta
to take me back to my room.

"Oh, boy," Silvano called. Simonetta and I froze. "There'll
be extra patrons each week, to pay for your outings," he
said. Simonetta clutched my hand to her soft bosom and we
raced back to my room. I felt as if I were racing from the image of Marco, bloodied and crippled. I was also fleeing my
part in his fate. As horrific as the patrons were, I almost
couldn't wait to travel to Santa Croce. The frescoes would
erase Marco, and perhaps my own guilt, from my mind.

WEEKS LATER I WENT OUT TO VISIT the Franciscan
church of Santa Croce. Winter was drawing on, the city was
cold and windy, and I walked with an ermine-lined mantello
wrapped around myself, the finest garment I had ever worn.
I walked about the interweaving flagstone streets of the
bustling, working-class Santa Croce quarter with my heart
palpitating and my nerves seething in anticipation: I meant
to stand before the frescoes to which I had journeyed so often. I passed wool-dyeing mills and justice courts and a market that I now frequented. Since Silvano had granted me
freedom, I had gone for walks, but I had not returned to my
old haunts. I did not want to see Paolo and Massimo. They
would despise me. I was changed now. I had always been different from the beggars, gypsies, and castoffs I met on the

street, but now I was different even from my old self. I was soiled to the core by the work I did, yet I was bathed and dressed in fine clothes. I was also no longer hungry, and shamefully grateful for that. And I had discovered within myself a secret and wondrous journeying that separated me still further from my old companions and former self.

I walked across the right transept of the church of Santa Croce into the Peruzzi Chapel. Finally, reverently, I stood in front of the frescoes of St. John. They were exactly as I had seen them in my travels. All the details—the musical clusters of figures, the harmony of people with buildings, the ravishing hues, the full-blooded liveliness of flesh and mien— were even as they'd been revealed. It was wondrous, miraculous, and I dropped to my knees in gratitude.

"Do they so move you, boy?" asked a kindly voice.

"Oh!" I was startled out of the rapture and sat backward, foolishly. I twisted around. A few paces back stood a stout and homely old man. He regarded me as curiously as I did him. Then I yelped with recognition. "That day at Santa Maria Novella—you're the ingegno man!"

"An honorific I hope to be worthy of," he answered dryly. "And I recognize you. You're the boy with the broken stick and the bastard dagger. . . ."

"The boy God laughs at." I nodded, scrambling to my feet.

"Don't take it personally," he said. "God laughs at all of us. Life is a divine comedy, and this is how we show our reverence for it." He indicated the paintings.

I nodded again. "They're holy, because they come from the beautiful place."

One of his graying brows lifted. "The beautiful place, eh? What is that?"

"You told me that Florentines had great souls, that there

were qualities inside us that made us who we are," I said. "The beautiful place is where whatever is beautiful comes from; it isn't inside us, but we can get to it from the inside. It's not from this earth at all."

"If the beautiful place isn't within us, how do we express it like this?" The older man waved at the frescoes as he trudged up to stand beside me. "Don't you think it must be within?"

"No," I said, but softly, so as not to offend him. "It's separate from us. The earth is full of ugliness. Like God's laughter is. But beyond that, there's beauty."

"What does a young hound like you know of ugliness?"

I thought of the patrons who opened the door to my room. I remembered the blank faces of people who'd walked past me when I was starving and begging for a penny, a scrap of food, anything. I recalled how I myself had silently willed Marco not to reveal my part in his escape attempt. Experience had shown me that there was more ugliness in most men than beauty. I wasn't going to say that to this man who crackled with quick intelligence, though I thought he would understand. "Ugliness is what we get for being human. It's the sin that stains us since the Garden of Eden. The beautiful place is God being kind to us."

He stroked his chin and stared at me. "I had a friend who would have agreed with you. He would have said that beauty expresses the grace of God, and that we see beauty when we are purified enough to see all of God's creation as one seamless unity."

"I'm not purified. I see a lot of evil."

"I daresay my friend Dante is spending a bit of time in purgatory himself these days." The man smiled and it was a soft illumination from his heart, a smile of love and loss that encompassed everything and rejected nothing. I marked it well, resolving immediately that I would one day smile like that.

"So he's dead. Was he a good friend?" I asked, turning to look at St. John ascending.

"Oh yes, a dear friend. A remarkable man and a poet like none other. I miss him still." He sighed. "More than I would miss my family, I think. They're a noisy and expensive lot."

"These are my family and friends." I stretched out my arms as if I could embrace the frescoes. "These will stick with me."

For a time we contemplated the frescoes in silence. Finally he turned to me. "I have an appointment to buy some pigments, boy. Then I must return to work in another city."

"I have work, too," I said, and the words were like ashes on my tongue.

He nodded. "I will return to Florence in a few months. I would like to bring you something. You remind me of one of my children, with these ideas that are bigger than you are, and far too old for your age. . . . If my paintings are going to be your family—"

I gasped. "You're *him*? You're the artist who painted these holy frescoes?"

"Giotto di Bondone, at your service, and almost worthy of this much adulation," he said dryly, shaking his grizzled head.

I fell to my knees. "Master, I didn't know, I would have been more respectful!"

"Nonsense, you silly pup," Giotto said gruffly. He pulled me to my feet with surprising strength in his liver-spotted hands. "Where do I find you, when I return?"

Not at the brothel, no, that would be unbearable. More than anything, I did not want this man whose smile bore a hint of the Lord's grace, this artist of miracle paintings, to know what I was. He would loathe me. I shook my head. "I'll find you, Master."

"See that you do, pup," he said. He cuffed my head playfully and took his leave.

A while later I stumbled out of the chapel, transported with joy at having been spoken to by Giotto himself, master of the frescoes that gave me solace while I was working. He had treated me with kindness and even interest! My feet skipped down to the shining river, under a bridge where I had often slept. I was standing close to the water, which was suddenly dappled and blue, full of mischievous currents and surprising peaks of winter light. Sometimes the Arno rose and washed away the bridges and carried away screaming people, but today it was peaceful in its playfulness, and laughter floated down from the bridge above.

After a while, I came to myself. I was being hailed. "Bastardo," a weak voice was calling. Propped against one of the bridge struts, his useless legs stretched out before him, was Marco.

"Marco!" I ran to him and hugged him tightly. He was pale and dirty, the scrapes on his face were full of pus, and he was much thinner. But he was alive. I asked urgently, "Are you hungry? I'll get food!"

He shook his head. "Not anymore. I was the first few days."

"I'll get you bread and meat!" I scrambled up, prepared to run off and get him something.

"Stay and talk with me, Luca. I always liked to talk to you." Marco made a weak gesture with his muddy hand. I sat down beside him. "He let you go outside. Our plan worked. For you."

My throat constricted, but I forced out the words. "Marco, I'm so sorry. I didn't know this would happen to you!"

"At least I'm not working anymore! That's something. You may be able to walk, but you still have to work." He laughed bitterly.

"Are you surviving out here? How is it?"

His long lashes fluttered down. "The streets of Florence are not kind to cripples."

"I know. But I'll bring you food every time he lets me out," I promised.

Marco opened his sunken eyes and smiled. "You would do that, I know. Bring me food and talk to me as if I mattered, as if I was still special."

"Of course you're still special! You matter a lot!" I said hotly. "Just because you live on the street doesn't mean you don't matter!"

"You're the special one now. You learned from me. You're keeping that thing alive inside you that would have you be kind."

"You were the kind one," I said. "You gave me candies and teased me so I'd laugh and told me how to take a beating so it wasn't as bad as it could be!"

"I did little things for you and the other children because it kept me alive in there. You have to do those things now. Help the other children. Give what you can. Don't hold back, give everything, anything! That's how you save yourself!"

"I want to save *you* now!" I cried.

"You can save me, but not with food." Marco's black eyes were like spears into me.

"Water? Wine?" I asked. "Tell me!"

"Freedom." He smiled as he said the word, then pushed himself upright with his bony arms. "Help me into the river."

"No!" I rocked back on my heels, shocked and understanding. "Don't ask that of me!"

"You owe me, Luca Bastardo," he said, with finality. "I didn't tell Silvano about you."

"This is no escape, Marco! You're alive! You said yourself, at least you're not working!" I grabbed his shoulders. "Marco, you have to try!" The words poured from my mouth in ragged pleas, but despair filled my gut. Marco's eyes were set and void. I didn't know why I hadn't noticed that before; Marco, who had found a way to survive the brothel, had now yielded to his mutilation. In some way, he'd already left himself, already died.

"I'm not alive," he said, his face distorted with savage anger, his voice like the weighted silk bag swinging at me. "This is a worse prison than Silvano's. The other beggars spit on me, because they know what I used to be. At least the patrons wanted me, even if it was disgusting!"

"You get used to the street. It's better than Silvano's, you're free out here!"

"I was freer at Silvano's! At least there I could command my own body, sometimes, when the patrons weren't using me."

"You can still command your thoughts!" I cried. "Like you told me, think about things that make you feel better! You can travel to wondrous places—"

"I'm a cripple on the streets with no way to get food for myself and no friends out here. I will die, slowly and suffering. You will do this mercy for me," he said coldly. "It's what I need. I would do it myself, but my strength has been gone for two days; in the cold, it won't return. Pull me to the edge and slide me into the river. If I bob up, hold me under."

"It's too terrible!" I cried. "I can't do it!"

Marco glared, holding my eyes with his empty, inscrutable ones. "Yes, you can. I know you, Luca Bastardo. You're the kind who can do whatever he has to. You won't pull back from the edge. That's how you survived out here for so long. That's why you didn't die the first week at Silvano's. Plenty do, you know. Not you. I have a feeling you'll be the only one of us to make it out of Silvano's alive! And not crippled. I can see it in your eyes. You've got something inside you, some quality that makes you endure!"

"You're asking me to kill you," I whispered. And would it matter if I did? No one but me in this world cared about Marco. In the next world, God was snickering; if I fulfilled Marco's request, it would only enhance His joke. There was a hard knot in my chest as we argued, but now it collapsed into waves of sadness.

"I'm asking you to save me! It's what you have to do to save yourself," he returned, in a tone both triumphant and bitter.

I'm not proud of it, but I did it. It was easy, in fact. Marco had only a sparrow's weight and it was nothing for me, strong and well fed as I was, to drag him to the water's edge. It was but a few minutes' labor.

"Go with freedom," I said to him, which was a kind of prayer for forgiveness.

So I rolled him over into the sun-stippled water. Life has a will of its own and wouldn't be denied so easily. Marco's arms splashed and propelled him to the surface gasping and sucking in air. I pushed down firmly on his black-haired head. I held him down until his thrashing stopped and his arms eased out. Marco was right: I was capable of doing whatever needed to be done, no matter how appalling. I had picked pockets and stolen fruit and extorted money for fake in-juries on the streets, and I had submitted to degradation by patrons at the brothel, but this was different, in magnitude and in kind. I willingly became a killer. I could steel myself to anything. To this day it is a characteristic of mine, whether for good or bad or both, and I've lived long enough to un-derstand that a man has to reconcile all sides of his nature. It's not that I don't weep later, just that I will pay the toll that the moment demands. Marco taught me this about myself, and I've never forgotten it or his kindness.

I let go of his head and sat watching the Arno carry his body away. I wondered if I would end similarly, a husk lapped by the river as it floated off. It might be soon; there was no predicting Silvano's whims. I wished with all my heart that someone who meant me well would be nearby, so that I did not die scorned and alone, as I had lived. Perhaps some friend would return the service I had just performed for Marco and yield me to the river. I did not know then that life had other plans for me, and that my end would come not through water, but through flame.

Chapter 3

AFTER MARCO'S DEATH, I took on more of the liberties that had been accorded him. I also took on his pastimes, stealing into other children's rooms to befriend them. Perhaps it was my way of keeping him alive, because I missed him; perhaps it was about assuaging my guilt and sorrow over his death; perhaps it was just that the longer I resided at Silvano's, the more I hated being trapped, and I was determined to wrest as much freedom from my situation as possible. I called on my old skills from the street, my quickness of foot and my ability to fade into the background as I snuck around the palazzo. I was largely undetected, except for once when Silvano caught me inside the room where he kept track of his business accounts. A large wooden desk sat atop a Saracen carpet along with a chest with painted doors that locked.

"Bastardo, you clever boy! You've found your way to the money place!" Silvano's gleeful voice rang out. "In all the years

I've run my beautiful establishment, I've never once found a worker here. You're the first. You are like me, smarter than most! Hungry for wealth."

"I'm not like you, sir," I whispered.

"I think you are. Otherwise, why are you here in the *ab-baco* room, my accounting room?" Silvano came up and caressed my neck. The room wavered in front of me like the air above a scorching hot flagstone on a summer day.

"Why is this room so important?" I asked.

"This is where I keep my abbaco book that records payments and expenses, of course." He smiled. "And my important documents. I even have one that concerns you!" He reached around me to pull out a large book. He opened it and withdrew a sheet of vellum paper. "If you can read it, since you're so clever, I'll let you run away to your room without feeling the kiss of my florins." He thrust the paper into my hands. "Go on, read it!"

I had never before held a sheet of paper, which was far too precious for a street urchin. It was soft and white and covered with strange markings. "What is this?"

"This is a letter that came to me when my condottieri robbed a messenger. Silly messenger was bearing far too much gold. It slowed his horse. My men relieved him of that little problem. And they took this. They couldn't read it, of course, but I could and I was delighted to have it in my possession. Can't you see how important it is? Why, the Pope himself would want to read it! Then hide it where it wouldn't be found for a thousand years! Someday I'll sell it to him. Not just for money, since I have that, but also for a full pardon, for a title, for influence! The Pope will want you enough to pay whatever I ask! I'll let him have you, for a fortune. But not until you grow to manhood. They can't use you before you're grown."

"Why would the Pope want me?" I whispered.

"You can't read it?" he asked, in fake dismay. "When you're so clever as to make your way to my abbaco room? Sneaking around like your old friend Marco? Well, don't worry, a whore like you is valuable for other reasons." He reached out to ruffle my hair. "You are a beautiful commodity, this orange-blond hair and those big dark eyes that are lush and almost purple, like plums, yes? Thank God for other men's lusts, for they make my business thrive." He released me abruptly. I went limp against the desk.

"I've heard other Florentine businessmen, noblemen of wealth and status, say that by exercising caution and vigilance over our affairs, by caring for even the slightest detail, we can avert disaster." Silvano walked around the room to the chest, withdrew a key from his *lucco,* and opened the lock. "I agree with them." He pulled out a lumpy silken bag, and I quailed. His narrow face twisted into a sneer. Then he swung his bag of florins with such force that it made the first beating he'd given me seem tame.

"Don't let me catch you in here again!" he said when he was done. I lay on the floor in a pool of urine, vomit, and tears. I felt pain and shame, but also vast rage. I knew Silvano cared less about my explorations in the palazzo than about the opportunity to beat me, so after a week of recuperating in my room with the walls closing in on me, I was at it again. Silvano's beating only strengthened my resolve to take what liberties I could.

The beating also sharpened my senses, or it taught me to pay exquisite attention to them, because I grew supernaturally alert to Silvano's approach. The lift of a few hairs on the back of my neck told me he was moving toward me. I learned to fold myself into a dark alcove or to twine myself behind the heavy drapery that shrouded all the windows.

There were times when I could have sworn he was thinking about me, because my stomach would tighten and feel light all at once, as if his very intent was a clawed thing reaching for me through the silent, dark palazzo.

As I explored, I looked for the little blond girl who had clung to my hand in the cellar, seeking comfort. I spied her one day when a door in the long hall opened and a big-bellied man, richly dressed, came out. I remembered seeing him at the market with his wife and children and servants. Behind him on the bed sat the little girl. She wore a torn white dress, her little face sagging into numb creases that a thirty-year-old would have worn better. I began to buy her sweets at the market when I went out. I would listen to make sure she was alone, and then I would crack open her door and toss in my offering. Her blue eyes would light up as her fingers closed around the sugared date or the pastry filled with *frutta di bosco*. Patrons often brought sweets to us children—something about a child licking sugar made them wild with lust—but I knew the little girl prized what I brought because I didn't want to do anything to her.

In the meantime, when I went out into Florence, I sought information about Master Giotto. He had said he would return and wanted to see me, and I believed him. He had an honor about him that was obvious even to a mongrel like me. When he came back I wanted to impress him with my knowledge of his incomparable work. On a cold day after Christmas, I went to the monk Friar Pietro, who had once taken me into the Church of Ognissanti to show me the glorious Madonna panel that Giotto had painted there.

"*Asperges me, Domine, hyssopo, et mundabor: lavabis me, et super nivem dealbabor. Misere mei, Deus, secundum magnam misericordiam tuam,*" I called brightly, when I spied him sweeping the path outside the austere stone facade of the old church of

Santa Maria Maggiore. I had no idea what the words meant, but I remembered hearing them at a Mass, and it amused him when I recited the liturgy back to him.

"*Salve*, Bastardo, it's been a long time." Pietro lifted his shaved head and smiled at me through a crowd of passersby. "I don't see you around anymore. It's been weeks since you tried to coax the leftover communion bread from me, or followed me around reciting the Mass."

"*Gloria Patri, et Filio, et Spiritui Sancto. Sicut erat in principio, et nunc, et semper, et in saecula saeculorum,*" I responded. I skipped toward him, winding my way through a perfumed quartet of laughing women who wore fur-lined mantelli that fluttered open to reveal shimmering *cottardite*, full-cut gowns of lavish fabric embroidered with pearls and appliqués. They stopped across the street from the church at a table of dyed wool swaths in the cluster of booths tended by merchants from the Oltrarno, the other side of the Arno, where enclaves of foreigners and Jews lived. I said, "I have some questions for you, Friar Pietro."

"What does an old monk like me know?" He sighed. "Not enough to advance in my order. I'm so incompetent, I'm lucky I can sweep the walk in front of a church on a cold day. I'm not even good enough to work at the monastery at San Salvi, with the other brothers of our worthy Vallombrosan Order."

"You're learned like a *professore*. You know a lot about Master Giotto," I said.

Pietro leaned on his broom, his breath making white fog in the air. His rheumy eyes stared into me. "Master Giotto? What do you want to know about this painter? He's too good for a filthy street cur like you!"

"Of course," I agreed, thinking that I wasn't so filthy anymore, at least on the outside. I wondered if he would notice how polished and plumped up I was, and take in the implications. "But I want to know about Giotto. You said his master was Cimabue. What else do you know?"

"Come." Pietro motioned. He leaned the broom against the wall of the church.

"Eh, monk, that's a pretty boy!" called a condottiere from a hulking pack of them by the church wall. He touched his dagger, hollering, "Look at all that silky yellow hair!" The others laughed raucously and another one whistled.

"Give me a nice tight boy anytime," another leered. "They're cleaner than women! I like 'em even better!"

"That's because no woman would have you," I yelled, even though they were but a short distance from us. He growled and lunged at me, but I darted into the church after the monk.

"Leave the soldiers alone," Pietro chided. "They're a brutish lot, but the city fathers think we need them." We settled into a back pew. "Giotto, eh? Why Giotto?"

"I like the frescoes at Santa Croce," I said.

"You should see the frescoes in Assisi," he said. "He painted a cycle of St. Francis—extraordinary. I hear the paintings in Padua in the chapel on the site of the old Roman arena are splendid, too: the *Last Judgment,* the *Annunciation,* the *Life of the Virgin,* all magnificent, with a physical presence that moves the spirit. But what do you like about the frescoes at Santa Croce, Bastardo?" he pressed. I shrugged. "The naturalism, the composition of his figures, the inventiveness of his allegory?" Pietro chuckled, not expecting me to understand. The language was difficult for me, but because of all the time I'd spent with the frescoes lately, I caught the gist of his meaning. My face must have stayed blank, though, because Pietro put his hand on my shoulder. "You think they're pretty?" he crooned. I nodded.

"I know a few good stories about Master Giotto," Pietro said. He rubbed his chin with a plump hand covered in sagging pale flesh. "I've seen him a few times, never spoken with him. He was born to a poor family in Vespignano, fifty-five years ago."

"Fifty-five!" I gaped. "He's lived a long time!"

"Well, time is different for everyone," Pietro said, his face puckering. "Master Giotto has aged well. Me, not so much, though I was born the same year." I looked at the droopy seams on the monk's face and agreed, though silently. "Of course, I have no vanity; our dear Lord would not want that of the humble monks who serve Him," Pietro added in a pious tone. "When Giotto was sheep-herding for his father, he would draw on flat rocks with a sharpened stone. He drew whatever he saw around him, or what he imagined. The great artist Cimabue happened by the pasture one day and was amazed! The untutored shepherd boy was a draughtsman the like of which Cimabue himself could not equal. He asked Giotto's father at once if the boy could come to live with him, to be instructed and developed as an artist. Just like that, Giotto's life was changed, his destiny set!"

"I've only ever known bad things to change people's lives," I whispered.

"Oh, accidents, catastrophes, yes, those alter lives forever, but miracles happen, too. Do you not think that the lepers healed by our Lord had their lives changed for the better?" Pietro asked. "Or the sick whose demons He cast out? Or the blind to whom He restored sight?"

"I never thought about it," I admitted.

"You need more catechismal instruction, boy," he said, in a tone of indulgence mixed with annoyance. "When you come around, I'll try to teach you. If a street rodent like you can be impressed by Giotto, there's hope for you. Just don't end up like your old amico Massimo."

"Massimo? What?" I jerked upright. Pietro surveyed me curiously.

"You didn't hear? He fought with some lout of a condottiere over possession of a florin. The condottiere said no deformed street urchin could own a whole florin and stabbed him. In the neck, here." Pietro tilted his head and indicated a pulsing spot on the line between his shrunken earlobe and his clavicle. "Poor ugly bastard spurted blood like a pig at the butcher. I put him on the cart to be taken out for a beggar's burial myself. A few months ago."

I closed my eyes and remembered all the times I'd huddled somewhere with Massimo, sharing a scrap of bread or inventing a game to keep ourselves warm in the winter. I wondered if those same memories had struck him when he sold me to Silvano. My stomach clutched up as if I'd eaten bad food, and I couldn't tell if it was because I felt badly for Massimo, or because I didn't. Didn't I owe him grief, after the time we'd shared?

"Don't dwell on it, boy," Pietro said, touching my shoulder. "Did you know that the Holy Father himself sent a courtier here to see what kind of man and painter this Giotto was? The courtier arrived at Giotto's workshop one day as he was hard at work. The courtier requested a drawing to take back to the Pope, and Giotto took out a sheet of paper and a brush with red paint, held his arm close to his body like so"—Pietro demonstrated—"and then, without any help from a compass, he drew a perfect circle! By his own hand!"

"What's a compass?"

Pietro snorted. "An instrument used to draw a circle, Luca Stupido. That's the point; Giotto so excels that he didn't need one. The courtier thought he was being made a fool of, and argued, but at Giotto's insistence, he sent the circle to the Holy Father, along with an explanation of how Giotto had made it. The Pope at once sent for Giotto. Giotto painted such beautiful works for him that the Pope paid him six hundred gold ducats!"

"So much money." I gaped. I tried to imagine a fortune like that, and the freedom and beauty it could buy, but my mind flitted out from within me as if I were trying to contemplate the boundless blue limits of the sky. I wondered if even Silvano could conceive of wealth on that scale.

"Indeed." Pietro patted my shoulder. "That's enough for today, Bastardo; you will strain yourself under the heavy burden of this knowledge."

"I have another question," I said, thinking of how Silvano hinted that he knew my origins. "I've been wondering about my parents. You hear what goes on in Florence, and you've been a monk here for a long time, do you know anything about them? Or where I came from?"

"I remember you only from the streets, Luca. It seemed you were always there, though you look more finely built than the other ragamuffins. The color of your hair is unusual; perhaps you are the son of foreigners. Ask in the Oltrarno, you might find someone who remembers something." He sighed. "I must go back to sweeping the walk, else the abbot will think I can't even do that right. He will use it as an excuse to blame me for how people give more money to the Franciscans and the Dominicans than to our order. Go along," he said. "A street mouse like you has a lot to keep himself busy with. Not that way, idiot," he called up to a novitiate polishing the incense box at the altar. "You'll damage the finish! The abbot will hold me responsible!" He bustled away. I sat for a while, thinking about perfect circles and moments of opportunity that change the direction of a life. I wondered if I would ever have a moment like that, or if my great moment would come at the sharp edge of Silvano's knife.

I walked along the Arno on my way back to Silvano's and stopped at a shop near the Ponte alle Grazie to buy some candied figs for the little blond girl. If I didn't grieve for

Massimo, I could at least feel pity for the little girl, who did not deserve the fate we shared. The door to her room was closed when I arrived, muffling the noises from within. My arms and the back of my neck were smooth, my stomach calm, so I knew that Silvano wasn't looking for me. I waited behind some draperies that made me itch until a prosperous wool merchant emerged from the girl's room. He was yawning and grinning and didn't bother to shut the door as he left. I slipped inside. The little girl stood beside her bed. Her cheek was freshly bruised and a thin line of blood snaked down out of her nose.

"I brought you this," I said, and tossed her the little packet of figs. Her expression remained blank as one hand reached for the figs. The other arm wiped her nose, smearing blood. She popped a fig into her mouth. I said, "My name is Luca. What's yours?"

Her little face brightened, like a candle being lit inside her. "I know you, you held my hand when I was scared and helped me. You are very good. I am Ingrid." She smiled and spoke softly, with an accent I didn't recognize.

"Ingrid," I repeated, smiling back at her. I felt fierce pride that she remembered me, that she thought of me as someone who helped her, as someone who was *good*. She smiled as she took a bite from another fig. I was transfixed by the sweetness with which she admitted to fear. She was like one of the heavenly figures from Giotto's fresco: holy. I couldn't stop myself from approaching her and wiping the blood from her face. We are all so hurt here, I thought, aching. I promised myself I would never let anyone else hurt her, then I felt foolish, because, after all, I was a slave here, too. With that came the familiar prickle on my forearms. I slipped out of her room and ran back to my own. I made it inside only a minute before a patron stalked in.

Later Simonetta came to lead me to the bath. Her pale face seemed more tired than usual.

"Why so tired, Simonetta?" I asked.

"Don't fret about me, Luca," she responded, stroking my hair. "Look at you, is that lice I see again? How is it you keep getting into trouble?"

"That girl Ingrid, where is she from?" I asked, after Simonetta had lathered my head.

"I wouldn't get too close to her." Simonetta frowned. Her long braid lay over one shoulder and I reached up to finger it.

"Why not? What's wrong with her?"

"What's wrong with any of us here?" Simonetta asked, with a rare bitterness. "I overheard Silvano. He's going to sell her to some rich cardinal for a kill."

"A kill?"

"Some patrons like to take a life. If they pay enough, a fortune, Silvano agrees."

I slid down into the warm water, struggling with nausea. It was hard to believe, after all that had been done to me, that something could still shock me. "Why would a cardinal want to kill a little girl?"

"The cardinal feels God wants him to punish women for Eve's sin. He is cleansing the world. He makes the girl suffer the agonies that Eve visited upon mankind. He takes his time, makes it slow and thorough, so it will be holy. He uses fire and blades. The girl must be young and innocent in order to be a proper offering for atonement. He has requested a virgin."

I was sickened. "Ingrid's not that."

"There are ways." Simonetta lowered her voice. She pulled me from the tub and dried me with a large rough cloth. "There's a surgeon who sews a little bit, and an

apothecary who provides a wash to tighten the parts . . . today is Ingrid's last day working. The surgeon is coming tomorrow, so there is time for her to heal before the cardinal
arrives." Simonetta's big face sagged. "She'll be bathed every
day in the apothecary's solution, in preparation."

"When?" I whispered.

"A fortnight, maybe two." Simonetta shrugged. "The cardinal is coming from Avignon."

I couldn't stop myself from remembering Ingrid's soft
hand in mine, and how she'd taken comfort from me. Then I
imagined her bloody and contorted in pain, like Marco
when Silvano cut him. I couldn't help Marco, but I have to
help Ingrid, I thought, stumbling back to my room. I could
barely see the way through the fog of my fear.

"Don't think about it," Simonetta whispered, tucking my
hand into her heart. We stopped in front of my room. She
put a soft plump hand on my shoulder. "Luca . . ."

"What?" I asked, breathlessly.

"Silvano wants me to ask if you enjoyed your old friend
Friar Pietro's lecture on Giotto."

My mouth dropped open. "He knows—how?"

"He knows everything," she cautioned, her birthmark
turning dark red on her round face. "Don't forget that, *caro.*
You must not endanger yourself the way Marco did." She
squeezed my shoulder and was gone, and I went into my
room wondering who Silvano's spies were. I promised myself that I would extend my senses until I could perceive
Silvano's minions as well as I could perceive him, and that
promise almost stilled the quiver of fear in my gut.

TEN DAYS LATER I ROCKED BACK AND FORTH on my
heels in front of St. John the Evangelist at Santa Croce. I was

trying to figure out how to save Ingrid. Time was growing short. I had no plan. I was desperate and sought answers in what I knew was wondrous: Giotto's paintings. If there was anything real in the stories that had inspired them, if there was any truth to the tenderness of color and line and expression, if there was a real saint who basked in the glory of these paintings, then surely that saint would help me. I had seldom prayed before, would curse at God more often than pray over the long years of my life, but I was praying at that moment. "It's not for myself, St. John," I murmured to the ascending figure.

"What's not?" an amused voice inquired. I whirled around.

"Master Giotto!" I exclaimed, so happy to see his short, stout form in the flesh. I learned later that people often had that reaction to him. Though he wasn't beautiful in the way beauty is thought of, and, in fact, his features were decidedly homely, Giotto had such a lively intelligence and such an expansive and humane spirit that he was a joy to behold.

"If it isn't the young pup, wagging his tail in front of my fresco, right where I left him," Giotto teased. His gray brows wiggled at me.

"I've been learning about your work," I said, words tumbling over themselves. "I've been asking the monks—"

"Be careful, you'll educate yourself out of an aesthetic appreciation." One corner of his mouth lifted in irony. "There's something about the natural response that doesn't mediate the truth. I thought I'd find you here. I brought something for you." He held out a small package.

No one had ever given me a gift before—except Marco, who had given me sweets—and I didn't know what to do. This thing was obviously not edible. It was wrapped in glossy, finely woven linen and tied with a red ribbon.

"It won't bite." Giotto gestured with the package. I took it and held it up. "Go on," he encouraged me. So I inhaled deeply and then untied the ribbon. The cloth fell open, revealing a square wooden panel. I stuffed the fabric into my shirt and ran my finger over the panel, realized it was actually two small panels, facing in toward each other. I opened them out and held them side by side. Each painting was about the size of two of my hands in length and width. A luminous Madonna in her starry blue cloak stared out at me from one. On the other stood the Evangelist, and next to him a small young dog, his adoring gaze on the saint.

I dropped to my knees. "Master, I don't deserve these."

"But they are your family," he said, flushing. "If my paintings are going to be that for you, you must have some to take with you wherever you go. I can't get away from my relatives; they adhere to me like tempera on wood, especially when they're broke."

"I have nothing to give you in return," I said, bewildered by his generosity.

"Your admiration is enough," he said, turning toward the large frescoes that graced the chapel. "They are valuable. See that you take care of them."

"I will!" I vowed. Slowly I stood and clutched the two panels to my chest. I was too dazed to say anything, even to stammer out the gratitude that rushed over me in waves as powerful as the Arno when it turns silvery gray and sweeps out of its banks.

"So what was not for yourself?" Giotto asked, his tone mild.

I was holding the panels in trembling hands, taking in every line, every color, every curve. The Madonna's radiant face was so delicately limned as to show both a real woman and a celestial being who could truly be the Mother of Christ. Her eyes were wells of compassion and love. I thought I could fall into them forever. I would have to hide these treasures from Silvano and his all-seeing eyes, find some safe spot in the palazzo to store them. I would have to search hard to find even a tiny inviolate zone in that place.

"Well?" Giotto's curious voice roused me from my reverie. I looked up.

"Freedom."

"You're asking the Evangelist for freedom for someone else? Because you're so free?"

I shook my head. "I have no freedom. But I have a friend who needs, well, freedom and kindness. A great kindness I don't know how to give."

"So you were praying." He nodded. "I see." He fell silent and I went back to the panels, devouring them with my eyes. Giotto said, "My friend Dante would have said that the greatest freedom is love, particularly the love of God. It's what moves the orbs in their spheres. We don't find it in this body. We find it when we surrender the things of the flesh for the will of God."

I thought about the men who came to my room and of Silvano, who did anything they wanted, even committing murder with impunity. I myself had killed a friend, and the only consequence of that act was my own guilt and sadness. God's will appeared to have nothing to do with love, only with pain. I doubted Giotto's words, but he was Giotto, so I took him seriously. I said, "Someone told me that death would give him freedom."

"That's an extreme case," Giotto said, in a somber tone. "Sometimes it's the only way, I suppose. This life on earth can be cruel like that, full of forces beyond our control and our understanding, until death releases us into heaven. I like to think my old friend is free now. But there are other ways to achieve freedom. Devotion, for one."

"What if devotion isn't the answer?" I asked, shuddering. It was the cardinal's devotions that were going to torment Ingrid.

"Then you're right, there's always death." Voices called out and a pair of men beckoned to him from the nave of the church. Giotto turned, sighing, and lifted his hand to acknowledge them. "Duty pursues me. I take leave of you, pup, you and your weighty questions."

"Will I see you again?" I whispered.

"I make my way back to Florence, despite the rich nobles who would have me always painting their portraits and tombs," he said dryly. He trudged toward the men, calling out hearty greetings and embracing them. I turned back to the two incredible paintings that had been so generously gifted to me. My gaze fell on the little dog staring up at St. John. I raced after Giotto.

"Master! Master!" I called. Then I noticed how richly dressed his friends were, and I was overcome with shame. I could not imagine what impression I made on them.

Giotto was unconcerned. "Excuse me, I must speak with my young friend," he said, clapping his companions on their backs. He stepped back toward me and raised an eyebrow.

I swallowed. "The dog . . ."

A sly, pleased smile spread over Giotto's face. "Yes?"

"It's, ah, blond. Like me. Its fur is dark blond with a little orange, like my hair!"

"So this young whelp they call Luca Bastardo is no fool," Giotto said, approving. "You'll find a way to help your friend, don't worry."

I drew myself up and held aloft the two panels. "Thank you," I told him, with all the dignity I had. He winked at me and rejoined his friends.

THE NEXT DAY, as I was working and my spirit was winging into the blue heavens with Giotto's Evangelist, it suddenly came together for me. Perhaps it was another mote of grace from the Laughing God, the deity whose hand was set upon me, alternately squeezing me and flicking me away like a piece of garbage. And like most of the moments of grace that came to me in my long life, it was laced with sorrow. But I suddenly knew how to protect Ingrid from the cardinal's ministrations: as I had freed Marco. But not by the river's auspices. I had to find a way so she didn't suffer, so she didn't even know, so her little heart wouldn't struggle in terror's vicious jaws. And I had to protect myself, as well; Silvano wouldn't forgive the loss of a fortune.

When the patron was done and Simonetta had cleaned me, I was free to go out. I went back to the loose floorboard behind the drapery where I had stashed one of Giotto's panels. I stored them in separate hiding places, in case Silvano discovered one. I touched my forehead reverently to the Madonna's beautiful face. I didn't know if there had been a virgin who had sinlessly borne a child; I didn't believe in anything immaculate. This earth was too tainted for anything pure to have existed upon it. But the beauty with which Giotto had painted her deserved my veneration. I slipped the panel into my tunic and left the palazzo. I hid in a nearby alley and watched to see if anyone had followed me, and when I was certain that none of Silvano's minions had tailed me, I sped on my way.

I knew where I was going because I had run an errand there once, back when I lived on the streets and would do anything for food. Anything except what I was doing now, that is. But once, a stoneworker ambitious to move up in his guild had sent me to a distant part of the city. He'd taken what I'd returned with, smiled, tucked a few soldi into my palm, and told me to forget I'd met him. Within a day, I'd heard that his competitor was dead.

It was a mild winter day with a speckled, milky sky like fragments of a broken robin's egg shell, so I walked along the

banks of the Arno with its wool-washing houses to the Ponte
Vecchio with its small wooden shops and sweeping views
up and down the river. I crossed there to the Oltrarno, the
other side of the Arno. I took a circuitous route to throw off
Silvano's watchers, walking around the church of Santa
Felicita and doubling back over the Ponte Vecchio, then back
to the Oltrarno over the Ponte Santa Trinita. I wandered past
silk workshops and goldsmiths, past the monastery of the
monks of San Romualdo, through narrow streets until I came
to a small bottega deep in the southern environs, the *camoldoli*
where wool carders, beaters, and combers kept their slum
shops and where the foreigners and Jews lived. The shop was
marked as if it were simply one of the dozens of tailors' shops
in Florence, though I knew it was not, and it was shuttered,
but I knew it was open. I rapped on the door impatiently.

A tall blond man opened the door. He saw me and his
eyes narrowed, then his square-jawed face changed. He was
a man from the distant north with a good memory, and he
remembered me. He ushered me into his shop. He slid a
heavy bolt into place behind us as I scanned the room. It was
empty of the assistants who should have been sitting on the
floor with laps full of fabric and thread. There was no long
table for cutting cloth and no wooden mannequins, no clasp
knife and scissors and needles, no bolts of the coarse linen
cloth that tailors used for fittings. There was only a small
rough-hewn table for conducting business and a few chairs.
The northerner turned to me with a sharp look.

"That thing I came for once before, I am charged to obtain more," I said softly.

"You have payment?" he said, in his slow, heavily accented
voice. I pulled the small panel from my shirt. My heart felt a
pang of reluctance and would have held on to the Madonna,
so I brought to mind the image of little Ingrid, cut and
burnt, and the torture that had led Marco to demand his

own death. Ingrid had called me good, the only person in my life to have done so. I had promised myself not to let anyone hurt her. I had to keep my promise. My hands thrust the panel at the northerner. The man exclaimed and sat down at the table, examining it. He ran his fingers over it as if he couldn't restrain himself. He murmured, "This will do."

It will more than do, I thought fiercely. It will buy you out of your unspoken business and send you back to the cold land you came from with a fortune in your hands. I thought about him returning to his distant homeland and remembered that the monk Pietro had told me to ask in the Oltrarno about my own origins. "Sir," I asked politely, "you've been in Florence for a long time?" He nodded, unable to tear his eyes from the panel. I continued, "I was wondering if you'd ever heard of someone losing a child. Years ago. Foreign people, nobles maybe."

He looked up with obvious reluctance. His pale blue eyes fixed on me sharply. "You think you were such a child." I shrugged. He nodded. "There was something, five years ago, maybe. A tale floating about the market. Something about a lost child, lost by the Cathars maybe. I didn't pay attention."

"Who are the Cathars?"

"Heretics, they believe in a good God and an evil God, so the Church kills them." He shook his head. "The parents weren't Cathars. I remember that. They had a secret that kept them in the company of Cathars. But I don't know where they came from or if they have any relation to you." Cradling the panel, he disappeared into a back room and then returned with a small vial.

"I have been told to ask if it can be mixed into a sweet," I said. I looked into the dark doorway beyond which lay my exquisite painting. A part of me mourned. I knew I would prize the remaining panel twice as much.

"It's best that way, it's sweet also," he said. He thrust the vial into my hand. "Use it all. It's one application, painless and undetectable." He unbolted the door and pushed me out onto the steps, into the cold evening of winter in Florence, with a moonless sky rippling into violet and plum clouds and a biting breeze promising a colder day tomorrow. I walked back through narrow streets overlooked by the tower houses and fortified residences, all the private dwellings where happy people lived lives of peace and safety with their loved ones.

At noon the next day Silvano summoned me. He sat at his dining table, sucking the marrow out of veal bones. "I am having a visitor today," he said. My eyes darted around the room, seeking the heavy silk bag. I didn't see it. Silvano tossed down a bone and scratched the underside of his pointy, bearded chin. "An important visitor. Unfortunately, the visitor will be disappointed. In fact," he continued, his tones growing acid, "I must return to him a substantial deposit." He turned his face toward me and his bladelike nose quivered, as if trying to sniff some truth out from me. "That does not please me!"

"Sir?" I said. I clasped my hands behind my back, gripping my palms tightly together, so I could feel myself in my body, alive and still Luca.

Silvano leapt up, pointed his face toward the ceiling, and screamed like a dog at the moon. "One of my girls was found dead this morning! A girl who had been paid for!" He threw his plate of bones at the wall. He howled again and threw a bowl of soup at my head. I ducked so that the bowl missed me, though the hot soup splattered all over me. Panting, Silvano held up his knife and shrieked, "Do you know anything about this girl's death, clever Bastardo?"

"How could I, sir?" I shook my head so hard that my chest rattled, or maybe that was fear batting around my heart the way a cat slapped a mouse before consuming it.

"Perhaps the frescoes at Santa Croce told you." Silvano waved his knife. His face was red with rage. "Perhaps someone at Santa Felicita told you! I think you know all kinds of things. I think you hide things. I think you stay awake at night and think things. I think you have secrets!"

"No, sir," I whispered, backing up to stand in the threshold so I could run, if necessary.

He slammed everything off the table with a sweep of one arm. As dishes clattered, he leapt toward me and held his knife to my throat. I held very still. He dug the tip of his knife in beside my Adam's apple. I felt something wet, a drop of blood, travel down to the hollow of my throat. I wondered if I was about to join Marco and Ingrid, after all; I was surprised at how calm I was. Silvano growled, "I am a very good judge of people, Bastardo, that's why I'm successful."

"Yes, sir," I whispered again.

"I would slit that white throat of yours, maybe gut you like the little pig that you are, even if you are the unholy get of some fancy foreign aristocracy. But I don't want to lose any more of my workers. We can't have our tender family destroyed, can we, Bastardo?" He threw back his head and snarled, his mouth drawing back around his teeth like a rabid dog. His blade shook in my flesh. He screamed, "I have lost a small fortune because of this child's death! It is unacceptable! My reputation for providing whatever my patrons want has been threatened! *Somehow you have caused this!* I know that you snuck into her room. I can't prove anything, but I am going to watch you. Closely. You're to stay inside. No more going out!"

He stepped away, still brandishing his knife. "I don't know where you went after Santa Felicita, but you won't go back for a while." I dipped my head, hiding my eyes so he couldn't see the tears of anger and contempt in them. I pulsed with fury, and with gratitude for still being alive. I also ached for Ingrid, whom I would never again see; something about Silvano's accusations gave her death finality. He didn't say anything else and I backed out the door.

"One more thing, Bastardo," he called. He slammed his fists on the table. "I already know about your parentage. But I'll find out more. I'll know what you know, and what you hide. I'm going to uncover your secrets. All of them!"

Chapter 4

DAYS CRAWLED BONELESSLY INTO MONTHS, which eased like a slow-acting soporific into years, and Marco's words bore fruit. I got used to the work. People get used to anything, if it continues for long enough. It was more than growing accustomed, though; there was also the way I numbed parts of myself to survive, and the way I focused on the tiny shards of grace that came my way: the journeys to great paintings, the freedom to go out when Silvano again granted me that privilege, the good food, the warmth in the wintertime. I thought little about the work itself. It was palatable only once.

A regular patron, a high-ranking member of the guild of furriers, banged open the door to my room, looked at me with lust, and then grabbed his thick left arm. He fell to his knees, groaning and panting. His eyes were wild and foamy spittle wet his beard. Curious, I watched from the bed. The pores on his broad face opened and rivulets of sweat ran down to where his cheek was pressed against the floor.

"Help me," he gasped. "Help me, boy." He had a thick country accent and I shrugged as if I didn't comprehend. I rose and drew aside the heavy crimson, cut-velvet curtain, the fabric of which had been meant for export to a harem in Turkey, but which Silvano had acquired for this establishment. After all, a brothel was the perfect place to flout the sumptuary laws. A triangle of brilliant yellow light bisected the patron's face. It was a late-summer afternoon, after the markets had closed and before dinner; a voluptuous time of day much in demand in this work. The furrier gagged a few times and vomited a small pool of green bile. His pale lips moved in the light, motes of dust spinning above his head, but his voice was no longer audible. I seated myself on the floor near him, drew up my legs, and clasped my knees with my arms, waiting. I was on friendly terms with Death and knew his approach.

I watched the triangle of light creep across the furrier's body until its tail like a scorpion's curved up on his torso and its head rested on the floor. Finally it lazed into a honeyed slant on the floor.

I searched the body. He had a purse with some silver coins. I reached inside his fine silk doublet, snapping off his neck the gold chain with its pearled crucifix that I had seen when he'd once bared his chest. I didn't take his rings; Silvano, who missed nothing, would have noted them. So I took some of the soldi, not all, and hid them with the chain in a hole mice had made behind the chest of drawers. Then I opened the door and called for Simonetta.

She came quickly, in her slow-seeming way, with a question in her eyes. Her glance fell on the furrier and she clucked her tongue and uttered some invectives interspersed with prayers. She turned the body over onto its back and laid her soft hand over the mouth.

"Trouble," she said. "I don't want you hurt, Luca!"

"I didn't kill him," I said, stroking her blond braid.

"Will that matter?" She made the sign of the cross and went to get Silvano. I sat on the bed to wait for him. This waiting wasn't as easy. The passage of time, though shorter, was frozen by the anticipation of pain. I wondered if I could send myself to Giotto's paintings while I was being beaten. Usually I couldn't muster the concentration when Silvano was swinging his sack of florins. But I had new hope: Giotto was in Florence, overseeing the campanile of Santa Maria del Fiore. The cathedral was meant to crown our glorious city, and everyone was excited that purpose had come to it again, after thirty years of lackadaisical construction. So I got to see the great Master every few days, though I didn't speak with him so often. He was busy with matters far more important than a scrap of street trash like me.

"You've killed a patron." Silvano's sly voice interrupted my reverie. He came down the hall in front of Simonetta, who had a fresh bruise under her eye. She kept her gaze on the floor. Her fingers twined together and jerked apart in her full blue silk sleeves. "How clever of you to get out of working! Did you enjoy it? Did you revel in the God-like power to take a life? I find it better than carnal climax. You're like me, Luca, one of the elite, without the qualms that weaken other people."

"I didn't kill him." I stayed where I was on the bed, out of reach of his hands, which could wield a knife faster than I could blink. There was still a tiny white mark on my throat from where he'd insinuated his knife into it when Ingrid had died.

"Too bad, I might have been proud of you emulating me, I might have rewarded you with money to spend in the mercato, you so enjoy that." Silvano bent over the furrier, examining him with quick, dispassionate poking. "You watched

him die for the better part of an hour, I'll wager," he said.
"And I always win my wagers." He opened the furrier's
purse and took the remaining soldi, then slid the rings off
the furrier's fingers, leaving only the signet ring, which the
man's family would claim. Finally he straightened and looked
at me. I met his eyes for a few beats, but it was too much like
staring into the frigid jaws of hell, so I turned away.

"Oh, you're not squeamish, Bastardo," Silvano mused,
stroking his chin.

"My work doesn't allow it," I said. He laughed, a wheez-
ing sound like bat wings against an icy wind, and it was more
terrifying than his words.

"You have an answer for everything," he sneered. "You've
been with me for more than four years, haven't you, boy?"

"Yes, sir." I nodded. Was four years too long? Did Silvano
mean to dispose of me now?

"Yet you look exactly as you did when you arrived: like a
boy of nine years," Silvano said. "You haven't aged a day. It's
not from lack of feeding. You eat almost as much as you
earn." He stepped over the furrier's body and grasped my
chin. He tilted my face up and bent close, as he had the first
day I'd met him. Then he pulled out my camicia and stared at
my chest as if searching it for something. I focused on the
gray in his beard, steeling myself not to quail as his perfume
assailed me. In all the years that followed, because of Silvano
and the patrons, I could never bring myself to wear perfume, even when I had the riches to buy the best of it.

"You should be maturing. You should have wisps of a
beard and a creaky voice. But no, you look exactly as you did
when I first took you. I know that you're the boy from my
document, your hair color is so distinctive, Bastardo, but
maybe it's not that you have special blood. Maybe you're just
a sorcerer. Do you know what we do with sorcerers?"

"They're imprisoned," I said flatly. *But prison would be better than this,* I thought.

"We burn them," he said, mirth in his voice. "A slow process to melt the skin and fry the brain in its skull, to extract every tiny bit of agony. . . . It's not pleasant to be a sorcerer, Bastardo. Lucky for you that I employ you here. Be sure you continue to please my patrons. If I put you back out on the street and give that document to the Church fathers, they'd burn you as an abomination and a witch."

"I'm not a sorcerer, sir. I'm just different," I said.

"Different? You're a freak who doesn't age as the rest of us do." His thin lips curled in a sneer. "And the rest of us do age. Like Simonetta here, she's aging. Isn't that right, Simonetta? You're getting old and you're worried you'll never have children? Isn't that what you said to Maria the other day?" He tossed the questions out without looking at her and she shrank back against the wall of my room, her mouth like a gash in her pale face.

Silvano turned my face from side to side. "Unlike you, I am getting older. Age makes a man think, if he's not a wastrel. I've been thinking. I would like a son, an heir. A son who will marry into one of Florence's best families and enhance the luster of the Silvano name. A son who will ascend to great social heights, when you finally do come to look like a man, and I sell you to the Pope for the social station I deserve!" He released me abruptly and stepped away. "My son will be respected. He won't be a freak whore and sorcerer like you, Bastardo. He will see to my old age." He turned to Simonetta. "There's an ufficiale, Alberti, who is a frequent patron, send for him. I'll explain the situation. And send for a doctor, one of the Hebrew doctors who can be persuaded to agree with my story. Promise him a florin if he says what he's told to. If he tries to refuse, threaten to have his family put out of Florence."

ALMOST ANOTHER YEAR PASSED, and still I hadn't changed. I took to examining myself in the dark mirrors around Silvano's palazzo into which patrons liked to look to tidy themselves before they left. My face remained boyish, unfuzzed, unaltered. What was wrong with me, that I wasn't maturing the way other boys did? Was Silvano right, was I a freak? An abomination? What did his document say, and why was he sure it spoke of me? I knew I wasn't a sorcerer. Was this why I'd been put out on the streets in the first place? Even Giotto commented on it, one day as I walked with him.

It was a summer morning, enlivened by good weather, and thick with the welter of sights, sounds, and smells of the Florence that I loved in those days: flowers blooming in window boxes and piled high on wooden carts from farms in the contado, the outskirts; pretty women in colorful dresses carrying baskets filled with produce like sweet figs and young beans or goods like swaths of our excellent Florentine wool; odds and ends with which regular people with families— whole people—defined their lives. Close to the front of the church of Santa Maria del Fiore, stones were being laid for Giotto's bell tower. The clanging rose up along with the clatter of horse hooves, the chiming of church bells, the creaks and rumbles of wagons, and the distant sussuration of the flour mills and wool-washing shops along the river. Giotto and I were headed for the construction site of Santa Maria del Fiore when the Master stopped, panting from our brisk trotting, and pointed to a stone.

"Do you know what that is, Luca Cuccolo?" His voice was affectionate as he called me "Luca Little Dog," but I knew the affection wasn't for me. It was meant for the flat gray stone in front of us. There were black letters painted on the stone, but I didn't read, so I just shook my head. "That is a timeless place of reverence, a sacred holy place like an altar," Giotto said. "I call it *Sasso di Dante,* Dante's stone. He would sit here for hours, watching the construction, writing his immortal *Commedia,* and thinking."

"Dante the great poet, who was your friend." I nodded. "So this stone is sacred because a great man, a perfect man, sat here often."

"My old friend sinned. In his great work *The Inferno* he admits to lust and pride—"

"Hell must be more crowded than Florence, if everyone who sins with lust and pride confesses it," I commented. A grin split Giotto's homely, wonderful face.

"We're all human. You'll be prey to lust, too, when you grow into a man."

"It isn't my lust that will damn me," I murmured, thinking uneasily of Silvano's insinuations that I was a sorcerer.

Giotto laughed, a deep resonant laugh from his belly that only he could produce. Passersby smiled. "Me neither, pup. That's what the grace of purgatory is for: purification."

"If you believe in purification," I countered dryly. It would take more than purgatory to fit me for heaven.

"I do," Giotto said. "It isn't perfection that makes this stone holy. Dante was a good man, but flawed, as we all are. Dante was even exiled because of corruption, though he wasn't guilty of what they accused him."

"It's about his genius," I reflected, running my hand over the rough surface of the stone. "His mastery as a poet. That's what makes the stone holy, even if he wasn't a perfect man."

"Exactly." Giotto clapped me on the shoulder. "There are no perfect men. Just men with sublime parts. You have good understanding, Luca."

"I don't know," I said slowly. "I thought only things the Church anoints were sacred and holy. Like the bread and wine of communion."

"That's an instance of holiness," Giotto acknowledged. "The deeper mystery of the sacrament, that moment of heaven entering earth, makes it so."

"I don't think heaven ever enters earth, the earth is too full of cruelty and ugliness. If heaven comes here, it must take on the taint of evil, like fabric dipped in dye. But then I haven't had any catechism. I don't even know that I've been baptized," I confessed, with a short laugh.

"Surely your parents had you baptized!" Giotto responded.

I shrugged. "I don't remember them or the life I might have lived before the streets."

"Luca, you must have some idea about your origins!"

I glanced around to make sure no one was eavesdropping. "I heard a tale about foreigners, traveling with Cathars, who lost a child." I had asked around in the Oltrarno about this, but Silvano had caught wind of my queries and made fun of me, so I seldom spoke of it.

"I've heard of the Cathars," Giotto said slowly. "They were a devout group full of Christian virtue. They cared for the sick and the needy, tried to live pure lives that reflected the most basic teachings of Jesus. I never understood why the Church called them heretics and tried to eradicate them. Perhaps because they had a strange idea about the Christ and baptism, that the Lord made the river Jordan flow upward, in reverse. It's a beautiful poetic image, but why destroy a people because of it?"

"Why destroy a people at all?" I asked, enjoying our discussion, as I always did. "Why not leave people alone to follow their own faith as they see fit?"

"There's a truly heretical belief: tolerance." Giotto laughed. Then he shrugged. "I considered many times this river flowing in reverse. I thought it was a demonstration of the Lord's mastery over nature, which is a great primal force, an original source. I go to nature first to find what is sacred and holy."

"The priests don't say things like this," I ventured.

"You're too clever to believe what priests tell you." Giotto laughed again. "You've been around for enough years to have your own thoughts." He tilted his grizzled head, stared at me with his keen eyes. "Though your years don't show in your face. You're like a painting, unchanging and timeless. There's a mystery to you, Bastardo," he said. "You have the face of a boy but the words of an old man who has spent too much time stewing in his own thoughts. Be careful that you don't burn for it. The Church doesn't much like those who think for themselves."

"No one does," I said, recalling Silvano's threatening words. But after all I'd seen and done, I didn't know how I was going to stop myself from stewing in my own thoughts. They were like the flotsam tossed about by a river, bobbing up and down within me, differentiating me from other people, and from the other whores, even more than my work or my youthfulness.

"Be careful who you confide in. I'd hate to see harm come to you," Giotto said, his mouth drooping as a rare air of sadness enveloped him. Then his stout body twanged like a viola string, and his jovial nature returned. "Come, pup, let's see my bell tower. The tribunal fathers complain about the cost, but beauty doesn't come cheap, especially beautiful marble inlay!"

Chapter 5

GIOTTO DIED IN 1337, and all of Florence mourned.
People who had merely heard of him went about with woe-
ful faces and dark vestments. He was buried in Santa Maria
del Fiore, whose walls were finally complete, under a slab of
white marble. I did not attend the lavish public funeral procession or the long Mass. I went a few days later and stood
near the white marble with Giotto's small panel of the
Evangelist and his peach-colored dog hidden in my shirt. I
didn't pray, I just remembered Giotto's paintings. I thought
of his homely face and the way he loved to laugh and how his
cheerfulness drew people to him. And I recalled, and savored,
each of our conversations over the years. My friendship with
Giotto had been the sweetest thing in my life. It made me
feel worthy. It inspired me with hope for other friends, better circumstances, a better self, and even, perhaps, one day,
a wife of my own. It was a lofty ambition for one such as me,
who probably wouldn't make it out of childhood. I didn't

even hope to free myself from Silvano. I had tried once, two years previously, partly as a result of a conversation with Giotto. The painful memory came up unbidden and unwanted, and showed how sorrow was woven into even the brightest tapestries of my life.

It had been an entirely spontaneous attempt at freedom. One afternoon I was out trailing Giotto from a small distance, ducking furtively behind people and rocks and carriages so I didn't bother the Master, when a tall man with a sweet face and lively eyes suddenly pounced up.

"See here, boy, why do you slink around after the Magnus Magister? Are you planning to empty his pocket?" The man's dark eyes danced as his hands held my shoulders firmly.

"No, sir!" I yelped. "I like to watch Master Giotto. I learn things."

"You learn things? What is it you want to learn?" the man asked, releasing me abruptly.

"Everything, I guess," I said, shrugging.

"Everything? A lofty peak to scale. What would be your motive for such an ascent?" He had a faint accent, as if he had come from Florence but didn't live here.

"Why does anyone climb a mountain?" I responded, with some asperity because Giotto had moved on and I wanted to follow him. "To see the view!"

"To see the view indeed!" The tall man burst out laughing. "But don't you think most people climb mountains simply to cross over them to the other side?"

"How would I know what most people do? I'm not most people, I'm me." I straightened my mantello. "May I go now?"

"Yes, by all means, and I shall ponder your desire to ascend a great height merely to see what it has to offer!" He waved me on. I darted after Giotto. I didn't find him at first, and when I did, he was standing with the tall man. Giotto spied me and waved me over.

"This young pup is a friend of mine," Giotto said, clapping me on the shoulder. "Luca, this is my friend Petrarca."

"A fine protégé"—Petrarca winked at me—"whose great desire is to learn everything!"

"I thought your great desire was for freedom, Luca," Giotto teased.

"Yes, that is what I want," I said, softly. "More than anything!"

Giotto laughed and ruffled my hair. "Go on about your rascally ways, then, and pursue freedom with all your heart! The Lord knows you deserve to have what your heart longs for."

Something about Giotto's affection, and his words, and Petrarca's approval, set me mindlessly ablaze with thoughts of freedom. Heedless of the consequences, I threw myself onto a peddler's cart going out of the city. Two condottieri who frequented Silvano's saw me right away. They hauled me out of the cart and dragged me back to Silvano's, hoping for a reward.

"Take your choice of my workers, on the house." Silvano waved, though he never offered his wares for free. He smiled. "This was very naughty, Luca! Simonetta, bring me Bella. And my knife."

"What do you want with Bella, sir?" I whispered, fear hardening my stomach.

"She's a pretty child, isn't she, Luca? Rather like little Ingrid who worked here years ago, with the big blue eyes and milky white skin. Though Bella's not blond. There she is." Silvano nodded. We stood in the carpeted foyer. It was daylight outside, but the windows were sheathed in heavy brocades, so the only light came from candles set in sconces on the wall. Bella was about seven years old, dressed in a sleeveless yellow camicia with her slender white arms bare and her brown hair unbound, as if she'd been sleeping.

"Bella, Luca here has done a very bad thing," Silvano said, taking his knife from Simonetta. Bella peeped at Silvano out of her sky-blue eyes. "He must be taught a lesson." Silvano raised Bella's hand to his lips. Then he held her hand out and extended her index finger. With his other hand, swiftly, he swiped his knife into her finger, and it popped off. Bella and I shrieked as blood spurted from the stump at her knuckle. Simonetta bowed her head, covering her face with her hands as her shoulders shook.

"No, no," screamed Bella, thrashing, trying to pull free from Silvano's grasp.

"Yes," Silvano said, holding out her thumb. "See, Luca doesn't care so much about his own life and limb." Silvano swiped his knife again, and Bella's thumb flew off. "He cares about other children, though, don't you, Luca?"

"Please, stop hurting her," I begged, sobbing. "Hurt me instead!"

"Wouldn't work, and I need you whole to sell to the Church," Silvano said, panting like a man in the throes of lust. He extended her middle finger, though she tried to curl it and begged pitifully for him to stop.

"Please kill me." I writhed on the ground in a pool of Bella's blood. "Bella, I'm so sorry!"

"This is tiresome," Silvano muttered, and a quick slash of his knife left a gaping hole in Bella's throat. It was a relief to watch the blank hand of death wipe her soul out of her eyes. "Luca, learn from this. If you ever try to escape, I will kill another worker, and I won't go easy on her, the way I did with Bella." He stepped away, wiping his blade on his lucco. "Simonetta, clean this mess. And you can go back out, if you wish, Luca," he called airily.

It was the one memory concerning Giotto that held anguish for me, and Bella's murder led me to forbid myself the whole notion of escape, of freedom. I even stopped inquir-

ing about foreigners with a Cathar connection who might
have lost a baby. It wasn't Giotto's fault, of course, and I
found great joy in all my other recollections of him. Only a
few months before his death, he'd shown me a panel he'd
painted for the nuns of San Giorgio. He'd ushered me before
the painting and said nothing until I yelped with delight.

"He has my face! That's me!" I said, pointing to a boy in
the corner, a reverent onlooker.

"A man who knows himself will go far in life." Giotto
laughed.

"I'm not worthy," I murmured.

"Of course you're worthy. Better your face than that of
any of my children or grandchildren. We're not a lot that
God has blessed with beauty, my wife and me least of all."
He rolled his eyes in mock despair. "At least we're a good
match for each other, eh? I don't know what you'll do for a
wife, Luca. There are few women whose beauty will match
your looks. It's a great blessing you've been given, though
you don't seem to value it."

"You have a greater blessing: you create beauty," I had
replied softly, happy to hear him mention a wife for me, as
if I were as worthy as anyone else in marriage-obsessed
Florence. So I'd started to think about how I might one day
earn the love of a wife, what I could do to deserve her. It became a secret motivation of mine.

In our last meeting, Giotto and I walked in the heart of
Florence around the octagonal Baptistery with its colorful
robe of bright marble. He recited from Dante's *Paradiso*:
"That which dies not and that which can die are nothing but
the splendor of that Idea which our Sire, in Loving, begets;
for that living Light which so streams from its shining Source
that . . . of its own goodness gathers the beams, as it were
mirrored, in nine subsistences, remaining forever one."

"That's beautiful, but I don't understand it, how three or

nine can be one," I said. I stopped to admire the facade's geometrical green-and-white patterns. They were encrusted
with the finest white Carrara marble and with green serpen-
tine stone that Giotto had told me was "verde di Prato."

"My old friend admired this ancient building, which was
a Roman temple devoted to Mars. It's so exquisite that we
can't let it alone, but keep making changes to it." Giotto
smiled and stroked his beard. "Arnolfo di Cambio added the
striped facing to the corner pilasters, and its precise forms
are perfectly in keeping with the rhythms of the wall surface." He ran his hand along a stripe, then turned to me.
"Don't fret over Dante's poetry, pup. You're intelligent, you
can think about it, and much will reveal itself to you; that's
the beauty of his art. He's talking about the nine orders of
angels, and how all creation, everything, whether mortal or
immortal, is a form of love streaming like light from the
mind of God. Dante thought of God as light."

"But how can creation, the world, be so filled with evil, if
it's a form of love? Unless the evil is God's joke. You told me
that God laughs, remember? That day on the Piazza Santa
Maria Novella, when I held a broken stick to fight the noble
boys," I said, earnestly. "The day you told me about ingegno.
I never forgot that, and have always tried to live up to your
advice."

Giotto's gray brows rose. "My words made a great impression, though they were scant."

"They were nourishing words!"

"They fell on fertile ground," Giotto replied swiftly. He
gave me an inscrutable look, and then, as if a haze cleared, I
knew what kind of look it was: one of respect.

"Dante's ideas about light make more sense to me than
what he says about love," I said, coloring. "I think it pleases
God's merciless humor to be reflected in beauty and art, and
those are the brothers of light. Like light glows in the marble

of St. John's Baptistery, and you render light in your paintings."

"Dilemmas, God's humor, art as the brother of light . . .
you come out with the strangest ideas. Keep them to yourself, pup. A man with these notions could run into trouble.
At least you're getting taller. You don't look so obviously different, though people will always notice your beauty. I don't
want people talking about you."

I was taller, and I finally looked older, like boys who were
eleven. My body hadn't matured enough to match my years,
but even a little aging allayed my alarm. Silvano still taunted
me with "sorcerer" and "freak," and he inspected my chest
regularly for something that never showed up, which irritated him. But Giotto had noticed me changing, and I was
pleased by it. As I stood at his grave, I remembered the flush
of pleasure his notice had brought. I repeated aloud the
words he had quoted from his friend's poem. I hoped they
were together in paradise, laughing and joking as Giotto was
wont to do. If there was any good in God, He would prize
beauty and light, and Giotto's rendering of those things
should admit him directly to heaven.

A few months later, after the harvest had been brought
in, when the small second figs were being served on tables
and the city was cooling into autumn, Simonetta bore Silvano
a son. He called a priest who frequented the establishment
to baptize the infant, which was proof that enough florins
gifted to the Church would buy anyone anything, even a
solemn baptism of the bastard son of a murderous brothel
keeper. The babe was called Nicolo, and even as a newborn
his features mimicked his father's: he had a narrow, thrusting
chin and a tiny sharp nose.

Simonetta was much weakened from a difficult confine-
ment, and Silvano was so pleased with her that he retired
her to quarters of her own in the private wing. He would

never let her leave, of course; the only way out of his brothel was death, we all knew that. He brought in another woman to take her place. She was a taciturn foreigner with high cheekbones, slant eyes, and thick arms and legs. She spoke little of the language and that only badly, and I didn't like her. She grabbed roughly where Simonetta had always directed with a quiet word or gesture. Still, I was happy for Simonetta. She had left the work without being killed. I snuck to her room to visit her, though it was forbidden for us to enter the private wing. I relied on my senses to alert me to Silvano's approach. Those senses were increasingly, unnaturally keen. I always knew where in the palazzo Silvano was. As time went on, I even knew where in the city he was. I would simply get still and empty, and an image would shimmer into my mind like a reflection coming onto the river as it calmed. I would see a piazza or a bottega or a mercato, and I would know with certainty that Silvano was there. It was as if my fear and hatred linked me to him so palpably that I could always perceive him, no matter where or how far away he was.

So the years continued. The work stayed the same but I seemed immune to it, as I was immune to time and illness. I lived in a kind of abeyance that felt natural to me because it was all that I knew. I was infirm only when I'd been beaten. Even then I recuperated rapidly. Once I was attacked outside the brothel. It was in the midst of the bankruptcies of the London branches of the Bardi and Peruzzi companies and the collapse of the smaller banks, which caused many merchants and small manufacturers of woolen cloth to go out of business. To add to the unrest, Tuscan crops were sparse. Florentines grew surly, angry, and fearful. Business was bad for everyone except Silvano, whose trade always flourished. I went one day to the church of Ognissanti near the Arno to look at the altarpiece, a Madonna and child painted by Giotto. The beautiful Madonna exuded a palpable spiritual gravity, while the baby Christ with his hand upraised in blessing was tender and sad, regal and graceful and open. Giotto had used colors of fabrics from the markets of Florence, which gave the Madonna a sweetly everyday feel. I stumbled out of the Ognissanti church as if my heart had been pierced, so powerful was Giotto's art. I bumped into a man, who snarled and shoved me away.

"*Mi scusi, signore,*" I murmured, and then recognized him as one of my early customers, a merchant who traded in the silks of Cathay.

"Wait! I know you," he snapped. He was a lean man with a stoop whose black hair had grayed since he'd left off giving Silvano his business. His eyes narrowed. "Are you still at Silvano's? That's been ten years . . . you've barely aged! You should be a man now, long since discarded by Bernardo Silvano!"

"You mistake me, signore," I said, trying to brush past him.

"Not so fast!" he cried, grabbing my arm and attracting attention from people walking toward the Ponte alla Carraia. "You're exactly the same as you were then, how is that possible? You haven't aged! This is magic! You're a witch, I say!" A crowd was gathering and I tried to wrench my arm from his grasp.

"You mistake me!" I cried.

"It's true, he's Luca Bastardo from Silvano's, and he hasn't changed in a dozen years!" another voice called. It belonged to a weaver who used to save his soldi for months to afford a visit to Silvano's. The weaver, too, had grown gray.

"Witch! Witch! Sorcerer!" cried several voices.

"It's witchcraft that has impoverished Florence!" cried an anguished voice. "Black magic that has struck down our banks!"

"Black magic has devalued our wools!"

"Black magic has blighted our crops!"

"We're starving and poor because of the witches!" The crowd seethed forward. People shouted and hands struck me. I didn't defend myself. I was used to being hurt, and part of me felt I deserved it. I also knew my body could heal from almost anything; that was part of my freakishness, it was something upon which I could depend. I was beaten to my knees and then gripped roughly by my arms and legs and dragged. I was thrown down in the Piazza d'Ognissanti, facing the Arno. A crowd tossed sticks into a heap.

"Burn him! Burn the witch!" voices were calling. Some people backed away to prepare the pyre and others surged forward to gawk at me. I curled up on my side, covered my head with my arms, closed my eyes, and let myself travel back to the Ognissanti Madonna.

"Audi partem alteram!" a fierce voice cried. "Hear the other side!"

A hush fell over the crowd, but I was only dimly aware of it. I was caught in my voyage. I floated in front of Giotto's beautiful Madonna with her strong, beatific body and the peaceful Christ child in her arms. I was basking in the angelic choir. "Madonna, Madonna," someone was singing. Then I realized it was me. I opened my eyes. A very tall man in his thirties with a sweet face and fine complexion stood near me. I recognized him as the man who had caught me following Giotto years ago—Petrarca, Giotto's friend. He motioned me to sit up. Slowly, painfully, I pushed myself up so I was kneeling. Ugly murmurs rumbled through the crowd.

"If we live good lives, the times are also good. As we are, such are the times," Petrarca said forcefully. He gave me a penetrating look out of impassioned eyes, then turned to the people thronging about us. "St. Augustine himself said that. Killing this boy will not make your wool cloth valuable. It will not make your banks strong again, or your crops flourish!"

"It will please God if we exterminate the witches!" a male voice hollered in response. "With the Lord's pleasure we will prosper again!"

"Yes, yes!" cried many voices.

"No!" Petrarca shouted. "Order your soul; reduce your wants; live in charity; associate in Christian community; obey the laws; trust in Providence—that is what you must do! This will improve your city's lot and make it strong!"

"He's right, this is enough, enough!" The deadly cool voice commanded attention—Silvano had appeared. He walked through the crowd, which parted as if before a snake. I was galled to my core to realize I was glad to see him.

"Signore Petrarca honors our city with his visit, and he is correct. Killing a whore will not bring our money back," Silvano was saying, with his usual sneer. "Go back to work; our business is what has made Florence great, and what will bring it back to greatness!" Silvano bowed to the tall man. "I have read your poetry, signore. I am moved by the delicate emotions of unrequited love you express so brilliantly!"

"I'm glad my poor words have touched you," he responded politely.

"Is it true you have received invitations from both Roma and Paris to receive the crown of the poet laureate?" Silvano asked, in a sycophantic voice.

"You are well informed, signore," Petrarca said, looking away. "I am en route to Roma even now to humbly accept the honors they would bestow on me."

"In my business, I must be well informed," Silvano said slyly. He motioned for the two condottieri attending him to stand me up.

"You're lucky I came for you, Bastardo," Silvano said as

one of the condottieri carried me away. "That prissy poet
wouldn't have been able to dissuade the crowd from a good
burning. It would have been amusing to hear you screaming
as the flames consumed you." His eyes gleamed. "Be grateful!" He touched the welts on my face and frowned. "You're
bruised, but you can still work."

And I was, and I did.

SO I GREW BUT SLOWLY, and by the time I should have
been twenty-seven years and a man well grown, I looked
about thirteen. Silvano's son, Nicolo, who was eleven, was
more developed than me, to Silvano's delight. Nicolo was
no taller, and he was as lean as his father, but he had a coars-
ened voice, a shadow of stubble, and red acne welts on his
cheeks. I sported only fuzz above my lip. At least it was
something. It made Simonetta smile and call me *porcino*,
piglet. Her hair had grown white and her face was now
seamed around her birthmark, though she was the same
quiet, sweet woman I had known for almost twenty years,
years that had passed as if I were asleep and dreaming, years
during which I did not try to escape for fear that Silvano
would kill another child, or perhaps Simonetta herself.

One spring business fell off sharply. I learned that illness
was rife in the city when a patron came to my room. He was
a wool-dyer who had done well and owned a few shops in
the city's more respectable northern outskirts. In the city
center, rich merchants and noblemen kept the rents high, so
most of the dyeing and finishing shops were located in the
worst slums of the Oltrarno. This wool-dyer had a good
opinion of himself because he'd located to better environs.
That kind always felt that I should be gratified by their interest in me. This one instructed me to take off my clothes be-

fore he even touched me. I complied, and he barked at me to turn slowly.

"No *bubboni*," he muttered. "Raise your arms above your head!" I did, and he nodded. "No swellings. Good. Cough, and then spit on the floor." It was not a command I'd heard before, but over the eighteen years that had passed, unusual biddings had become the norm. People were creatures of twisted desires; if man had been created by God and in His image, only an evil deity could sire these lusts. I forced a cough and spat. The wool-dyer eyed it. "No blood," he said, relieved. "You'll do, boy." And the rest of his hour proceeded as usual.

Afterward a new foreign woman came to clean me. I didn't care for her. She was cold and scrawny and spoke in harsh cadences, poking me to get me to obey her. Today I looked her full in the face and asked, "Woman, is there a pox about in the city?"

She shivered. "There's a terrible illness about, Bastardo. It's reached the outskirts of Florence. People are afraid. They're staying indoors, even leaving the city!"

"What kind of illness?"

"They call it the Black Death," she whispered. "Some people have a terrible fever and spit up blood, and they die by the third day. Others get black swellings, bubboni, before they die. They say in countries in the East, more than half are dead! Even as many as eight in ten!"

"There was a plague eight years ago, and many survived it," I said.

She shook her head. "This one kills everyone who takes ill. Everyone!"

The next month, with spring easing into summer, Silvano called me into the dining room, where he and Nicolo sat playing at dice. "I'll teach you not to play stupidly, son!" he was saying, and boxed the boy on the ears as I entered the room. Nicolo saw that I'd witnessed his chastisement and he flushed and looked away.

A sharp squawk made me jump. In the corner of the room, in a gilded cage, was a brilliantly plumed bird. I gaped at it.

"Do you know what that is, Bastardo?" asked Silvano.

"Of course he doesn't, Papa, he's an ignorant whore," said Nicolo.

"It's a bird," I said, stiffening.

"Not just any bird," Silvano said. He went to the cage and took the bird out, held it on his finger, and crooned to it softly. He stroked its red head and green wings. "This pretty fellow is a special bird that I will display on festival nights, when many patrons come. He's a rare bird from the Far East. No one else in Florence has anything like this!" He looked exultant and then replaced the bird in its golden cage. "Bastardo, you're to go out into the city."

"Shouldn't you beat him first, to make sure he returns?" sneered Nicolo, adjusting the slits in the sleeves of his crimson tunic to show the blue silk *farsetto* underneath.

"Luca knows what I'll do if he doesn't return." Silvano laughed and scratched his beard, which had grayed almost to white. "He's to gather information."

"You want to know about the new plague," I guessed.

"The bird merchant says it's ravaging the city," Silvano said. "Has the plague really made inroads into Florence itself? Are people dying in swarms? A piece of street trash like you can get around in all sorts of clever ways, find out what's going on, how bad it is. You're good at sneaking around and observing things, aren't you, Bastardo? It goes with your freakish agelessness." He pointed at me. "Go. See if the sick die quickly and horribly." He angled a glance at me, and I saw that his eyes were dimmed with a thin milky glaze. It startled me; I always thought of Silvano as the irreducibly potent, malevolent man I'd met in the market years ago. I noticed now, with wonderment, that his beard wasn't the only sign of his age. His face had grown leathery and lined, and his pink scalp peeked through a monk's tonsure of white hair. I gazed studiously at the dice on the table. It wouldn't do for Silvano to see that I'd picked up weakness in him.

"Don't worry, you won't catch the Black Death." Silvano snickered, misreading my expression for one of fear. "You're the hardiest, most resilient thing I've ever seen. You don't even catch the clap, and I have to put down a whore every month who gets it."

"But it's very odd, don't you think, Father? That he barely ages and never gets sick," Nicolo whined. "It's unnatural. Some kind of evil sorcery. Maybe you should kill him and throw him into the river." Nicolo smirked at me. "It's been months since we've had good sport."

"Nonsense, son, he's useful to me, he's still popular among the patrons." Silvano smiled fondly at Nicolo. "Besides, I have bigger plans for him. He will mature, and when he does, we will have a new life of honor and station!" He leaned over and ruffled Nicolo's hair, and I noted how Silvano's hand was draped in loose gray skin. He added, "If you want some sport, you can have the new Spanish boy." He rose and motioned for his son to follow him. I stepped back into the wall as they passed me.

"Really, this Bastardo is too arrogant, I don't like him," Nicolo whined, pausing in front of me. He tilted his head and gave me a look of contempt down his bladelike nose.

"Beat him if you like, then, but not so much that he can't go out in the street," Silvano said from the hallway. Nicolo brightened. Before I knew what I was doing, I stepped toward him. It wasn't a big step, barely even a hand's width, but at the same time, my strength, like the waters of a river rolling

into a wave, gathered in my arms, and the muscles of my
chest and shoulders tingled with blood. I met his eyes
square-on. It was a subtle thing, taking power into myself.
I'd done it with snarling dogs on the street, when to show
weakness would invite attack, but never with a person.
Perhaps my fear of what my abnormal agelessness meant,
and my humiliation over my captivity, and my dread at the
terrible acts I had committed, had kept me from it; power
was not for such unwholesome ones as me. But today, having spied weakness in Silvano, I refused to be beaten by his
son. Nicolo paled. He stepped back hastily and then darted
after his father. I was amazed at myself. I would probably
pay dearly for it later, when Nicolo coaxed his father into
beating me. But this moment, I'd been prepared to defend
myself with force. I hadn't known I had it in me, and it
heartened me. Perhaps I wasn't so despicable, after all.

I LEFT THE PALAZZO IMMEDIATELY. It was early May,
with cool moments before summer swoops in and the sun
roasts the valley of the Arno. Few people walked the streets.
Doors were barred and windows were shuttered. Shops,
factories, and even taverns were shut down. Florence was a
city of tall towers, though not as tall as in the past, when
they had been over one hundred twenty *braccia* in height.
The city fathers had decided to restrict the height of private
dwellings for greater public security, but still they were imposing. Now the towers were closed up and dark. The warning bell in the austere Palazzo dei Priori pealed out in
somber tones and the air was threaded with a foul odor.
Soon I saw the cause of the odor: bodies lay scattered on the
street. Black flies buzzed around them and crows swooped
overhead, cawing. Rats skittered around the streets but
avoided the bloating bodies. Most of the dead looked like

poor wool and dye workers, still wearing their *foggette*. Some were children, small bodies heaped together in twos and threes, tiny, wasted arms intertwined or flung out indiscriminately. The city had become a vast charnel house.

One corpse looked different, a young woman with her hands folded across her bosom, as if she'd died praying. She was distinguished as a noblewoman by her sumptuous brocade gown. Black spots covered her delicate cheeks and neck. Her belly was swollen under her gown; she must have been with child. The plague had killed two here.

"A terrible pestilence, and just beginning," said a somber voice with a southern accent. It was a lean, dark-haired man who, despite the Neapolitan intonations, had a sculpted Frankish cast to his face.

"You think it will get worse," I said. He nodded.

"Don't get too close," he said, jerking his chin at the dead woman. "It's transmitted with evil speed from the dead to the living and from the sick to the healthy." He moved away. The few people about were huddled into themselves, throwing suspicious glances at other pedestrians. I trotted after the man and fell into step with him.

"Can't the doctors cure it?" I asked loudly. The man turned and gave me a half smile.

"Haven't I seen you before today?" he asked.

"If you patronize Bernardo Silvano's establishment."

"No, no, I prefer to take my sport for free," he murmured. "Somewhere else."

"Around the market?" I offered. His intense eyes perused my features, then he smiled.

"Your face is reminiscent of a face in a panel in the abbey at San Giorgio," he said. "Though that boy is two or three years younger. But you are very alike, indeed, an older twin."

I was afire with pleasure. "You know the glorious work of Master Giotto!"

"As do you, evidently, though I wouldn't have expected as much from one of Silvano's charges," he answered. We halted when rags sailed out of a window above us. There was a bang as the shutters slammed before the rags even landed in the street. I would have gone to look, but the man laid a cautionary hand on my shoulder. "Those probably came from some poor soul who died of this pestilence," he warned. "People are desperate to rid themselves of anything that was even touched by the dead." Two gaunt pigs raced up to the rags, took them in their teeth and hairy snouts, and shook them, the way pigs do. We stood watching as they snorted and grunted through the rags.

"To answer your original question," the man said, "no, the doctors can't cure it. Either its nature is such that it can't be cured, or the doctors are so ignorant that they don't recognize its cause, so they can't prescribe the proper remedy."

"Is it true it comes from the East?" I asked.

"Yes, but it has changed along its journey," he said. "In the East, those who were ill bled from the nose and then died. Now it shows its first signs by a swelling in the groin or the armpits. The swellings grow to the size of an egg." He glanced at me. "Take care that you stay away from patrons with those swellings." He spoke with knowing, but without judgment.

I shrugged. "I may not have that luxury."

He shook his head, frowning. "Silvano, that vermin. How the city fathers can allow him to operate, I don't know. There's no need for such an abomination of an establishment. A man with unslaked lust can always find some other man's wife with which to satisfy himself, if he has a mind to it. Women are mindless, like baubles. They're easily seduced creatures."

"Some of the city fathers are Silvano's patrons."

A thunderous expression crossed his lean face. "Sometimes I believe that God's just wrath has visited this plague upon us, for our iniquities. Sin flourishes in Florence, and everywhere else; this plague cannot be simply the result of an unfortunate star. It would be a fitting expression of God's justice if Silvano succumbed to the plague and died horribly!"

"You speak like a cleric, but you don't look like one," I observed. He was well dressed but simply, in fabrics any Florentine would recognize as fine: a dark woolen mantello over a narrow, cotton-linen tunic, and ordinary but well-constructed black hose.

"I'm a poet, though my father would have had me in law or business." He smiled.

"A poet like Dante?" I asked. Having always the gift of perfect mimicry, I recited Giotto's quotation: " 'That which dies not and that which can die are nothing but the splendor of that Idea which our Sire, in Loving, begets . . .' "

His thick dark eyebrows wagged. "Giotto, Dante, is Silvano running a school?" I laughed. The man pointed. "Look!" I followed his finger to where the pigs convulsed, squealing and frothing, eyeballs rolling in their wasted heads. In a few moments they stiffened and died.

"From the clothes of the dead," the man marveled. "The animals died in mere minutes from the rags a dead man wore!" We resumed walking, giving the dead a wide berth.

"Will someone come to bury them?" I asked, twisting to look at where a father and son lay on the ground nearby.

"Not their families. The city has hired porters called *becchini* with biers for the poor and middle class," he said. "Priests are reluctant to approach the bodies, so civilized customs of holy rites for the deceased are being shortened. It won't be long before those customs are suspended altogether." He shuddered, gathering his dark mantello closer around his shoulders. "Some people are already throwing themselves into wild licentiousness, while others maintain the strictest regimens of denial and abstinence. This plague will bring an end to custom and law as we know them."

"It will be hard to keep from getting ill if the pestilence spreads through clothes and animals," I observed. "Many will die. Whether licentious or abstinent."

"Indeed," he said. A coach with its curtains drawn raced past us, the team of chestnut horses running full-out. He nodded at it. "They have the right idea, I think, in leaving the city."

"Won't the plague follow them into the *campagna,* or meet them there?" I asked.

"Probably, but those who flee have a better chance. I will be leaving the city."

"I would like to do that," I mused. "Leave the city, leave Silvano's establishment far behind. In its way, it's as bad as the plague."

"I've heard stories of murdered and disfigured children." The poet nodded. "It's said that Silvano kills those who try to leave."

"Would anyone stay otherwise?" I asked, bitterly.

He laid his hand on my shoulder. "If you could leave, go anywhere to escape Silvano's and the plague, where would you go? What would you do?"

"A game of fantasy." I smiled warily. "I don't indulge myself."

"Fantasy can be a strong wind, blowing open the doors of your mind, or a support through a dark time. It is more than diversion. You must bring yourself to it," the poet urged. I looked at him with large eyes, never having considered such things. When patrons came to my room and I soared toward Giotto's frescoes, I did so literally. Or so I believed. And the fervor of those experiences convinces me even as I wait in my stone cell for my executioner that they went far beyond fantasy. There's a dividing line between the real and the unreal that breaks sometimes and allows the two halves to mix, like fluids in an alchemist's alembic. It has been my lot in this long life to plunge often into that mixture.

Back then, so long ago, I spoke of the simple things in my heart. "I would go out to the hills where I can hear the cicadas in the olive groves and see the pastures turning green. I've never been beyond the city walls, but I hear that in the campagna, the wheat fields move in the breeze like the Arno does. I would go to nature to find what is holy." Then I looked at him, remembering Giotto. "I would go with a friend, and sit at his feet and listen to him, for ten days straight. I would just listen to him."

We fell silent, passing through the large grassy Piazza Santa Maria Novella, the very place where I had first met Giotto. Pious Dominicans still preached here on the grassy lawn in front of their church, but none were in evidence now. For all their piety, priests feared the Black Death as much as anyone else. Where were their Holy Trinity and nine orders of angels in the face of this pestilence? A tangle of bodies lay at the edge of the square.

"Ten," the poet muttered. "Unshriven, unburied." Cries arose from the web of small streets to the west behind the church. We exchanged glances. The shouts grew louder and thrummed with an ugly tension. Words of hate and murder lifted above the clamor.

"They are screaming about Jews," he noted. "The crowd will make scapegoats of them."

"The Jews didn't bring the plague. Why should they be scapegoats?" I puzzled.

"People will have someone to blame for their suffering."

The poet shrugged. "It's in our nature. Someone else, preferably. Few can long tolerate blaming themselves."

"But, if anything, God brought the plague—you said it was His wrath!"

"We cannot blame God, nor are Florentines likely to look in a mirror and repent. Florentines are a proud lot. Whoever those Jews are"—he waved his hand toward the growing outcry—"they will be blamed and likely killed. The plague will indirectly claim more victims."

"It's not right that people blame Jews, or witches!" I said, remembering how close I had come to being burned that long-ago day.

"There are many good and honorable Jews. I have known some myself." The poet's brow puckered. "But their souls are lost to hell through lack of faith. Does it matter when they die?"

"Every life matters." I quickened my step. "What kind of faith would say otherwise?"

"Perhaps a longer life would give them a chance to turn to Christian truth," he agreed, not quite keeping pace with me, "to kneel before the clergy and be baptized and redeemed."

"It will give them more time to see how false the clergy is," I snapped, thinking of the friars who made their way to Silvano's.

"I have to go," I said, gesturing toward the uproar. "I know what a crowd will do when they blame someone for the city's problems."

"Then I take my leave of you, young admirer of Giotto and Dante," he said. He smiled and placed his hand over his heart and bowed. "I hope you will find my humble work as worthy of your admiration. I am Giovanni Boccaccio, and I will see that my poetry finds its way to you."

"My name is Luca Bastardo, and I can't read," I admitted.

"But perhaps one day you shall read, Luca Bastardo," he said. He pointed. "Go, to whatever destiny awaits you." His portentous, perhaps facetious, words were accurate: my destiny was about to change, dramatically and forever.

Chapter 6

BY THE TIME I REACHED THE SOURCE of the uproar, the crowd had grown to about sixty strong. They were an ugly, swarming mass, having boxed against the stone wall of a neighborhood church two figures: a bearded man and the child sheltered in his arms. The crowd seemed to share one mind, and that mind was filled with hate that pressed against the man and child like walls moving in. I wondered how it was that I so often bore witness to people at their worst. Was it because I myself had committed unthinkable acts?

"Dirty Jew!" one man was screaming.

"You brought the plague on us!" screamed a poor dye-worker wearing coarse robes and a frayed foggeta. He trembled as if with fever, but I knew it wasn't from the plague but from anguish: many had been lost in the crowded slums around the dye houses. After the plague there would be few left to labor in the cloth industry on which Florence depended.

"I can't take care of my children, or I'll die!" a woman

screeched. "My children are dying alone! Dirty Jews, you brought the Black Death!"

"Your filthy people killed our Lord and brought the plague!" shouted another man. He was rawboned and tanned, a farmer come in from the campagna, and he held a pitchfork that he waved in menace. Shrill shouts of affirmation went up. Someone threw a small rock. The Jew turned to cover the child's body with his own. The rock bounced off his shoulder and thunked on the cobblestones by his feet. Another rock flew at him, this one larger. It hit him in the ribs. Even through the waspish catcalls and screams of the crowd, I heard him grunt in pain. I crept down a side alley and circled around to get closer, and as I came out to the side of the Jew, he was frantically turning again and again to protect his child from the hail of rocks. I envied this child who knew the kind of parental protection that I had never received, and I wanted to help.

Around the Jew were scattered fist-sized and larger rocks, and his nose poured red roses of blood onto his beard and mantello. I glimpsed the child's terrified face. Tears ran down her soft white cheeks, on which was cast a shadow that looked like a bruise. The man with the pitchfork threw it, and before thinking, I darted out to deflect it. One sharp tine scraped my arm. I felt too much fire in my blood to pay attention.

"Bubboni!" I yelled, pointing toward the back of the crowd. "That man's sick! He will infect us all! Bubboni!" Cries of "Where, where?" and "Bubboni!" rose up.

"No one here has the plague!" howled the farmer. "It's a trick!"

I pointed insistently. "Bubboni! The Black Death! He's coughing! He'll kill us all! Run, run, or die!"

Panicked cries went up and two women broke from the crowd, shrieking and running. A hoary old man hobbled

after them. Suddenly the whole crowd erupted in pandemo-
nium. People ran everywhere, screeching in confusion and
fear. I turned to the Jew, saying "This way!" I motioned him
to follow me into the alley. From my old days on the street I
knew of a sewage gutter that came to an end at a brick wall,
but the wall had an uneven surface with good handholds and
footholds and it could be scaled. Behind the wall was another alley that ran to an outlet opening onto a parallel street.
The Jew immediately sprinted after me, clutching his daughter to his chest. I came to the stone wall and scrambled up,
sat astride it, and then reached down.

"Give her to me so you can climb over!" I said. The man
with the pitchfork and three other men carrying sticks had
followed us, undeterred by my ploy. The Jew glanced over
his shoulder and passed her up to me with large, trembling
hands. Her arms reached up and wound tightly around my
neck. Her cheeks were smeared with her father's blood.

"I'll hold them off so you can take her to safety!" he whispered.

"Climb, you'll both be safe!" I urged him. Another rock
whizzed toward him, spinning up at an angle when it hit the
wall. "Come on!" I said to the Jew. He scrambled up and I
leapt down on the other side, sinking to my knees with the
little girl pressed against me. A moment later the Jew landed
beside me. On this side of the wall, the space of the alley
opened up so that blue sky poured in and a slice of the sun
was visible over the tops of the tall stone buildings.

"You saved my daughter's life. And mine. I am indebted
to you forever."

"I don't want your debt," I said.

"I owe you," he insisted. "More than I can ever repay.
Look, your arm is bleeding. I can help you, I'm a *physico,* a
physician," he said. "Come with me to my home and I'll tend

it." He grasped my arm gently by my wrist and laid his other hand alongside the long, weeping gash. A warmth flowed from his palm into my arm—the first healing touch I had ever experienced. Something in my chest eased. The wound clotted and stopped dripping. I looked at the Jew in surprise. His thick dark brows lowered over his sharp blue eyes. "It's deep. You don't want to trifle with it, especially with this plague about. I can stitch it and give you an unguent so it doesn't take an infection. You don't want to die of an infection."

I pulled my arm back, but reluctantly, because the warmth of his hand had been so comforting. "I never get an infection. I always heal. I don't need your services."

"Why, because I'm a Jew?" He straightened and looked full into my eyes, a grave and intelligent look that insisted I tell him the truth.

"Because I'm a whore," I said bitterly. "I wouldn't bring shame to your home!" I indicated the little girl, who clung to her father's torn mantello. She stared at me with luminous blue eyes, her thumb stuck in her mouth.

He shook his head. "It doesn't matter. Come with me, let me care for your arm."

"It matters to me." I drew myself up.

The Jew stroked his daughter's hair. Finally he asked, "Which establishment?"

"Bernardo Silvano's."

A look of revulsion came over his angular face. "They'll kill me surely for what I am about to say . . ." The apple of his throat bobbed as he swallowed, then plunged ahead. "I saw how you handled yourself today. You look thirteen, small for your age, but shrewd. You conduct yourself like a man. You can take care of yourself. You don't have to stay there. You don't have to be . . . to do that anymore. I've heard what

Silvano does to children who try to leave him. But you can defend yourself. You'll think of a way. Do you hear me? *You can defend yourself!*"

"Against a troop of armed condottieri?" I retorted.

"Look around. How many condottieri are left in Florence? People are fleeing. War with Pisa or Lucca isn't important when people are dying on the streets. How many soldiers are left in Silvano's employ? Not many, I'll wager." He was gazing into my eyes as if there was something I should understand, but didn't.

"It's not me I worry about," I said. "Silvano will kill one of the other children if I leave."

"With the condottieri gone, Silvano is left defenseless, and he's not young and vigorous like you. You could make sure he couldn't hurt anyone else." The Jew's voice rumbled with a heavy undertone. The import of his words struck through my core like a lightning bolt. I literally stumbled, then steadied myself with a hand on the rough stone wall. It wasn't just the Jew's hand that had healing power, his words did, too. My trembling stilled and a terrible calm took over.

"I have been afraid for so many years that I didn't notice I didn't have to be afraid anymore," I whispered. "But where will I go? I came from the streets, but there's no one to give alms to the poor with the plague about."

"To my home. You will live with me and my family."

It was almost too cruel an offer because of its impossibility. I was torn between knowing that the stains at my core made me worthless and feeling as Adam might have felt if God had laughed with compassion instead of retribution, and invited him to kill the serpent to reenter Eden. I shook my head. "I wouldn't dishonor—"

"The greater dishonor would be mine, if I didn't reciprocate after you risked your life to save mine and my daughter's," he said, in the calm resonant voice that I would come to cherish. "You wouldn't have me dishonor myself, would you? What's your name?"

"I am Luca Bastardo."

"Good, Luca." He gripped my shoulder, his serious eyes peering deeply into mine. "This is Rebecca, and I am Moshe Sforno. I live in the Oltrarno, in the Jewish section. Everyone knows my home. You free yourself, *do whatever you need to do,* and then come find me. You have a home with me." He scooped up his daughter. "I don't care about the past. Today you saved my daughter and me from a terrible death. That's all I need to know." He stepped out into the street with little Rebecca in his arms. I watched them from the alleys. Even back then I knew what I have experienced so tragically since then, that mobs of people turn mindless and act quickly to effect murder. When Sforno and his daughter reached the Oltrarno, I turned. It was time for me to return to Silvano.

IT WAS LATE AFTERNOON when I arrived back at the dark palazzo. I looked with fresh eyes at my surroundings. As Sforno had guessed, there were no condottieri in evidence. I tried to recall when last I'd seen them; it had been months. And there had been fewer in the last years than the previous ones. Why had I never noticed? What was it about the dead time in this shuttered place that had cozened me into complacence? I had let fear freeze me like a figure in a painting into the moment when Silvano was beating me, or the worse one where he was cutting Marco. I banged on the door and the skinny foreign girl opened it.

"Out of my way, woman," I commanded. She shrank back. "Leave the door open!" I said. I marched to the window by the door and yanked at the thick velvet drapes. Clouds of pale gray dust swirled out. With a creak, the drapes came down in my hand. The honeyed light of afternoon poured into the foyer, illuminating the spiral dance of dust motes, and the girl gasped. I dragged the drapes down the hall so they made a sibilant sound.

Silvano was alone in the dining room. His abbaco ledger lay on the table in front of him. His graying head snapped up at my approach. I threw the drapes onto the floor. Blood dripped from my arm, pooling on the floor, but I paid no attention to it.

"I won't be staying," I said. Silvano rose from the table, but stiffly, I noted with satisfaction. His knees had grown sore with age. How had I failed to observe that?

"I wondered when the cub would grow some teeth," he said coolly. His nostrils flared. A knife flashed in his hand, but I wasn't afraid. I was going to defend myself. I was going to end my long indenture. I felt a solid column of light snap into a straight line in the center of my body, from the soles of my feet to the crown of my head: a pure expression of this moment *now*.

He stepped out from the table. "You'll be sorry, Bastardo. You can't imagine the pain you'll suffer. Your fancy parents would be ashamed. Your people have pure blood, but you've corrupted it and shamed them!"

"Don't talk about my parents," I warned.

"They knew from your birth that you were an unholy abomination who would never age as he was supposed to, and that's why they lost you. They wanted to! Think how they would feel if they knew what you did to Marco!" He sneered. I stumbled backward, shocked. "You think I didn't know about that, Bastardo? I have many spies. I know what you are. A killer, like I am! You hate me, but you're like me!" He was gloating and moving toward me.

"I'm nothing like you!"

"You're just like me, but worse, because you're a whore, and damned by black magic, which keeps you young. Your parents saw their blood was spoiled in you and that only evil could come from you." As he approached me, he tossed his knife back and forth from hand to hand.

"My parents loved me! They were good people, real people, who searched for me!"

"I should have sold you to the Church long ago, with the document and the story about the heretics. I never forgot your mother's hair and eyes, they were exactly like yours, and even if you hadn't matured to bear the mark of heresy on your chest, I could have convinced the Church that you were the boy in that letter! The Church would have rewarded me well, it gets so worked up about the good God and evil God nonsense. As if God could be anything other than everywhere. The Kingdom of the Father is spread out upon the earth, and men do not see it."

"Because there's evil on the earth, evil men like you!" I cried. "There's no God in you!"

"I'm not a freak whore bastard who won't grow up, like you," he crowed. "Who's really the godless one? I thought I'd get more money for delivering you as a grown man with the mark the letter describes, but you wouldn't mature! All my plans for Nicolo and me had to wait for you, and you've always been trouble! You'd live forever with your dark sorcery until you're burnt at the stake for being a witch, but I'm going to kill you now!"

"No, I am going to kill you!" I shouted. All of my senses tingled and intensified. Suddenly I could hear, see, smell, taste, and feel as never before: the sibilant squawk of the exotic bird Silvano had bought, the tiny skitterings of a mouse running under the floorboards, the harsh scent of the lye used to clean the floor, the sobs of a child upstairs, Silvano's clove perfume, the increasing tempo of his heart, and the frantic flow of blood through his veins: they were louder, stronger, more vivid to me than anything ever before had been in my life. It was like another world, another cosmos, was present within this one.

Shapes and forms dissolved. The outlines of objects smeared out, and what was left was glazed with light and separated into dancing motes and juicy scrims of color. Even the walls fell away, and I could see outdoors: flowers and trees and other *piazze,* all of them flying apart like a handful of sand thrown into the wind. I could have seen anything, anywhere, but I focused on Silvano. He was surrounded by a haze and he seemed not to move. After what felt like an hour, he was still advancing toward me. It took an eternity for him to reach me. His hand was so slow that it was easy for me to grab his wrist and shake the blade from it. The blade clattered onto the floor, and a disjointed cry went up—Silvano's? A strength I had never known before possessed me. I felt a lush crunch as the small bones of his wrist gave inward. I shivered with delight. His other hand swept toward my face, fingers outstretched as if to jab my eyes, but it was slow. I knocked it back. The wrist I was holding went floppy. Silvano dropped to his knees. He pawed vainly at my hand with his free one. I kept squeezing. There was a sound in the background and I realized it was Silvano screaming.

"Stop, I beg you!" he was pleading, his pale face turned up to me. "I'll pay you anything, anything! More gold florins than you can carry!"

"A bag of gold florins? Like the silk bag you beat us children with?" I asked, fury building again within me. I released his wrist abruptly and wrapped my hands around his neck. It was intoxicating to have his life in my fingers, to feel the blue veins throbbing against my hungry palms, to know that his pulse would soon dwindle into emptiness, into my freedom. He would stop breathing and all the horrors of the last eighteen years would die with him.

Satisfaction thrummed inside me like the glorious song

of a lyre in a pageant. I had killed before, knowing only the sickening burden and shame of it. For this one time, for this one evil man who had hurt so many children, I knew the intoxicating pleasure. Since that day, I have killed many men, but none with the same gusto. Just as I was going to wring Silvano's neck like a chicken's, something hit me. It was Nicolo.

"You leave my father alone!" he screamed. I punched him, hard, sent him flying across the room. All those years ago when I lived on the streets, Paolo with the dark gypsy looks had taught me how to punch, and I never forgot anything I learned. Nicolo grabbed his father's knife from the floor and leapt at me. He appeared, like his father before him, slowed down to my preternaturally heightened senses. I slammed my fist into his jutting chin before he could reach me. He crumpled into a heap on the drapes. I turned back to Silvano, who was gasping and writhing on the ground. His pupils were huge with my reflection.

"Don't kill my son," he whispered, clutching his bruised throat. "He's just a boy!"

"Bella was just a little girl when you cut her throat," I said. I wrapped my hands around Silvano's head and twisted, hard. There was a crack and his body went limp.

"Papa!" Nicolo cried. Weeping, he fell upon Silvano's body.

"I'm going to free the other children," I said. Nicolo attacked me again, throwing himself hard against my back. I whirled around, flung him off. He landed with a crunch against the gilded cage, and the red and green bird inside it screamed to complain. It beat its wings against its bars. "No one will be left imprisoned!" I vowed. I ran over and freed the bird. It flew around the room, shrilling and flapping its wings. I took up Silvano's knife. "I'll release it outside!"

"No! You won't get my papa's bird!" Nicolo shrieked. He jumped up and grabbed at the bird, caught it with a quick swipe and then wrung its neck, just as I had wrung Silvano's. He swung the limp bird by its feet, laughing maniacally. "Ha, ha, Luca Bastardo, you freak whore!"

I went a little mad. Not as mad as I have been since the great tragedy that has come to define my life, but with something of the same blind hallucinatory rage. "You can't take away its freedom!" I screamed. I danced around the room, waving the knife. "You can't do that!" I stopped in front of Nicolo. "Since you've killed it, you're going to eat it! Now!" I held Silvano's knife to Nicolo's throat. He picked up the bird, trembling. "Eat it! Eat it!" I screamed, over and over again, pressing the knife until a drop of blood appeared on his scrawny throat.

Nicolo jerked the bird to his mouth and bit into its neck. He chewed, swallowed, feathers and all. He lifted his pimply, tear-smeared face to me. Bubbles of snot and blood coagulated on his wisp of a mustache. His sharp nose and thrusting chin made him the image of his father, and I was tempted to kill Nicolo, to see them both closed away in small boxes, unshriven, unmourned. What stayed my hand was the thought that Nicolo was still a child, and I would prove myself unlike Bernardo Silvano, who had killed so many children.

The bird's blood dripped down Nicolo's chin. He vomited violently onto the carpet, forcefully ejecting sodden red feathers. I laughed, and picked up one of the red feathers. I thrust it against his forehead, and because it was wet, it stuck to his skin. I laughed and laughed.

"I will never forget this! I will never forget you, and what you have done, Luca Bastardo! Someday I will avenge my father's death. I swear it on my own blood, on my father's body! I will make you suffer, you will die a horrible death!" Nicolo rose up on his knees and shook his fist at me, the red feather still clinging to him. "I curse you and curse you!"

I shook my head. "I don't believe in curses said by little girls wearing red feathers." I stepped over his father's body and went to confront the patrons and to open doors for the children. If I had known then how potent cruel intention is when joined to blood fury, I would not have discounted his words. Curses have power, and Nicolo's curses ripened, marking my life forever.

Chapter 7

SHAKING, I STOOD AT THE LARGE DOOR, the carved portone, to Moses Sforno's house. It was a typical Florentine home of the time, three stories high and constructed of stone, with evenly spaced windows under arched lintels, so ordinary that it awed me, unnatural creature of the streets and the brothel that I was. The pale gold light of a candle streamed out from a window with an open shutter and made a monstrous shadow of me on the street. I reached up to grasp the doorknocker, a brass plate shaped like a six-pointed star with a ring through the center for banging. The full moon gleamed on the blood slicked all over my arms. A succulent, oniony smell wafted from the house like a deep breath blown out; it was dinnertime. How could I, a stranger covered with gore, intrude on this intimate family time?

I was stepping away without knocking when the door opened. Sforno stood there, outlined in the yellow candle-light. "I heard something, or maybe I felt it," he said, stroking his beard. "I thought it might be you."

"I'm free of Silvano," I said quietly. My chest felt hollow, which surprised me. I had no idea freedom would feel so empty, after all the years that I had longed for it. What was left, if the prison was gone? How would I now fill my days? Was living with strangers really the answer?

"Come in."

"I'm not clean," I demurred, with a sharp spurt of the familiar fear that had dogged me at Silvano's: the fear of breaking the rules and being harshly punished. Sforno pulled me gently into the house. I stood in a foyer on a threadbare blue and gold carpet of Saracen design. The walls and ceiling were bathed in a warm lucency by lamps set on old carved wooden chests called *cassones.* A dark-haired woman wearing a patterned blue dress and a yellow *cappucci,* a cowl, swept into the foyer.

"Moshe, who is it?" she asked sharply. She stood beside Sforno, staring. She had high cheekbones, a cleft chin, and a strong nose, was full-bodied and womanly, handsome in the way in which little Rebecca's prettiness would mature. Small crow's-feet radiated out from wary dark eyes that scanned me intently, taking in my bloody arms and clothes.

"My friend Luca, who saved Rebecca and me today," Sforno said.

She smiled. "You have my gratitude. Few Gentiles would do as you did today!"

Moshe nodded. "He's staying with us."

"For dinner?" the woman asked.

"He's going to live with us, Leah," Moshe said, in a quiet, firm voice.

"What? Moshe, he's—"

"Wife, set a place at the table for him while I take him to clean up," Sforno said. There was a warning note in his voice and my heart plummeted.

"I don't want to cause trouble," I said.

"Looks like you've already done that," a merry bass voice rumbled. A thick-bodied older man came up by Mrs. Sforno. He had a full gray beard that reached to his belt, and a wild mane of gray-and-black hair. His face was broad and lined and graced with the largest nose and most cunning eyes I'd ever seen. He crossed his arms over his sturdy chest and laughed.

"You look like a wolf cub who had his way among the lambs."

"I killed no lambs today," I growled, nettled by his implication.

"Would it be so bad if you had?" He raised a grizzled eyebrow, challenging me. "Isn't it necessary sometimes, for the lamb's sake?"

"You killed someone?" asked Mrs. Sforno. She turned her face away, distressed. "There will be ufficiali after him!"

"Luca saved my life. And Rebecca's. We owe him more than we can ever repay." Sforno laid a hand on his wife's shoulder. Her full mouth compressed into a thin line, but she tilted her head to lay her cheek on his hand and her face softened. Then her frown reappeared. "We'll send the ufficiali away," Sforno said. "We don't need to know what Luca has done."

But if I was going to live here, Sforno's wife should know the truth. I didn't want to conceal any acts that could ripen into danger for these good people. "I killed the proprietor of a brothel where children were kept as prostitutes," I said directly to the woman. If she had raised her eyes, I would have met them squarely. She didn't. In fact, she kept her gaze from mine for the many years I lived with her family.

"Is that all?" she snapped.

"I also killed seven patrons who were using the children. I stabbed two in the back, as they lay on the children. I cut the throats of three, and two I slit in the stomach," I admitted. I was secretly pleased to have discovered such peculiar strength in myself; at the time, it seemed far more useful than unending youthfulness. I knew my actions made me appear unnatural, but I wasn't silenced. For years Silvano had preyed upon my abnormalities to keep alive my fear of persecution by the outside world. I realized with a shock that that old fear was gone, washed away in the blood of my oppressors. But in the absence of fear and in the presence of these good people, I felt not peace, but the weight of humiliation and guilt over what I'd done during my long indenture. That would take far longer to overcome than the fear.

"I would want you at my back in a fight." The older man laughed. "Wolf cub indeed!"

"He's not some stray dog we can take in!" the woman objected. "He's a Gentile who has killed Florentines. There will be people looking for him! I will spend my life being grateful to him for saving your life and Rebecca's, but we have to be practical. No good can come of us harboring him. We could be forced to leave the city, or worse! They could harm our children! As Jews, we are already too vulnerable to take in a murderer!"

"Leah, without him, I would not be here. Nor would your baby," Sforno said soothingly.

"Wolf cub, what did you do after all that stabbing and slitting?" the older man asked. His eyes sparkled at me as if it was all an amusing anecdote, as if I hadn't basked in a sea of warm coppery life essence.

"Gave the children the money I found in the brothel and told the maids to care for them. I drove out the son of the proprietor. I told him I'd kill him if he came back. He knew I meant it."

"You must be hungry after all that," the older man said. "Come have dinner."

"I should wash first," I said.

"Come, I'll take you," Sforno said. His wife started to speak, but he held up a warning hand. He took a lamp and led me through the foyer to another hall, and out a side door. "My Leah's a good woman," he said slowly. "Don't judge her. It isn't easy for us Jews."

"It's not for me to judge anyone," I said quietly. "Is that other man a relative of yours?"

"Not that I know." Sforno shook his head.

"What's his name?" I followed along a path lit by his lamp. The path led to a small crude barn of the kind people built in the Oltrarno, where not all the land was built up with homes.

"I don't know that he has one. He's a wanderer. He knew my father. He seems to know everyone, and he brings news of my brother and cousins in Venice. He shows up and we feed him." Sforno threw the sash to the barn door and motioned me to enter. Two bay horses whinnied and a cow lowed as we went in. Sforno led me to a trough filled with water and placed the lamp on a small three-legged stool. "Here's a bucket and a brush, clean yourself, Luca." Then he went out.

First I took from within my red-spattered vestments Giotto's precious small panel—the only thing I had brought with me from Silvano's. I looked around for a hiding place, saw a small ledge above the door. I overturned a bucket and used it to climb up to the ledge, and then pried away a board and secreted the panel in a hollow between the barn's outer shell and inner walls. The panel was wrapped in oiled calf-skin, so I knew it would be safe from mice. I climbed back down and doused myself. The water ran onto the rough wooden floor in pink rivulets. I dumped a few more buckets over my head. I picked some horse hair out of the brush and then used it to scrub out the blood dried in my hair and the flesh caked beneath my fingernails.

Sforno returned carrying a threadbare camicia, a patched woolen doublet, hose, and a short mantello. "We'll have to have garments made for you," he said. He sighed. "Leah won't like spending the money, but it has to be done. This is an old farsetto of mine." He swung the mended vestcoat doublet back and forth. "It'll be large, but you'll be decent."

"When I lived on the streets, I found clothes in the garbage, and I folded and rolled them and tied them to fit," I said. They were old memories but still clear, perhaps more vivid now, with Silvano's prison torn asunder. I found myself awash in the old images, Paolo and Massimo and the spot under the Ponte Vecchio where we had often huddled together for warmth in the winter, games of chance and skill and begging for coins for a meal and going to the market with an empty belly . . . Sforno's voice severed into the past, and I realized he was speaking to me.

"Before Silvano's?" he asked. I nodded. "You don't look like the usual street urchin," he observed. "You're not deformed, an idiot, or dark like a gypsy. The yellow hair, your features, your strength and cleverness—you could be a nobleman's son. I'll wager that you are, and there's some strange twist in your history. There are probably people looking for you even now."

"I have often wondered about my history. But wouldn't my parents have found me long before now, if they were looking?" I asked bitterly. I gave him a sharp glance and did not confess the secret abomination of my long youth and hardiness. Sforno was a physico, he would probably observe those for himself.

"The world is strange and full of crooked paths." Sforno shrugged. "You're here now. Come back in when you're dressed."

Cleaned and dressed and filled with anxiety, I made my way back into the house. Overwhelmed by how different I

was from these people, by both blood and experience, neither of which I could ever wash from myself, I walked
timidly along the hall. Wooden beams ran above my head,
and paintings of the flowing canals of Venice were hung on
the walls. Everything about the place sang with the ordinar-
iness of a cozy family, something I had never known. Even
among an exiled people, I stood out, a bruised fruit in an or-
chard of flowers. Moshe Sforno was taking me in out of a
sense of obligation, but I couldn't stay here forever. I would
have to form a plan for myself. I didn't want to go back to
the streets, especially with the Black Death slaughtering
more wantonly than I had this night. Nor would I ever go
back to the work I had done at Silvano's. I heard voices, high
girlish timbres interwoven with Sforno's resonant tones,
and I stepped into a dining hall. The conversation ceased.
Before me stood a tall wooden chest painted with faded
grapes beneath an arching of strange letters. Beside it, the
dining table was a long rectangle, with plain, columnar legs
but made of well-polished walnut. There sat Sforno, his wife,
four girlchildren, and the Wanderer. A plate was laid down
between Sforno and the Wanderer. They all stared at me except for Mrs. Sforno, who studied the table, which was set
with lit candles, silver goblets, a roast fowl, fragrant sautéed
greens, a golden loaf of bread, and a carafe of plum-colored
wine. Rebecca, the littlest daughter, slid down from her seat
and skipped over to hug me. Her breath on my cheek was
warm and milky.

"Look at him, a Gentile through and through." Mrs.
Sforno threw up her hands. "What are the neighbors going
to say? They'll think badly of us for having him around our
daughters!"

"Whatever they say, you aren't saying kaddish. Sit down,
Luca." Sforno's resonant voice was kind. Rebecca led me to
the empty spot on the bench next to her father.

"Four daughters," I murmured. The four girls inspected me in open fascination. They were unabashed and unashamed, completely unlike the cowed and beaten girls I had known at Silvano's or the unheeding ones I had witnessed on the streets. I flushed and stood straighter, fidgeted with Sforno's farsetto to pull it to a tighter, better fit.

"Even the great Rashi had four daughters and no sons," Sforno said, with an air of both love and resignation. The girls giggled. Their laughter was such an exotic sound that I gaped. For many years, I had not once heard the bright laughter of girls. The poet Boccaccio whom I'd met on the street earlier today was wrong: women were not trivial baubles. Even the young ones were far more than that. They had a special grace because divine music played in their laughter. Sforno stroked Rebecca's cheek. He sighed. "One accepts God's gifts as they are given."

"What's a killer whore?" six-year-old Miriam asked in a lilting voice. Sforno groaned and slapped his hand over his eyes.

"Hush, Miriam!" the serious eldest sister, Rachel, said.

"Someone cruelly used, who decides to change his fate," I answered grimly.

"Change is the only constant," the Wanderer said. "I think I'll stay for a while, Moshe. I'll make the kiddush, yes?" He held up his goblet of wine and sang some words in a language I did not understand.

And so began my first meal with the Sfornos, and the beginning of my living in a family. It was tangential to real domestic intimacy, it wasn't my family, and I was an alien thing still. But it was the closest I'd ever come.

THE NEXT MORNING I AWOKE FROM A NIGHTMARE of fire and ache, dead patrons and freed birds, and a beautiful

woman with a fragrance of lilacs sinking beneath black water. It was dawn and I lay on a pallet of straw. My heart was
stuttering in my chest, which was no longer numb with submission, and an ordinary green garden snake was slithering
away through the straw. I gulped air, and then, as the
rhythms in my body slowed, I unwrapped myself from the
woolen blanket Moshe had given me. The gray barn cat
who'd slept purring in my armpit darted off after a field
mouse, or perhaps after the little snake. I stretched and took
a deep breath of earthy animal scents, sweaty fur and dusty
feathers and fresh dung, mouse droppings and insect carcasses and damp straw. Here the air was not scented with
perfumes and there was no bed with fancy linens like at
Silvano's. I wondered when the smell of those perfumes and
the luxurious hand of those fabrics would dissolve, or if
they'd cloy my senses forever. I felt confusion and gratitude
toward Sforno, and then the anguish of the dream reared up
like an unruly horse. It reminded me of my promise to his
wife, to be helpful. I grabbed a shovel and started cleaning
out the horses' stalls. I worked awkwardly, having practiced
other skills these last many years. I hoped this new work
would shatter the dream that encased me like dark glass.
Then the Wanderer came in, his wooden clogs clattering on
the unfinished timbers of the barn's floor.

"You look pale, Bastardo," he said. He grabbed a brush,
let himself into a stall, and briskly curried a donkey that was
stabled with the Sfornos' two horses.

"Bad dream," I said, trying to keep my voice from being
surly.

"I sleep little and dream less." He shrugged. "Who can
sleep when God's creation is emanating all around us with
such goodness?"

"I've seen little goodness in God's creation."

"So what kind of dream was this, that blinded you so?"

"The kind that traps you even in the light," I muttered.

"A dog that is beaten will stay in his cage even if the fence is removed," the Wanderer said. "Because the fence is inside him."

I stopped and rested my chin on my hands on the shovel. "I thought I was a wolf cub."

"You can't be both?" he asked, and it was such an intimate question that some cool reserve within me dissipated, and I felt myself completely understood in his presence in a way I'd never felt before with anyone else, not even Giotto. The Wanderer stood in profile to me as he brushed the donkey, which nickered with pleasure. I was struck by the man's huge, beaked nose and the way it dominated his craggy face but didn't detract from it. Rather, it enhanced the intelligence of his mien and the seriousness that didn't go away even when he was laughing.

"What are you looking at?"

"Your nose. It's the biggest I've ever seen," I said.

"A man's got to have something to distinguish himself." He snickered, rubbing his nose proudly. "We can't all be beautiful golden-haired wolf cubs!"

"I thought I was a beaten dog," I said.

"Again, what seem like opposites aren't. You need a new way of seeing, Luca, so your eyes reveal to you the goodness woven into everything, even what seems on its face to be evil."

"What eyes will show me goodness in a life where I was abandoned to live on the streets, then sold into a brothel by my closest friend?" I asked bitterly. "The only life I've known is one of cruelty and humiliation. What goodness is in that?"

The Wanderer's sharp eyes drooped. "I'm just an old man without a home, what do I know? But if I were to know something, I might answer that your life is teaching you. It's a gift, a great education. And perhaps you suffer now so that great joy can come to you later in life, and the suffering makes you worthy of it. I might know this, if God were to whisper it to me."

"God doesn't whisper, He taunts us. At best He laughs. Do you have a name?"

"What do you want to call me?" He winked at me. "I'll answer to whatever you wish. As long as you tell me more about this humorous God of yours."

"What do I know about God?" I rephrased his question back to him and returned to shoveling manure. "I've heard priests speak, but their pious lectures have nothing to do with what I've seen and felt."

"So your mind is empty. Good. Emptiness is a place to find the Master of Hiddenness."

"I always thought God was found in fullness," I said slowly. "Like in the richness and beauty of a master's paintings. God is found in that beauty, in that purity."

"Only in purity and beauty and fullness? God is not in stain and ugliness and emptiness? Why do you limit Him that way?"

I stopped again and stared at him. "Why do you call God 'the Master of Hiddenness'?"

"What would you have me call Him?" The Wanderer shook his unruly mop of hair.

"Don't the Jews have a name for Him?"

"How can Jews give a name to what is unlimited? Or Christians or Saracens?" The Wanderer straightened his coarse tunic over his barrel-shaped torso. "Names evaporate in that fullness and beauty you hung on the Lord like a mantello, boy-who-looks-like-a-boy-but-is-not."

"You speak in riddles," I muttered. "It's beyond me. I just want to live a new life, a good life, and someday have a wife and family of my own. God's not very nice; I don't want to worry about Him and His names. I just want to stay out of His way."

"Be careful what you wish for." The Wanderer's broad face creased into a teasing smirk. "In giving a name, we're trying to enclose in form what is formless—a terrible sin. Original sin. Do you understand sin?"

"I know about sin." I looked with as much arrogance as I had ever mustered into the Wanderer's face. I was a killer and a whore and a thief. If anyone knew about sin, it was me.

"Wonderful, what a blessing! Soon you'll be crowned! What need have you for names of God? Why go down a wrong path when you've had such a wonderful start to your journey?"

"You think that naming God is a way of limiting Him, and so it's wrong?" I puzzled.

"We have a name for God. But we never speak it aloud. Words have magic and power, whether written or spoken, and names are the most sacred and powerful words of all!"

The Wanderer gestured with the brush at the manure, which I'd managed to spread everywhere, not knowing exactly where I was supposed to put it. He said, "You're not very good at that. You've made a big mess."

"I'm bad at this," I agreed. I threw down the shovel. "I have another idea, for something that doesn't require so much skill. I'll talk to Sforno about it."

"You could probably learn to shovel manure, with lengthy instruction and a few weeks' practice," the Wanderer said dryly. "Collect the eggs from under the hens and take them in with you, eh? There's a basket hanging by the door."

Inside the house, Mrs. Sforno in her voluminous blue dress bustled about the kitchen. She was seeing to the oil jars, pouring off luminous chartreuse olive oil from a large jar with a tap in its side into smaller jars. The piquant nutty scent of the oil wafted out from her hands. Her auburn-haired daughter Rachel stood at a wooden table, slicing bread. Rachel gave me a grave, searching look, then an ironic smile. I smiled back uncertainly. "I, uh, brought in the eggs." I held the basket out to Rachel, but Mrs. Sforno quickly shut off the tap and took the basket from me. Miriam skipped in wearing a patched pink nightdress. She snatched a piece of bread from the plate at Rachel's elbow. Rachel clucked and pretended to slap at her. Miriam's long chestnut braids flew out as she spun around and saw me. Her impish face lit up.

"Good morning!" she lilted. "Here's some bread!" She tore her purloined slice in half and gave it to me with a grin. "Now that you live with us, are you still a killer whore?"

"Miriam!" chorused Mrs. Sforno and Rachel.

"No." I flushed, though I didn't mind the girl's honesty. I preferred it, even, to the unasked questions. I fidgeted with the women all staring at me. "Is Signore Sforno around?"

"Just returning from morning minyan," Sforno answered, striding in. He wore a long white shawl which he playfully gathered around Mrs. Sforno as he embraced her. She smiled and pushed at him, but he kissed her with relish before he let her step away. He bussed Rachel's cheek and tugged Miriam's braid. Miriam giggled and flung herself up into his arms. Sforno staggered back as if bowled over by her weight, which elicited peals of laughter from her.

"Luca brought in the eggs," Rachel said.

"Isn't that kind!" Sforno exclaimed. He looked toward Mrs. Sforno but she didn't seem to notice, and he and Rachel exchanged a pointed glance. He clasped my shoulder. "How are you this morning, Luca?"

"I've a plan for earning money," I told him. "You and Mrs. Sforno can have my wages."

"I do well as a doctor," Sforno said. "It isn't necessary for you to give us money." He took a piece of bread from the plate.

"Papa!" Rachel chided. "There'll be no bread left for breakfast!"

"I have always worked," I said. "Now the city is hiring becchini to cart away the bodies of the dead. I can do that. It takes no skill, and I have none. It just requires strength. I have plenty of that." I shrugged. "And I never get sick. I can do this."

"He'll have to be taught to read," Mrs. Sforno commented, not looking at me.

I gasped with surprised delight. "I could read Dante!"

"He'll need a trade," she went on. "It's the only way we'll get him out of here."

"My Leah, you're so practical." Sforno caressed her cheek.

"In the meantime, I can work for the city," I said.

"He mustn't bring the contagion here," Mrs. Sforno said. "But he could bank his earnings until he has enough to begin a life for himself."

"Leah's right, the contagion spreads like fire." Sforno frowned. "You'll have to do what I do when I return from tending the sick: scrub yourself with lye soap and change clothes before you come indoors. Even clothes can transmit the plague."

"I can do that," I said eagerly.

"I can teach him how to read," Rachel offered.

Sforno was nodding, but Mrs. Sforno turned and gestured at her daughter. "I think not," she said sharply. "His wages will hire a tutor!"

A tutor, for such as me? I boggled at the thought. It was all too much. "I'll go then," I said, backing out of the kitchen. I turned and fled down the hallway, past the staircase where the other two girls, shy Sarah and little Rebecca, were playing with a doll, into the foyer and out the large carved door on which I had not been able to knock last night. I wasn't sure what drove me at such velocity out of the Sfornos' house. It had something to do with the way Mrs. Sforno averted her gaze from me while delineating a new life for me, and something to do with the way Miriam laughed in her father's arms. It had something to do with the little green snake curving sinuously away. Perhaps most of all, it had to do with beaten dogs and the fences in their minds.

Chapter 8

THE DAWN SUN OF MAY shed a blanched light like a watery mist over the city, and the bodies of the dead lay everywhere, cast without ceremony from their homes. But for the black bubboni, many could have been Florentines sleeping outdoors in unnatural positions, as after some infernal carnevale. From the number of bodies and the stench, I could guess that there weren't enough becchini in the city to keep it clear. It would get worse as summer went on and the relentless heat arrived earlier and earlier in the day. I crossed the Arno, which undulated in a lazy silver ribbon under the bridges, heedless of the contagion and death sweeping the city.

A few beggars and some common thugs waited in the courtyard of the Palazzo del Capitano del Popolo, a severe, imposing stone building with arched windows and a high tower rising above its three stories. It looked like a fortress from the outside, with its massive, rough-hewn stone walls, but the courtyard where I waited was handsome, with columns supporting a spacious vaulted portico and a ceremonial stairway leading to a grand open loggia on the first story. Those who were gathered eyed me, but I was too young and simply dressed to arouse their interest; it was clear that I didn't have any money. We were joined by other men and boys whose threadbare clothes marked them as dye-workers. A handful of women also arrived, common prostitutes whose work had been eliminated by the plague. Those of us who weren't sick still had to eat. I gave my name to a notary, who nodded wearily and recorded it in a ledger, and then I leaned against a stone wall and watched people gather. My ears pricked when I overheard a man say, ". . . and we walk right into the homes where everyone is dead."

His companion nodded vigorously. "You have to watch for ufficiali, though. Yesterday a man died in the door of his palazzo, and I went in to get his wife and babies and found three gold florins! The palazzo was empty, no maids or anything, and I could have taken more, but two ufficiali on horses came to watch me load the bodies. I had to tie the little ones onto their parents to get them stacked properly. Too bad about the ufficiali, or I would have taken a fortune!"

The first man shook his fist. "They think they can command the city, even while everyone is dying or fleeing. We deserve to take what we find, if we have the balls to handle the dead. We risk our lives! The city owes us."

A burly, balding man standing nearby shrugged. "Servants are making the real money now. They can charge anything they want for their services, and nobles will pay. The nobles who are left in the city. Most have fled."

I goggled to contemplate finding an empty palazzo with its riches laid out for the plucking, and fair game because the owners were dead. I could acquire money and jewels, silks and furs, silver goblets and pearl necklaces, enough to take care of myself for a long while. I was pleased to find myself thinking in the old resourceful ways of the street, as I might have done had I remained free of Silvano, had I been spared years of savage indenture. . . . Then I remembered that I was now living with the Sfornos. This sort of planning was unnecessary, perhaps unseemly. Nor could I imagine Mrs. Sforno with her high cheekbones and averted gaze being pleased with anything I obtained in this fashion.

A slender magistrate with an overly coiffed beard came out of the palazzo onto the loggia and then strutted down the steps. He wore giant red sleeves of brushed velvet which swooshed out around him as he swung his arms with his stride. Such adornment seemed obscene, when so many lay dead in the city. If it wasn't a transgression of the sumptuary laws, then it should have been. His gaze flitted over the crowd and in a condescending voice he called out the terms of the work: how much we would be paid, how we should work until sundown but take a break at midday for a meal, where to find biers and planks on which to load the bodies, where to deposit them. Horse-drawn carts would take the bodies to the city boundaries, and when the church bells chimed vespers, we would meet there to dig burial trenches. Above all, he informed us, we were not to loot the homes of the dead and dying or we would be put in prison to rot with criminals who were already succumbing to the Black Death. Finally he suggested that we stuff our shirts with garlic and herbs, both to combat the fumes and to discourage the contagion. For this purpose, there was a wheelbarrow filled with the herbs beside the wooden planks, another one loaded with garlic bulbs. Then he walked through the crowd pairing people for the work.

"You." He pointed at me. At the same moment we recognized each other. Both of us flushed. I threw back my shoulders and stood straighter. I refused to be shamed ever again. Nor could I quell the joy I felt, knowing that just yesterday I had killed his ilk: men who went to church, drank wine with their guild-mates, and dressed their wives in fine dresses, who lived with self-contentment like God-fearing people, but then forced themselves on enslaved children. My fingers itched to wrap around his throat, and the bloodlust hummed in my belly like a long-denied hunger. News of my rampage through Silvano's brothel must have spread. Florence was ever a city that reveled in gossip, even during the plague. And most of the patrons had had families, wives and parents and friends. I wondered how the city fathers planned to react. Perhaps Mrs. Sforno was right and soldiers would follow me to her door.

Then the magistrate dropped his eyes, and satisfaction like a cool wine spurted through my chest. He meant to pretend that we'd never met, that he'd never climbed astride me, overlooking my silent tears of rage and violation, and paid handsomely for the pleasure of doing so.

"What of me?" I challenged him. A deeper scarlet suffused his face.

"You're with that boy." He flicked his finger and trotted off in haste.

"Let's get a bier," I said to the other boy. Then I turned and saw a white-faced Nicolo staring at me. Unthinking, I leapt at him. My hands closed with inhuman strength around his throat. Last night I meant to spare him because he was a child, but that intention had fled my mind. Nicolo grabbed my wrists and tugged as his face turned blue and his feet slapped against the flagstones. The burly, balding man swatted me. I wouldn't let go of Nicolo. He went limp and the man grabbed me under the arms and pulled me off him. Then he boxed my ears.

"Are you stupid, boy, attacking someone on the steps of the Palazzo del Capitano del Popolo?" he demanded, laughing. The little hair left on his head was red, and his short beard was teased with white strands. Somehow the red hair made his complexion pleasing and ruddy, rather than pale. He said, "This place is swarming with ufficiali and ministers and magistrates! They'll throw you in prison before you can earn your soldi!" I shook him off and glared at Nicolo.

"You crazy cur," Nicolo hissed, rubbing his throat. "You killed my father, and I nearly vomited out my life with those feathers! I'm going to get you! I'll make red feathers the last thing you ever see!"

Before I could reply, the burly man dragged me away. "You'll come with me. You're young, strong. I can use such a partner." Around a corner we found a stack of wooden rectangles. They were hastily made biers, three or four planks nailed together with another nailed crosswise at the top as a handle. The man released me and I stumbled, rubbing my shoulder.

"I didn't need you to intervene," I said. "It's not your affair."

He smiled, revealing a rotting blue front tooth. "I saw you save the Jew and his little girl yesterday. It was good of you. I don't know if Jews are guilty of everything they're blamed for, but I don't like to see people killed. Enough people have died in the last few months." He shrugged. "I didn't want to see you thrown in prison. They'd have had to lock you up if you'd killed someone out in the open, even scum like Bernardo Silvano's son."

I eyed the man coldly. "Were you a patron of his establishment?"

He shook his head and the warmth faded from his eyes. He went to a nearby barrel and grabbed a handful of cut greens, mostly wormwood, juniper, and lavender, and stuffed them under his camicia. "Before the plague, I had a wife who was good to me. I had no interest in the evil things Silvano's place offered."

"How did you know that was Nicolo Silvano, then?" I challenged him.

"All Florence knew Bernardo Silvano and his son. Everyone who's still alive here is talking about his slaughter last night. Only Nicolo mourns him. Silvano got the justice he deserved. So did his patrons. But what a man can get away with in a brothel is different from what he can do in public." He grabbed a plank and dragged it past me, its shadow barely sweeping the ground in the early sun. "Revenge has to be private. Grab the other side, will you?"

An ufficiale hailed us. "Rosso, ragazzo! Clear the bodies in the streets along the right-hand riverbank near the Ponte Santa Trinita!"

"Rosso, my daughter used to tease me with that name," the burly man called back, laughing. So we set off westward toward the river, where the streets were densely inhabited and the bodies would be plentiful. Other pairs of becchini headed in other directions. Their voices, joking and grumbling, trailed along behind them, the only vital sounds in the sick and dwindling city. We passed the grain market at Orsanmichele, its recently rebuilt loggia crowned with two stories for storing grain, a reminder of the rich and bustling times Florence had known. Now the market was empty except for a few vendors from the contado.

"I'm sorry about your wife," I said.

"Me, too," he answered in a low voice. "And about my children. I had two sons and a daughter. My older son was about your age, thirteen years. My daughter was ten, a pretty thing. I could have married her well, to a high-ranking guildsman or even a lesser noble. She had a nice disposition and pretty hands, would have bred well and brought honor to her husband. And my youngest son was full of trouble and fun. I miss them."

"When did they die?"

"A month ago. My poor daughter's hands were completely disfigured with black spots, and they hurt her terribly." His broad face was writ with a despair so complete and so accepted that it took me a moment to identify it. Then I realized I was seeing the same kind of unalloyed hopelessness I'd seen in the barren eyes of the children at Silvano's, when the body continues to live though the soul has expired.

"You've lost everything," I said quietly. He nodded. I asked, "Do you wish you'd never been married and had children, to spare yourself this mourning?"

"Oh no. I had fifteen sweet years with my wife—we were very happy. Our parents arranged the marriage, but we were well suited. We soon came to love each other."

"I have sometimes hoped to have a wife of my own," I said shyly. "A pretty wife who loves me as I love her."

"Love is a great blessing, the greatest gift that the Lord gives us," he said solemnly. "It makes a man whole in a way he couldn't imagine before." He sighed. "I only wish the plague had taken me, too. But then"—he paused, his balding head drooping—"because I was spared, I could bury them. They didn't have to lie around and wait for a stranger to throw them onto a bier like this. After I buried them, I closed my shop and came to do this work, until the plague takes me—most of the becchini fall ill and die. Everyone is dying."

"You buried your family with your own hands?" I couldn't imagine how painful it must have been to have a wife and children, to love them and then to lose them.

He nodded. "I couldn't get a priest to give them the offices of the dead, so I built coffins and took them out into the hills by San Romolo and buried them and prayed over them myself. I hope that's good enough to send their souls toward heaven."

"It must be," I assured him. "What could be more sacred than a father's love for his children?"

Rosso shrugged. He paused to wipe off the sweat beading on his face, and then pulled off his mantello, folded it, and tied it like a voluminous belt around his thick waist. I followed suit, because I was perspiring, too. He said, "It's warm, after a cool spring. The priests would have us believe that no one comes to God except through them."

"What do priests know?" I said, remembering several at Silvano's. "From what I've seen, they're gluttons or drunks, horny or grumpy or both, and looking to sell relics and indulgences and to advance in their order. No one's going anywhere through them except straight to hell."

Rosso laughed mirthlessly. "Keep those thoughts to yourself. Men have burned for less." I shrugged and we trudged through streets littered with bodies toward our assigned section. When we arrived, he told me to work on one side of the street while he worked the other.

"We'll get, oh, four bodies on the bier, depending on size," he said. "We'll pile them there, that's where the cart will pick them up." He indicated a small piazza where two streets joined. "It's simple work. We just go back for more bodies and clear as many as we can."

So I crossed over to my side of the street, where a body sprawled facedown on the cobblestones. When I rolled it over, I saw that it was a blond boy about my age. His features were coarser than mine, and his vacant eyes were blue, unlike my dark ones. His cheek bore a raised black welt as big as a hen's egg. He was wrapped in an expensive green velvet mantello which fell open, revealing black bubboni all over his naked body. As I gripped his arm to move him, I noted that he was still warm and his limbs were still soft and pliable. I dragged him over to the bier, upon which Rosso was

heaving the bodies of two men. They reeked of a putrid
stench and I screwed up my face and pinched my nose shut.

"You get used to it," Rosso said, with a raise of his
reddish-brown eyebrows. "Almost."

"People can get used to anything," I agreed, thinking with
wistful irony that it was better when they didn't have to. I
paused, taking in the quiet street with its gray flagstones and
shuttered windows and disfigured corpses whose clothes
seemed to melt in the humidity. In the background, the
river burbled and sluiced under the bridge. All things came
to death and destruction; eventually, I must, too, even if I
didn't age the way other people did. And my freakish agelessness would, perhaps, give me opportunities that other
people didn't have. I was gifted, and if I was also cursed, at
least I could promise myself that I would never again capitu-
late. I had bought myself this right by killing Silvano. From
now on, when I didn't like my circumstances, I would change
them.

I went back for another body. Near the boy lay two
corpses, a withered old woman whose white head rested on
a middle-aged man's belly, a similar cast to their faces: mother
and son. One of his hands gripped one of hers. If it hadn't
been so awkward, I would have dragged them together to
the bier, to preserve their intimacy, which I envied. If the
plague took me this day, no one would clasp my hand and accompany me. Was my birth similar, attended by some blem-
ish that caused my parents to want to lose me, as Silvano had
taunted? If I really was the lost son of foreign nobles with
pure blood, why hadn't they found me long before now? I
stood out; I was not being arrogant when I acknowledged
that. My striking looks were unusual, the shade of my hair
rare.

Had my parents, indeed, known their blood to be spoilt

in me? Had they ever loved me as Sforno and Rosso loved their children? Over the years, I had wondered only rarely about my parents this way. On the streets I was too busy securing food. Marco had piqued my interest in my parents, but at Silvano's, I was occupied with the ignominy of the work, with the ecstasy of the paintings that saved me, and, above all, with the knowledge that if I attempted to escape, as I surely would have if I'd discovered my parents, other children would have paid for my deeds with their lives. I could not let that happen. Now I was free and I could explore my origins and find out about myself, learn why I was different from other people. I would fulfill my other dreams, too: earning money, learning to read, even marrying. Above all, I would avoid the attention of the evil God who sent children into slavery, prospered murderers and rapists, and cursed the earth with lethal plagues. I didn't know how I would accomplish this, I was just determined to do so.

I was ruminating on this when a soft tapping caught my attention. I looked up; a man whose face was obscured behind a gauzy, billowy curtain in a second-floor window was waving. His hand like an imp called me to him. I glanced around for ufficiali. When I saw none, I gently laid down the bubboni-crusted twin toddlers hoisted upon my shoulders. I went to the door under his window. Inside I saw a small hallway which led to spiral stairs. I climbed to the second floor, where a door swung open for me. A finger of saffron smoke poked out of the door and curled, as if beckoning. Curious, I entered.

Inside the room were several tables set with wondrous equipment: flasks and alembics and small pots breathing up flames that licked the bottoms of bubbling flasks. There was a profusion of objects whose names and functions I did not know. I looked around in wonderment.

"You're intrigued by the appurtenances of my art," the

man said softly, from his seat on a bench by the window. "That's a start. You've the minimal intelligence to be curious."

"I've never seen anything like this," I responded, and turned my attention to him. He was of middle age, short, slim, and lithe, with coarse black-and-white hair and a narrow, beardless face. He wore a black tunic, and the slits in his sleeves revealed a black camicia underneath. Across his lively eyes stretched some apparatus that sat on his nose— another marvel. He saw me staring and tapped the thing on its side, by the outside edge of his thick black eyebrow.

"Don't stare, boy, speak up and ask. These are eyeglasses. Invented more than sixty years ago, but not yet worn by the *popolo*. They enhance the vision."

"Who are you?" I asked.

"An alchemist. You may call me Geber," he said. "The hand of fate is upon you, and it commanded me to speak to you. Otherwise I would not have taken the time from my work; I must have done something wrong to be so afflicted."

"How could you tell that about me from up here?" I circled the room, staring at the moving sea of objects washing over the tables as if by some magical tide. Little implements for poking and cutting and stirring lay alongside mortars and pestles, vials of dye, lumps of clay, needles and thread, books with illuminated pages, parchment and quills and ink pots, small tin boxes filled with powders both coarse and fine, stones of all colors, bottles of colored liquids, a bag of salt, and jars full of oils. The scents of sweet clove and anise mixed in with the acrid odor of sulfur, which still smelled better than the dead. A beheaded rat lay on one table, a cloth-covered jar of beetles on another, and on yet another was a pigeon with its wings neatly cut off. I stopped to stare at the pigeon because the cuts were so precise and the body was neatly sewn up where the wings had been removed. One of the wings was fanned out alongside the body.

"Distance is no obstacle to knowing," he said with a sly smile. "Distance is just a fabric that dissolves in the acid of merging. You know. You've traveled great distances to see things."

I started. His words seemed to allude to the traveling I did when I worked at Silvano's, but I had never spoken of that to anyone. I would not have confessed it to God, if I were the kind to confess, for fear that He would end my journeys for His own private amusement. It simply wasn't possible that this Geber could have guessed about them. I gave him a sharp look. "Is magic your art?"

"Nature is my art, and it will reveal everything to one who looks with the eyes and sees with the heart," he replied obscurely. "Heaven is spread upon the earth, but men do not see it. Nor, of course, do minimally intelligent boys."

"Hell is spread upon the earth now, with plague-stricken bodies everywhere." I shuffled over to another table. On this one lay an open book, a heap of dried violets, the furry brown paw of some small animal, an earthenware cup filled with white eggshells and another filled with blue shards, and a bowl with a translucent triangular stone soaking in cloudy water.

Geber sighed. "This is an evil plague. But so are all things of the earth." I had begun to finger a device of three interconnected glass vessels, when he barked, "Careful! That's a three-beaked still, exactly to the specifications of Zosimos himself. It's for distillation . . . the release of the spirit from the matter which has entrapped it."

"Like death," I commented.

He nodded. "Death isn't the end of the story in alchemy. The spirit, the pneuma, can be reintegrated into the body after purification. On that table, I have built Zosimos's *kerotakis,* for sublimation . . . Come, let me look at you. Even with this wondrous invention, my eyes are weak." I hesitated, running my fingers over the delicately colored pages of a book, and he beckoned impatiently. "Come, boy. I'm ill, but it will take the plague some months to kill me. And you are immune to it, as you know."

He seemed to know so much about me that I obeyed, warily crossing over to him. He examined me with thoughtful blue-green eyes. I reached out to touch the things that rested on his nose. A round piece of glass, secured by metal wire, hovered in front of each eye. "How do you know I'm immune to the plague?"

"You wouldn't be working as a becchino if you weren't," Geber said, pulling down the lower lid of my left eye, then my right. He stuck his index finger into the corner of my mouth and I opened it. He inspected my teeth and then picked up my hand and looked at my nails. He turned my hands over and traced some of the lines on my palm. He laughed shortly and tapped on the mount of my thumb. He seemed satisfied as he crossed his arms over his middle.

"There are many becchini," I noted, stepping back uneasily. What had he seen in his examination? What secrets of mine did his eyeglasses reveal to him? I spoke to distract him. "Many becchini will get the plague." I thought of Rosso. "Some of them want to die."

"Not me," he said shortly. "I've spent years laboring to cheat death. Only to find the plague cheating me of the fruits of my hard work."

"None of us can cheat death."

"You'll make a grand effort, though," he said, with another short laugh. "Your parents were magicians of the second race of men. You've inherited their talents, though you've not had anyone to guide their development. It'll take some effort on your part to earn them."

I jumped back, shocked and confused. "How do you know about my parents?" I cried. Had he met them? Did he know secrets about my origins, and if so, would he tell them to me?

"There is a light that pours forth from people, and that light is who we are," Geber said fiercely, leaning toward me. "This is what alchemy is about, truly. Ignorant folk think it is about turning base metal into gold, or perhaps manufacturing the elixir of life. But these are the grossest veneer. Alchemy is the search for what not yet is, the art of change, the quest for the divine powers hidden in things! The divine powers reveal themselves as light . . . he who properly cultivates himself will see the yellow light shine forth as it should!"

I didn't know how to respond to his strange and passionate words. It seemed to me that few things could be more important than turning base metal into gold, which sustained life. I could believe in a light that poured out of people, because didn't Giotto paint people thus, luminous? I looked away. I said, "You don't look ill."

"Don't judge by first appearances, it makes you seem common," Geber said sharply. He raised a lean arm and indicated his armpit. "Go on, feel for yourself. Direct experience is always the highest!" So I reached out and felt a squishy lump under his black tunic. "The plague's just beset me. I can resist it, but not forever. I will succumb." He spoke calmly, without fear.

"Maybe not. Some people recover, you could be one of them."

"I won't recover. I've seen it." He shrugged. "My own light has been tainted, weakened. As the light from within goes, so the body inevitably follows. You can see it, too, son of magicians, and so verify my words with direct experience. Look around my arm and head." He spoke softly and with elegant command. I found myself gazing almost sleepily at the outline of his outstretched arm and the roll of his shoulder into his neck, and then there was a pulse of blue light out from his head. He was murmuring, "As above, so below; as within, so without." Another blue pulse traveled along his arm and then the light widened into a yellow umbra shimmering out from his form, but the yellow luminosity was speckled with black spots—

"Stop!" I cried. "I don't want this, it makes me stranger than I already am!" I stumbled backward against a table. Geber brought up too many odd topics, most disturbingly, my parents. I blinked at the mist rising above a bubbling pot. The mist flowed into soft shapes like a river. My eyes followed the little pipes draining off into a closed flask. I wondered if this alchemical boiling was part of changing lead into gold, and if I could get this Geber to teach me how to do that. It would be a useful skill. Geber didn't seem to value it, but I knew the importance of gold in a man's life. If I could persuade Geber to teach it to me, I would never again have to fear hunger or being indentured into a corrupt life. Geber had to be saved, he had secrets to teach me. I said, "I know a physician, a good man. I can bring him to examine you."

"No physician can help me."

"You can let him examine you. You have to try to live," I argued.

"Because life is valuable even with hell spreading itself upon the earth?" he asked. He shook his head. "I won't waste your good doctor's time. I've stretched my allotted years long enough. But I will talk more with you. Come again tomorrow. Bring me something."

"Bring you what?" I asked.

He smiled. "You'll think of something." Dismissing me, he looked at the door with eyes which I did not believe to be weak. I fled.

———

LATER, SCRUBBING MYSELF IN SFORNO'S BARN by
the weak light of a single oil lamp, I looked up to find the
Wanderer watching me. I knew immediately that he wasn't
titillated, but still, I didn't want him there. I had had enough
of men watching me perform ablutions. I'd only been free of
Silvano's for one day, after all.

"I'd like to be alone," I said. My head was full of sensu-
ously textured and richly colored fabrics, raised black welts,
the yellow light around Geber's body, the sickening odor
that seeped out from corpses, and the raggedness of the row
of bodies we'd laid in trenches, sprinkled over with quicklime, and then covered over with another row of the dead.
My arms, back, and shoulders ached from carrying, dragging, digging. My stomach roiled and I wasn't sure I could
eat, though I was famished in a way I hadn't been in years,
and I could smell Mrs. Sforno's good cooking from out
here. But this was a refuge: the dark barn with a milky scrim
of starlight flowing into its windows, the golden bubble of
light radiating outward to blend into the stars, and the bleat-
ings of warm-blooded animals around me. I didn't want the
fragile peace disturbed.

"You stink," the Wanderer said, combing his long beard
with his fingers.

I gestured with the chunk of lye soap in my hand. "I'm
scrubbing."

"No." He leaned against the stall of the gray donkey, for
whom he seemed to have a fondness. "You smell like sorcery
and immortality." He grinned wolfishly at me as he stroked
the animal's ears. "You reek of splendor and the hidden way,
like someone who has crashed into the tree of life and
knocked down an apple. Do you have a bump on your head,
lucky cub?"

"Today there was anything but life and immortality around

me," I replied wearily. "And nothing fell on my head. See, no bumps." I ran one lye-greasy palm over my scalp.

"So literal! Well, there'll be things to see later," the Wanderer chortled, and when I looked back up, he was gone, with his laughter still ringing in the barn.

Chapter 9

THE NEXT MORNING I WOKE to find Rachel standing over me, staring. Her auburn hair was neatly combed back into a single long braid that she'd wound around the back of her shapely head, emphasizing her slim white neck. She wore a simple sleeveless yellow *giornea* over her green *gonna*. "I'm going to teach you how to read and write, Luca Bastardo," she said, in her serious way. In one hand she held a small wooden board with squiggles carved into it; in the other hand, she held a wax tablet. "Get up. We're starting now."

"Right now?" I sat up slowly, dislodging the fat gray barn cat and wiping stray pieces of straw off my face. The air was cool and pearly gray, as if the sun was just under the horizon. "Does your mother know you're here?"

"Papa does. Come by the window, there's better light here. We don't have much time before breakfast and I want to show you the letters. Papa says you're clever and that you'll learn quickly. We'll see." She sat down by the window. I kicked the blanket away and went to sit beside her, but not too close. Her presence unnerved me. She was a girl but on the brink of being more than that, and that something more floated around her like rose perfume. She was all soft rounded lines, soft red-brown hair, and not-so-soft self-confidence. I wasn't used to girls like her. I wasn't used to any girls, really. I was getting more nervous by the second.

"Your father said I was clever?" I asked. I was pleased by the compliment, but it made me feel more tentative, because now I had something to measure up to. No one had ever expected much of me before. Silvano had thought the worst of me, Giotto had thought the best of me, and patrons had expected only that their lust be slaked.

"Uh-huh, Papa thinks you're probably the lost son of a nobleman. Sit here, or you won't be able to see," she ordered, pointing to a spot closer to her. I scooted closer. She held the board so I could see its face. "This is *la tavola,* the hornbook. I'll show you the letters, and then you'll copy them on the wax tablet, with this." She showed me a small implement like a sharpened stick. "I don't have a quill and ink and parchment for you, so we'll have to do it this way. I'll teach you *rotunda,* which is the easiest form of script."

"Rotunda?" I asked, staring at her mouth, which was pink-lipped and full.

"Yes, because the letters are rounded!" she snapped, and I could tell her patience was already wearing thin. I took my eyes off her disturbingly pink mouth and trained them on the tavola, sat straighter, and sucked in my stomach. She went on, "When you've filled up the wax tablet, you'll smooth it out again."

"Fill up the tablet?" I repeated stupidly.

She gave me a sardonic look from dark eyes much like Mrs. Sforno's. "I would rather find my father right about you than my mother, but so far, you're not impressing me, golden hair or no. Maybe you're the lost son of an idiot."

"I'll try harder."

"See that you do. Now, this is the alphabet." She pointed to the squiggles.

"That's a cross," I said, pointing to the first mark on the hornbook. I was glad to know something, anything, though I was surprised to find the mark of a cross in the home of a Jew. "I thought Jews didn't revere the cross?"

"Christians think if they show us enough crosses, we will see their truth, give up our ancestral beliefs, and convert," Rachel said, her voice wry and delicate. "Now, for every sound there's a letter in the alphabet. Let's start with your name. What sound does it begin with?"

"Bas?" I offered.

"Bastardo isn't your name, and that's more than one sound," she said. "Try again."

"Bastardo is my name," I argued, though softly, because I wanted to please her.

"No, it isn't, it's sort of a description because you don't know your parents. Think, *Ll*uca," she said, emphasizing the first sound.

"*Lll?*" I offered.

"Good. That's the letter *l*. It looks like this." She showed me the *l*. "Now you." She put the wax tablet on my lap and then laid the cutting tool in my hand. I was looking at her pink mouth again instead of her hand and I immediately dropped the tool. She clucked her tongue.

"I'll get it," I said hastily, diving onto the floor. The tablet flew up in the air and Rachel caught it with an impatient ex-clamation while I scrabbled between the floor slats until I'd retrieved the cutting tool. I sat up with a foolish grin. "Here it is!"

The lesson wasn't long, but it was unbearable. I couldn't do anything right. Every time I attempted to copy Rachel's letters, I dropped the tablet or the tool, or I said something stupid. I persistently copied her small fine letters backward. My hand of its own volition reversed the letters, making her cluck and mutter. I squirmed with despair. It was my first lesson in the power women have over men, though we men may wield the greater power out in the world. Later in my life I was to encounter the greatest power a woman wields: her love. But that was more than a century into the future, and on this day, I could only exclaim with relief when the lesson finally came to an end.

"That's enough for today, Stupido—I mean, Bastardo," Rachel said, rolling her eyes. She tucked the tavola under her arm. "We'll try again tomorrow. Perhaps you'll do better."

"Maybe the day after tomorrow?" I asked hopefully. "I need to rest. Reading is hard!"

"You need two lessons a day, not rest," she sniffed, and flounced out of the barn, leaving me with the cutting tool clutched in my sweaty palm. I looked down at it and thought of Geber, who had asked me to bring him something today. Now I had something.

THE DOOR TO GEBER'S APARTMENT SWUNG OPEN, and threads of blue smoke trickled out, like fingers on a hand averting the evil eye. I entered and crossed over to where he stood at one of his long, profusely laden tables. "I brought this for you—" I began.

"Hush!" he commanded, so I replaced the tool in the waistband of my hose and watched as he carefully poured a golden stream of liquid out of a heated pot into a cool one. To hold the hot pot, he wore thick leather gloves with extra leather pads stitched over each finger. "Do you know what I'm doing?"

"Is that gold?" I asked in response.

"It's yellow, heavy, brilliant, extensible under the hammer, and has the ability to withstand assaying tests of cupellation and cementation," he answered.

"Huh?"

"It's gold." He nodded. "I'm going to purify it with nitric acid."

"Why?"

"Think, young man, what is the point of purification? To dissolve impurities, to reach quickly the perfection that nature intends . . . Purify me, O Lord, renew in me a right spirit," he murmured. His eyeglasses had slid down his nose on a small sheen of sweat. "Do you remember what I told you yesterday about the purpose of alchemy, or will you grunt at me again?"

"You said, 'Alchemy is the search for what not yet is, the art of change, the quest for the divine powers hidden in things,'" I quoted.

"Very good, no grunting. Do you understand what you've just said?"

"No, and I don't feel like answering any more questions because I spent the morning appearing stupid to a girl who thinks she knows everything," I said, sulking.

"A pretty girl?" Geber inquired with a laugh. I gave him a sour look and wandered over near the window, where gauzy curtains blew in to fan over a table's surface. A small black-and-white dog with its legs amputated had been cut open in a long straight line from its throat to its penis, its skin cunningly held out around its body by pins so that the muscles underneath could be seen. I was intrigued by the way the muscles wove in and out together and fat veins ran over them like rivers over hills.

"You've cut this dog open so you could see its insides?"

"Yes, but don't touch anything," Geber warned. "It's called

a dissection. I've begun by opening the skin, and I'll examine fascia and muscles and skeleton in turn."

"Why are you doing a dissection to a dog?"

"There is so much to learn still, a hundred fifty years is not enough." He sighed.

"Are you really so old?" I asked in wonderment. "How is that possible?"

"How is it possible for a person almost thirty years old to look like a boy of thirteen?" Geber glanced at me. "The thinking man questions himself first. For me, time is running out."

"Maybe the physico can help you," I said uneasily, dodging the issue of age and time, though I wondered at his secret source of knowledge that revealed to him my true age. I was determined to wrest answers from him, though I could tell he wouldn't yield them easily. I would have to use ingegno and circumspection with him. Changing the subject, I asked, "Can you really turn base metal into gold?"

"Any good alchemist can," he said dismissively. "A dog trained in alchemy could."

"I want to learn how!"

"Soon. There are more important concerns, with the plague consuming me as I stand here. I want to create the perfect philosopher's stone. . . . I want to revivify the dead, I want to generate a homunculus and to master nature and to avert chaos, that is the end of alchemy!"

His words were so fiery and ambitious, so unlike the false, pious platitudes mouthed by priests, that I was intrigued. "Isn't nature everything? How can that be mastered?" I asked.

"Many agree with you: 'art's so naked and devoid of skill that never can he bring to life or make it seem that it is natural . . . He'll ne'er attain to Nature's subtlety though he should strive to do so all his life. . . .' " Geber winked at me. "So it says in the story of the love of a rose."

"I love roses," I said, thinking of how pretty noblewomen held them in their gloved hands. "The color, the smell, the softness of their petals. They're beautiful and good."

"Do you not love painted roses more? As if from nature but with man's artfulness applied to it?" Geber asked. I shivered, wondering if he really did know about my singular travels. He went on, "The mistake in your logic, if you can call what comes out of your thick head logic, is separating my work from nature. I do nature's work for her and with her, so she submits to me."

"If Giotto had painted a rose, I would love it more," I admitted. "But Giotto turned to nature to find what was sacred and holy. He copied figures from nature, people as they really move in life. As God made man. It's part of what gives his paintings such power and holiness."

"Neither is alchemy an unholy art," Geber replied. "Though demons attend it, as they do everything in the material world, even saints and magicians with thick-headed sons."

"Do you know about my parents?" I demanded. "Who they are, what happened? Why did you call them magicians before?"

"What if I did?" Geber asked.

"Then you must tell me!"

"Must I? Would I really be helping you if I did?"

"Bastardo, Bastardo," called Rosso, a faint voice from outside.

"I have to go," I said. "Why won't you tell me what I want to know?"

"Why would I deprive you of your journey? He who fails to keep turning the wheel thus set in motion has damaged the working of the world and wasted his life, Luca."

"You speak in riddles," I grumbled. "Everywhere I go lately, riddles. No answers!"

Geber smiled. "Maybe you're asking the wrong questions."

"Then tell me about yourself," I said. Maybe if he revealed himself, he would let slip other answers. I said, "Where did you come from?"

Geber nodded slowly. "I belonged to a people who are mostly gone now. We were the guardians of secrets that the world needs, but isn't ready for. We were trying to purify and perfect ourselves. We called ourselves Cathars."

"Cathars, I've heard of them," I said, remembering a long-ago day in the Oltrarno, an uncaring northerner, and a beautifully crafted vial of poison for blue-eyed Ingrid. "I heard that the Cathars were a heretical sect that the Church killed."

"Not a heretical sect! One that possessed the secret teachings of the Messiah, for which the Church largely exterminated us," Geber said bitterly. "The things we taught—direct experience of God, tolerance, purity, the equality of man and woman, unyielding devotion to the true ministry of Jesus—threatened the secular power that the Holy Roman Empire craves. There was no room for us in their corrupt doctrine of the lust for wealth, hate, and exclusion! They coveted our secrets and our treasures while pretending to worship the Lord of love!"

"Luca Bastardo!" called Rosso, more loudly and with exasperation.

"But Cathars still exist," I said hurriedly. "Some were in Florence twenty years ago."

"You want to know about the connection between your parents and my people."

"I want to know who I am, where I came from, why I'm different from other people, and what it means! I want to know the secrets of my origins, and if I'm different even from my parents!"

Geber looked at me for a long moment. "The Cathars knew many secrets. We kept treasures. Our purity made us worthy. What makes you worthy, Luca?"

"I have struggled my whole life to answer that question!" I cried.

"Could it be that the struggle itself is your answer? That it's not for me to shorten your quest?" Geber asked steadily. "Does not your personal quest progress history along toward its end, allowing men to be the swords with which spirit wages war? What, after all, is history: the great swaths of events or the sum of individual lives? Which is more important?"

"Luca, now!" Rosso shouted.

Geber and I regarded each other. I realized that, today, he would not answer my questions, except with questions of his own which I could not begin to answer. "You asked me to bring you something. Here." I held up the sharpened stick and then laid it on the table.

"A pointed stick?"

"For copying letters into a wax tablet, a task which is purgatory on earth," I said. Rachel's merciless face flashed into my head. She was a hard mistress.

"An alchemical gift." Geber looked pleased and surprised. "Thoughts transmuted into signs, which become spoken words and thoughts again: the richest alchemy . . ."

"Bastardo! Ufficiale!" Rosso called urgently. I waved goodbye to Geber and fled down the stairs. Rosso waited outside the door, nervously rubbing his hand through his bristly, balding red hair. We walked toward some bodies, dead condottieri, on the cobblestones. Three ufficiali on horseback cantered up to us. The two in the lead stared at me, and I stared back defiantly. I was free now. I didn't have to drop my gaze and slink off like a guilty mongrel at the approach of the police. My boldness must have unsettled them, because they pulled back. The one in the rear drew his dancing horse alongside me, then spat at me. I looked up into Nicolo Silvano's narrow face. For a moment, furious and appalled and a little terrified that some diabolical alchemist had re-united Silvano's pneuma with his body, I saw his father's mien. But then it was Nicolo, dressed in the red of a magis-trate with an elaborate rolled cowl around his neck.

"The city must be desperate for ufficiali if they're making magistrates of scum like you," I sneered.

"There is witchcraft about you, Bastardo," Nicolo hissed. "I'm telling people about you, and we're watching you!" He dug his heels into his horse and trotted off with the other uf-ficiali close behind him. Furious, I picked up a stone and flung it after him.

"Beware, Luca," Rosso warned. "You've an enemy in Silvano. Fear runs alongside the plague, and people are quick to kill what makes them uneasy." I shrugged, stifling my anger. We each took a bubboni-spattered body by its armpits, lugging it to the ubiquitous heaps of the dead.

OVER THE NEXT FEW WEEKS, my days fell into a rhythm. Rachel woke me before dawn and taught me let-ters, or rather, attempted to. I possessed the gift of auditory recall and verbal mimicry, and I never forgot a painting or a sculpture that I saw even once, but the meanings of the little squiggles she drew eluded me. It made no sense to me that those scratches cut into wax meant something. Rachel took to pinching me with her elegant, strong fingers when I for-got how to form a letter or drew it backward—which was almost always.

I escaped her schooling as soon as I could, ran from the barn to the house, bade the other Sfornos and the Wanderer good morning, and then took some bread dipped in olive oil and a chunk of cheese with me to meet Rosso at the Piazza del Capitano del Popolo. While we collected bodies, he would tell me stories about his wife and children. I liked hearing how his oldest son had copied him, how his second son had teased him, and how his daughter with the pretty hands used to help her mother sew his lucco. Once the girl had sewn his hose closed as a joke, and laughed until she wept when he hopped around on one foot trying to get his other foot in. When Rosso went to rest and take his midday meal, I ran off to see Geber.

One day Geber met me at the door laughing. "At this rate, you'll never learn to read, my fine ignorant sorcerer," he said. His face and black tunic were smudged with grainy ocher powder and he emitted the scent of salt and wet leather. Behind him, tendrils of dun-colored smoke scrolled about his room, weaving through the plethora of strange objects. "I'll give you a lesson as well, perhaps spare your arm some pinching!"

"How do you know so much about me?" I demanded. In truth, the inside of my upper arm was black-and-blue because of Rachel's slim strong fingers.

"The philosopher's stone tells me," he said mysteriously, chuckling. He gestured me in impatiently and set about giving me a second lesson. From then on, we would stand at the end of the table where his three-beakered still bubbled as he painted letters, and then combinations of them, onto small linen squares. When I read the square correctly seven times in a row, he let me toss it into the fireplace and watch the ink, like magic, paint the flames purple and green.

Despite myself, after a few months, as Florence baked in the natural oven of the Arno valley and then cooled again, and the number of corpses swelled like the tide and then finally began to wane, the double lessons began to work. Through no merit of my own, letters surrendered their mystery and spoke to me, first in whispers and then in clear, reasonable tones. As I read first syllables and then whole words, Rachel began to scribble numbers and sums alongside sentences. Before the plague, and hopefully again after, Florence with its banks and merchants abounded with people who could cipher well. As Silvano had told me, this skill was called abbaco, it was much valued in commerce, and I was pleased to learn it.

As my reading skills quickened, Geber spoke of other things. He showed me weights and measures, demonstrated the properties of metals and herbs, lectured on the four elements of fire, air, earth, and water, and the four qualities of hot, cold, wet, and dry, and explained how all ores come from mercury and sulfur. He discussed with me the transformation of matter, such as when water, through evaporation, becomes air, and through condensation becomes water again. He instructed me in the difference between the purely mimetic art, which copies nature, and the perfective art, which improves upon it.

"The alchemist must use what nature uses, and restrict himself to that; the naturalness of his products depends on his imitating the workings of nature whenever possible!" he insisted as if I were arguing with him—which I was not. I had the sense of an old argument that persisted in his head. He ranted on about the need for experimentation, for a consistent witnessing of the alchemical art without taking anything for granted beforehand. "Not all alchemists agree with me. But I write down my observations, all of them, in detail," he confided. "I have made a great book of them, the *Summa Perfectionis.*" Then he gave me a sad look, and I saw his sadness as an opening to ask him again about the Cathars.

"We were a group of worshippers devoted to God. We believed not in faith but in direct access to God, without the intervention of clergy."

"And?" I prompted him slyly.

"And because we were devoted, we had access to the indivisible point within, the grain of mustard seed like a radiant blue pearl. . . ." Geber's voice softened and his eyes grew distant.

"Where did the Cathars come from?" I persisted.

"Directly from Lord Jesus," he said sharply. "Our teachings are pure and perfect and come from Him. We knew, for example, that there is a feminine component of God in the soul of the world, that this material world was created by an evil God and that it is our task to escape material trappings through following the star within! That Judas Iscariot was no traitor, but was a beloved intimate of Christ and did only as the Lord asked in order to fulfill His mission on earth, that Judas was the only one to possess full knowledge of the truth of the God within—"

"Judas betrayed Christ, even I know that, and I have no catechism!" I argued.

"If Judas hadn't handed over our Lord, would there be salvation?" Geber snapped.

"I don't know." I shrugged. "But I meant what place did the Cathars come from?"

"Woolly-headed boys don't think much." Geber gave me a piercing look over the rims of his spectacles. "Cathars have been in all places and all times. We were intimates of the Sethian race before we received Christ. The Sethian race is the secret, incorruptible race of man, who carry the great knowledge and hide—"

"Am I of that Sethian race?" I interrupted, excited. "What does it mean, if I am? Do they have marks on their chests, and should I have one, too?"

Geber's face smoothed suddenly. "I am not the one to reveal these things to you, boy."

"Then at least teach me how to turn base metal into gold!"

"Not today." He shook his head. "You will learn, eventually." It was a promise he dangled before me, and with gold as the goal, Geber found me a willing student. He covered many subjects. He unrolled a great map on one of his long tables and showed me the Republic of Florence's position on the boot of land extending into the Mediterranean, with the Tyrrhenian Sea on the east and the Adriatic Sea on the west. When I came to him with news of how a roving band of soldiers had killed three men and raped their women in the countryside and nothing was done about it by the city fathers, who had been decimated by the plague, he explained the city government and its history, how the nine-man *Signoria* which led the city was now jeopardized by the plague.

"Even the great Florentine *casate* are foundering, which is a measure of the plague's devastation," Geber said. "The casate originated hundreds of years ago. These ruling families are the Uberti, the Visdomini, the Buondelmonti, the Scali, the Medici, the Malespini, the Giandonati, most of whom had moved into the city but maintained their country lands with their patronage rights in their ancestral zones. They also nurtured a spirit of vendetta, which has haunted Florence, and which erupted into violence at a wedding banquet in 1216. There, a Buondelmonti wounded one of the Uberti with a knife. A marriage was proposed as reconciliation, but Buondelmonti chose vendetta. He was ambushed, and ended up a bloody corpse on the street by the statue of Mars."

"The Uberti had their vengeance, problem solved," I noted.

"It was the beginning of more than a century of problems!" Geber snapped. Everyone in Florence took sides, and the city was torn apart. Those who supported the Buondelmonti became Guelfs, supporters of the Pope, while Uberti supporters were Ghibellines, who supported the emperor. The two vied cruelly for power until the Ghibellines were finally broken.

"Which led to the Neri-Bianchi struggles in this century," Geber continued. He looked up as if preparing his thoughts, and I saw the small black spot on his throat. I made a small sound, pointing, and he nodded. "The plague has marked me. Now let me tell you about the Donati. . . ."

THAT NIGHT I WAS IN THE BARN scrubbing the stink of plague off me, listening with only half an ear to the Wanderer. He was prattling on about how the universe was a balance of light and dark forces that seemed to be separate but were really all a part of the great formless Oneness. I drifted into my own thoughts because, after all, the Wanderer couldn't teach me how to make gold and wouldn't pinch my arm if he caught me daydreaming.

"I have been out tending to the ill. I hear your name being spoken in the city, Luca," Sforno said seriously, as he came in and took the strong lye soap from me. I knew now from Geber's lessons that the soap contained potash for the cleansing.

"What name do they call him?" the Wanderer asked. He sat on the tripod stool and stroked the fat gray barn cat. "Ah, but the question really is, and the right question is everything, do they give him a name or take away from him a name? Because to lose his name is perhaps the first step in the long climb up the tree of life to its Source."

"I don't want anyone to take away my name," I said stubbornly. "Luca Bastardo may make me less than other people, but it's mine. I intend to do great things with it!"

"The ultimate essence isn't limited by name," the Wanderer commented, "though for our convenience it is referred to as the *Ein Sof,* and one who contemplates it is annihilated in a sea of light and passes beyond control of his natural mind."

"They call him 'sorcerer,'" Sforno answered.

"Divine names unfold in accordance with a law of their own." The Wanderer shrugged, combing his great gray beard with his meaty fingers. The warm-blooded animals in the candlelit barn swayed and uttered their moos and clucks and whinnies, and the gray cat even mewled, as if in response to his words.

Sforno dipped the scrub brush in the trough of water. "They say he practices black magic to remain youthful and beautiful, that no ordinary boy could have killed eight men in one night."

"Do they say he kills Christian babies and drinks their blood, as they do about us? Do they give you satanic horns, too?" the Wanderer crowed. "Welcome to the tribe, wolf cub! God has chosen you, too, and tribulations and struggle await you!" He clapped me on the shoulder.

Sforno shrugged. "Silvano's son is telling tales. Those left alive in Florence are listening. Florence is a meddlesome place. People are quick to believe nonsense when they're afraid."

"They can't do much now, it's hard enough to clear the bodies of the dead," I said. Sforno shucked off his tunic and camicia and lathered himself with the soap. His broad chest was solid and covered with hair, and though I had seen many men unclothed, I turned away.

"It's best for you to avoid groups of people," Sforno said. "A crowd can turn murderous."

"Ten men turn into a community of God," the Wanderer said.

"There aren't ten people who would gather together," I noted. "They fear the plague. Half the city is dead. Signore Sforno, there's a man I know who needs a doctor. Will you come?"

"I'll come," the Wanderer said, yawning. "I need a diversion, and I hear the sound of chariot wheels turning. Moshe, do you think your pretty wife made lamb for dinner?"

"I don't know what she found at the butcher shop today." Sforno frowned. "Or if she found any meat. She trades with the other women and the one Hebrew butcher still working."

"Jews are lucky they have each other to trade with. There's little food," I said. "You can comb the whole city and not find three eggs. No one's coming in from the contado with new food and meat. The markets are deserted. People are hungry."

"There'll be problems when plague survivors begin to die of starvation," Sforno said. He and the Wanderer exchanged a grim look.

"Jews are the scapegoats of the world," the Wanderer said wearily, his mirth dissipated in an instant. His face seemed to melt like wax held above a flame, and he looked old, impossibly old, centuries old; he looked as if he'd seen more pain and suffering than any man could possibly observe and remain sane. Then his face reassembled itself into its usual ironic lines. "Think what a service we provide for those who must have someone to blame! They ought to thank us while they burn us."

"Jews aren't the only scapegoats," I said. "Witches are blamed and killed. Cathars, too."

"Cathars? There's a name I haven't heard in many turns of the wheel," the Wanderer boomed. "They might as well have been Jews, for all the kindness they received at the hands of their fellow Christians. Indeed, they were friends to Jews. They lived alongside us in France!"

"Do you know where they came from before that?" I asked.

"They wandered the earth, seeking safe haven, even as

we Jews do," the Wanderer said. "Centuries ago there were Jews among the Cathars, though the Cathars called themselves by other names then. There aren't many of them left."

"The ones who are left have secrets," I said. "And treasures."

"Don't we all?" asked the Wanderer. "The Cathars made no secret of their belief that the material world was evil, ruled by an evil God, while heaven and souls were the good God's domain. They split in two what we Jews believe is one: 'Hear O Israel, the Lord our God is one.' "

I was uninterested in abstruse matters of philosophy. "We all have secrets, yes, treasures, not necessarily," I said, then remembered that I, too, had a treasure: Giotto's panel.

"Depends on how you define treasures," said the Wanderer, with his sly grin. "There are treasures of the mind and heart, treasures of a life lived so that it means something both to the individual and to the community. . . ."

"Jews have to have portable, countable treasures in the form of gold, precious stones, and a trade," Sforno said darkly, "for when exile calls us again, as it inevitably does."

"There'll always be a new country to flee to," the Wanderer rejoined.

"Next year in Jerusalem," Sforno muttered.

"So be it," the Wanderer said.

Chapter 10

THE NEXT MORNING, I brought Sforno and the Wanderer to Geber's. I led them up the stairs and through the door that always mysteriously swung open at my arrival. The usual pulsing array of objects littered the tables, with pots boiling and beakers rattling and pink mist tapping against the ceiling and sweet, pungent scents intermingling in the air. Geber stood with his back to us. His shaggy black-and-white head was bent over a large illuminated manuscript with a brown leather binding; a vellum page covered with rose and quatrefoil miniatures peeked out from his elbow. When he turned to face us, he and the Wanderer cried out at the same moment. The next moment, they were hugging and exclaiming and pounding each other on the back.

"My old friend! The last time I saw you, you were shimmying down Montségur in the Languedoc with a treasure on your back!" the Wanderer roared. "You were weeping over the power of Satan and flesh, and railing against the terrible war between good and evil!"

"March 16, 1244, the day after my wife and friends, the other Perfects, were burned alive in a wood-filled stockade. Along with children and infants. 'Kill them all. God will recognize his own,' that's what the Pope's representative said." Geber's narrow, intelligent face contorted into a mask of pain. "I still hear her praying in my dreams, as I know she did in death."

"Love is seen as heresy by the Church and brings down the bloodiest wrath," the Wanderer said, squeezing Geber's slight shoulder with his big hand. At a table by the window, two doves flew against the door to their cage and broke it open, and then they flew around the room, cooing and weaving in and out of the crackling pink fog.

"Was it that the Pope despised our beliefs, or that he coveted our treasure?" Geber asked, bitterly. "The Languedoc was rich and fertile, sparkling with education and tolerance, radiating Cathar ideas out into Flanders and Champagne and München. The Church couldn't have that. It was never about faith. It was about secular power, as always!"

"You two know each other?" I interjected. The space between them vibrated with old memories and fresh feelings, debated ideas and shared jokes. I was, as always, on the outside, looking in at other people's tender connections.

"I've known—what are you calling yourself these days, my Perfect friend?" the Wanderer asked, with rough affection in his voice.

"Geber."

The Wanderer laughed. "Abu Musa Jabir ibn Hayyan would be pleased!"

"Maybe, maybe not." Geber's face softened and lost some of its anguish. "I've expounded some principles which he might not approve of, though I didn't know him as you did. And you, rogue Wanderer, have you taken a name?"

"I would not put one on; I would not give to others the

means to any magic over me," the Wanderer said seriously, and it was the only time I ever heard him answer a question directly. He said, "Geber, let me introduce you to my good friend, the physician Moshe Sforno."

"I am honored to meet any of the Wanderer's friends," Sforno said, with a serious smile that reminded me of his daughter Rachel when she was most intent upon something.

"Well met, physician. You've come at Luca's request," Geber said, looking at me.

"He said he had a friend who was sick." Sforno's eyes went to Geber's throat. "I see the plague is upon you."

"I don't want you to die," I said to Geber. "Signore Sforno is an excellent physician!"

Geber shook his thin, ink-stained finger at me. "You take too much upon yourself, boy. I would have spared you the trip here, physico. There is nothing that can be done for me. Though I am greatly heartened to see my old friend!" He squeezed the Wanderer's arm.

"I should have guessed you were the boy's teacher!" the Wanderer said. "He comes home bursting with more self-importance than dragging corpses around ought to earn him."

"I am not self-important!" I objected hotly. "I'm doing honorable work for the city—"

"The world is full of impudent boys, which convinces me that my old beliefs were correct, and evil is equal to good. From what I've seen of this particular boy, time won't be enough to make a dent in his thick head," Geber said wryly.

"He'll have enough of it for the attempt to be made," the Wanderer said, with great mirth. "He is one of those that your people protected?"

"A son from one of those families of whom we were the guardians." Geber nodded.

"What families? Whose son?" I demanded. "Why did the Cathars protect them? Are you talking about the second race of man? What does it mean to be of the second race?"

"All these questions, as if answers would solve anything." Geber sighed. "He may be studying with me, but he's not learning."

"Answers solve questions!" I said. "I want to know about my family!"

"The right answer creates more questions," the Wanderer said. He looked at Geber. "I wish I'd known earlier that you were in Florence!"

"The Inquisition burned Cecco d'Ascoli at the stake only twenty years ago," Geber said. "He was a fine fellow, though he shouldn't have made a fuss about the star of Bethlehem being a natural event. The priests protect their miracles. They made a big fire and smiled as the flames melted the flesh and fat from his bones. It's better for alchemists to stay hidden."

"But I would have liked to spend time with you," the Wanderer said, sadly, staring at the black spot on Geber's throat.

"Why don't you come near the window and let me examine you in the light, Signore Geber," Sforno said, gently leading Geber over to the window. "I would like to check your pulse and hear your history, and if you've some urine in your chamber pot, I'd like to see that."

"My heart is beating, my history is health until the plague contacted me, and my urine is the stinking piss of men with the Black Death upon them," Geber grumbled.

Sforno stifled a smile. "Your history is something more complicated than that, if you're really more than a hundred years old. Is it true that alchemists have discovered an elixir of life?"

"Even as Hermes Trismegistus himself instructed: use the intellect to render oneself immortal," Geber answered.

"If this elixir was part of the Cathars' secret knowledge, that would be one reason the Church persecuted your people," Sforno said. "They see immortality as their domain."

"Secret knowledge, treasures, ancient artifacts, our friendship with the Sethians; they had many reasons to hate us," Geber grumbled. He sat on the bench by the window and Sforno bent over him, looking into his eyes and throat. They conversed in low, private voices.

The Wanderer went to Geber's illuminated manuscript. "In every word shine many lights," the Wanderer said, running a bulbous index finger over the delicately limned page. Flowers and little animals trembled at his touch. "Do you know what this word is, Luca of the many questions?"

"Pan-ta-rhe-a," I read haltingly.

"Everything flows," the Wanderer said, stretching out his thick arms to indicate the whole world, almost bursting the twine that belted his gray lucco over his big gut. "Even your reading. You owe Moshe's daughter a debt of gratitude, though if her mother discovers what the two of you have been doing, there'll be trouble. Not that Leah Sforno has anyone to blame but herself; this is what comes of educating women."

"We've been doing nothing," I said stiffly, though the image of Rachel's mouth flashed before my eyes. "Rachel is an honorable girl." I moved to the next table and fingered the pyramid of flat gray stones that lay beside a heap of chestnuts and a row of dried apple cores with faces carved into them. Beside the apple cores was a tiny shriveled head—and I wondered if it was really the head of a small human, as it appeared to be. There was never any telling what I would find lying on one of Geber's tables. There was always something new and strange, and never the same rare object twice. I wondered where Geber obtained his objects, or if he simply manufactured them in his stills and flasks as he wanted. I asked, "Why did you call Signore Geber 'perfect'? He doesn't seem so perfect to me; do you consider him perfect?"

"Who am I to judge another man's perfection?" The Wanderer smiled, thumbing through the manuscript. The gilded edge of a white vellum page flashed as it stood vertical, then fell flat. "Do I look like the living embodiment of the Sefira of Gevurah, divine judgment?"

"I guess not," I said, wishing the Wanderer would simply answer my questions, instead of throwing more questions at me like stones that must shatter the glass containers in my head.

"Wrong," he said promptly. "I'm the living embodiment of Gevurah. I'm the living embodiment of all ten sefirot, the holy emanations or attributes of God, as all men are, each of us formed like Adam Kadmon in the image of God."

"You speak with formal phrases, like a priest canting," I said fiercely. "And what do priests know of God? A great master told me that God was laughing at me, and he was right. God, from His great remove, laughs at everything. We know that because something wonderful happens in the midst of something too terrible for words, like a vision of a painting when an atrocity is happening. Then something terrible unfolds in the midst of joy, like the plague killing a man's beloved wife and children. There's contradiction everywhere. Remorseless contradiction. In some way, when you subtract everyone's feelings, it's funny. Bittersweet, and funny."

"Finally," the Wanderer said, staring with admiration writ openly on his big-boned face with its shrewd eyes and full, shaggy beard.

Moshe Sforno came over, shaking his head. "I'm afraid Signore Geber is correct, there's not much I can do for him. I'm sorry for you, Luca. And for you," he said to the Wanderer.

"It will be a while yet," Geber said, straightening his black lucco as he joined us.

"Such a waste." The Wanderer sighed.

MOST NIGHTS I RETURNED to the Sfornos' home late. There were so many bodies to bury that we becchini were kept outside the city walls digging graves well past sundown and long after dinner was served. Mrs. Sforno made no secret of not wanting me around, so, after scrubbing off the stink of death in the barn, I crept as though invisible through the house to the kitchen. There I scrounged up a leftover slab of chewy bread and a wedge of soft, strong-smelling cheese or slice of herb-roasted chicken breast. Sometimes there was some flavorful white bean, black cabbage, and old bread crust soup left out in a bowl on the table, or a savory stew of beans and garlic and tomatoes, or a plate of peas cooked with oil and piquant parsley. Mrs. Sforno also made a wonderful soft omelet with artichokes. She was a very good cook, though she followed an arcane set of Hebrew rules for food. I was grateful for whatever she put aside for me. As quickly as possible, I took the food with me and went back to the barn. There I took out Giotto's panel from its hiding place and beheld it while I wolfed down my meal.

One night I was still hungry after a plate of fresh spinach sautéed in olive oil and I went back into the house for more. I ate in the kitchen, wearing only camicia and hose. By the pale gold light of a lamp on a chest in the foyer, I saw Moshe Sforno coming in from the barn after me. He looked grim and weathered, his beard down on his chest and his shoulders slumped under a mantello that looked huge and black in the shadows.

"*Ciao,*" I murmured, and he lifted his head and smiled tiredly.

"Do you have a good word for me, Luca? I just told a man that his wife and children were dying of the plague and there was nothing I could do for them. The best advice I could give him was not to catch it from them," he whispered.

"Your wife made excellent spinach," I whispered back. There was nothing more I could say; tomorrow I would bury the good folk he had examined today. Sforno waved good night.

"Moshe?" murmured a soft voice. "*Caro,* come to me." It was Mrs. Sforno, and her voice was so sweet and sensual as it carried down the stairs that I flushed. Age and weariness fell off Sforno like a discarded cape and he stood a little straighter. He didn't glance at me; he smiled and hurried up the steps. I was thunderstruck, imagining a woman calling to me like that, her arms soft and warm for my arrival. I knew at once that I must have that kind of sweetness for myself someday, just as, years ago, I had known that I must someday be able to smile Giotto's smile of knowing acceptance. Life was full of pain, sorrow, and horror, but a man could handle anything with a call like that awaiting him at the end of the day.

MONTHS WENT BY, and victims of the plague grew fewer. Rosso met me at the Palazzo del Capitano del Popolo one morning with a black swelling on his full cheek.

"No, not you." I was dismayed.

"It makes you wonder; will everyone die? Will man perish from the earth, every last one of us laid out on the ground, our bodies covered with black spots, our own blood on our lips?" He smiled, showing the rotting blue front tooth. "If this plague kills everyone, if everyone dies, the earth will be left empty, without music or laughter or children who play jokes, and what will be the point? We will have loved and labored and constructed in vain."

"Not everyone will die," I said. He gave me a keen look.

"No, this plague won't take you, Bastardo. And for me, it's not so bad, I'll join my family at last," he murmured. "If I know my wife, she's waiting with ten important chores for me to do in heaven, and a soft embrace when I've completed them. My daughter's hands will be beautiful again, and she'll have a joke to tell me, some funny tale that Santo Pietro himself whispered in her ear. I can accept what is coming. I welcome it, even. God is good."

"May it be so for you," I said, humbled by his surrender. I couldn't see myself surrendering so easily; I had promised myself I would stand and fight. Nor did I believe in Rosso's heaven, or a good God for that matter, but if those beliefs comforted Rosso, who had only been kind to me, I was happy for him.

Two days later he didn't show up for work. I searched until I found him lying on the stoop of a once-prosperous bottega. On the street, two shops were open, and a man even walked past and gazed into the window of one of them. Windows were unshuttered and the bells were pealing again for Mass, not just to warn of the plague. In a sunny autumn of cerulean skies, this city of gray and dun-colored stone palazzi, ancient Greek and Roman statuary, and bridges swept away periodically by the Arno, was taking its first few breaths of new life.

But Rosso wasn't breathing. His blood-rimmed eyes were glazed over and vacant. He must have died only minutes before I arrived; he was still warm, and the enlarged facial pores around the bubboni still oozed. Black spots stippled his sturdy neck and strong hands, the front of his lucco was stained with vomit. He had died in pain. I was sorry I had not been there to ease it for him.

I dragged his body inside the shop, into a spacious, white-plastered room with two long worktables and many shelves set with dyestuffs and small bolts of fabric. Dust had sueded over everything during the long siege of the plague. I sat down on a bench and looked at Rosso's empty body. Outside a pair of horses trotted by, pulling a wagon. Ufficiali rode in it, but I didn't worry about them harassing me. They were busy rebuilding the city, now that the plague was loosening its grip. I remembered Rosso's stories about his wife and children. He had asked me what it would mean if everyone died. I thought the point would be amusing God, and that an empty earth with all of mankind dead would be a great joke for Him. What did He need us for? After a while I stood and looked out the window. The tall gray stone houses across the street obscured all but a sliver of azure sky, which was hazing over with the lush honeyed light of afternoon.

"Laughing God, let his soul join his loved ones," I said. Then I dragged the corpse back out to the street and laid it on the bier. I folded his hands in a prayer over his heart, because I knew the limbs would soon stiffen. Over the next few hours, sweating in the harvest sun, I dragged the bier through the twisty cobblestone streets, out the brick and stone city walls with their battlements that had seen armies march past so many times, past cedar trees and olive groves and neglected vineyards with heavy grapes dragging down sun-burnished vines, all the way into the rolling hills of Fiesole with its cool breezes, Roman ruins, and views of the city's stone towers and red roofs. I stopped near the cathedral of San Romolo. Rosso had told me he'd buried his family near there. I knew I would not find the exact location of the graves in the tall autumn fields of lavender and the groves of pine and ilex, and, indeed, there were many graves there now, as well as rotting unburied corpses, but I might get close to the bones of his beloved. It might lend some comfort to his spirit. I borrowed a shovel from an abandoned farmhouse near the church, and when I found a place that seemed restful and the sky seemed especially blue and open, like something Giotto might have painted, I set to work digging. My arms, shoulders, and back had grown strong over the last few months of digging graves; I made short work of it. I laid his body in the grave as gently as I could and then covered him over with dirt. I packed it down well so no dogs or wolves could get to him. At least I would cheat God of that laugh.

I MADE MY WAY BACK TO GEBER's brimming with purpose. I meant to confront him about his knowledge of me and of my origins, of good and the loss of good people, of God's need for people. It was dark and cool, a star-filled night with a full white moon whose dreamy seas were illuminated. I walked through the city without fearing the curfew. Once I saw some ufficiali on horseback. They approached, but stopped short when they caught sight of my face in the silver light, and then cantered away. I was not to be provoked this evening.

For once, Geber's door was closed. I knocked, but there was no answer; I called his name, still no answer; then I tried pushing, but the door refused to budge. I beat on the door and kicked it, but it didn't give. I leaned my back against it and then slid down until I was seated on the floor with my back resting against the door.

After a while—maybe hours, maybe minutes, for time seemed stopped up like a river with a boulder blocking its

current—I went down to the street. The wooden bier I had
used to haul Rosso to his grave lay beside the door, and I
worked at the iron nails on the handle. My fingers grew
ragged and bloody, despite the thick calluses I had earned
from months of hard labor. Finally the nails gave and the
handle came off the top of the bier. I brought it upstairs to
use as a battering tool. As I swung the plank back for the first
thrust, the grainy surface of the door rippled like a cloudy
mirror, or like the Arno. Bernardo Silvano's pockmarked
face looked back at me. He grinned, that knowing sneer of
all the years of my indenture in his establishment, and I
swung the plank at the door, at his face with its narrow nose
and thrusting chin. Silvano laughed at me. He knew that I
would never be able to forget him. He knew that he would
live forever inside me like a worm perpetually rotting an apple. A fury vaster than the horizon rose up inside me. I
howled like a wolf and went berserk, battering the door
with the same supernatural strength I had summoned to kill
all those men at the brothel. The rough board splintered
in my hands. Silvano laughed again. All of my rage and frustration and bitter dregs of humiliation slammed into the
wooden door. It groaned and then banged open. I strode in.

Inside, instead of Geber's familiar room with its playful
smoke and seething curiosities, a cave greeted me. It was
stony, dank, and dim, and smelled of animal droppings and
old air. I had to duck my head to enter. The hem of a familiar
crimson mantello fluttered ahead. I felt a shock of recognition. Anger surged through me. Carrying the long jagged
stick from the ruined bier handle, I bolted after the red
mantello. I ran through a maze of low tunnels dripping with
moisture, and finally trapped the red-clad figure against a
cave wall. I swung the splintered wood, and he turned—his
face was invisible, swathed in a luxuriant red cowl—and he
parried with a sword. It was no ordinary sword. It was one

of the costly, elegant longswords made by northerners, a nobleman's sword, the kind I had seen strapped on the sides of honorable men with the wealth of their wives, families, friends, and name. We fought that way, my wooden shard against his gleaming sword, until his sword stuck in the wood. Instead of stepping back, I pressed forward. Ingegno, as Giotto had advised me long ago. I swung my left hand up and punched him in the throat, hard. He coughed and loosed his sword, and I spun the stick away so that sword and stick came away together in my grip. The sword flew off, and I plunged the jagged point of the wood deep into his chest. Spraying blood, he fell, first on his knees, and then to the floor. I leaned down to rip off the red cowl, which was of the softest wool I had ever felt. I gasped, because the glassy-eyed face that stared back at me wasn't Nicolo Silvano's. It was mine.

As I stood in shock, the gray smoke of the cave drained away. Geber's room emerged, with all the tables bare but for candles, except one, which bore a still. Standing shoulder to shoulder were Geber and the Wanderer. They were clad in plain white lucchi instead of their usual garb, Geber's black lucco and the Wanderer's coarse gray tunic belted with frayed twine.

"It's time for you to encounter the philosopher's stone," Geber said.

"I see no stones," I said, looking around. "The stone caves I thought I saw are gone!"

"It's not a physical stone," Geber rebuked, slapping the back of his hand into his other palm for emphasis.

"Then why do you call it a philosopher's stone?" I asked.

"It's an image for transformation! Pay attention, boy! You are to be ennobled."

"Ennobled, me?" I laughed bitterly. "An urchin off the streets, a whore, a killer?"

"I know, you still have a long journey ahead of you," Geber agreed, weariness lacing his voice. "But you're as ready as you're going to be in the little time I have left." There was a new bubboni on his cheek and purple half-moons beneath his lively eyes, and I knew that the plague had started to fatigue him.

"The ways of the cosmos are splendid," the Wanderer added. "You are the bridegroom encountering the light. Your body has grown strong, now it's time to strengthen your soul."

"What is this all about?" I asked, looking from one man to the next. "Are you finally going to teach me how to transform base metal into gold?"

"The name of God transforms everything," the Wanderer answered solemnly.

"First, the sacred marriage," Geber said. He held out his hands. In one was a plain beeswax candle, in the other a silver winecup, engraved with the symbol of an upside-down tree with its fruit webbed together. "Fire is the element that multiplies; the cup fills and empties." He laid them in my hands and then motioned me to follow him. I trailed along behind him to the table set with one of his rattling stills. He reached over and plucked some hairs from my head. I grunted, but he ignored me and pulled off a chunk of nail from my torn fingertip. Murmuring "Into the retort," he took the stopper out of the bubbling flask and carefully dropped the hair and fingernail into the boiling liquid.

"What are you doing?" I asked.

"There are four worlds of being: emanation, creation, formation, and action," the Wanderer answered. He came to stand beside me. He chanted in a language I could not understand and rocked back and forth with his chanting. Then he said, "We can see a pattern. But our imagination cannot picture the maker of the pattern. We see the clock.

But we cannot envisage the clockmaker. The human mind is unable to conceive of the four dimensions. How can it conceive of a God before whom a thousand years and a thousand dimensions are as one?"

"I can conceive of a God who plays cruel jokes, and I think he's doing it right now," I said uneasily. I looked toward the door, but it was closed, without even a seam of light to show where it was cut into the wall. Instead, there appeared the face of an horologe of the new mechanical kind seen in the past few years on towers around Florence, which always, like a vain woman, prided herself on having the latest, best appurtenances.

"That's the laughter of the Trickster." Geber's narrow intelligent face relaxed into a smile. The Wanderer chanted and swayed, his wild mane of hair fluttering around him in gray and white fringes. Geber poured wine into the silver cup with its strange tree and gestured for me to drink. I sipped, the wine was sweet with a sour finish. He said, "The Trickster leads you to feel the nothingness of human desire and the sublimity and marvelous order which reveal themselves both in nature and in the world of thought, of art. The Trickster shows you that your own existence is a prison. He instills in you the desire to experience the cosmos as a single significant whole." Geber lit the candle and put on his leather gloves with the extra pads sewn onto each finger. "Pay attention to the Trickster, boy; he's your only hope for escaping prison."

"I'm not in prison now, now I'm free," I answered, a little stubbornly, because I was confused and I did not like the feeling of confusion. "I freed myself. And I'm going to stay free!"

"To substitute nothingness for chaos is to guarantee freedom," the Wanderer said. "Within the King, this abyss exists along with unlimited fullness. Thus is His creation an act of love freely given. It is written thus. 'In the beginning, when the King's will began to take effect, He engraved signs into the heavenly sphere,'" the Wanderer recited in the bold voice of a storyteller. His large hands made dramatic gestures to illustrate his words.

"Do you remember what I taught you, boy who lusts only for gold?" Geber asked, his voice holding a faint tone of mockery. "About the distillation process. From the retort, through the condenser"—he ran a gloved finger along the pipe leading out of the retort flask—"and into the distillate!" He removed the distillate flask and uncorked it. Something shining and white flew up, wings fluttering noisily so close to my face that I exclaimed; Geber sighed, the Wanderer laughed. Geber produced a gold vial from his white lucco. He shook out two drops of some thick, oily liquid into the distillate flask. In a melodious voice he chanted, "One nature rejoices in another nature; one nature triumphs over another nature; one nature masters another nature!"

Within the distillate flask a spark lit up. It began as a tiny iridescent point of light and then grew spherically until it filled the flask. As it grew, it shimmered with colors in sequence: first a curious black light, then white, yellow, violet. A sharp crack like the strike of lightning against a tree echoed through the room, and the point of light bulged until it exceeded the flask, then flared out to fill the room. It threw rainbow slicks of color on all the surfaces: the tabletops, the rough-plastered walls, our clothing. Looking through the light, I saw Geber's bones, but not his flesh. The Wanderer, too, was visible as a skeleton, but not as a person. I held my hand up and saw the narrow phalanges spreading out before me. My hands tingled as if full of running water.

"What is this magic?" I breathed, and the light dwindled,

and the room was as before, lit with the soft lucence of many candles. Geber poured steaming liquid from the flask into a small earthenware cup, and handed it to me.

"Before the world was created, only God and His name existed," the Wanderer said. "As you are rectified by the stone which is not a stone, repeat in your mind a word which I will speak into your ear, a word which you must never utter to another person. It is one of the sacred names!"

"*Prima materia*," Geber said. "Drink, and return to your essence!"

I held the cup in both hands. It was a small brown cup, painted with green leaves, and oddly frosty to the touch. The Wanderer leaned forward and whispered into my ear, and with his whisper ringing in my head, I swallowed the bitter elixir.

Geber and the Wanderer vanished. They were simply not present, as if they'd never stood before me, the Wanderer with his maddening riddles, Geber with his sharp-tongued instruction. Geber's room remained as it had been: lit with dripping wax candles set on bare wooden tables, a central table displaying a still which rattled while it boiled. I gagged. Weakness seized my limbs, and I pitched forward. I was able to grab the edge of one of the tables, but it steadied me only for a moment. My knees crumpled—kind, doomed Marco must have felt this way all those years ago, when Silvano hamstrung him and we children watched in horror—then I was lying on the floor. With the last strength in my arms, I pulled myself upright against the leg of the table. A shudder went through the room, and my body was fragmented into parts: hands burned and flew off into a deep blue void, while my limbs separated from my torso, from head, from breath, from the thoughts that scrambled about in my head like objects tangling up inside a peddler's sack. Everything was disjointed, and the center fell away. I knew I was going to die.

There was sorrow that I was dying alone, having hoped for so many years, with death dogging my steps at Silvano's, that I would eventually pass peacefully, with someone kind at my side. I thought of Rosso and wondered if his spirit lingered nearby and could greet me. He had surrendered to death so gracefully, when he knew it was inevitable, that I decided to follow his lead. I sighed—or would have, if my frozen chest could have moved—and let it come.

A ragged frisson of pain went through me, and my breath stopped weaving in and out. The steady pumping of my heart, which I was so used to, stuttered into silence. A body fell over, and as I looked down at the lean blond boy curled up on his side on the floor, I realized that I was no longer inside that body. It was a fine body that looked as if it would soon have ripened into manhood: it had clean, strong limbs, long rounded muscles on the shoulders and back, a pleasing, symmetrical face, staring dark eyes, and shaggy reddish-blond hair, but it no longer contained me. Darkness in the room was pushed back by dawn, and Geber came in, crying out when he saw my empty form. He knelt to feel for a pulse in my throat, murmured with sadness when his fingers failed to find the river of life streaming through me. Grunting with effort, he dragged me downstairs to the street and waited until becchini came with a wooden bier. They piled my corpse atop the bodies of an old man and a pregnant woman, the last few victims of the plague. Geber left, and when the becchini had dragged me outside the city walls to a burial site, Geber returned with the Sfornos. The Wanderer was not with them. They huddled together while a group of becchini dug a trench and laid in it a dozen bodies, including mine. They threw quicklime over us and then shoveled on the good crumbly brown-red dirt of Tuscany. Rachel, Sarah, and Miriam wept softly; Moshe Sforno chanted, while he held Rebecca in his arms; Mrs. Sforno looked out over the rolling

lavender hills to the tall stone walls of Florence with its dark
towers rising against the endless blue autumn sky.

Suddenly I was liberated. I could go anywhere. Joy spilled
through me: I could see more of Giotto's frescoes. I could
see the glorious cycle of St. Francis in Assisi that Friar Pietro
had told me about. And just like that, I was floating over a
high hill with a white marble double cathedral, one church
built atop another. Peace emanated from the hill. The great
rose window of the upper basilica faced east, and I was
drawn to descend down through the rose window into the
transept of the church. I found myself hovering before a
painting of St. Francis preaching to the birds. St. Francis was
a gentle and lively figure in a monk's brown mantle, gesturing tenderly to birds both in flight and at rest. His hands
were calm and holy, expressing goodness even to dumb animals, and compassion shimmered in the humility of the great
saint.

I couldn't linger because a brilliant force pressed against
me, whatever "I" was now. The force opened like a door into
a timeless, placeless whirl. Images like water sluicing off
eaves ran past me: the cobblestone streets of Florence, dirty
and silent and emptied by the plague; the market with bar-
rels of grain and baskets of ripe apricots; the faces of people
I'd known, dark-complected Paolo, and Massimo, who had
betrayed me, and Simonetta with her birthmark; the faces of
people I'd killed, the men in the brothel, Marco with his
long black lashes, blue-eyed Ingrid; unknown faces which
closely resembled mine; the bed with its horsehair mattress
in the little room at Silvano's; Giotto's beatific St. John ascending; the hay in the Sfornos' barn and the fat gray cat that
mewled until I let her sleep in my sweaty armpit. . . .

The images arced past and then I was observing great
swaths of time, like an illuminated manuscript whose pages

were flipping rapidly to disgorge its secret illustrations: strange faces and bloody wars and new weapons that spat fire and floods and plagues and famines and huge new cities in faraway lands and marvelous machines that flew through the air or dove deep under the water and an arrow-shaped vessel that thrust itself toward the very moon.... A panoply of unimaginable sights opened up before me; it seemed there was nothing that man's art could not create, sustain, and then destroy. I could only witness in wonderment, much as I had witnessed Giotto's frescoes during my secret journeying, when I worked at Silvano's. All the while, the Wanderer's sacred word pealed in my mind like a distant bell ringing.

My heart wrenched open. The dark flame from within Geber's distillate flask burned through me. It scoured open canals within my woven-together sense of "I." It left me soft, wrung out, awash in sadness and loss and pain and my endless hidden yearning for love. It was raw and exhilarating, to be stripped bare in a way my nakedness at Silvano's could never presage, because this was nakedness of the heart. I was reveling in the translucence of being undefended when a small, slender woman's form approached me. She was dressed in a fine blue and orange cottardita and wreathed in silver light, but her face and hair were concealed by shadow.

"You have a choice," said a voice that was not hers. Indeed, the voice was neither young nor old, male nor female, Florentine nor foreign. It came from nowhere and everywhere and it simply spoke. In the voice's resonance, I saw myself grown to be a man. I was still lean and of medium height, though I was well muscled. I approached the woman. I took her delicate hand, kissed the soft palm that smelled of lilacs and lemons as if she'd been gathering flowers in the clear light of morning. I embraced her. Her slender body melted into mine. She was my wife, my life, the sum of everything I had ever wanted: family, station, beauty, freedom, love. Unbearable aching happiness pulsed through me.

"You can have the great love you long for, but she won't stay—" and I saw, felt, myself alone. My throat was raw with anguish, the dark fire that had opened me now scorched my heart without mercy, and my own aloneness pressed in on me like spiked iron walls collapsing inward to crush me. Giotto's paintings couldn't soothe me, nor could the ravishing paintings by painters still unborn that had revealed themselves during my flight through time. It was suffering on a scale that even I had never imagined possible, and I knew suffering. My tongue felt bitter and shriveled from cursing God. My own nails excoriated the flesh on my palms. Then all was still.

"—and your love will lead you into loss and a premature death. Or you can live without ever meeting her, and live hundreds of years longer," said the voice. And the man that I became strolled casually, his expensive woolen mantello fluttering as if I were walking down a country road with a soft wind at my back. Gold florins weighed down my money purse, and I knew I was wealthy. Indeed, I was peaceful, content, expansive, but somehow incomplete. My hands felt cool and still. There was open space around me, a soft, expansive freedom. I would live to see with my own eyes the wondrous machines that had been shown to me earlier. The voice finished, "You must choose now."

"That's no choice," I heard myself say aloud. "Love, of course."

There was a rush, and then I was gagging again, choking, and vomiting onto Geber's wooden floor. The Wanderer was supporting me while Geber wiped my face. I coughed and vomited some more. I wiped my face with my hand and was surprised to smell the fragrance of lilacs clinging to me out of my vision. The fragrance wasn't subtle. It was strong, as if I'd dumped a vial of perfume on myself. It was a tangible artifact of an inconceivable journey, and it shocked me. I was disoriented, disquieted, unsure what to make of what had happened to me. Was it real? If so, then what, indeed, was real? My own bizarre agelessness, and the marvelous journeys I had made to Giotto's frescoes to escape the horrors of the work at Silvano's, had led me to question things that other people took for granted. This vision dissolved boundaries even I had believed to be firm.

"Welcome back," the Wanderer said cheerfully.

"Good journey?" Geber asked, his thin, beardless face quizzical. I looked from one to the other, a thousand questions trembling on my tongue, then leaned over and retched again.

"I've a donkey downstairs, I'll get him home," the Wanderer said. He heaved me up over his broad shoulder and trudged downstairs, his clogs clattering on the steps and making my head ache. Geber followed us with a rag to clean up the bile when I vomited again. A braying donkey was tied up at a bronze fixture outside the door downstairs, and the Wanderer threw me unceremoniously over the smelly beast with my head hanging down one side and my feet down the other. Waves of nausea rippled through my throat and belly and I threw up into the animal's dusty gray fur.

"Luckily my friend here doesn't insist on cleanliness as Moshe's pretty wife does, or you'd be wiping him up and apologizing for your bad behavior," the Wanderer joked. "Get rid of it now, wolf cub, because if you puke on Sforno's floor, his lady will beat you with her broom!"

My head was lolling helplessly, but I picked it up to look at the two men. Questions clattered in my head like pebbles rattling against each other, but only one emerged. "Can I change lead into gold now?" I croaked.

"Possibly," Geber said, rolling his eyes. He picked up one of my hands and eyed it in the silvery moonlight, ran his finger over the lines graven into my palm. I noted with wonder that there seemed to be an extra crease radiating out from the mount of my thumb. In a pleased voice, Geber said, "Yes, very possibly. Not tonight, though, impatient boy."

The Wanderer snorted. "Real gold is understanding, and I doubt you've sublimated that!"

"At least he's persistent," Geber said. "We have to admire that. He can fix on a single notion, minimal intelligence and all."

"I find much to admire in our young cub." The Wanderer laughed. "The question is, can he find it in himself? Will he continue to see the enemy within, or will he finally see the Friend? Before his opportunity to repair the world is finished?"

"Why must I repair the world?" I groaned again as I maneuvered myself around to sit astride the donkey. It craned its head and snapped at me. The Wanderer smacked its flank, but with obvious affection. I said, "After what the world has done to me, I don't feel like I owe it anything!"

"Just when I think he shows potential," Geber snorted.

"Wolf cub, it's not what the world does to us that matters," the Wanderer said in a kind tone. "It's what we do to the world. We're not taught that, but you've been given the grace of a life on the streets, so you've been taught little. There's hope for you. We must become ignorant and be, instead, bewildered. That's when eyesight becomes vision. Do you see yet?"

I laid my head down on the donkey's neck. "I don't know what I've seen," I confessed. "I don't know if it's real or shadows. I don't know what's real anymore."

"Then there is potential," Geber said. He waved goodbye and the Wanderer led the donkey on, and the rhythmic

clip-clop of the beast's hooves on the flagstones lulled me
into a state close to sleep. I surrendered, thinking that there
would be time later for all my questions, time to get answers
from Geber and the Wanderer about what had just happened
to me and what it meant. I was wrong. Time is not what we
imagine it to be. Its span is ungraspable, immeasurable, unexpectedly brief, even for a man whose life stretches many
times what most men are allotted.

Chapter 11

AT DAWN THE NEXT DAY, Rachel flounced into the barn to rouse me for our usual lesson. I groaned and rolled over with my head wrapped in my arms. The gray cat screeched.

"Get up, Bastardo, you're going to read Aesop's *Fables* today," she commanded, poking me with the toe of her shoe. It was not a dainty poke.

"Ergh," I responded, burrowing my head deeper into the blanket and straw. My tongue was furry and swollen, my muscles ached, and the slightest noise instigated a vicious thudding pain in my forehead like footsteps stamping with iron-spiked clogs. I had buried Rosso, whom I liked. Then I myself had died. It all confounded me. The visions of the prior night replayed in my head and instigated strange notions and amorphous yearnings. Geber said I was to be ennobled by the philosopher's stone, and I felt as if, in some way I didn't quite merit, I had been. First I'd been shattered, and then I'd been bettered. It left me wanting to do loftier work, work in which I could take pride, work which would have an impact on the world. Work which would bring honor to the love who was promised me in the vision, if, indeed, the choice offered in that vision ripened into fact. Such an ambition was far outside my purview, but it waxed rather than waned. I was at a loss about how to fulfill it. So I didn't get up until late in the afternoon when Moshe Sforno came to get his street clothes. He pulled his lucco off a peg. An image leftover from the visions of the philosopher's stone flashed in my head, and I saw myself trailing along behind Sforno as he went out to tend the ill.

"Wait, signore, I have to go with you," I said, struggling to sit up. "You're going to tend someone who's sick. Someone with the plague?"

"Not this time. There's a nobleman's son with an infection in his arm from a sword cut."

"May I go with you?" I asked. "I could help you, carry your tools or something." The idea was intriguing enough that some of the wool cleared from my head and I lurched to my feet.

"Well, I never thought of you helping me out," Sforno said in a musing tone.

"I can't go on as a becchino forever," I pointed out. "The city doesn't need them now that the plague is receding. And you have four daughters and no son to accompany you."

"No son to teach what I know." Sforno sighed.

"Besides, you'll need help holding down the boy if his arm needs amputation."

"It's true, you work hard, you're strong, and you're not at all squeamish," he said. He smiled. "You would make a fine assistant, perhaps even a physico someday. Get dressed."

I shook out the brown woolen blanket I always slept in, folded it, and then patted my camicia to rid myself of hay and cat hair. My working clothes—hose, farsetto, and mantello—were hung on a wooden peg by the door. I pulled them on, saying "I never considered it before this moment, but I might like to be a physico. It's good work."

"It's hard work," said Sforno. "There's much to learn."

"I'm not afraid of hard work, and I'm ready to learn," I said. In fact, I was more than ready. The months of lessons with Rachel and Geber had built up an appetite in me. And, after the philosopher's stone, I wanted a new direction in my life. I said, "I'm hungry to learn!"

Sforno perused my face, then nodded. "You'll start off as an empiric, learning by watching me and then practicing while I oversee you. If you show talent, I'll find Galen's works for you to read, and of course Aristotle's treatises, and I can send for a copy of Avicenna's great *Canon,* too. He wrote about important medical topics, like the contagious nature of phthisis and tuberculosis, the distribution of diseases by water and soil, and the interaction between psychology and health. You'll have to learn Latin. Most of the great medical writers were Saracens; some were Greek, and their work has been translated. I'll find a tutor for you. You'll learn quickly. Rachel says you do, despite yourself," Sforno said with a wry smile. The autumn air was cool in the barn and he pulled his heavy mantello closer about himself. "But, again, I warn you, don't imagine that being a physico is easy."

"No work's easy, that's what I've learned," I said quietly. Being a physico had to be easier than prostitution or gathering and burying dead bodies. It surprised me how quickly my past came up for me, even after a night like last night. I was still haunted by my history. But I had to be comfortable with it, since it was what I had. The Wanderer had asked me if I would find the friend within. I didn't know how to do that, other than to be that friend.

Dressed, I went with Sforno along the stone path through his garden into his house. Inside we stopped at the kitchen, where I took a slab of cheese and a chunk of dark bread. There was a honey cake baking in the fireplace. Signora Sforno stood by the table talking with another Hebrew lady. Moshe gave me an amused look. "My wife is a ruthless negotiator, I love watching her," he whispered.

"I can offer you a large bowl of my dried apricots," Signora Sforno was saying.

"These apples are fresh and ripe, there aren't many nice pink apples like this in the city, people were too ill to attend to their crops!" the other lady responded, indicating a basket of glossy-cheeked apples. She was plump with dark hair curling out from under her yellow headdress. "Besides, I accepted your dried apricots for the wheat flour yesterday, and Signora ben Jehiel told me afterward that she would have given me dried meat for it!"

"What do you want, Signora Provenzali? What do you think I have left? Do you think people have been paying my husband for his services, when they die as soon as they see him? Meanwhile, your husband's pawnshop has stayed open during these terrible plague times. . . ." Signora Sforno let her voice trail off suggestively. She took two apples from the basket and tossed them to Sforno, who handed one to me.

"My wife, she has some spirit," Sforno said mirthfully as we went out into the hall. "She's had to work so hard these last several months. But the serving girl will be back soon to help, I heard she survived. Anyway, as I said before"—Sforno crunched a bite of apple with some gusto—"this is not an easy profession. There are always ignorant village healers who think they know more than a trained physician, and who offer amulets and incantations instead of medicine. I think there would be more magicians now, preying on people's fear and superstition, except that the plague has killed so many of them. And don't forget you have to have the stomach to remove limbs and tumors, to cauterize wounds, and to cut out gangrene if that's what's necessary." He plucked up a large calfskin bag from the stairs. He opened the drawstring and indicated his instruments: knives, razors, lancets, a silver cannula, a cautery iron, various needles, and grasping tools. He pulled out a bloodstained steel saw. I nodded, and with a grimace he replaced the saw in the bag.

"People distinguish between medicine and amulets," I said, following him into the street.

"Never," Sforno snorted, spewing white apple crumbs into his beard. "Sometimes. Worse yet, incantations work as often as anything else. Some priests offer exorcisms as medicine, and no Jew can gainsay a priest, or he risks burning! And there are barber-surgeons, for whom the cure to every disease is bloodletting, and I'm not sure that bloodletting ever cured anything."

"People die when they lose a lot of blood," I commented. I had seen that myself, during Silvano's demonstrations.

"That's what I think, too," Sforno confided, tossing his apple core into a gutter. We walked out of the Jewish enclave and through the narrow bricked streets of the Oltrarno, where the new palazzi of nobles and wealthy merchants had been halted in mid-construction with the plague's incursion. There were the usual bakeries and artisans' shops, mostly closed—but not all of them. Three children followed a pair of women who were gossiping about the market; ufficiali on horseback trotted past; a man wearing the crimson of a magistrate strode in a hurry toward the blacksmith, from which arose a busy clanging. Sforno commented, "People are returning to the city, now that the plague is receding. But the Wanderer didn't show up for breakfast. He'll be back. He's like a wart that never stays away."

"I thought he was your friend," I said.

"Is that troublemaker anybody's friend?" Sforno asked, so

sarcastically that we grinned. "He sets off Leah every time. He started in with Rachel and really got her going the other day. She's a thoughtful kind of girl who doesn't like to be challenged. I thought she was going to throw a cup at him."

"He's some kind of trickster, with those questions," I said slowly. I had no way to make sense of my experiences of the previous night, of the cave and the battle with Nicolo who turned out to be me and the vision of the future. I decided to do what I always did: focus on the work at hand.

"The Wanderer will show up when it's most inconvenient. Meantime," Sforno said briskly, "you must learn about herbs. I know a woman in Fiesole who's an expert herbalist. There are some excellent women healers," he told me in a confidential tone of voice. "Most university-trained doctors dismiss them, but I prefer a woman healer to a bloodthirsty barber-surgeon. And every physician has to have a good midwife to work with; a doctor can't be there for every popolo grosso cow who's calving." He clapped me on the back in good spirits. "There are few good Gentile medical texts, but a Christian woman named Hildegard wrote some very nice ones. That's what I mean about women, don't discount them in medicine."

We came to a new palazzo near the Ponte alla Carraia, where carts crossed into the city from the country, and I had a bittersweet memory of Marco from so long ago, and how we'd planned to meet on this bridge after escaping from the brothel. I rarely thought of Marco, or Bella, but on this day of memory after a night of foreseeing, I wondered if I would ever truly forgive myself for my part in their deaths. Perhaps, if I did actually find the love offered to me in my vision, I deserved to lose that love. I wondered how I would survive the loss of something I'd longed for my whole life. Perhaps I'd made the wrong choice at Geber's. And why was I given this choice? Why had Geber singled me out for the

fantastic journey of the philosopher's stone? Because of my
family's connection with the Cathars? I knew Geber's time
was short, and I was determined to wrest from him answers
about my parentage. Also the secret of turning base metal
into precious gold. My musings were interrupted by Signore
Soderini, who stood at the door, waiting.

"I've been expecting you, Signore Sforno," said the anxious nobleman, a stout, black-haired man. He gesticulated
wildly with arms wrapped in voluminous gold sleeves. "You
must help my son!" He led us through his richly appointed
home to an upstairs bedchamber where a boy of about thirteen lay tossing on the bed. He was wiry and had his father's
black hair and high forehead. His oval face was pale with
fever. His mother, a tiny, plump woman with a pale green
headdress over her chestnut hair, bathed his face with rags
dipped into a bowl of water.

"You're the Hebrew physico who studied in Bologna,"
she stated, giving Sforno a determined sideways glance. "My
cousin Lanfredini speaks well of you. He urged us to return
to the city and send for you to care for Ubaldo."

"Your cousin is a good man," Sforno said politely. "Signora,
will you step aside so I may speak with the young signore?"
She rose, clenching her lavender silk skirts together in one
hand. Sforno set his calfskin bag by the bed and took the
woman's place at the boy's side.

"He's our last child," she said in a low voice, her chin trembling. "Two other sons and a daughter died of the plague. You
must save him!"

Sforno gave her a compassionate look. "I have children
myself. I will do everything in my ability to save your son,
signora." He gestured for me to stand beside him. I watched
as Sforno greeted the boy in a friendly voice. "I'm going to
examine you, Ubaldo. This is my apprentice, Luca," he said,

pulling the boy's lower lids down to look at his eyeballs. He placed his ear close to the boy's chest, listening, and then grasped the boy's swathed right arm. Ubaldo moaned and licked his lips. His black eyes, like his mother's, sharpened, but he didn't cry out. Sforno unwrapped the bandages.

"You're a brave one, Ubaldo," Sforno said, as the smell of rotting flesh reached our nostrils. He pointed at the festering slash mark on the boy's forearm, but I didn't need a physico to show me that it was infected. The wound was surrounded by purple- and bronze-colored skin that graduated into swollen reddened skin, and dark red lines radiated out from the swelling. Even as we watched, the boundaries of the infection spread farther down toward his wrist and up toward his elbow, and more of the bronze skin surrounding the gash deepened into purple. Ubaldo moaned and tossed his head.

"Ubaldo, I'm going to speak with your parents," Sforno said gently. He gave me a significant look, which I understood to mean that the arm was lost.

"You're lucky, your parents really care about you," I whispered, when Sforno stepped away. I didn't know if Ubaldo would or could answer.

He picked his head up and made a brave, agonized attempt to smile. "Don't all parents? Yours must, too. You look about my age. I was playing at swords with my cousin. He didn't mean to hurt me. He's not more than a baby. I was careless, not expecting his strength."

"Does it hurt?" I asked, looking at the wound. My hands tingled as they had last night at Geber's. The dreamy images of the time to come flitted before my eyes, and yet I was fully awake. I felt heavy. My breath came slower.

"It only hurts when I'm awake." He tried to smile but moaned instead. "You've probably never had something like this, you were probably never foolish enough to get cut this way."

"I know pain," I said. My hands burned. An uncontrollable impulse to touch Ubaldo swept over me. Of their own volition my hands went to his arm. I gripped his arm with one hand at his wrist, one at his elbow. The heat in my hands increased until they were flames of flesh. Then a streaming sensation like sweet water pumping up from an underground well flowed between my two palms. The purple-and-bronze flesh around his wound bulged like a bladder being inflated, and then it wept. Sweet-smelling reddish-brown goo leaked out and drained down his arm, staining the white linen bedclothes. Not knowing why, but trusting my intuition, I kept a firm hold on his arm and fixed my eyes on the wound. After some moments, the goo thinned into a milky liquid and then ran clear, and before my eyes the swelling receded, like a tide going out. The reddened skin paled, and the bronze-and-purple skin softened into red, then pink, like a sunset climbing backward out of night, or a river reversing its course to flow upward. "Ah," said Ubaldo. His head lolled to the side and his black eyes closed.

"So this is why the arm must be amputated," Sforno was saying, in the sad, firm voice of an experienced physico. He stepped back with Ubaldo's parents and pointed to the boy's arm. Then he gasped. "Luca, what are you doing? What is this?"

"Should I stop?" I cried in dismay, my grip on the boy's arm loosening.

"No!" Sforno shouted. "Whatever you're doing, keep doing it!" So I returned my attention to Ubaldo's arm, where the deep hues were still dwindling, the swelling still ebbing, and the crimson lines retracting into the gash like thread being wound up around a spindle. Ubaldo's mother uttered a soft cry. I focused on the arm, watching as it slowly returned almost to normal. The cut was still there, but the skin around it was pink and pliable.

"Holy mother of God," Signore Soderini exclaimed. *"Grazie Madonna!"*

"A miracle," the mother breathed. "A woman in Fiesole uses her hands to stop bleeding, and priests calm disturbed people with prayers, but I've never seen anything like this!" She kissed Ubaldo, who snored loudly. She pressed her cheek against his, and I felt envious that he would receive such gentleness. "No fever," the mother cried. "His fever has broken!"

"You must be blessed by God," Soderini exclaimed, "to have the power to do this! I've heard people claim you were in league with the devil—that verminous son of the brothel keeper Silvano has been spreading malicious tales about you, calling you a sorcerer—"

"Nicolo Silvano lies," I said, alarmed. I backed away and angled myself toward the door, in case I needed to escape. I remembered all too vividly what had happened last time people called me a witch, at the Piazza d'Ognissanti: I'd almost been burned at the stake. "I'm not a sorcerer," I said uneasily, but with a flicker of fear, because the journey of the previous night might have been brought on by sorcery. Geber would say that the alchemist's art was not sorcery but careful methodology and application with the elements; I was not sure anyone but Geber would believe that. "I'm not a sorcerer!" I repeated.

"No sorcerer would heal a child this way, and I will proclaim that!" Soderini thundered.

"Maybe you shouldn't talk about this," I suggested.

"People will want to know," Ubaldo's mother said breathlessly. "Florentines talk, and things that have been said about Luca Bastardo are enough to get him hung or worse."

"The less said about me the better," I said tightly.

"Luca is right," Sforno interjected. He was blinking rapidly and wore a bemused expression. "My young apprentice is very talented. Luca is no sorcerer, he does not engage in diabolical exchange. He's an intelligent young man who's had a difficult start in life."

"I will support your wishes. If you wish us to be silent about Luca's abilities, we shall be," Soderini said, his voice breaking. "Physico, I can never thank you and your apprentice enough. We are so grateful that my son's arm can be saved and he will be whole!" He grabbed Moshe Sforno in a strong embrace. Sforno grunted and struggled, and finally, a tearful Soderini released him. Soderini came at me, but I ducked beneath his arms and hid behind Sforno. I had no taste for the embrace of men. I looked for the door. I was ready to leave.

"We are happy to have been of service," Sforno said, straightening his lucco. He bent back over Ubaldo and examined the arm. "There's no need for a dressing on the wound now. You don't even need an unguent for it. Just watch it to make sure it doesn't get infected again."

"Since you won't let us defend Luca's good name, you must take this." Soderini pressed two gold florins into Sforno's palm and then closed the physico's fingers around the coins.

"That's well above my fee," Sforno demurred.

"Many physicos have profited handsomely from the plague, and they couldn't save anyone," Soderini said. "You brought your apprentice who cured my son!"

Sforno shook his head. "I have no wish to profit from the plague."

"You must accept this," Ubaldo's mother said earnestly. "It's small recompense for the life of our only remaining child!" She laid a quivering hand on Sforno's arm. He bowed, acquiescing. Around his head she gave me an overly sweet smile. I cowered behind Sforno.

"Luca," he said, "we should let these good nobles tend to their son."

"We will speak well of you, as a Jew," the nobleman said then, in the tone of giving a great gift. It was a generous concession, because everyone knew that Jews were blinded by the devil and so didn't recognize the true faith. I decided in that moment that I was lucky to have lived on the streets. My life there, and in the brothel, with all its hardships and humiliations, had cultivated only the simplest notions of God, whose baleful grace I saw for sure only in paintings by the masters. I wasn't encumbered with preconceptions and so I wasn't required to denigrate other people for their beliefs.

"You are most kind," Sforno said, quickening his pace down the steps.

"And we will always champion residence permits for Jews," Soderini assured him. We had reached the foyer at the bottom of the stairs and Sforno turned to look at Soderini.

"Not every unusual boy is a sorcerer, and not all Jews are callous moneylenders with high interest rates," Sforno said brusquely. He and Soderini stared at each other, a hard-eyed stare which encompassed both their similarities as parents and their different identities as Jew and Christian, outsider and city father, ambivalent Other and secure Florentine. Then there was me, who was both and neither, and always alone. It was a gift from my life on the streets that I could see both positions. The Wanderer was right: my humble origins were valuable.

"Of course not," Soderini said quietly. He clasped Sforno's hand. "Let me know if you ever need anything, physico. I am in your debt." He turned and twinkled at me. "And you, boy

who is not a sorcerer, are ever welcome here!" He opened
the door and Sforno and I stepped out into the cool autumn
afternoon. I looked at Sforno, but he wasn't talking. He
walked back along the streets we'd come, stroking his beard
and wrinkling his brow. Finally he turned to me with puz-
zlement writ on his large-boned face. "Luca, how did you do
that?"

"I don't know," I murmured. I was glad to help the boy,
but unnerved again by the strangeness that kept coming
forth from me, unbidden. I had seen nothing like this even in
the visions of the previous night. But it felt related to them.
I was transformed more than I realized by Geber and the
Wanderer. I shook my head. "But I know who to ask." Sforno
scrutinized me intently, then nodded. I waved farewell and
fled down another street.

GEBER'S DOOR SWUNG OPEN, and his room was back
to its usual disarray. The wooden tables were again littered
with objects strange and wondrous. I didn't see the wineglass or earthenware cup from last night. And there was a
disconcerting silence; the stills were cold, no vividly hued
smoke tapped along the ceiling, and the profusion of objects
was quiescent. Geber was not in the room, and when I
called for him, there was no answer. I wandered about, and
eventually saw a small flight of stairs in the corner that I'd
never noticed before. I'd been in this room often, and I
could swear that the stairs had not been here. I ran up and
found a windowless room with Geber lying on a small pallet. He was covered by a thin cotton blanket, beneath which
he was shrunken and collapsed into himself. His eyes were
deeply sunken in a face marred by bubboni. His eyeglasses
and a stack of papers tied with a purple cord lay next to a
flickering beeswax candle on a small stand beside his pallet.

"Don't just stand there, put out the candle," Geber said softly, "the light is painful."

"Signore, are you well?" I asked anxiously, kneeling beside him.

"That depends," he said, opening his eyes. The sclera had yellowed and his pupils were hugely dilated in the shadows thrown over his sweaty face. "If you mean that by dying, I complete my purification and attain perfection and rejoin my beloved wife, then I am well. Otherwise, no, and you can see it for yourself. It's obvious: I'm covered in bubboni and my flesh is withered. Don't ask questions when you know the answer yourself, or can discover the answer yourself. Anytime you can learn for yourself, experience for yourself, apprehend directly and with no intermediary, you must do so! Remember that, boy, when I am gone!"

"Can't it be undone?" I made a small disconsolate noise. "You have so many potions and elixirs, isn't there one that will prolong your days now?"

Geber coughed and his small thin frame shuddered. "Even the best elixir finally fails."

"I have so much left to learn," I said, dismayed. "I have many questions for you!"

"At least you know that you have much to learn," he answered with a weak smile. "That's the beginning of knowledge. The questions, as I told you, you must pursue on your own. That will make the journey all the more intriguing, won't it?"

"But you have the answers," I said in dismay.

"I have my answers, you have to find your own."

"How will I ever find out about my parents, my family?"

"When the time is right, you won't be able to avoid discovery." He turned his head toward the wall and coughed again, then turned back to me. "I would have you learn the zodiac, and the meanings of the constellations and lights. On

your journey, astronomy will be important. I see you teaching it to someone who is dear to you, a beautiful woman. . . .
You will find a few books on the subject among my things."

"Your things?" I asked.

"Pay attention," he commanded, with some of his old asperity. "You're the inheritor. My possessions and the deed to
this place go to you. I have notarized it so with a lawyer."

I rocked back to sit on my heels. "I don't want your possessions!"

"You want my secrets." He laughed, a wheezy sound that
dwindled into shallow gasps. After a few soundless moments, he said, with satisfaction, "You want my knowledge."

"Yes," I admitted. "I want to know what the Cathars know
about my family!"

"The Cathars have many secrets. We possess artifacts that
the Church and others would kill for, powerful artifacts
written about in the Bible. We are the guardians of alchemical secrets and treasures from the ancient world. Because we
have guarded these artifacts with our very lives, we have also
been entrusted with other secrets."

"I'm not interested in the Bible," I said. "I want to learn
how to turn lead into gold! I want to know what happened
last night, and what you know of my origins!" I gripped his
shoulders in my enthusiasm, and when I saw my hands on
him, I thought of Ubaldo Soderini, and why I'd come to see
Geber. "Maybe I can help you," I said with excitement. I held
up my hands. They'd worked magic once today, they could
again. I laid my hands gently on his chest. I stared expectantly, waiting, but nothing happened. They didn't tingle.
They didn't burn. The sensation of water flowing didn't
pulse in them. Geber laughed again.

"Your *consolamentum* won't help me," he whispered. "And
you won't get to the consolamentum like this, anyway. It's
about surrender, fool, when will you understand that?"

"But I want to help you!"

"Help yourself, you mean," he said. He smiled. "If you can invoke the consolamentum, you will be able to do what it is you aspire to. They are the same."

"The consolamentum—is that the warmth in my hands that healed the nobleman's son today?" I asked. "How did I do that, and how can I make it happen again?"

"The consolamentum surpasses warmth and healing. It encompasses completion and perfection." Geber's frame was wracked by coughs, and then he turned his head away and spat blood on his pillow.

"Is that why the Wanderer called you 'perfect'?" It was easier to return to the give-and-take of our lessons than to watch him waning before me. And I had the silly, vain hope that I could coax him into staying, into living, if I refused to relinquish him as my teacher. "Because you can use the con-solamentum, not just for healing, but to change lead into gold?"

"We don't use the consolamentum, it uses us!" Geber spoke with a ferocity that blazed in his ragged eyes with their twin yellow reflections of the dancing candle flame. He pushed up on one elbow as if to roar at me, but only dropped back, overcome and spent. I was sad to see him so weak and reached out my arm to hold him up, but he pushed me away. "The Wanderer used a term from the Cathars' beautiful faith, the faith of my wife, though she and I no longer lived as husband and wife when we took the vow to give up the world of flesh. . . ."

"Why? I've seen the comfort a woman can give a man in difficult times," I said.

"This realm of flesh is the realm of Satan," Geber whispered. "The worst sin is to perpetuate the world of flesh. So we offered up the fleshly joining of husband and wife, to perfect ourselves. Our love remained, as love always does, but not the carnal dross that gives service to the king of the world. You see, boy who will live longer than I have, men are the swords fought in a mighty battle between good and evil, light and darkness, spirit and matter. These two sides are equal, and the God of light is pure spirit, pure love, untainted by matter, and entirely separate from material creation. The king of the world is matter itself, and is evil."

"No, this realm has beauty," I insisted. "It's a sin not to enjoy the beauty that surrounds us! It may be the only good we know!"

"How like the Jews." Geber smiled. "No wonder you've found your way to them; you were meant to. They would tell you that enjoying His creation is one of God's most sacred commandments. 'And God saw that it was good.'"

"God's creation may be good, but what of God? It's best just to stay out of His way," I said, with some grumpiness because the secret to making gold was slipping out of my grasp with the expiring of this alchemist's breath. And with that secret were going the answers to all my unasked questions, about last night, about my origins. . . . Under the grumpiness was a terrible ache, but I didn't want to give it space. It might hasten Geber on his way. I said, "Chance led me to the Jews. I ran into a crowd that was stoning Moshe Sforno and his little daughter."

"There's no such thing as chance," Geber said. "Beneath the surface of everything is a tightly woven fabric of meaning!"

"Meaning is a cruel joke, and it's on us!"

"When I come back, I'll argue the point with you," Geber said hoarsely.

"I think you're not coming back this time, Master Geber," I said softly, unable to deny the ache any longer. "You're too far gone. I've seen death so often that I know his approach."

"Coming back is certain for those of us who still have desires," he wheezed. "Remember that when the lust for gold overtakes you." Then he coughed up blood all over his chin and cheeks, too weak now even to turn his head, and I used his coverlet to wipe his feverish face.

"Would you like some water, signore?" I asked softly. I realized with a pang that I should have been tending him, not arguing with him; some physico I would make. Geber shook his head. "How about something to ease your pain? Wine with some of that distilled liquor from the poppy flower? You showed me where you keep it."

"All my life has been given to me that I might learn how to die," he whispered. "Why would I dull my mind at the crux of the journey?"

"Because death is certain, but suffering is unnecessary," I said sadly. "I would release you from it."

"You'll be a good physico; you want to release conscious beings from their suffering. Remember that when . . ." Geber's whisper trailed off. He smiled slightly and looked at me with luminous eyes. I wondered if I'd ever before seen his eyes without his strange eyeglasses framing them. Then I understood that he could no longer speak. I slipped my arm under his neck to support his shoulders and held his hand with my free hand, because I would want that kind of contact if I were dying. Of itself, with no prompting on my part, the tingling warmth entered into me. It ran through my chest and down my arms and out my hands into him. His eyes sparked briefly, and then dulled as a shudder went through his body. His breath came more and more shallowly, until it was the tiniest puff on the tip of his tongue, like the fanning of a butterfly's wing. Just at the end he smiled and squeezed my hand.

It was still daylight when I went outdoors with Geber's body wrapped in the bloodstained coverlet. I was surprised, because his little room had been so dark and closed that I assumed the sun had gone down. The Wanderer was waiting with his gray donkey.

"I thought you were gone," I said as I draped Geber's body over the donkey. Just last night I'd been the one in this position. But now I was walking around while Geber never would again, and for me, it was another precious friend gone.

"I thought you'd need help," the Wanderer said, patting Geber's back gently.

"I'm not the one who needs help," I said, both bitter and sad. I had replaced the eyeglasses on Geber's face, thinking to bury him as I had known him, wearing that strange visual apparatus, but the Wanderer pulled them off his face, folded them, and held them out to me.

"Don't you think he would want you to see as he did?" the Wanderer asked slyly.

"I will always see the way I do, and not as anyone else does," I said. I placed the apparatus awkwardly in the inner pocket of my farsetto, thinking that I would keep it with Giotto's panel. Then I took out the bundle of papers from Geber's nightstand; I had fastened my farsetto over it before bringing Geber down. I gave the bundle to the Wanderer. "He would want you to have this, I think. You two understood each other."

"*Summa Perfectionis Magisterii,*" the Wanderer read from the cover page. "How like my old friend. I know who to give this to." He took the donkey's lead rope in his big, gnarled hand, and trudged alongside me. "Death is merely moving from one home to another. If we're wise, and my Perfect friend was, we'll make the latter the more beautiful home."

"Do you believe visions are real?" I asked. "Last night, this thing happened to me, a journey, and I was offered a choice, was it real?" My face was wet as I grabbed the Wanderer's sleeve.

"The purpose of mourning is to empty the self of the self," he replied, squeezing my hand. "Then, slowly, drop by drop, you refill yourself with your Self. It takes time."

But time for me was different from how it was for other men, and now there was no one to ask why that was so. I would miss Geber's sharp-tongued lessons. I would miss the sense of being in the company of someone else who was different, like me.

"Let me tell you a story, since you asked about what's real and what's illusion," the Wanderer said, brightening. "There's a man, he's walking down a road, he sees——"

"What's his name?" I interrupted. Despite the ache of Geber's loss, I couldn't quell the urge to tease the Wanderer back. Two could play at the trickster game. Geber had once told me that I had the minimal intelligence to be curious. I could use that curiosity to repay the Wanderer in kind.

"The man's name? It doesn't matter."

"It matters to me," I said stubbornly.

"Giuseppe." The Wanderer threw up his hand. "He sees a woman——"

"What's her name?"

"Debora." He rolled his eyes. "He sees Debora, and she's beautiful. He's struck by lightning, he must have her. So he goes to her father's house—the father's name was Leone—and asked for Debora's hand in marriage. The father agrees, the two are married. They are very happy. In due time, the couple have three beautiful children——"

"Whose names are?" I prompted.

The Wanderer muttered a few sentences in another language. I didn't need to translate to know they were imprecations. Then he intoned, "Avram, Isaac, and Anna. The

father-in-law, who is wealthy, dies, and his property comes
to Giuseppe. Giuseppe has everything: a beautiful loving
wife, beautiful children, a beautiful home, land and sheep
and cattle and gold."

"I like this story."

"Yes, well, one day a flood comes, a vast, terrible flood
that covers the land—"

"Like the flood of November 1333," I observed. "That
was terrible. The rain came down without a break for four
nights and days, with fearsome lightning and continual
crashing thunder. Were you in Florence then? It was an
amazing sight, and a sound like I've never heard before or
since," I continued. "All the church bells rang continuously.
A monk named Friar Pietro told me that it was an invoca-
tion for the Arno not to rise further. And in the houses, they
beat kettles and cried to God, *'Misericordia, misericordia,'* but
God only laughed. The water kept rising. People in peril fled
from roof to roof and from house to house on makeshift
bridges. And the din people made was so loud that it almost
drowned out the thunder!"

"Loud, yes, and in my story—"

"The bridges were all swept away, you know," I said, as if
confidentially. "I saw the Ponte Vecchio go, with shopkeepers still inside the little wooden shops. It was a terrible
tragedy!" I gave the Wanderer an innocent, wide-eyed look
and he stared back as if I were the village idiot. I knew I was
irritating him. I gave him a cheeky grin.

"The flood was no better for the Giuseppe of my story,"
the Wanderer said, gnashing his teeth. "The waters came and
washed away his home, his crops, and his animals, all his possessions. Then a giant wave appeared on the horizon and he
grabbed his children and wife, he put one child on his head,
and held two together with one hand, and held his wife with
the other hand. The wave crashed upon him, and the child

on his head was ripped away, and when he reached for her, the other children and wife were lost into the waters. Then the wave cast him back on the shore. He'd lost everything. That's illusion," he finished with a flourish.

"Which part of it?" I cried, dismayed.

"Which part of it isn't illusion?" The Wanderer chuckled, looking pleased with himself for delivering the punch line. "It's all illusion. What he had, and what he didn't have."

"I don't like this story," I growled, disgruntled.

"You should like it, it's the story of your life. Of everyone's life, really."

"Life should be different."

"How can life be other than what it is?"

"Full of death and loss and unanswered questions," I said sadly. We fell silent. As the light faded and the setting sun spread orange clouds through the sky and the cool autumn air turned lavender, we walked through narrow streets overshadowed by fortresslike dwellings, severe gray facades crowned by crenellated cornices, high brick towers, and red terra-cotta roofs, black iron rings for torches set into rough bosses of stone, until we came to the stone wall twenty braccia high encircling the city. This was the third circle, Geber had explained during one of our lessons, because it was the third enclosure built to protect the city. The first, an irregular square, was built by ancient Romans. Stretches of it still ran through the city. The second was built by the commune in 1172, when the *borghi,* the suburbs of the city, spilled out along the roads from the four original Roman gates and the citizens didn't want invaders to burn the borghi. This third circle was completed two decades ago. We paused there because three horses were cantering toward us. Nicolo Silvano in his red magistrate's sleeves sat astride the lead horse.

"You won't get away with anything, Bastardo, no matter what you inherit," Nicolo said, circling me. "I know what

you are: a sorcerer. A Jew-loving sorcerer," he spat at the
Wanderer, who studied the flagstone. I stared at Nicolo, at
his narrow ugly face with its protruding chin and thin,
sharply angled nose. The other horses caught up with us.

"You are the boy called Luca Bastardo, who was employed by the commune as a becchino for the last several
months?" one of the ufficiale asked. I nodded. "You've received an inheritance," he said. He paused and looked at
Geber. "Whose body is that on the donkey?"

"Geber," I said.

"Antonio Geber, the merchant. Two inheritances, then,"
he said pleasantly, as if he were telling me that the sun was
shining. "There will be taxes. Come to the Palazzo del
Capitano—"

"Two?" I puzzled.

"One from this Geber, and the other from Arnolfo
Ginori. You were seen taking his body for burial. Both men
left you their possessions, bank accounts, everything."

"Ginori?" I wondered.

"Someone you put a spell on, sorcerer," Nicolo sneered.
"Someone you cozened with your witchcraft, the same witchcraft that keeps you young when you should be a grown man!"

"Ginori left you a bottega, a shop for dyestuffs," the ufficiale explained. "Before the plague, it prospered; Ginori was
a cousin of an old family and had excellent customers."

The dye shop—Rosso. "I never knew his name," I murmured, touched that he'd thought of me this way. Was it only
yesterday that I'd buried him, and today I was burying Geber?
The last two days seemed like ten years. Time felt all askew,
stretched in some places and wound up in a tight skein in
others.

"You're wealthy now," the ufficiale said with a smile. "You
should look for a wife."

"A wife?" I repeated slowly, almost dazed. The philosopher's stone had given me the choice for one, and now perhaps the means had come to me.

"That's right," the other ufficiale said. "There's a flurry of betrothals taking place right now. Those who've survived are desperate to marry their daughters. You're young, but you can get yourself betrothed to a girl who's wealthy and beautiful, perhaps even one of the lesser nobles. You can make your way up in the world. There's great opportunity now, for those who've survived the plague."

"He's not as young as he looks," Nicolo hissed, glaring at me.

"Take care of the legal matters and the taxes," the first ufficiale advised. He flicked a glance at the Wanderer. "You have real estate now, you don't have to live with Hebrews." He turned his horse around, saying "I've other inheritors to notify." He and the second ufficiale set off in a sprightly trot together, matching their horses' gaits. I heard the second one say, "Do you really think he's some kind of sorcerer?"

Nicolo remained behind. He heard the question, too. "I can't kill you now, Bastardo; the city fathers who remain alive are determined to protect the rest of the living. My ambition must take precedence. But eventually, I'll get you!" He wore the same sneer I had seen on his father's face, the sneer that had made me a prisoner. A wave of anger pulsed through me. I wished I had killed Nicolo when I'd had the opportunity and the resolve, with the blood rage upon me. Then I realized that I had seen too much death and was thoroughly sickened by it. Even for vengeance, I didn't want to partake again of that poisoned feast. I would settle for wiping the sneer from Nicolo's face.

I drawled, "Your father smiled that way just before I wrung his neck and killed him like the rat he was."

Nicolo howled. "Enjoy it now, Bastardo. Soon I'll take everything away from you!"

"You can't harm me," I said. I looked away nonchalantly. I wanted to belittle him, to make him feel as worthless as I'd felt at his father's brothel. "If you try, I'll find another bird for you to eat. This one won't be red, though. Do you think it will taste as good?"

"I'll make you sorry you ever saw a red bird, sorry you were ever born! People will know that you're an abomination. Florence doesn't like freaks. You'll burn, Bastardo!" Nicolo kicked his horse with the sharp spurs on his boots and set out after the other two ufficiali.

"That charming fellow didn't offer you congratulations, but I will," the Wanderer said. "If I know my old Cathar friend, he had abundant florins. You're a wealthy man. It's what you've always wanted. So here's a question for you, since you like them so much: what do you do when you get what you want?" Grinning, the Wanderer put the donkey's lead rope into my hand and closed my fingers over the rope. I had a sudden flash of long ago at the Mercato Vecchio, Silvano closing my friend Massimo's fingers over a coin. "I win!" Massimo had whispered, all those years ago. But he hadn't, unless winning was dying by a condottiere's greedy hand. I'd endured agony, shame, wretchedness beyond what most people could imagine, but I'd won. I'd won because now I would never have to worry about hunger or poverty again. The Wanderer stood watching me raptly, as if my thoughts were transparent to him. He took a pack off the donkey's back and hoisted it over one thick shoulder. I suddenly knew that he was leaving. "Will I ever see you again?" I asked.

"Do you think it's so easy to get rid of me?" The Wanderer shook his shaggy head with its black-and-gray mane of hair. "Long from now and far from here, we will meet again, Bastardo."

"I wish you well, Wanderer," I said. He raised his hand in

farewell and shambled back down the cobblestone road into the city. A few steps later he looked back over his shoulder.

"Take care of the ass, eh, Bastardo? He's an old friend, too," the Wanderer called. I made a vaguely obscene gesture which provoked a laugh in the Wanderer. Slowly I grinned back. Then the Wanderer went on his way, and I resumed my walk back out into the Tuscan hills, to bury yet another friend.

Chapter 12

I FOUND MYSELF WITH MONEY to surpass my farthest dreams. I went to the Palazzo del Capitano del Popolo on the afternoon of the day after burying Geber and discovered that the Wanderer was right: Geber kept a substantial account of a thousand florins, which was augmented by investments in a wool factory and ownership of a vineyard in nearby Anchiano. Ginori, whom I'd called Rosso, had a third that many. However, Ginori owned the building that housed his shop and home, and he had an inventory of dyestuffs, bolts of fabric, and the other appurtenances of his trade. I was now wealthy, with all the tools of an established business. There were taxes to be paid, but I could take possession of Geber's belongings and Ginori's home whenever I chose. With half of Florence dead, legal matters pertaining to inheritance and bequest were being hurried along. Those who were left wanted to get back to the woolen cloth industry and international commerce, the grain trade and the artisanal profiteering, the banking and investing, the carnevales and the art that had made us Florentines, according to Pope Boniface, the fifth element of the universe.

I walked out of the palazzo in a kind of stupefaction. This inheritance meant freedom on a scale I had longed for but never thought I'd have. I had the means with which to support myself honorably. I would never again have to follow anyone's directives. I would choose where I went, when. Hunger and cold were behind me, and more than that, I could even gratify myself.

It was a cool, wintry day with a vast yellow sky like buttermilk, and I held in my hand a sheet of linen paper with writing on it that noted my inheritance and gave me the right to withdraw funds from my new accounts. Outside on the piazza, a breeze sucked the paper from my hand and flipped it onto the ground. As I bent to retrieve it, a horse cantered up. Just as my fingertips grazed the paper, the tip of a longsword, the mighty spada da una mano e mezzo, landed on the paper a hair's breadth from my fingertips. Nicolo Silvano was leaning down, sword arm outstretched, sneering.

"Collecting your inheritance, sorcerer?" he asked. "How long do you think you'll have it before people realize what you are, the spawn of some unholy, long-lived evil? My father said he rescued you once when a crowd would have burned you for never aging!"

"Your father didn't rescue me. Your father never did a good act in his miserable life," I said coolly. "A great man rescued me and your father happened to be around to collect me."

"My father was a great man! What was your father, a freak like yourself? Don't you ever wonder, Bastardo, what kind of evil thing could sire a beautiful abomination like yourself and then lose you?" Nicolo laughed. "My father speculated about it!"

"What I wonder is none of your concern," I said. I eyed his posture and seat. He held the sword awkwardly, as if it

were new, and I knew he'd never had lessons in swordsman-
ship. I straightened in a quick burst and kicked it. It skittered
up off the linen paper and almost clattered out of Nicolo's
hand; only his ungainly lurch forward on the withers of his
horse kept him from dropping it. I squatted and grabbed the
paper, simultaneously dancing out of the way of the horse's
clomping iron-shod feet.

"You may hold a sword, but you'll never be a nobleman,"
I taunted him. "You'll always be the son of a lowlife brothel
keeper who enslaved and killed children!"

"I am a nobleman, the city fathers have made me one," he
said, righting himself on the horse, regripping his sword,
and circling around me. "My father would be proud of me,
I will fulfill his dreams!" Nicolo tried to steer his horse at
me, but I slapped its rump and it shied back, nearly unseat-
ing him.

"It takes a snake to be proud of a snake."

"You're jealous because I have a father," Nicolo cooed. He
straightened on his horse and smirked, gathering the reins
in his sword hand. "I went back to my father's palazzo,
Bastardo. I took a certain document that pertains to you. A
certain letter that I will show to the Church fathers when
the time is right. And then they will burn you!" Then he
leaned down and punched my face with his free hand. Fury
erupted within me. The superhuman strength I had called on
before surged through me, and I reached up and pulled him
down off his horse, tearing apart his leather stirrups. He
screamed and tried to thrust the sword at me, but I knocked
it away. Kicking him to the ground, I grabbed the sword. I
aimed the tip at his throat.

He was panting, his eyes wide and red-rimmed. An acrid
scent threaded through his cloying perfume: the odor of
fear. I could kill him. I wanted to. I pressed the point of the
sword into his Adam's apple. A drop of blood beaded up. My

hand trembled. I remembered how his father had once
pressed a knife into my throat in the same manner. I did
not want to be like Bernardo Silvano. And more than that,
though that was powerful motivation, I did not want to attract divine attention to myself.

God was usually cruel, that much I knew from my life.
I did not know whether He would be pleased or angry if I
dispatched Nicolo, who was the spawn of cruelty and evil.
Either way, killing Nicolo was likely to provoke His laughter. And I had had enough of God's mirth.

Not from compassion but from fear of divine notice, and
the suffering it engendered, I stepped away. I did not know
how much greater my suffering would be in sparing Nicolo.
I would not now be in this tiny cell, broken and bleeding.
But I do not question my journey, because as Geber said, he
who fails to keep turning the wheel thus set in motion dam-
ages the working of the world and wastes his life.

"You're weak," Nicolo sneered. "Your weakness will be my
victory, Bastardo!" He mounted his horse, it reared up and
I jumped back to avoid its hooves, and he sped off, laughing.

I returned to the Sfornos' with a torn lip and black eye.
Moshe Sforno stood in the kitchen by the fire. He raised his
eyebrows, then set down his wineglass and came over to examine my lip and eye. His hands were gentle but firm as they
probed the wounds, and I resolved that, when I was a
physico, my hands would be friendly like that with my patients. The residue of tension left over from my encounter
with Nicolo eased away with Sforno's kindness.

"Wash up and you'll be fine," he said. "Nicolo Silvano?"

"Yes. Signore, I'm wealthy now. I have a home. And a
business, a bottega for selling dyes."

Sforno smiled. "Very good. Will you be moving out and
operating the bottega?" He went to the wine cask and poured
off a cup for me.

"There's no hurry for Luca to leave," Mrs. Sforno said. She entered the room wearing a plain brown apron over her dress and carrying potatoes, cabbage, and carrots in a basket. She did not look at me but set to work shaving and chopping carrots with her skillful paring knife, and soon had a pile of translucent orange shavings. Her yellow headdress was bent over the table. "You're still young, Luca. It's best for you to stay here and learn what Moshe has to teach you. He says you have talent and you'll make a fine physico."

"Thank you, signora," I murmured, pleased to be accepted, even so offhandedly.

Mrs. Sforno went on, "Besides, you don't know how to cook or clean and there are few servants about in the city for you to hire. You can rent out the dye shop——"

"You know about that?" I asked, surprised.

"Just because women stay indoors most of the time doesn't mean they can't get information," she said tartly, sounding like Rachel. "So you'll rent out the dye shop."

"It won't be easy to find renters, with so many dead," Sforno noted.

"In a few months it will be," Mrs. Sforno said. "Half of Florence is gone, but people will move in, immigrants from all over. Many places are decimated by the Black Death, and people will come to Florence to rebuild their lives." She sounded certain and reasonable as she continued with her work. "You'll bank the rental income. Your money will stay where it is, in the bank. I don't want you wasting it on gaming and dice or"——her white hand with the knife paused, and then went back to chopping——"or on any other unworthy pursuit."

"Yes, signora," I said solemnly, because I knew what she meant, and she needn't have worried. I had long ago sworn to myself that I would never pay for sexual favors, if I ever wanted them, which seemed unlikely after my history.

"When you're grown, you'll move out, and you'll have an honorable profession and good savings," she finished firmly.

"Leah, you're so practical, and kind, too." Moshe Sforno wrapped his arms around his wife's waist and nuzzled her. I turned away. I felt both flattered that she cared enough about my welfare to decide for me this way and a little irritated that, yet again, someone else wanted to oversee my life. This was a gentler binding, of course, than Silvano's. But I wondered if I would ever again be as free as I was on the streets, and if I would always harbor, like a sore tooth, this gnawing sense of not belonging. "Luca," Mrs. Sforno said. Her voice held a warning note and I snapped around to face her. "Hire a tutor for your lessons. Rachel is not to go to the barn and be alone with you again. It's not seemly!"

I was astonished, and a little afraid of the signora's wrath, and it took me a moment to answer. I swallowed. "Yes, signora!" Then I fled to the barn.

After I washed up, I went back out into the city, to the once-crowded, now-desolate narrow street on the river-bank near the Ponte Santa Trinita where Geber had lived. I climbed the stairs to Geber's apartment and was struck again by the emptiness emanating even into the stairwell. The door didn't swing open for me of its own accord as it used to, but it did yield to me when I pushed it. I looked around at the room where I had spent so many confusing, stimulating hours. Outwardly, everything was as it had been: the tables were laden with strange objects and stills and bags and boxes and dead animals and stones and mortars with their pestles, but now, instead of everything being in motion, as if the room was somehow breathing its contents, everything was frozen, lifeless, vacant. I went to a table where a large orange butterfly lay with its wings spread wide. I picked up the dead insect and held it to my face to examine it closely.

As my breath touched its antennae, it turned to fine brown dust that fell from my fingers and scattered on the table and floor. I cried out in astonishment, and at that moment, other objects on the table disintegrated: dried flowers, spools of thread, lumps of clay, a dead snake, a bowl filled with clear liquid—all turned to piles of dust. I whirled around, and the same thing was happening at all the other tables: bowls holding herbs or liquids, vials of paint or ink, linen squares, and beakers all evaporated into the fine brown dust. It took only a few heartbeats. Then the room was left with plain wooden tables which were bare except for dust, Geber's illuminated manuscripts, and stacks of paper that he had written on. Even Zosimos's three-beakers still, of which Geber had been so proud, was gone. I gathered the manuscripts together onto one table and went back to the Sfornos'.

FOUR YEARS PASSED that I lived in the barn and apprenticed with Moshe Sforno. I began as an empiric, learning by watching Sforno work. He saw patients with every disease and disorder imaginable, from leprosy to dropsy to bad breath, from broken bones to catarrh to epilepsy. I helped him set bones, tend fevers, dress and cauterize wounds, amputate gangrenous limbs, treat earaches through the insertion of a probe, use heated cups to draw humors to specific areas of the body, and administer purges and emetics. I learned about herbs and medicines, was instructed in the preparation and usage of plasters, poultices, fat-based ointments, unguents, and philters, though their preparation was mostly to be left to a trusted apothecary.

I hired a tutor to teach me Latin and Greek and then read Galen's lengthy *On the Usefulness of the Parts of the Body, On Complexions,* and *Ars parva,* among others; Avicenna's million-word *Canon;* and Hippocrates's *Aphorisms.* Sforno went to great trouble to obtain the laboriously copied manuscripts for me, and insisted that I read the works in their entirety. I read more recent medical authors, too, such as Gentile da Foligno, who had died during the plague from attending the sick; Albertus Magnus, who wrote about human anatomy; and Arnald of Villanova, who discussed the function of air and baths, activity or exercise, sleep, food and drink, evacuations, and the emotions, in maintaining health. In Hebrew, I read Hunain Ishaq's *Ten Treatises on the Eye,* Haly Abbas, Rhazes, and Maimonides's treatises.

I enjoyed reading, and found that I could read for as many hours as an oil lamp burned into the night, still waking in the morning feeling rested and buoyant. But I didn't forget my more practical concerns. I engaged a sword master, and went to his residence near Santa Croce to practice with sword, dagger, and staff. This activity occasioned much teasing from Sforno and his daughters; it wasn't the sort of thing Jews were wont to do. But I was always aware of Nicolo Silvano's avowed enmity. By tacit agreement, neither of us wanting to jeopardize our newfound stations, we stayed apart for these years. I studied and he worked in the city administration. He seemed to have stopped, probably only temporarily, spreading tales about me. And, whether through my old acute senses developed in the brothel or through my knowledge of the man, I didn't have to watch Nicolo at it to know that he, too, was practicing with his longsword. He intended to use it on me on the day that we came together decisively.

In four years, though I was over thirty, I looked and felt like a youth of eighteen. I was still lean and only middling tall, though I was well muscled. I still had reddish-blond hair and I wore it long and tucked up under an ordinary foggetta, which I chose over any other hat for its humbling effect. I never wanted to let myself forget who I was and where I'd come from: no one and nowhere. My chest was bare, without any mark to indicate heresy, as Silvano had once told me I should have. I wondered if I actually did belong to the nobles he had seen, even if the woman did have hair with the same unusual color as mine.

One dreary day, when winter had slicked over the gray stones of Florence with damp and locked the chill into the narrow streets, I went out, as I often did, with Sforno on a call. I didn't know it, but it was one of those decisive days during which my whole life would change. We walked around the vast unfinished Santa Maria del Fiore. We came around to the other side of the long cathedral, almost bumping into a group of men who were talking, as groups of men often did in the city's piazze.

"Is there really a need for this confraternity?" a tall, stout man in fine clothes was saying. He was familiar looking and stood facing me, flanked by a lean, dark-haired man whose face also tugged at my memory. Facing him, with their backs to me, stood three red-cloaked magistrates.

"Signore Petrarca, the Confraternity of the Red Feather will do important work for the Church, stamping out the seeds of idolatry by identifying sorcerers, astrologers, prodigies, alchemists, augurers, spellmongers, satanists, and witches of all kinds!" one of the red-cloaked men facing him said hotly. "We will burn them and cleanse Florence!"

"Those things don't exist except in the fantasies of ignorant folk, so why do we need to found a society to find and fight them?" Signore Petrarca asked. He was an older gentleman with an expressive, handsome face, and I suddenly recognized him: he was Giotto's friend, the man who had intervened years ago in the Piazza d'Ognissanti, when the crowd had been about to burn me as a witch. He had aged since then and looked to be about fifty. "There are more im-

portant concerns: the unification of Italia, the return of the
papacy to Roma, where it belongs . . ."

"I know of a witch who uses his black art to perpetuate
his youth," said one of the men who had his red-cloaked back
to me. I recognized that loud grating voice with its hint of a
whine. I felt for my sword, but it wasn't by my side.

"If he were truly practiced in black arts, he would have
cast a spell on you, Nicolo Silvano!" I exclaimed. Nicolo
whirled around, flinging his red mantello over his shoulder.

"Bastardo!" he gasped. "This is the very sorcerer! Doesn't
the devil always know when he's being spoken of?" He
looked at me with a sneer curling his lips, the very image of
his father: thin, knifelike nose, prominent chin, carefully
coiffed beard cut close to his pockmarked face. The same
perfume wafted out around him. Hatred scalded me from
my toes to my scalp.

"Look well on the face of this sorcerer," Nicolo spat. "It
will not change!"

"Better my face than your ugly one," I taunted.

"He doesn't look like a sorcerer," Petrarca mused, cock-
ing his head and narrowing his eyes at me. "He looks like a
rather handsome young man with poor taste in hat wear. See
here, young man, can't you find something a bit more dash-
ing than a common foggetta?"

"How long will he look exactly like this?" Nicolo shouted.
"He looked like a boy of twelve or thirteen for almost twenty
years while he worked for my father! It's witchcraft!"

"That's older than your age, isn't it?" Petrarca returned in
a measured tone. "How would you know what he looked
like before you were born?"

"I've heard rumors of his unusual youthfulness," a man
beside Nicolo said. He was pudgy with oily skin, and when I
raked him with a contemptuous glance, I noticed the garb of

a Dominican under his red magistrate's mantello. He stuck his nose into the air.

"Rumors are like the fantasies of little girls," I said, more calmly than I felt, "unreal. Are you a little girl, Friar, that you place your faith in them?"

"Exactly," the stately Petrarca said. "We should doubt what we hear until we can verify it as truth. Indeed, we should embrace doubt itself as truth, affirming nothing, and doubting all things except those in which doubt is sacrilege!"

"Luca, we should be on our way," Moshe Sforno urged me, jostling my elbow.

"But I can prove it, Signore Petrarca," Nicolo said slyly. "I know of a letter that discusses his parents' search for him, and how they kept the company of heretics, and this letter was written thirty years ago!"

"With all due respect, a thirty-year-old letter proves nothing," demurred Petrarca.

"Look at his chest! He's supposed to bear the mark of heresy on his chest!" Nicolo cried. The Dominican with him raised his eyebrows at me, and even Petrarca tilted his head in curiosity. I smiled coldly, parted my mantello, undid my farsetto, and slowly lifted my camicia. My chest was unblemished. Nicolo was not to be dissuaded. "He conceals the mark with black magic! Look closely at his face, and go examine a panel kept by the nuns of San Giorgio. His face is there, only a few years younger than he is now!"

"His is a fair face that a painter would want to paint." Petrarca shrugged.

"Giotto painted it!" Nicolo cried, with a flourish. "Giotto, who died a decade before the Black Death! You can see he doesn't age as normal people do, he's some sort of freak, a demon in human form! He cast a spell on the great Giotto to paint him!"

Nicolo drew his sword, flicking the tip of it onto my

throat. But I felt no fear as I met his gaze. He wouldn't kill me with these other men looking on. It wasn't Nicolo's style. He would wait until we were alone and my back was turned to run a sword through me. It was my task to be sure he didn't find me thus. Nicolo pressed slightly, nicking my flesh. A drop of blood ran down over my Adam's apple.

"Put your sword away before you hurt yourself with it, Nicoletta," I sneered.

"I've left a gift for you at my father's brothel," he said, so only I could hear him. "Be sure you collect it!"

"This ugly episode has gone too far," Petrarca said, stepping between us. He placed his index finger on the flat of the blade and pushed it aside. Nicolo let the sword drop, but he kept his stony eyes on me.

"The Confraternity of the Red Feather cannot be stopped," Nicolo shouted. "We will hunt down and burn witches and sorcerers, destroying evil in Florence!"

"What about snakes, Nicolo?" I asked. "You'd better leave room for them in your charter else you'll be exterminating yourself!"

"You would do well to rethink your position, Signore Petrarca," the Dominican said. He gave me a scathing look. "If we rid Florence of the evil creatures in her midst, perhaps we can prevent a recurrence of the Black Death!"

"I am not inclined to believe that solution will work," Petrarca answered mildly.

"Come, Silvano, your plans intrigue me," the Dominican said. "I know a cardinal, beloved of the Holy Father Innocent VI, who would be well pleased with your confraternity. It's his passion to cleanse the world so that God's will can be established. He's personally wracked with sorrow over the stain that Eve's sin has visited upon mankind, and has worked for decades to eradicate it!"

"I will support you with all the power at my disposal,"

added the first magistrate. He drew Nicolo away, with the Dominican alongside them.

But Nicolo turned and called, "Bastardo, give my regards to Simonetta when you see her. Tell her you'll soon be joining her!" He threw back his head and laughed.

What had he done to sweet Simonetta? A red haze clouded my vision. I growled and lunged, but Moshe Sforno and Petrarca held me back.

"Let go, I won't follow him," I snarled in frustration. Sforno released me.

Petrarca was staring at me raptly. "If you good gentlemen will excuse us, walk with me, young man!" He placed his arm around my shoulders and led me off toward the Baptistery. He said nothing until we stood in front of Giotto's bell tower, and the silence allowed me to calm myself. By the time I stood looking at the beauty which Giotto had created at such great expense to the city fathers, I was almost smiling, remembering Giotto's humor and kindness.

"You look like a man caught in memory," Petrarca observed. "I have a memory, too. A memory from a dozen years ago, when I stopped in Florence on my way to Roma." He scowled and fingered his mantello. "I remember a boy of eleven years, being readied to burn at the stake. A boy who was clearly indentured to an evil man. Would it be possible for such a boy to be only eighteen now, all these years later? Even if this boy doesn't bear some mark on his breast?"

His words were ones I feared but, this time, I didn't contract with fear. I stayed soft in my chest, undefended. "My life is a tribute to God's cruel humor, starting with my residence on the streets of Florence, continuing with my life in a brothel of perversions, and then as a guest of Jews, who themselves hold a precarious place in Florence. As for my origins, I only know a few fragments of a story, and some of the pieces don't fit. I don't know for sure."

"You have the aura of the elect. Surely you are the son of refined people. You are too intelligent not to be!"

But of course, I would sound intelligent. The doors of my mind had been opened by the likes of Master Giotto and Moshe Sforno, Friar Pietro and the Wanderer and Geber the alchemist. Even Bernardo Silvano, loathsome as he was, had managed to impart something to me. "Of my origins, I remember nothing except begging on the streets of Florence."

"It matters naught. 'Memory brings forth not reality itself, which is gone forever, but the words elicited by the representation of reality, which as it disappeared impressed traces upon the mind via the agency of the senses.' Augustine said that. I agree," Petrarca said seriously. "Through our thoughts and our writings, we give form and meaning to our journey. You will tell your story one day, Luca Bastardo. In telling it, you will find meaning. That's how you will uncover who and what you are."

He reached into a leather pouch hanging from his shoulder by a strap and took something out. "Here," he said, tossing it. "A gift for you. For your memories. I wish I were going to be around to read them!"

I caught Petrarca's gift in midair. It was a lavish gift for a stranger: a calfskin bound book with blank white vellum pages. It was thick and beautiful, the calfskin soft and supple, a pleasure to hold in my hand. It still is, as I sit in my small cell with the walls pressing in again. The pages are nearly full now; I have filled them as I await my execution. The time here, though short, would have crawled if it weren't for Francesco Petrarca's gift and Giotto's small panel of St. John, both of which were brought to me by Leonardo il Maestro himself, after the soldiers of the Inquisition dragged me to this cell. Back then I thanked Signore Petrarca profusely; such notebooks were rare and costly. He laughed off my stammered words of gratitude in his mercurial way.

"We stand before Giotto's brainchild, and were you not his protégé? I knew the Master only briefly, but his was an honorable friendship, and I have cherished it faithfully. If you were beloved of him, that more than suffices for me."

So he remembered me from Giotto's side, too. I swallowed. "You know my secret, and you don't think me a sorcerer? You aren't tempted by Nicolo Silvano and his confraternity?"

Petrarca shook his head. "He is, ah, rather unappealing, with that heavy perfume and superstition." He shrugged. "If the Author of all times and ages permits you to wander for a longer time than most, who am I to question that? Who are you to gainsay the grace of His gift?"

It was the first time my agelessness had been presented to me in the light of God's grace, and I stared at Petrarca, unable to speak at all. I saw myself whole in an entirely new way. He laughed again and took my arm and told me that we must now be good friends, since we had both been befriended by Giotto.

LATER, AS EVENING WAS COMING ON, after I had spent a few hours grimly ruminating on what Nicolo had meant about a gift, I went to the brothel. I was reluctant to do so, but also, with the contradictory logic of the heart, I wanted to. I wanted to see my old prison from the perspective of freedom. And I had to face whatever it was that Nicolo had left for me. So I sped off toward the city walls on the eastern end of town, running through twisting streets where chasms created by tiny cottages wedged in between massive towers let small dapples of light onto the damp and dark cobblestones. Finally I came to the palazzo that I had promised myself I would never again enter. The front windows were bare and let the light in; I had pulled down the

drapes all those years ago. The place seemed deserted, as so
many buildings still were, four years after the first onslaught
of the plague that had devastated Florence. As I slowly ambled toward the door, the tiny responsive hairs on the back
of my neck lifted and pulsed. Something was terribly wrong.
As I pushed open the door to the brothel, my hand trembled.

Inside it was silent, as it had been during Silvano's long
dominion. I had not left it thus. When I walked out with the
blood of eight men on my arms and chest, children openly
milled about and talked and the maids gossiped as they
cleaned up the bodies. In killing, I had brought life to the
palazzo. Simonetta hugged me and wished me well in my
new home, and I assured her that Nicolo would not come
back, because I'd threatened him with dire consequences.

I called out, but no one answered. I went through the
foyer into the hall and became aware of the sickly sweet
smell of rotting flesh. All the doors were closed, and when I
opened the first one, I saw a small form on the bed. "No!" I
shouted. My heart thumped as I ran to the bed. It was one of
the small, delicate children from Cathay, one of Silvano's last
acquisitions. She hadn't been in the palazzo long before I'd
liberated it, and her spirit hadn't yet been broken. She had a
sweet laugh like little bells trilling. She had barely grown in
the years I'd been gone, and now, her slanted eyes stared un-
seeing out of her triangular yellow-skinned face. Her throat
had been cut.

I vomited, then lurched out of her room. Next was the
room of a young blond boy and he lay crumpled in a heap,
facedown, on the floor. His throat, too, had been slit. I was
crying as I ran upstairs into the private wing. I banged open
Simonetta's door, saw her plump form on her bed. She lay
as if asleep, her long blond braid trailing off the luxurious
velvet pillow that was one of the features of this palazzo.

Her chest wasn't moving, and her eyes with their engraved crow's-feet were peacefully closed. There was neither blood nor mark on her neck, but she was dead. Her sweet seamed face with its red birthmark was rolled to one side, and her worn hands were folded at her breast. Nicolo must have given her poison. I collapsed on the floor. Simonetta had been kind to me, and now she was dead for it. Nicolo, vile thing that he was, had killed his own mother. It was an unthinkable atrocity. If I hadn't left to live at the Sfornos', perhaps she would have been saved. I should not have abandoned her. Regret and rage wouldn't save her now. I didn't try to stem the tears that dripped down my face.

Night fell with its sticky plum shadows arching out of alcoves. A cold wind wheezed at the windows. I went through the palazzo, lighting lamps and candles. In almost every room a child lay dead, either on the floor or on the bed. The throats of most had been slit, though some were stabbed. None had resisted; I knew from bitter experience that they had been taught not to, and even years of liberation were not enough to remove the fences in their minds. I saved my own room for last. There was a shape in my bed. It was a small reddish-brown dog, a mutt of the kind often seen scampering about the city, begging for food. The muzzle of its severed head hung open, its long pink tongue lolling out, and the head lay next to its torso, which had been stabbed through several times. Its legs and genitals were missing. It was a clear warning to me. Instead of frightening me, it angered me. I should have killed Nicolo when I had the chance. If I had been the sorcerer he said I was, I would have killed him with my thoughts in that moment.

There were almost fifty bodies here to bury, a few days' work were I to do it alone. But I was done burying the dead; my time as a becchino was over. The Laughing God, seeking a new joke, had batted me as a cat does a mouse into another place in life. It was a while of sitting in contemplation on the bed next to the mutilated dog before I knew what to do. Then the answer came to me in all its crimson simplicity. It would require a huge sacrifice from me—exile—but it was the only fitting response to this moment. I took a torch out of a wall sconce and held it to the heavy drapes that had blocked the light from this little room, my prison of so many years. They lit quickly and orange flames raced up them to lick at the ceiling. I held the torch to the bed with its horse-hair mattress and the linens whistled as they caught fire. A small trickle of flame ran along the dog's muzzle, and I ran upstairs and set Simonetta's bed on fire. I watched for a while as the flames wrapped tenderly around her body like a blanket for sleeping. I left before the smell of roasted flesh could nauseate me.

I entered into room after room, setting fire to the linens and drapery. I didn't pray because I was angry at God again for allowing Nicolo to commit so many murders. I simply trusted the fire to guide the children into a better afterlife, whatever that afterlife might be. I doubted it was the boring heaven vaunted by priests. But there was probably something. Better men than me, baptized men, had been certain in their faith of a heaven.

Soon the palazzo crackled, groaned, and shrilled with fire. Black smoke poured in flumes along the ceiling and fierce hot blasts of air struck my face. A golden glow suffused walls and ceiling and it reminded me of the radiant, expressive halos in the work of Giotto's master Cimabue. Cimabue had painted the exquisite altarpiece of the Madonna at Santa Trinita. The Madonna was shown as a queen upon a rich and monumental throne, with eight adoring angels attending her and four stern prophets below her. She existed

in the gold that was the ground of her divinely maternal being, holding on her knee the Christ child with his hand upraised in blessing.

Perhaps it was the smell of smoke and burning meat that
confused my senses, or perhaps it was Cimabue's powerful
Madonna that exalted them, but I was thrown back, for a
moment, into the unbounded state of the philosopher's
stone. Time spun loose like a wheel rattling off the axle of a
cart, and scenes from the past sprang to life before my eyes.
The flames vanished like clouds scattering from the surface
of a river and I saw myself, a scrawny, dirty boy, being led
through the door by a sneering Bernardo Silvano. I saw the
first patron walk into my room, and the countless other patrons who had followed him—I saw each and every one of
their richly hated faces. I still hated them. I still felt the fire
of anger scorching through me at what they had done to me.
It tormented me and I felt violated all over again.

Suddenly time stopped gyrating and the forty-eight
children whose bodies I had consigned to the fire stood
around me in a semicircle. They were quiet, solemn, reverent. They wore plain blue silken camicie and golden halos,
like Cimabue's angels. The little girl from Cathay stood
nearest me; when I met her eyes, she nodded. Ingrid, to
whom I had fed poisoned candy to save her from the ministrations of a cardinal, joined the children. Blue-eyed Bella
appeared, with her hands mercifully whole, and then Marco
stepped into the semicircle. He was as he had been before
Silvano had brutalized him: handsome, elegant, radiating
kindness. I was so happy to see him looking well and luminous that I called his name. He winked at me with his old
esprit. A sound like a song went up from the children's
throats, exalting me, and Simonetta stood among them. She
was young again, but without the stripes from Silvano's

whip that she had often worn. She smiled at me and pointed—

Crack! A falling beam landed close enough behind me to throw blue sparks at my face, startling me out of my reverie. I laid the torch on the carpet and turned and strolled out the door. I walked some distance, making sure I could still see the palazzo's scarlet umbra reflected in the night. I scaled the wall of an abandoned palazzo near the Porta Santa Croce, which, like all of Florence, was closed for the night. Heedless of the curfew and any passing ufficiale, I shimmied up onto the roof to watch the spectacle of Bernardo Silvano's brothel burning to the ground. It was, after all, my life that was also burning. I wasn't sorry to see it go. A better life, a better Luca, would emerge from the ashes. Perhaps for the fence to finally leave the mind of a beaten dog, the fence had to go up in flames.

It was worth it, though I now had to leave Florence. The city fathers would disregard Nicolo's slaughter of innocents, but they would never forgive my act of arson. Arson was a hanging offense. Florence's buildings were precious, far more valuable than fifty familyless children and an old woman who took care of them. In fact, the Signoria would probably be grateful to Nicolo that he'd rid the city of pestiferous outcasts, embarrassing reminders of a vice in which too many city fathers had participated. But burning a building which could have been reclaimed for civic purposes: that was an unpardonable outrage. Knowing this to be so, that neither God nor men would avenge the children whose funeral pyre I had set, I could no longer believe in any God at all. Even a cruel God must harbor tenderness for enslaved children and for a sweet soul like Simonetta. Clearly there was no God apart from the evil in men.

Dawn broke cold and damp. The first tentative rays of

sun shattered the indigo horizon, and the city gates opened. In came peasants from the contado with their carts laden with produce for the markets. Mingling in the streets with the carts and pack animals were devout folk hurrying to early Mass. I had to return to the Sfornos' home to pack my things, and by the time I arrived, a light rain was falling. I went quietly through their house and out to the barn to wash myself. Rachel was waiting. She sat on the hay where I had slept for so many years, but would never again. Her knees were curled up against her chest and wrapped in my woolen blanket.

"I've been worried about you, Luca, I didn't see you come home last night," she said. Her full pink lips were drawn in concern, and her long auburn hair spilled around her shoulders in a glossy sheet, wisps of it curling around her face. Her large eyes were smudged under with purple crescents. Strong-minded Rachel seemed oddly vulnerable, even to my exhausted eyes. She had grown very beautiful over the last four years, with her high cheekbones and fair skin and eyes that shone with intelligence and spirit.

"Rachel, your mother doesn't want you alone with me," I said softly. I stopped in the doorway and pulled over the little tripod stool to sit on, to wait for her to leave.

She asked, "Where were you?"

"Out. I think you should go, so your mother doesn't get angry with me."

"You disappear sometimes," she murmured, hugging her knees closer to her chest. "Where do you go, Luca Bastardo? Do you go to the market, to visit friends from your past, to look for the parents you've never known? Mama says we're not to ask you questions about your life, that someone who's done what you've done has secrets that the rest of us must never learn."

"I'm leaving," I said, looking away. "Something has happened. I can't stay in Florence. It isn't safe for me. Or for your family; ufficiali will come here looking for me."

"No! Luca, why?" She jumped to her feet, dropping the blanket, standing in front of me in her plain peach-colored gonna, the sheer undergarment women wore. I wanted to look away because it wasn't at all appropriate for me to see her thus. A woman wore her gonna only in the most domestic settings, with the most intimate family members. But the dawn threw a soft luminescence that made Rachel's gonna diaphanous, revealing the lift of her full breasts and the indent of her small waist underneath the sheer silk. I was aroused, and stunned and shocked to find myself so. I couldn't tear my eyes away.

"Luca, what's wrong? What's happened? You must tell me! We can help you, I can help you!" Rachel cried. She ran over and pulled me up off the stool. I was breathing heavily, almost shaking. "You're not alone anymore, you have us!" She grabbed my shoulders, shaking me, and as she did, the silk of her gonna was sucked inward to outline the curving shape of her body. A strange lassitude coursed through my being. I went slack though my blood was boiling. I knew all about desire, of course, having had it wielded against me during those years at Silvano's. But I had never before experienced it in myself. I had not expected it to feel this way, insistent and luscious and warm. My cheeks burned. I felt ashamed. Desire was cozening my brain, as I had seen it fool men with wives and children of their own into despicable acts of rape and abuse. So what difference was there between them and me? It was a galling question. I did not want to hurt Rachel as I had been hurt, especially not this day of new self-possession. I hung my head.

"Luca?" Rachel asked. Softly she placed her hand under my chin and tilted up my face. She searched my eyes with her own.

"You have to get out of here," I said hoarsely. "Now!"

I stood to the side to let her pass. Instead, before I could react, she clasped my face in her hands and kissed me. I noted that she was as tall as me and didn't have to stretch up on her toes, and that her lips tasted sweetly of butter. Then she parted her lips to let me feel her soft, lush tongue, and all thought left my head. After a few moments, Rachel pulled her head away from me.

"You're so beautiful, Luca," she murmured. "I've wanted you for so long!"

"Really?" I asked hoarsely, surprised and grateful. "You wanted me?"

"But only if you want me, too," she whispered, and right then, I knew the difference between me and the patrons: Rachel wanted me as much as I wanted her. I had never invited patrons into my room, I had submitted to them with anger, despair, and contempt. There was no submission in Rachel, just reciprocal tenderness. I couldn't speak, so I kissed her some more.

Somehow she was soon lifting off her gonna, and I was scrambling out of my camicia. All those years at Silvano's, I had never imagined that I would be in a hurry to remove my undershirt! I fumbled and Rachel giggled, and then she stroked me and I could only groan. Over the next hour, she took pleasure in my body, as so many had before, but she also unstintingly gave pleasure to me, with her hands, and her mouth, and all of herself. Something was healed that had been damaged by my prior work. I would never be unscathed by what I had done, but I could let myself be a man now, with all that implied. It was a great gift that Rachel gave me.

"You're not going to leave now, are you, Luca?" Rachel asked, after a while. We were lying in each other's arms in the hay. I was nuzzling her, marveling at her beauty and sweetness and strength. Somehow I knew she wasn't the woman promised to me during the night of the philosopher's stone, but I still felt grateful and tender toward Rachel.

"If I don't leave, I put you in danger," I said, and guilt assailed me as I took in the full import of my words. Now more than ever, having loved Rachel, I couldn't bring harm to the Sfornos. Jews were only grudgingly tolerated in Florence. My heart sank as a second recognition seized me: what Rachel and I had done would not be condoned, not by Jews, not by Gentiles, and most of all, not by her parents. "Not just because of what I did last night, but because of this." I stroked her breast softly. "Your parents will kill me when they find out. And you!"

"They won't find out, we won't tell them," Rachel said, her tone pleading.

"Your parents aren't stupid, they'll know at a glance what we did," I said. I rolled away from Rachel and gazed up into the rafters. My heart ached. I had discovered this wondrous thing with Rachel, and it was already lost. We'd betrayed her parents' trust and broken a great taboo. This on the heels of my setting fire to a building, which would bring the city's wrath upon me. I couldn't bring myself to be sorry about our lovemaking, because it felt whole and right, but others would judge and condemn us, her more than me. She could even be killed. I took a deep breath. "Moshe and Leah will be shamed. They'll feel that you've brought dishonor to them, to your family, and to your community. Your family could be ostracized."

"No one will ever know," Rachel repeated, stubbornly. I kissed her forehead.

"People always find out," I said. It hurt me, but I had to leave her, for her own sake. I scrambled up and searched for my camicia. "And men will come here looking for me, and I don't want your family to get in trouble. I did something last night—the ufficiali will hang me! They won't wait for a trial. They already don't like me because of Nicolo Silvano and his new Confraternity of the Red Feather."

"Did you kill Nicolo Silvano?" Rachel stared at me with round eyes.

"I wish I had!" I said. "I wish it was that simple." I was finished dressing and I stood on the stool to retrieve my Giotto panel from its hiding place. Rachel watched me with curiosity in her intelligent eyes. I packed the panel with Petrarca's notebook and Geber's eyeglasses in a portmanteau I'd bought recently at the market, and then shrugged into my mantello.

"You don't have to go, Luca," Rachel said. "Please, don't go! I love you!" She leapt to her feet and clung to me.

"I want to stay, Rachel," I said, running my hands through her luxuriant auburn hair. Just for a moment, I let myself imagine remaining here. I could hold her . . . but her parents would hate me for shaming them in the eyes of their community. And then ufficiali would come here looking for me, holding me accountable for arson, a far worse crime than the murders Nicolo Silvano had committed. And what if the city fathers blamed the Sfornos for sheltering me? What if harm came to Moshe and Rachel because of me?

"I have to go, Rachel, because I care about you," I said, my voice cracking. "If I don't, the ufficiali will hang me, and they may well punish your family. You know how they treat Jews. You could be kicked out of Florence, or worse! Just like your mother has always feared. I won't endanger you."

"Please, Luca, stay," she whispered. But I kissed her one more time on her full red mouth, and then I walked out of the Sfornos' barn. I left Florence and went into exile.

PART 2

Chapter 13

IT WAS A LETTER that brought me back to Florence. Not
one of Petrarca's letters, though he wrote regularly until he
died in 1374. Somehow his letters always found me wherever I was: captaining a pirate ship on the Adriatic Sea, supporting Edward the Black in Spain, battling Tatars at Kulikova,
transporting luscious fabrics and exotic spices over the Silk
Road traversed by the Venetian Marco Polo, salvaging ancient texts from monasteries in Greece, helping expelled
Jews escape Spain and resettle, fishing in Portugal. I worked
first as a physico, that being a skill I possessed that was valuable enough for other men to pay me for. I was also curious
about other professions. I worked as a condottiere, though I
stringently avoided killing anyone, as I'd seen too much of
that already. Instead, I fought for the pleasure of knocking a
man off his horse. I was also a bandit, a merchant, a fisherman, and a dealer in antiquities and forgeries and in anything else I could buy and resell for a higher value. There was
no limit to what I could do except my own conscience,

because I was unencumbered of notions of heaven and perdition.

So, for the decades between 1353 and 1400, I lived from my caprice, exercising all the prerogatives of a free man. I did what I wanted and went where my fancy took me. I traveled the world. I saw its wonders both natural and artificial, met great men, and bedded beautiful women. It seemed unnatural to deny myself pleasure when pain and suffering hovered nearby, ready to pounce and demand their due. So I responded to women's invitations and cherished each of them, though none were The One from my vision. I was no longer certain that I deserved to have the woman from my vision. But I knew I would recognize her instantly, smell her lilac and white light scent, and never again want to touch another woman. There was an underground awareness in my reveries that wouldn't go away, a knowing that whispered across my skin like a warm breeze, that I would find her someday. I had made a choice that fate would honor. What I didn't know was if I could honor fate. I didn't realize until later that the time I spent waiting was empty. Nothing tethered my heart into life. I was floating, dreaming, half asleep, because love is what wakes us up.

DURING THIS TIME I made and lost fortunes, though I never let myself become penniless. I was scrupulous about banking part of my proceeds. Through his Church contacts, Petrarca knew of a bank in Florence run by a young but capable man named Giovanni di Bicci de' Medici who came from an old Florentine family. I liked about this Giovanni that he had the common touch. He was sympathetic toward the rebel poor of the city, probably because his father had eked out a living from a modest patrimony and from the interest on loans to peasants in the contado. He was at home on the streets of Florence and was well liked by the general populace, though his political leanings were usually out of favor with the elite. In burgher-laden, florin-conscious Florence, to be rich was to be honorable and virtuous, and to be poor was to be subject to misery. I was also impressed by the way this shrewd young man diversified his family business and took on the management of farms, the manufacture of silk and woolen goods, and international trade. I regularly sent agents to the Medici bank with funds to deposit.

I took Petrarca's advice about banking, but I did not discipline myself to study as he suggested. I sent him ancient manuscripts as I recovered them in Greece and Egypt, but I did not peruse the classical authors as he urged me to in his missives. There were some romantic poets I liked because they appealed to my secret nostalgia for the woman to come, and I learned to play a *viola da gamba* badly. I practiced sword-fighting and knife-play with any man who had a good, strong arm. I also sought out artists to examine their work. I had a notion that someday, when I returned to Florence and married, I would collect paintings.

I made discreet inquiries about Cathar-connected people who had lost a son. I also asked casually about people with unusual longevity and a mark on their chest. No answers were forthcoming. I confess that my efforts were halfhearted. In this uncomplicated in-between period that passed without the presence of any deity, I did not want to question myself or my origins. Questions were contrary to the simple life of pursuing my pleasure. When they cropped up, they drove me onward, as if I could silence them by traveling to the next town, the next occupation. I wanted only to keep gainfully employed and to keep moving, both because my native curiosity prompted it and because the appearance of my unending youth inevitably aroused comment and consternation. I looked to be a man of twenty-five years and did not age past that, nor did I fall ill, and any wounds I received healed with a rapidity which did not characterize other men. I accepted that I was different, as I always had been, and I left it at that.

However, if I tarried too long in one place, people gossiped about me. Their words drew the attention of the growing but secretive Confraternity of the Red Feather, which considered itself a covert arm of the Holy Roman Inquisition. Members tied a small red feather onto their clothing and greeted each other with secret gestures. It was always my experience that fear and the instinct to scapegoat were more contagious than the plague. Sometimes the aging Nicolo Silvano and his son, Domenico, a red feather sewn onto their farsetti, would follow the rumors to me, whether I was in Roma or Vienna or Paris, as if they possessed the same strangely acute senses that used to tell me where Bernardo Silvano was—only now those senses were fixed on me and my whereabouts. I learned to slip out of town the moment a Silvano arrived. And soon the very first whisperings about witchcraft were the call for me to move on, so I could avoid Nicolo, and eventually his son, Domenico, altogether.

Throughout those years, I kept abreast of what was happening in Florence. The year before he died, Petrarca wrote me that Boccaccio had read *The Divine Comedy* in the *chiesa* of Santa Stefano, and that educated men in Florence raged against him for serving Dante to the masses as if it were common crusted bread. The Black Plague struck again in 1374, and a few years later the *Ciompi*, wool-workers who wore clogs in the factories, revolted after being given impossible production quotas. In the same year, 1378, an antipope was elected, which caused anxiety in papist Florence. The rich Albizzi family controlled the city through a network of friends and nominees in the Signoria. They acted with typical Florentine ingegno in expanding Florentine territories. And Pisa and Milan threatened Florence at the end of the century.

At that time I was living on the northwest coast of Sardegna, in Bosa, a little fishing village on the banks of the Temo River. There I had taken up again my old skills as a physico. I had sailed in with a Genoese merchant ship to trade for coral, and discovered many Bosans ill with dysentery. The local physico had died of it. I pitied the Bosans and made them as comfortable as I could. By the time the town recuperated, I was enchanted with Bosa: with the luxuriant orange and olive groves and sweet berry thickets; ancient cork-oak forests and rich vineyards for the delicious amber Malvasia wine; the griffon vultures and peregrine eagles soaring over high volcanic cliffs; the red-, yellow-, and blue-painted fishing vessels; and the way the pink-stoned city hugged the hill above the sparkling blue sea in a sweeping crescent, climbing upward in narrow lanes and stairs toward the rosy-colored fortress of Castello Malaspina. I bought a small home off the city center, which was an intricate web of alleys, porticoes, and small squares where women worked busily at their looms and embroidery. One hot afternoon in early summer a familiar voice boomed in through my front door.

"Is this the abode of a wolf cub?" called the voice.

"I could not prevent him from coming in, Luca," whispered Grazia, my maid, assistant, and bedmate, appearing in the doorway. She was a small, pretty woman, dark-haired and with a Castilian mien. She had a lively charm and quick intelligence and her menses had ceased at a young age, so pregnancy wouldn't be a problem. I'd let her initiate the bedding, of course, and then I'd enjoyed her without guilt and paid her well for her work around my home.

"It's fine, Grazia." I smiled. "There's just no keeping the Jews out of anywhere!"

"Why would anyone try?" she sniffed, flouncing her skirt. "They bring education and commerce wherever they settle!"

"True," I murmured. I had just finished stitching up a cut a young fisherman had sustained on his arm when a fish thrashed unexpectedly, causing his knife to slip. That was his tale, though I suspected he had been arguing with another young hothead. I was about to warn him to stay away from the other youth, but Grazia pointed behind herself.

"Come in unless you fear getting bit," I called. The Wanderer strode in and I leapt up, whooping with joy, and hugged him. He squeezed me and then stepped back to examine me.

"A cub no longer," he observed, grinning. He pinched my biceps. "Look at these muscles, grown hard from use. Luca Bastardo the wounded blond cub has grown to be a dangerous animal!" But he looked the same: big burly shoulders carrying a bulging sack, thickly muscled arms and thighs, a long, wild, gray beard, and deep crow's-feet radiating out from dark eyes that luminesced with play, sadness, and time lived too long.

"You look the same, Wanderer," I said, and I was glad to see it. I wasn't the only one with an oddity when it came to age.

"I always will," he returned lightly. "As will you, now that you're a wolf fully grown."

"Strange quirk to have as a trait, like an arrow with too many feathers in its quill," I commented in a low voice, to keep our words private.

"Some people have unusual gifts," Grazia said airily, to

no one in particular. "Tommaso, go, and don't argue with Guglielmo anymore! Next time it may be more than your arm that's cut!" The young man protested as Grazia took him by the arm to usher him out. She was useful as an assistant this way; she was practical and firm and the Sards respected her.

"What is time, that we should be mindful of it? What seest thou in the dark backward and abysm of time?" the Wanderer asked, spinning his old questions like a net that would capture me. I was so delighted to see him that I just grinned and shook my head.

"It's something you and I have a lot of that other men have less of. Why should that be?"

"Why shouldn't it be? Because you fear it? Fear that we're from the land of fairy, of heart's desire, where nobody gets old and godly and grave, where beauty has no ebb and decay no flood, and time and the world are ever in flight," he chanted, with his particular grin that I had missed more than I realized.

"Riddles about things I haven't thought about in years." I chuckled.

"You don't want to," he replied crisply. "So they've come knocking at your door. What did you do with my donkey, eh? Did you eat it, wolf?"

"That donkey was kept in high style in Florence, and damned if the stubborn, sordid old creature wasn't still alive when I had to leave!"

"So that's what you do with my gift, you abandon and denigrate him?" The Wanderer laughed. "And here he's one of us, cursed by God to outlive his usefulness! You should have brought him with you. He's loyal and dependable, a good ally to have at your side in a fight!"

"He's a prince among asses," I said, rolling my eyes, "but I'm sure he's dead now."

"Don't you ever question your certainties?" the Wanderer asked. "What are you doing in this little fishing village in the middle of nowhere, anyway?"

"The finest fresco cycle in all of Sardegna is here, painted by a Tuscan from the papal court in Avignon. It boasts an Adoration of the Magi that will make your heart stop beating—"

"You're joking, yes? A fresco cycle? Listen, I have a story to tell you—"

"A story?! I haven't seen you in, what, fifty years? And you want to tell me a story?" I exclaimed. "If I'm going to listen to one of your infernal stories, we'd better be drinking good wine! Come upstairs and I'll ask Grazia to prepare us a meal."

"That woman is small but formidable, she's as pretty as Moshe Sforno's wife, and probably faster with a knife," the Wanderer said. "I wouldn't want to cross her!" I laughed and agreed, then led him upstairs. We sat at my dining table. Grazia brought us a jar of wine.

"Are you the first of your people to come to Sardegna?" she asked. "I hear the Jews are looking for places to settle. Bosa's a good choice; there are open-minded folk here. Perhaps smarter than open-minded. Many Bosans see the advantage of a community of Jews here."

"Jews are always looking for places to settle," he said gravely. "It's God's will for us."

"How can anyone know God's will?" she challenged him. He grinned widely at her.

"And you, what are you looking for?" he replied, answering a question with a question, as always.

I didn't expect Grazia to answer. She had a lively charm that was all her own, but she was a typical Sard, courageous, hardworking, and remote, wary of revealing too much of herself, suspicious of strangers. To my surprise, she grew

still. She tilted her small head and her fiery eyes softened.
The Wanderer could have that effect on people, of course;
I'd seen it before, decades ago. "Love," she said softly, "a
child. Myself. What do you want, Jew?"

His craggy, bearded face took on a rare pensive expression. "Peace for my people," he said softly, surprising me for
the second time. "Peace for the earth."

"Then our wishes are brethren," she said. "If everyone
had what I want, there would be peace." Her fine Castilian
face shuttered over with its usual Sard stoicism. "I'll get
food."

I was silenced by the grace of Grazia's response; I'd never
thought to ask her about her longings. Longings were incon-
veniences I'd avoided these past decades. She hurried about
gathering food with her cheeks slightly pink. I poured a glass
of wine for the Wanderer and myself. He lifted his cup in a
silent toast to me, and we both drank a long draught. I
plunked my cup on the table, so that some of the fine amber
liquid danced up inside the brim. Then we both sat in the silence. I grew aware of the myriad sensory impressions
around me: Grazia clattering about in the kitchen, the fragrance of nearly ripe apricots from the tree outside my
home, the shrill call of a gull winging down toward a rock
on the coast, the distant laughter of men working in a field,
the bleating of a herd of sheep crossing along the street in
front of my door. I settled into a fuller, richer moment than
I had experienced in many years, as if all the time spent diverting myself was only a flickering shadow of what life
could be. I felt my kinship with the Wanderer, who sat with
me, alert and still.

"You came all the way to Sardegna to tell me a story?" I
asked finally.

"Wouldn't it be a worthy journey?"

"That depends on the story," I said slyly, and he chuckled.

"Isn't there a gift at the end of every good story? Let me ask you, you're a physico like old Moshe Sforno was—"

"Was?" I cried, as the implication of the past tense sank in.

"Moshe died twenty years ago," the Wanderer said. "A good death; he was alive when he died. Now, you're a physico, you'd heal someone who was ill who came to you, wouldn't you?"

"If I could, of course, always," I said, remembering with a pang that cleft my heart Moshe Sforno's many kindnesses to me. I thought of Rachel lying warm and sweet in my arms. Somehow I'd neglected to keep track of the Sfornos these many years, and now that I knew that Moshe was dead, I wondered why. Had I simply let my heart lapse so that the time like a frozen flower wouldn't elapse, when all along other people, people for whom I cared, were living in the summer of lives that yielded inevitably to a harvest? Wasn't there a better use of these extra days I'd been allotted? "What of Rachel?" I asked, feeling suddenly breathless.

"I have no word of her," he said. "But I do have that story I promised you. A certain man—"

"What was his name?" I prompted him, eliciting the Wanderer's hearty grin.

"Some things don't change, eh, Bastardo? But I won't ruin a good story by confining it to specific names, not this time. Suffice to say the man was ill and in terrible pain, so he went to a great rabbi. 'Rebbe, heal me,' he said. The rebbe was greatly saddened by the man's suffering."

"Of course; suffering is unnecessary," I said flatly.

"Suffering is part of life, it's unavoidable," Grazia commented, setting a platter before us with the mild soft country cheese of Sardegna, prosciutto made from wild boar, salty sardines, olives, early figs and orange cherry tomatoes, a bowl of chartreuse olive oil, a little cup of salt, and two round flat loaves of bread. I tore off some bread and dipped it into the olive oil.

The Wanderer nodded as he combed his thick beard. "Part of being alive is to see the suffering in the world and our own suffering and to stay whole through it and because of it. We can't be whole without including suffering. We cannot cleave God in half!"

"God, what God? If there were a God, man would be too puny to cleave Him!" I said.

"Luca doesn't say prayers," Grazia told the Wanderer, shaking her head.

"Prayers say 'Luca,'" the Wanderer told her. He looked at me. "Oneness is everything."

"I wouldn't mind being a half," I joked, "to have avoided what I've been through!"

"Isn't it just that you've eaten freely from the Tree of Life, so you've also been given the bittersweet fruit of the Tree of the Knowledge of Good and Evil?" he asked, holding up his callused hand. "Is there any suffering in your life that you have lived through that you would give up now that you're on the other side of it? Hasn't it made you who you are?"

I stared out the window where a hummingbird buzzed around the flowers that Grazia had planted in the window box. I thought of Silvano and the years in the brothel, Massimo and Paolo and the years on the street, Moshe and Rachel Sforno and the years in their barn. The past was still strong, still making me hungry, but it didn't have the same old hooks anchoring into me. I could hold it as the air had held the hummingbird, without clenching. Something about my time of wandering had allowed my history to sit more spaciously inside me. Even my part in Marco, Ingrid, and Bella's deaths had eased its stranglehold. "You ask questions that no one has put to me for many years, Wanderer."

"The questions are always waiting," he said. "You can exile yourself, but it's always there. It reigned before anything was created and will do so after all things shall cease to be."

"It hasn't been exile. I do not regret this time. I've enjoyed it."

"Joy is the foundation of the worlds." He shrugged. "Shall I return to my story? The rebbe felt sorry for the man but answered no, he wouldn't heal him. The man was terribly disappointed and lamented miserably. At last the rebbe sighed and said, 'Go see Rabbi So-and-So. He can help you.' Now, the second rabbi was a lesser rabbi, not as wise, not as learned, not as discerning. But the man went to him, and the rabbi healed him."

"What is the point of this story for which you have traveled a great distance after many years to tell me?" I asked impatiently. I bit on the chewy, sour flesh of a green olive, spat the pit out into my hand, and tossed it onto the table. Grazia, who hovered nearby, eavesdropping, clucked at me. She brought a cup for the pits and gave me a look that meant she'd scold me later. I smiled, disarming her. Then I looked at her as if seeing her for the first time. The Wanderer had asked her questions of substance, and she had answered with honesty and intelligence. It had never occurred to me to engage her that way, though I had treated her with kindness. If Grazia wasn't the woman from my vision, she was a kind soul. She deserved something real from me in return for what she gave so generously of herself. I wondered if I had kept her at a distance so I wouldn't have to face how alienated from her I was, and from everyone, not only through the differing span of our days, but through my understanding of the power of evil, which nothing held in check.

The Wanderer leaned toward me, rapping lightly on the table to get my attention. "Now, why do you think the great rebbe wouldn't heal the man, but referred him on?"

"The man didn't offer to pay him enough?" I asked. The Wanderer gave me a stony look.

"The great rebbe discerned something important about the man's pain," Grazia answered. "But the great rebbe knew the lesser rabbi wouldn't!"

"Yes! The great rebbe knew that the man's suffering was God's grace, and he didn't want to deprive the man of it," the Wanderer said, thumping his hand on the table. "God's grace!"

"God's cruel laughter, you mean!" I cried, unable to refrain. I poured more wine for myself and gulped it down. "Another one of God's mean-spirited jokes!"

"Luca, God's jokes are embraces of love," Grazia said in a pitying tone. Her pretty face softened again, but I was stubborn in my knowing.

"That's not what I've seen," I said.

"Then your eyes aren't working," the Wanderer said. "But this woman sees clearly. The man's illness balanced out a debt he owed. God was allowing this man to work it off, so he could return to Oneness!"

"Debt? What debt?"

"I should tell you everything?" The Wanderer shrugged. "A debt from this life, from another life, who knows? The great rebbe knew that the debt was being paid off through suffering, and thus the man would advance toward transformation. The rebbe did not want to deprive the man of that opportunity. Nor did he want to leave the man in pain, and he knew the lesser rabbi would not discern the grace in the suffering." He leaned back in his chair and crossed his arms over his chest, stretched out his heavy legs and wagged his feet, as if relaxing.

"Another life? What life?"

"Didn't Geber talk to you about the transmigration of souls?" the Wanderer asked, sounding surprised. He took a deep sip of wine and then plucked a tomato from the platter and popped it into his mouth. Spewing tiny seeds, he said, "Geber read the *Sefer Bahir,* the book of brilliance. He knew that souls must return to earth over and over again until their tasks are completed. I suppose his time was cut short, he couldn't teach you everything you need to know. You're supposed to teach yourself, you know. That was the point of the philosopher's stone."

"I needed to learn how to turn lead into gold, and his time was cut off before he could teach me," I said, with the edge of a sulk in my voice. It was an old regret of mine that I had not mastered Geber's ultimate secret. I rose and paced distractedly around the room, which suddenly seemed too small, too far from the center of things.

"Are you so small-minded, Luca Bastardo?" the Wanderer chided me. "Gold, bah, that's easy to come by. I am talking about the education of the soul! I am talking about human destiny and divine order! I am talking about each soul fulfilling every commandment with proper intentionality and sacred language, because if some spark of a soul has not fulfilled even one aspect of the three—deed, speech, and thought—it must transmigrate until it fulfills all of them!"

"I heard about the transmigration of souls as I rode a camel into Cathay, of souls putting on new bodies the way we put on new clothes. I'm not convinced! It's a pretty tale to soothe people. We're just little toys made of dust and blood, playthings for a cruel God who doesn't exist. Who are we to deserve new lives? Who are we to deserve life in the first place? It's miracle enough, or a rich enough joke, that we are ever born. More than that, we cannot hope for!" I said passionately. "Our greatest joy is to behold beauty. Your story is not for me, Wanderer!"

"Do you want to decide before you've seen the gift that it

brings?" he asked. He withdrew something from his mended gray shirt: a letter. I snatched it from his gnarled, thickly veined hand.

"It's from Rebecca Sforno, dated recently," I said, in amazement. My heart beat harder at the thought of hearing about Rachel. "Things are not good for the Sfornos. The plague visits Florence again, and war is snarling at the city gates. Two of her grandchildren are sick. She's asking me to come back and help! She remembers what her father said of the consolamentum, that I had the gift of healing touch. She asks me to give it to her grandchildren."

"I'll wait while you pack a bag," the Wanderer said. "There's a ship that's leaving tonight. The captain owes me a favor or two."

"I didn't say I was coming," I said. "I want to help Rebecca, she's an old friend, the Sfornos were good to me, they changed my life, and I've always wondered what became of Rachel. . . . I guess I abandoned them, but I didn't want harm to come to them because of me. . . . There are people who want me dead in Florence."

"How can you turn your back on old friends?" interjected Grazia, in her piquant, meddling way. "When you came to Bosa a few years ago, your hands gave sweet relief to many who were ill. That must be the consolamentum your friend is asking for. If you can help her grandchildren, you must. I'll gather clothes for you." She bustled out of the room before I could respond. The matter was decided in her mind. I thought she was probably right. I had been called back to Florence, the bonds of old friendship had been invoked, and I must go. I was reluctant but also excited. It had been many years since I'd been home.

"Have that pretty maid with the good vision pack us some of these tomatoes, eh?" the Wanderer said. "In fact, have her pack a full basket of food. This island has delicious fare."

So I took some clothes and my Giotto panel and Geber's eyeglasses and Petrarca's notebook and put them into a portmanteau that had seen dozens of ports in the last fifty years, years that suddenly seemed as empty as the pages of the notebook were. Grazia packed food. Before I left, I tore a sheet of vellum from the back of Petrarca's still-blank notebook and wrote a letter deeding my home and belongings to Grazia. I gave it to her with all the money I had in the house and a quick kiss. To my surprise, she took my face in both her hands, and kissed me long and gently on the lips.

"You've been good to me, Luca Bastardo," she said.

"How can I have been good to you when I didn't even know you?" I asked softly.

"Did you know yourself?" She smiled. "Go now. I always knew you would leave. Your parents must have been travelers who bore you under a restless star." Her fine Castilian face was pensive, her dark eyes limpid. "If I didn't let you leave, it would be wrong. I would be trying to make you into someone you aren't."

"Good-bye, Grazia," I said softly. For a moment I enclosed her in my arms, feeling her small warm body with its strong bones. I wished her well; I wished for her that she would find the love and the child that she was looking for. I thought she already had herself, though it was interesting that she had included that in her list of longings. If I had stayed, I would have asked her what she had meant.

I set off with the Wanderer down the steep hill toward the seacoast. We walked through cobblestone alleys and down stairs cut into the side of the hill, passed through groves of fig, olive, and almond trees, startled wildcats and wild boars and partridges as they prowled through the lush foliage, and eventually came to a curving beach with dark sand that was claimed by the locals to possess healing properties. I had heard that people with stiff joints would lie on a blanket on the sand and feel better, looser, and more flexible. Nature was full of marvels. Considering that, was it so odd that nature would choose a few men for special longevity? Was it so strange that time would pass differently for some men than for others? I pondered this as we followed the coast around. It was a long trek under the relentless Sard sun.

"Now don't you wish you had kept my donkey with you, Bastardo?" the Wanderer asked.

"He would have been dinner in some of the places I've been over the last fifty years," I said, wiping sweat off my forehead. "Now's the time to distract me with a tale, Wanderer."

"Do you imagine that I can simply regurgitate a tale for you at will, like a dog who barks on command?" he asked, indignant.

"Then tell me about this book, the *Sefer Bahir*. What does it say?"

"What do you want it to say?" he asked. "Don't men read books and take from them what is already in their own hearts?"

"That's right, you insist on answering questions with questions. Over the last fifty years, I'd forgotten how satisfying that is," I said, with some sarcasm.

The Wanderer grinned his wily grin and leaned close so that his wild gray locks flopped against my cheek. "It says that the union between a man and woman is a pathway to the divine. Has the lovely Grazia brought you closer to God?"

"Oh yes, there were times when I was with her that I called out God's name," I said facetiously, and then winked broadly.

"A sacred union, then," he answered solemnly. "So to have had such a union and not to have raised a child together means that you will both transmigrate to come together again and raise a child. That will fulfill the commandment."

"If I am going to transmigrate to be with a woman, it will not be for Grazia. She is lovely, but she is not the one, The One. Do you understand, Wanderer? The One who was promised me. Promised, during that crazy night of visions inspired by the philosopher's stone with you and Geber! I have saved my heart for that promise!"

"Saved your heart or hidden your heart?" he asked. It was the question which seemed to have awakened me, and I couldn't answer it. So we continued in silence until we reached a Catalan ship, where we were taken aboard and treated as royalty.

I WAS BACK IN FLORENCE. Florence: the center of the world, the city which inspired madrigals to sing of its silver walls, declared by a Pope to be the fifth element of the cosmos. Of course the city was scorching. Under the summer sun, the gray stones heated up and baked the streets like an oven. And naturally the plague was about. Still, I was home. I was breathing Florence's air, smiling at her fashionably dressed women. I would dine on bread-and-bean soup, fresh spinach sautéed in Tuscan olive oil, and roast beef on the bone. I was going to salute the city's health with the noble wine of Montepulciano. I was walking through the Oltrarno, marveling at the many new palazzi built for wealthy merchants and guildsmen. Via San Niccolo, which connected Porta San Giorgio with Porta San Niccolo, was built up almost to a solid facade of brick and stucco without a breach. The dwellings were high and narrow, rising four or five stories, and deeper than they were wide, as was common. The streets were still a vibrant mélange of palazzo and cottage, of cloth factory and bottega, of church and monastery. Stonemasons and shoemakers rubbed shoulders with bankers and traders, artisans and prostitutes. The plague cast a lull over the street, but it wasn't as desolate as the first time the Black Death had swept through the stone walls. People had learned they could not hide when death stalked them.

I came to the Jewish enclave and made my way to the Sfornos' carved *portone,* the massive recessed door to their home. I knocked with the brass knocker and a moment later, a hunched-over grandmotherly woman opened the door. "Luca!" she trilled.

"Rebecca?" I asked, with some hesitation.

"But of course." She laughed. "Come in, get out of the street before the plague finds you, and let me look at you." She tugged on my sleeve and I stepped into the foyer, which was much the same as the first time I'd entered this house, more than fifty years ago. Rebecca stood close, smiling up at me. Her curly hair was white now, her face deeply seamed, but her eyes were as clear and joyful as ever and her voice did not quaver. I could feel the vibrance and sweetness of the young girl whom I had first seen clasped in her father's arms, ducking away from murderous stones. I wondered what it was like for her to see her old friend still young. I wondered if it would make her envy or hate me. My differentness from her would be all the more apparent, and it made me more alien to her than even Gentile was from Jew.

"I came as soon as I received your letter," I said, feeling tentative. I looked past her to see if Rachel was inside this house, even though I knew Rachel must have her own home.

"You must have flown here," she marveled. "Where is our old friend the Wanderer?"

"Tormenting someone else with his questions." I smiled, shrugging. "He disappeared the moment we came through the city gates."

"Isn't that just like him, coming and going when he's not

expected!" Rebecca grabbed a fistful of my sleeve and tugged happily. "I am so glad to see you. I knew you'd come, even though we hadn't heard from you in so many, many years!"

"Of course I've come," I said softly, moved and pleased by her welcome.

"Grandmother, who is it?" asked an unsmiling young man, who came into the foyer and gave me a hard stare. He was tall, taller than me, broad-shouldered and strong, with dark curly hair and a long oval face whose high cheekbones reminded me of Leah Sforno. He narrowed his blue eyes at me, scanned me up and down.

"This is Luca." Rebecca smiled. "The one who saved me and then was trained by Papa as a physico! I asked him to come heal your brother and sister, to give them his consolamentum!"

"Really?" the boy grunted. "He'll be hungry. Why don't we show him to the table?"

"Of course, Aaron, you're right," Rebecca said, her face lighting up. "How silly of me to stand here gawking. Come, Luca, you must remember where the table is!" Spry and giggly, she darted down the hall. I followed, but the boy stopped me with a hand on my shoulder.

"If you are who she claims you are, then there is unholy magic involved, and you are a golem, with parents who are demons," he said in a low voice. "If you are not him, which is what I think, then you are an adventurer trying to get money from an old woman with a weak mind."

"I don't need her money," I said, pulling away. "I came to help your brother and sister."

"My brother and sister are beyond help," he said. "I buried them a week ago. And Great-Aunt Miriam, and my parents, and my aunt Ruth, Miriam's daughter. The plague struck us hard this time, perhaps because it spared us all the other times. Grandmother and I are the only ones left. She can't remember that, though, so don't tell her. It would only upset her."

"I would not cause her pain," I said, saddened. I went into the dining salon and sat on the old bench and let Rebecca fuss over me. She put down a plate of cool boiled chicken and a fried artichoke and poured me a cup of white wine. As she bustled around, she touched my hair and pinched my cheek. Aaron stood in the doorway, arms folded, staring balefully.

"Tell me, what's the news with Rachel?" I inquired, my heart racing suddenly.

"Rachel, Rachel. She left, she's been gone," Rebecca said, drooping.

Aaron shook his head at me, and asked Rebecca to get some bread. When she left, he said, "My great-aunt left this house decades ago. I heard from Miriam that it was a month after you left. She thought Rachel had gone after you. Everyone was scandalized." His eyes were cold on my face.

"I never saw her again," I said, looking away, wondering what had happened to Rachel. Did she still live somewhere with friends? Had she had a husband and children and a full life somewhere outside Florence? I hoped so; Rachel deserved happiness. It occurred to me that she could also be dead, that she could have died alone in some strange place. Sorrow sat heavily on my heart as I remembered the spirited young Rachel with her quick mind, sharp tongue, forthright ways, and beautiful strong-boned face. I remembered her tenderness as we'd held each other. I hoped that she was vigorous and beloved somewhere, and if not, that she'd had a good death, an easy death, and that the Wanderer would say she was alive when she died, as her father had been. It occurred to me that this unexplained longevity of mine wasn't necessarily a gift. I still carried the hungry streets and the brothel within me like a living homunculus always looking for more, but somehow, along the way, despite my roaming, I was accumulating people to care for, and I was going to watch them die.

Chapter 14

I STAYED FOR A FEW NIGHTS in the Sfornos' barn, though now Rebecca had a different last name. The place was the same, and the resident cat was an orange tomcat who sat in the rafters, flicking his tail and watching me with unblinking amber eyes. The space in the wall where I had secreted my Giotto panel was still there. I had to examine it, and I found in it a wooden doll that must have been hidden there by a child. I chuckled to think that some young Sforno girl had discovered my hiding place and used it; my old secrets were always being discovered. I spent a lot of time with Rebecca, who was alternately lucid and dreamy. Sometimes she would ask me the same questions over and over, "Did you just return, Luca? Have you eaten?" When she repeated herself, I would hold her hand and talk about the old days, and she would slowly come back to the present, or as much of it as she could tolerate, with her sisters, her children, and most of her grandchildren dead of the plague. It was a bittersweet time that wrung my heart in unexpected ways. Then I had a day that sent me into hiding again, this time for sixty years.

The day started and ended with confrontation, and during the middle, there was death, as in so many of my days. At dawn, Aaron entered into the barn with a braying donkey following him. "A friend of mine kept this mangy beast while I cared for my family. He belongs to you."

"No," I groaned. I sat up and rubbed hay out of my hair. "He belongs to the Wanderer!"

"Family legend says he's yours and you'll claim him—if you are who you say you are. So here's your noble steed, and don't let us keep you from your journey." Aaron spoke with cold purpose and a determined thrust of his stubborn young chin.

"I haven't upset your grandmother."

"Yes, you have," he said firmly. "She's in a ferment, with her memory all jumbled up and time looping around on her. You have the same face as a man she knew in her childhood—"

"I am that man," I said quietly.

"Perhaps the Red Feather should hear about it," Aaron said tightly. "They're looking for witches and prodigies. A Jew who turns one in would curry favor for the entire community. We need as much goodwill as we can get. Jews are the first people blamed for the city's troubles!"

"I'll be out of this barn today."

"Take the animal. It's older than I am, but the thing won't die. I don't want it in my family's stable," he said. "If they come looking for sorcery, they could come to our door to ask about it, and it won't go well for us. That murderous confraternity is intent upon mayhem." He paused for a moment. "They might even have their sights on us already. Miriam told me of a rumor that Rachel was taken in by

Nicolo Silvano, who kept her prisoner and then beat her to death some years later."

I was stricken and stared at Aaron in shock and horror. Was this possible? What could have been Rachel's reason for leaving her family and falling into such a terrible fate? What had happened to Rachel that she would willingly go to Nicolo Silvano? Had I somehow done something to her? I felt a terrible unease and guilt. "I never heard such a thing."

"My great-aunt never told her parents, and only told me on her deathbed. It surely has something to do with Silvano's enmity with you. You've caused this family enough misery. Get out before you bring more to us." He tossed the lead rope at me, turned on his heel, and strode out.

A FEW HOURS LATER, under the vibrant blue sky of the morning harvest sun that had not yet risen far above the horizon, with a light breeze ruffling my mantello, I went walking with the donkey through Florence. I was looking for an open boardinghouse with a stable. Because of the plague, most hotels were closed. Foreigners weren't welcome when the Black Death was about. Much had changed in Florence, and, at the same time, much hadn't.

I led the donkey in desultory fashion across the Ponte Vecchio, where all of the little shops were closed, then I ambled toward the city center. I was aimless, brimming with a dozen contradictory feelings. I was happy to be back in Florence, and sorry to have bade farewell to Rebecca Sforno. I would never see her again. I wondered what had happened to Rachel and if I had one more thing to feel guilty about. I had thought that I'd pick up the threads of my old relationship with the Sfornos as a woman picks up the pattern again when she sits back down at her loom, and I was wrong. Time as I lived it was different from how it was for others. I didn't want to see the consequences of that, but the consequences were there, ineluctable, making me feel melancholy and alien even as I rejoiced in my return to my incomparable Florence. And then there was the rumor about Rachel, which left me feeling queasy and sick about her possible fate. It renewed my old fury toward Nicolo Silvano.

A well-dressed boy ran awkwardly toward me, his eyes wide and his face pale. There was something strange about the fearful way he moved, so I glanced around to see what was alarming him. Two beefy-looking, dirty-bearded men in coarse, torn farsetto came barreling after him. Days of the plague always brought out criminals, who rightly suspected that there were fewer ufficiali to patrol the streets when citizens were dying en masse. The boy stumbled across my path and I threw my arm around him and tossed him up onto the donkey. I never could bear to watch a child get hurt, and it was clear that the ruffians meant to do him harm.

"Please, they're going to hurt me," the boy squeaked. I held my finger to my lips and sang a loud, raucous song and bobbled on my feet as if drunk. The two ruffians slowed to a swagger. With gusto, I screeched out lyrics about a bosomy Napolitano woman and my extraordinary prowess as her paramour.

"The boy is coming with us," one of them said, as they got closer. I sang louder and swayed, gestured broadly in front of me with the hand holding the lead rope while my other hand snuck around to pull out the dagger I kept strapped on my thigh under my lucco. I didn't go for my short sword, my *squarcina,* because that would have been too obvious.

"And she loved my MASSIVE tool so she never EVER denied me her favors," I bawled, easing the dagger out of its sheath and holding it behind me.

"Look, he's drunk," the other ruffian said, sneering. "You

knock him down and I'll grab the boy!" The first ruffian smirked and reached for me. I twisted as if intoxicated, kicking the donkey while I seemed to fall at the ruffian. The man made a soft grunt of surprise as my dagger found him in the center of his chest. I twisted the handle and pulled it out even as he toppled over. The second man turned to see why his comrade had grunted. He barely had time to utter an exclamation when my dagger caught his Adam's apple. I stabbed quickly, and just as quickly withdrew the blade. The lout fell, and I wiped off the knife on his muddy mantello and left them where they lay. The becchini who came for the plague victims would add these two to their biers.

"They deserved to die. They were going to kidnap me," the boy said fiercely, in a high, sweet voice. I looked at him and nodded. He was a thin, sallow child with fine light brown hair and an angular nose, not comely, but with an honest, quiet mien that gave him poise beyond his years. The donkey calmed and the boy started to dismount, but I stopped him.

"I'll take you to your family," I said, "you can ride." He smiled, and light came into his serious face. "Where to?" I asked. The boy pointed in the direction of the Baptistery, so we set off toward the domed octagonal structure that was the very heart of Florence. All at once I was hungry to see the Baptistery, with its harmonious geometrical forms in green and white marble. It had been decades since I had feasted my eyes on the south doors with their exquisite sculpted panels of the life of St. John. They were designed by Andrea Pisano in 1330, cast in bronze in Venice, and fit on the southern entrance in 1336, back when I was still a boy in the city.

"They planned to ransom me back to my father, he's very rich," the boy said.

I looked at the boy's clean face, well-kempt hair, and precisely cut clothes. "He'd have paid."

The boy nodded. "And they'd have killed me anyway. That's the problem with having money; people want to take it from you. It's best to stay out of sight if you're very rich."

"Perhaps so, if people know you're very rich." I shrugged.

"But then what do you do if you stay inside all the time?" he asked, as if posing a question of weighty philosophical import.

"I had a friend who told me to read and study the great men of the past, the ancient Greek and Latin thinkers who were very wise about the nature of man," I said.

"Yes, that makes sense, to learn of the nature of man from the ancient masters," the boy said, in a considering tone. I smothered a grin lest it offend his dignity, which was very great. Petrarca would have liked this young boy. Petrarca had been disappointed in his own son, who was intelligent but not bookish; this solemn, thoughtful boy in front of me had the affect of a scholar, and would have pleased him. "What's your name?" the boy asked.

"Luca Bastardo."

"My father knows a man who is on the council that is the Six of Commerce, who might be Gonfaloniere soon and who is friendly with the Podestà, and once I heard that man tell my father that he had been looking for someone named Luca Bastardo all his life."

"Ugly man, with a skinny nose like this"—I made a peaked gesture with my fingers—"and a chin that sticks out?"

The child nodded. "My father called him Domenico. Are you his Luca Bastardo?"

"No relation," I said shortly, concealing my alarm. I glanced around warily. So Domenico Silvano, despite being the grandson of a brothel keeper, had come up in the world. He had power and influence. He was serving on the prestigious Six of Commerce; he might be elected Gonfaloniere, the head of the Signoria that governed Florence; he was friendly with the Podestà, the chief of justice in the city. Nicolo Silvano had indeed seized the opportunities presented by the plague to improve his family's fortunes, as he'd said he would so long ago, and his son, Domenico, was reaping the benefits. The Confraternity of the Red Feather must have aided him in his ambitions, as it was favorably looked on by the Church. I changed the subject. "What's your name?"

"Cosimo," he answered sonorously, squaring his little shoulders. At that moment the donkey decided to sit on its hindquarters, so that the boy almost tumbled off. I caught him and steadied him, and he smiled at me. I tugged the donkey's tail to get it to stand, which it did, reluctantly. We had arrived at the Baptistery, and I looked around covertly for anyone with a red feather tied to his farsetto or lucco. Seeing no one, I stopped in front of Pisano's beautiful bronze doors, each with fourteen square panels. Of the twenty-eight panels, twenty showed the life of St. John the Baptist, and the other eight showed the virtues: Hope, Faith, Charity, Humility, Fortitude, Temperance, Justice, and Prudence, all the great qualities to which Florence aspired but failed miserably to attain. The most laughably failed virtue had to be Temperance; Florence was always a city that violently took both sides of an issue. But to have these ideals before our eyes, expressed in sculpted figures that moved like real people dressed in draperies that fell convincingly like folds of real fabric around their bodies, made it plausible that Florentines could embody them.

"Your eyes are wet," the boy said. He had clambered down from the donkey and stood next to me. He took my hand in his small one.

"The most important thing is art, the beauty that art shows," I said reverently. "That's the only heaven that we can glimpse. If there's such a thing as grace, it's in the work of these great Masters: Pisano, Giotto, Cimabue . . . ."

The boy stared at the panel of the "Naming of the Baptist." "That's the Virgin who presents the babe for naming; I can tell it's her by her halo." I nodded, and the boy mused, "It is a great honor for the Baptist that the Mother of Christ presents him. It gives him a higher status."

"I never thought of that," I admitted. "But look how she bends so tenderly over the child, as she would for any child, since she's the mother of the world. And look how strong her shoulders and arms look under her robes, so she can bear the world's suffering."

"Yes, I see that," he said, in the wondering voice of one who newly understood something. "In this panel, John baptizing Christ, the angel is struck with awe, and he's the only one watching, so it makes us think how holy the moment is! And here, Christ speaking to John's disciples, he blesses them sweetly with his hand, but he has no halo, because the disciples haven't yet realized what John realizes, that Christ is the savior! In a moment, they'll understand that, and everything will change!"

"You have eyes for seeing art, Cosimo." I smiled. "Go look at Giotto's paintings in Santa Croce. They'll amaze you."

"Giotto's paintings are as beautiful as these?" He indicated the panels.

"Giotto was the teacher of this sculptor, and his paintings are sublime, almost too beautiful to believe," I said. "Florence would not be what she is without Giotto's paintings and Pisano's reliefs, without all the great artists who come here to make the city rich with color and form and texture, to fill the city with beauty that the rest of the world envies."

Cosimo drew me around the Baptistery and pointed at the north doors. "Why don't we have something beautiful on these doors, too? We should have equally grand doors here!"

"Because it must be paid for," an energetic voice said,

"and because an artist must be found to do as exquisite a job as Pisano, and how could we pick the artist?" It was a stoutish young man with a round face who addressed us. He looked not even twenty yet, but his hair was already thinning. I perused his dress for a telltale red feather, but didn't spy one. The young man bowed slightly. "I saw you two admiring Pisano's doors. Their beauty breaks my heart!"

"With the plague about, there's plenty of idle time for everyone except becchini," I said.

"I come here despite having work to finish." He grinned. "I am Lorenzo."

"I have a little brother named Lorenzo. I am Cosimo," the boy told him, sounding at once both lofty and sensible, a neat trick.

"I'm Luca Bastardo," I said. "Are you an artist, Lorenzo, to be so sensitive to beauty?"

"I'm a goldsmith, but, ah, I also paint," he said modestly, his round face coloring. "It's my dream to create a set of sculpted doors to rival Pisano's and add to the luster of Florence!"

"What would you do?" I asked. "What scenes?"

"Whatever was required." He waved off my question. "It's not what I would do, so much as how. You see how much stillness there is in Pisano's work; I would make exuberant figures, with life spilling out of them! I would fill the space and yet make the space an important compositional element. . . ." He stood in front of the plain doors, gesticulating as if he had created his own set of bronze doors. It was a trick of light, but for a moment, I could almost see Lorenzo's doors: twenty-eight panels, with the first panel on the top row showing a masterful Jesus carrying the cross. . . . Then I blinked, and the image was gone.

"Perhaps you will execute these doors," I mused, "since you have such ideas for them."

He chuckled. "I am an unknown goldsmith. If anyone gets a commission to do these doors, it will be some famed master artist!"

"You never know what life has in store. Powerful dreams have a way of coming true." I shrugged. "Perhaps there will be a competition for the commission, and you'll win."

"A competition, I like that!" Cosimo cried, placing his hands on his hips and thrusting his chest out as if he were a grown man. "My father has close friends in the Calimala guild that maintains the Baptistery, I'll talk to him about it!"

Lorenzo rubbed his thin hair. "A commission, now? With Milan barking like a rabid dog at our gates, and the Black Death murdering our citizens? Would the guild spend the money?"

"Maybe not right away," Cosimo said thoughtfully. "But I will mention it to my father for later. He listens to me, you know."

"I'm sure he does," Lorenzo said, without a trace of mockery. Cosimo had that effect on people; though a child, he possessed a reserve that caused them to take him seriously. In later years, I was to see him exercise his unique gravity even more effectively as an adult.

"Art in Florence has always been a matter of civic pride," I added. "The money offered by the Calimala guild would be well spent invigorating the city in the face of these troubles."

"This is so, art is the soul of Florence," Lorenzo said.

"Art and money," I corrected him, and he gave me a sardonic grin that I returned.

"Art and money and the people of Florence," Cosimo corrected us both.

"Wisdom out of the mouths of babes. . . . I must return to my workshop. People want necklaces even when they are growing bubboni." Lorenzo sighed. "To impress their neighbors from their caskets, I suppose."

"Don't forget your dream, Lorenzo. . . ."

"Ghiberti. Lorenzo Ghiberti." He bowed in courtly fashion, then set off toward the Arno.

"I like him, Luca. I want him to make the doors, I just know he will make them as beautiful as the gates of paradise!" Cosimo gave me an intense look. "One day I will rule Florence," he said, in the sure voice of a man making a vow. "When I do, I will bring the best artists here! You believe me, don't you, Luca, that I will rule Florence?" the boy asked fiercely. "I know I look on the outside like a skinny boy. But you can tell, can't you, that I have something special inside me? What's on the outside is the least of what people have. It's the qualities inside us that really matter!"

Giotto's words from long ago came back to me. How had I forgotten the first thing ever taught me by Master Giotto, the thing that had changed and preserved my life a thousand times?

" 'What's inside you is the gate to everything. It's what you become, what you make of your life,' " I agreed, repeating Giotto's words as if waking.

"Exactly!" Cosimo cried. "You understand! So you believe me when I say I will rule Florence and make her greater than ever?"

The boy's eyes were so filled with luminous conviction that something in my heart melted. Yes, with such precocious wisdom, this boy would rule Florence. I knelt beside him in a posture of fealty. I stared carefully into his sallow young face, so that he would know I spoke honestly. His features plucked at my memory, and the architecture of my mind moved like glass shards falling. I had a flashback to Geber the alchemist and the night of the philosopher's stone. After seeing myself dead, when time winged forward before my eyes, I saw many faces. One was of a puissant man, a ruler, who had grown out of the young Cosimo. It confirmed for me that this boy was unusual and gifted. In Petrarca's terms, Cosimo had the aura of the elect.

"I believe you. And when you rule Florence, Cosimo, you must never forget that her beauty, her art, belongs to all Florentines, rich or poor, no matter what their class!"

"I will remember. And you will be my friend when I am ruler," he decided. I rose, clasped my hands together at my chest, and bowed. It was not facetious. The face from my vision was Cosimo's; I had always believed that the vision granted me by the philosopher's stone contained truth. And there had always been destiny in Giotto's words. All these years that my caprice had led me across the earth, I was not quite living. Now that I was back in Florence, caprice dropped away like a fluffy mantello and something else, something richer and more substantial, took its place: purpose. I was here for *her*. The woman from my vision. I didn't know if I was worthy of her, but once again, I felt the unquenchable pull of that youthful longing for a wife and a love of my own. I felt as if she would walk up and greet me where I stood, by the Baptistery. I looked around for her with my heart racing. Then I caught myself and laughed. With wonder, I sensed the warms strains of divine laughter, too. I was on the path to meet her now, even if I had wandered for decades.

"Cosimo, Cosimo!" cried a voice. "Son, where have you been?" A stocky man wearing the finest green and orange lucco raced up to us. He was flanked by dozens of men: retainers, condottieri, ufficiali, and priests. Concern made his features haggard, but as he scooped the boy up into his arms, his hard features melted and his hooded eyes softened. "We were worried that you'd been kidnapped by ruffians. One of the slaves saw men grabbing you. . . ."

"Bandits took me, but this man saved me!" Cosimo cried, hugging his father tightly. The father gave me an intense look of relief and gratitude over his son's shoulder. "Two mean men threw me into their cart, and they were going to take me out of the city, but I bit one and jumped out of the cart and ran even though my knees hurt from jumping, and they chased me! They were very big and dirty. This man killed them, and I was so glad he did! They deserved to die because they tried to hurt me. It was scary, Papa, but I tried to be brave!"

"I'm sure you were, Cosimoletto," the man murmured. He set the boy down and looked at me seriously. He had a substantial nose and a big chin, but was made appealing by the thoughtful stateliness which he had passed down to his son. He said, "I owe you a great debt, signore. I am Giovanni di Bicci de' Medici. Command me, and I am your servant!"

I shook my head. "You owe me nothing. Any man would help a child in need. And your son is a brave boy, signore. But you may want to send some men to clean up the bodies, to prevent any misunderstandings. Toward my role in their deaths, that is."

"I'll make sure you aren't hassled for the service you have done me and my son," he said, and his sharp eyes narrowed. "There's something familiar about you. May I ask your name?"

"Papa, let's walk a bit," Cosimo said in his high, fine voice. He looked purposefully at all the men within earshot. They were a large group, murmuring with excitement, waiting with sycophantic eagerness to congratulate the father upon his son's safe return. Then Cosimo looked back at his father. Tacit understanding passed between them, and the father took his son's hand and clasped it tightly in his own.

"Come, signore, let's walk with my son," he said. He held up his free hand with great majesty. "The three of us will walk!" A sibilant sound of disappointment passed through the crowd, and many hungry eyes fixed on me like sucking mouths. I pulled my mantello closer despite the warmth of this late-summer day with the sun climbing high overhead.

"This way," Giovanni said. He held his son's hand and led us toward the still-unfinished Santa Maria del Fiore with its eccentric pattern of green, white, and red marble rectangles and flowers. Giovanni muttered, "We must do something about setting a dome atop this enormous cathedral!" He wiped his hand over his hard-featured face. "It is not fitting that the most beautiful and honorable temple in Tuscany should stand practically in ruins!"

"A competition, Papa, to find someone who can build it," Cosimo said. "But first a competition for new doors for the Baptistery."

"A competition, eh, little man?" Giovanni smiled, tweaking his son's nose. "Not a bad idea." He turned to me. "Signore, is there some problem with your identity?"

"I like my identity just fine."

"Papa, my friend's name is Luca Bastardo!" Cosimo said anxiously.

Giovanni looked at me with the frown lines between his thick eyebrows deepening. "I've heard the name spoken in ways that would discomfit me, if I were you. But I've also seen the name on records for regular deposits in an account held by my family's bank. You're a prudent man, Bastardo, saving your money so carefully, over such a long period of time."

"Not prudent enough to have avoided making enemies," I said. The Wanderer's donkey brayed loudly, refusing to move forward. I slapped its rump. The wretch snapped at me, then reluctantly moved forward. The harvest sun was warm in an endless cerulean sky, my shadow had shrunk down to a small inky puddle at my feet, and I took off my mantello, rolled it, and stuck it in the portmanteau tied on the donkey.

"The Confraternity of the Red Feather would be happy to have you," Giovanni said unhappily. "They claim to have an old letter about you that proves you were born of heretics with special powers. Unsavory powers. Perhaps your prudence would urge you to leave the city."

"I have been gone so long already, and I am a Florentine!"

"I myself don't care for a society founded upon superstition and torture." Giovanni shrugged. "There are more profitable activities for a Florentine. But the Church is well disposed toward the Red Feather. Ever since the first occurrence of the Black Death, the Church has smiled upon penitents who flagellate themselves to atone for our sins. The Confraternity of the Red Feather hopes to obtain a papal bull that will declare them an arm of the Inquisition, and give them immunity for their persecutions—just as the bull from Alexander IV a hundred and fifty years ago allowed any kind of torture for suspected heretics, as long as it was attended by at least two priests. And your name is mentioned as a favorite target!"

"I know how to hide on the streets of Florence," I said stubbornly.

"On the streets of Florence, a florin will buy you anything, especially the whereabouts of an enemy. And you have an implacable one in Domenico Silvano and his ruthless old father, Nicolo." Giovanni made a frustrated sound in his throat. "Is it true you're so old, Bastardo? Our records show deposits going back at least thirty years, and yet you look like a young man! Is it possible the confraternity's letter about you is accurate?" I met his gaze steadily, and after a while Giovanni shook his head. "Perhaps I don't want to know, if you're going to create a debt for me by rescuing my son and then refuse to take yourself out of harm's way. Your parents must have been great mischief makers, to have begotten so unreasonable a son!"

"I never knew my parents, but I know that the Silvano men are bad to their core."

"Luca's not a bad man, Papa. He saved me, and there

were two of them, and they were much bigger than him!"
Cosimo said anxiously. "He didn't use witchcraft to kill
them, he was just so much more clever than they were, and
he's very fast with his dagger!"

"Oh, Cosimo." Giovanni clutched his son's head to his
chest and closed his eyes. "I was worried about you. Under
other circumstances, Bastardo, I would feel as much alarmed
as puzzled by your eccentricity. But you've brought my son
back to me unharmed. . . . I must urge you again to consider
leaving Florence. It's said that Domenico will soon be
Gonfaloniere for a term. Florentines have long memories of
their friends but even longer ones of their enemies."

"I won't tell him that we met if you don't," I said.

"Son, what do we do with this stubborn rescuer of yours?"
Giovanni asked, gripping the boy's shoulders with a show of
seeking his advice. For a moment I envied the two. Giovanni
had a singular son to be proud of, and Cosimo was much
loved and appreciated by his father. I wondered if I would
have a child with the woman from my vision, and all my old
longings for a family of my own rose up in my chest like a
great bird with its wings beating. I resolved not to squander
the time I'd been given anymore.

"We should help him leave the city when the Red Feather
comes after him, and take good care of his money, so that he
will have plenty of it whenever he needs it," Cosimo said
promptly, showing again his unusual perspicacity. "Send letters to all our offices so that he can access his money wherever he goes, without questions being asked of him."

"There you have it, Bastardo, a plan! An excellent plan,
from my most excellent son! Cosimoletto, may I amend
your plan to include inviting our friend Luca here to a meal?
All this discussion leaves me hungry, and you must be famished after your ordeal! Luca, too, after the dirty work of

dispatching ruffians. It's the least we can do to show our gratitude!"

"Oh yes, Papa, let's have him come for dinner!" Cosimo clapped his hands together. "He's ever so interesting, you should hear him talk about Giotto!"

"I am honored," I said. "Since you are so gracious, signore, I will ask you one favor. . . ."

"Anything!" Giovanni swore.

"Stable this ass," I said, laying the lead rope of an ill-tempered, long-lived donkey in the hand of one of the richest and most powerful men in Florence.

IT WAS EVENING when I returned to the street, and this time without the damned donkey. The sky was deepening into a royal blue with pink at the edges, like a fine mantello. My belly was full from a lavish meal of fresh green melon, ravioli in garlic broth, roast guinea fowl covered with the cinnamony red sauce known as *savore sanguino,* spiced veal, and sautéed leeks and beetroot. We had eaten in intimate surroundings, as the family did on ordinary occasions, at a trestle table near the open garden door, to catch the delicious breeze as afternoon stretched into evening and the light grew honeyed and tinted with lavender. We sat on the lids of chests as musicians played softly in a far corner. It was such a sweet moment, full of the laughter of Cosimo and his brother, Lorenzo, and the warm appreciation of Giovanni, with Giotto's words ringing again in my heart, that I thought that maybe I'd been too quick to dissolve God into the evil in men's hearts, as sugar is dissolved in hot brew. Surely, where warmth and love like this were present, so was God. One God, anyway. Perhaps my long-dead friend Geber the alchemist was right, after all. There were two Gods, a good one and an evil one. And if I had fallen under the sway of the lesser God in revering caprice and believing only in men's capacity for evil, I could still seek out the good God, the God who laughed with tenderness instead of cruelty. There was still time for me.

Giovanni invited me to stay the night, but I didn't want to bring trouble to his home. I told him it was enough that he hosted my donkey, and I set out again for any kind of inn that was open. If I didn't find one, I could sleep under a bridge. I still knew how to do that. I'd slept in worse places than by the silver Arno in the last fifty years.

A birdcall sounded. It caught my ear because it was out of context: a real bird's call wouldn't sound at this time of day. It was someone whistling, communicating, trying to be discreet. It provoked a lift of the hairs on my neck and prickles on the flesh over my triceps, which tightened in anticipation of holding my sword. I kept walking, but I turned abruptly down the next street. A soft set of footsteps shuffled to my left. I walked faster, and the tempo of the accompanying steps increased. I heard another soft clomping to my right. The sky had darkened into indigo and the city's lamps had not yet all been lit, so long fingers of purply-black shadow raked over the cobblestone streets, obscuring movement. I started to trot and to zigzag through the narrow stone streets, under stone arches that supported tall buildings and around half-built new palazzi and decayed old cottages that looked ready to be cleared for new building.

Footsteps clattered behind me, faster, closer. I turned a corner. Two shadowy cloaked figures stood halfway down the street, outlined in flaming orange light by torches set in bronze holders on the gray stone building behind them. They held unsheathed swords. I reversed direction and raced out toward the intersection. Three more men approached me from the other side. I twisted around, looking for an alley, a lane, anything. I was near the old Palazzo del Capitano del Popolo and I sprinted south past it, toward the Arno. I burst out into the piazza by the Palazzo della Signoria. There waited six cloaked figures in a semicircle. The three men chasing me closed in behind me, and two more ran in, trapping me.

"Are you the man called Luca Bastardo?" bellowed a sonorous voice in the dark.

"Who wants to know?" I asked. I reached for the dagger in its sheath at my thigh. Two men grabbed me from behind and, not bothering to handle me gently, wrested it from me. One of them unbuckled my sword belt. I was disarmed. On each side of me, a man roughly gripped my arm. More men converged on the scene from the dark surrounding streets.

"I do," said a querulous old voice. Torchbearers lifted their flames, and when the flickering yellow light reached him, the man pushed down his hood. If I had not recognized him by his sneering, nasal voice, I would have known him instantly from his face, despite its aging. The deep seams and sags of time could not erase the prominent chin and sharp, angular nose that were so like his father's and that repeated again on his son's face. Nicolo Silvano grinned. "I say you are Luca Bastardo, a witch who uses black arts to defy time and death! And I have a letter from eighty years ago that identifies your parents as sorcerers who keep company with heretics!"

"I have pursued Luca Bastardo for thirty years, and I say that you are that man, who has not aged since I was a child," declaimed another voice. More torches lit Domenico Silvano's countenance, and my breath was sucked into a cold void of fear in my gut. "Witchcraft keeps you youthful! Witchcraft prolongs your youth, and your sin brings down the wrath of God upon Florence!" I wanted to answer, but when I opened my mouth, the man to my right punched me hard in the gut, and I bent over, retching. "He does not deny it!" Domenico cried. "We don't have time to subject this witch to the rack or the *strivaletto* to obtain his confession. We must act now to cleanse our city of this scourge of evil! Bind him, and prepare the stake! The letter my father has safeguarded for so long will serve as his indictment!"

I was seized by many hands and dragged forward. My hose tore against the rough cobblestones, and the skin over my bruising knees was cut into bloody stripes. I heard the harsh scraping of wood, and when the men briefly parted before me, I saw beams being laid down in the Piazza della Signoria. One of the beams was roped off and pulled erect. A dozen men worked on the scaffolding; it was only a few moments until the executionary apparatus was ready. I was pulled to my feet, many men spitting on me and pummeling me. I heard rather than felt two of my ribs crack, though I don't know how I could have heard them when so many were screaming "Witch!" and "Sorcerer!" Wearing little but rags and blood, I was thrust against the post. A thick rope was wrapped around my shoulders and chest.

The angry crowd parted. Nicolo Silvano made his way toward me, hobbling with old age. He didn't speak until he was close to me. "I knew this day would come, Bastardo. Think of my father as the flames nibble at your feet, then lick up your legs to fry your balls, then consume you entirely! It's just punishment for your act of arson against the palazzo that was my inheritance!" He leaned closer so that his foul breath fanned my cheek. "I hope you enjoyed the gift I left there for you. Give my regards to Simonetta and the other whores when you see them in hell!"

A red haze obscured my vision, and then the old cool, clean desire to kill Nicolo spurted through me. Suddenly I was without hate or fear, without any emotion at all. "I should have killed you when you were cowering over your father's dead body." Then I spat at him.

"Your Jewess whore spat at me when I beat her to death," Nicolo said. Rage boiled through me and Nicolo saw it. He laughed. "Yes, I enjoyed killing her." Then he screamed. "Burn him! Burn him slowly, so that he suffers!" He laughed maniacally. Chunks of wood and kindling sticks were piled up around me. A man with a torch approached, to the cheers of the crowd. He gave the torch to Domenico Silvano, who licked his lips and smiled at me.

Then, rising up into the dark night as if from the stones paving the streets of the city, there was song: "She loved my massive TOOL so she never ever denied me her FAVORS," chorused raucous drunken voices whose heavy accents declared them to be foreigners. The men around me turned to look. Through a gap in the line of their heads, I saw a group of condottieri weaving drunkenly, their arms wrapped around each other for support. The torchlight on their mantelli illuminated the colors of mercenary soldiers from the north.

"Hey, it's a party!" a wheezy voice cried. A persnickety bray trumpeted out; the mercenary at the end was leading a gray donkey.

"Be gone!" shouted Domenico Silvano. "These are private proceedings!"

"We like parties! I don't see no women, but we can send for 'em! If we can't find any women, I don't have a problem with them fluffy Florentine sheep!" the condottiere hollered. His comrades whooped. He let go of the rope and slapped the donkey, hard. It bucked up and then raced forward, snapping its teeth and kicking and causing consternation in the crowd around me.

"My donkey, get my donkey!" hollered another voice.

"Damn it, you said you'd hang on to it, Hans, you small-dicked lout!" There was the rasp of a sword being drawn, and the condottiere who claimed the donkey leapt at the hapless Hans. Hans drew his sword in response and the two fell to fighting viciously. A third condottiere yelled, "I'll get the donkey, I'll get 'im, his legs are like Karl's sister, she's a nice piece of tail, only the donkey's got a prettier face! Course, it don't matter if you're getting her from behind!" And with that, one of the condottieri broke from the others and charged into the crowd after the donkey.

"Hey, whadda you know about my sister?" cried Karl. "I'll cut your heart out if you stole her flower!" He drew his sword and charged into the crowd. Bedlam broke loose. Condottieri drew their swords and charged each other, screaming and running into the crowd of men around me. The donkey brayed and layed about with its teeth and heels. Nicolo's cohorts drew back, murmuring and unsettled, unsure of how to stop the melee.

Domenico swore. "Get back, get away!" he cried, waving the torch. He had to pull it back because the screaming soldiers were everywhere, intermingled with his own men. In the dark it was impossible for him to swing his torch with any accuracy. The condottiere chasing the donkey leapt close to me, swinging his sword as if to parry Karl's strokes. Karl, a big man with blond hair, winked at me. Then, while looking forward, he sliced backward with his sword. It chopped into the ropes binding me to the post and they fell away. His sword moved so fast that it seemed almost a blur in the starlight, as if the stroke that freed me hadn't happened at all. All the while he was screaming insults: "Stefan, you limp dick, yer mama's even uglier than your sister, what're you worked up about? Don't tell me you ain't got some of that good stuff, too? She'd had plenty of tool time before I got there!"

I didn't wait for a formal invitation but leapt over the kindling, taking advantage of the moment when all attention was focused in other directions. A condottiere handed me a rolled-up bundle. "Put it on!" he snapped, then stepped in front of me when Domenico's torch would have irradiated my face. The condottiere bawled out my song about the bosomy Napolitana lady and thrust his sword about in wide arcs that kept Nicolo's men away. I unrolled the cloak, a mantello in the colors of the foreign mercenaries. I shrugged it on and pulled the hood up and then down low over my face. The donkey trotted up, and behind it came another condottiere who fell on me in a soppy embrace. "Friedrich, you're a good lad! I wouldn't want anyone else at my back when we're fighting those flea-bitten, lice-covered Milanese!" He covertly pressed a short sword into my hand and lifted his head so that his hard-bitten blue eyes blazed into mine. "Don't use it!" he whispered, without the trace of an accent.

He blubbered an apology, and suddenly all the condottieri grabbed each other and hollered apologies, and I knew what I had to do. I threw my arm around the condottiere's shoulders and laid my head on him, as if muttering an apology. With the other hand I grabbed the donkey's lead rope. I staggered out of the crowd as if drunk, my face pressed into the condottiere's muscled shoulder while he rambled apologies. Through the slit of my hood, I saw Nicolo standing a few feet away. I didn't need to see him, though. I would have felt him even if I were blind: the frigid empty presence of evil. My flesh crawled and my fingers burned with lust to stab my sword into him, to pay him back for Rachel's death, and for the deaths of Simonetta and the children in the brothel, by spilling his blood all over the cobblestones. The condottiere felt me tense up. He pinched my cracked rib as he kept sobbing out regrets. Nicolo must have felt me, too, because he turned to look at the pair of us, me and the weepy condottiere. He said nothing, though he scowled in suspicion, and my heart beat so loudly that I was sure he could hear it. We walked past him while he stared straight at us.

In a few steps we rejoined the group, who were all linking up arms. One of the condottieri grabbed the donkey's rope from me and another one hollered, "Hey, I know where there's a real party! They have the prettiest women in town, well, most of them have all of their teeth, okay, some of them don't look like Karl's grandmother, but hey, they're fun!"

We increased our pace into a trot, the donkey clip-clopping alongside us. A second later we heard furious shouts go up from the piazza.

"Game's over," the blue-eyed condottiere said to me. "Come with me!" He sprinted off at an angle away from the other condottieri. I followed him and we ran west along the Arno toward the Ponte alla Carraia. We got to the bridge, and instead of going over it, he led me down below to the water, where two figures waited with a small boat that bobbled up and down on the rollicking moon-slicked surface of the river. One of the figures was much smaller than the other.

"Cosimo," I panted as the condottiere and I joined the two, "you got the melody wrong!"

Cosimo put down the hood of his mantello. "That's right, you sang with the emphasis on 'massive,' not on 'tool.'" He grinned at me. I ruffled his hair.

"There are florins and weapons in the boat," said Giovanni di Bicci de' Medici. "My man Alberto here will get you out of the city. I'll make arrangements so that you'll be able to get money from any of my agents or offices anywhere in the world."

"It's good of you to help me, signore," I said. "You, too, Cosimo. Was that your plan?"

"Partly." The boy nodded, looking delighted, and his father smiled and put his hand proudly on his son's shoulder. "You are my friend!"

"He would have been *arrosto* if we hadn't arrived when we did," Alberto said grimly. "They had him tied to the stake and were lighting the tinder."

"A timely arrival," I commented. Indeed, the perfection of the timing led me to suspect divine merriment, because what hand other than that of the kindly God whose presence I had felt earlier could arrange my rescue with such exquisite deftness?

"You brought my son back to me alive," Giovanni said. "I'll always help you."

"So will I," Cosimo said. "Luca, I'll get that letter for you, the one that Papa says the confraternity has. I'll give it to you and you'll be safe then."

Giovanni squeezed his son's shoulder fondly. "But now, Luca, it's time for you to leave Florence, and my advice to you is—"

"I know," I said, "don't come back." It comforted me to find myself in the company of a deity again, after decades of absence. I knew that with this companionship, though fragile and suspect because of its divinity, my purpose and my longing would not fade to extinction. So I got into the little boat with Alberto and passed at midnight from the city I loved.

Chapter 15

"I WANT TO GO IN, but I'm afraid," the boy said in a musical voice. He stood with his back arched and his hand on his knee, and then he angled his golden head back toward me so I saw his face for the first time. It was strikingly beautiful, and I was nearly overcome by a spasm of a memory that was in fact a nightmarish fantasy; I could see Bernardo Silvano, with his bladelike nose and jutting chin, putting his venal hand on the boy's head in delight, crowing at the thought of the money he would bring in. I shook myself to escape these strange thoughts, focused again on the boy. It's not vanity but simple observation that leads me to say that my own face was the handsomest I had ever seen until the very moment that I laid eyes on this gracefully shaped boy of eleven or twelve.

Recalled to Florence after six decades by my protector Cosimo de' Medici, I had come first to Anchiano, outside Vinci. I wanted to check on the vineyard bequeathed to me over a hundred years ago by the burly, red-haired Arnolfo

Ginori with whom I'd worked as a becchino when the Black Plague first struck. The fine day had enticed me on a trek up Monte Albano, which on one side descended toward the Arno Valley and Florence, and on the other rose toward craggy heights filled with great boulders, cold streams, and mysterious caves. In wandering, I'd stumbled on the boy, who now turned back to the mouth of the cavern, his hand shading his eyes from the bright early-summer sun. Its glare was partly absorbed and partly reflected by the scree field and overhanging rocks around us.

"What are you afraid of?" I asked the boy. I knelt beside him.

"It's dark and threatening," the boy answered, and abruptly sat down beside me.

"But there might be marvels inside."

"Yes. Yes!" he cried. "I want to see if there's something marvelous inside!"

"That's the question, isn't it? To brave the dark, closing in all around with its ominous possibilities, in order to discover the marvels within?" I asked. I plucked a few blades of grass and ripped them into long green threads. "Shadows are very important. They give depth to the light."

The boy puckered his brow. "You're not just talking about this cave," he said. He wound a finger through a golden ringlet. "The question is, are you talking about yourself, or about me?"

"So he's clever as well as beautiful!" I laughed. He joined in, his trill spilling out into the air, and it was as if the sun came out from behind storm clouds. I couldn't help but stare at him, amazed by his looks and his lyrical voice.

"You're beautiful, too," the boy said. He had widely spaced eyes set in a perfectly sculpted face. "But you're not just beautiful; you're lively, with many expressions. I like faces like yours, that are interesting, whether beautiful or ugly. Tell me, signore, would you change the way you look? Are you grateful to your parents for giving you such beauty? How has it shaped your life? Have you found more love because of it? Has it been a curse or a blessing for you?"

I gazed into the dark cave. "Both." This boy asked questions that probed too deeply into my unresolved heart. The danger from the Silvano clan had kept me away from Florence for six long decades this time, but the instant I returned, so did the questions. Somehow the stony Tuscan city of my boyhood always insisted that I confront myself. It had imprisoned me as a child in Silvano's brothel, yet given me wings with Giotto's art. It had given me an education through the alchemist Geber and the Hebrew doctor Moshe Sforno, and then it had cast me out, not once, but twice. It promised me a grand destiny of love and passion, but then held that in abeyance. It forced me to witness man's inherent capacity for murder, evil, and betrayal, and to know that I was capable of those things, too. And here I was, almost within sight of the city walls, with the old ineluctable questions spiraling back to tear at my shielded heart with renewed ferocity: what were my origins and what did my gifts, my differences, mean? When would the promise of the night of the philosopher's stone manifest itself? Questions, questions, still no answers. I would like to introduce this interesting child to the Wanderer, I thought; they could question each other.

"I faced a dark cave once," I said.

"What did you do when you faced the cave?" The boy sounded intrigued.

"I went in, and I fought with myself," I said, closing my eyes and clenching my fists. "I had an amazing vision. A vision of things to come."

"Tell me your vision!" he commanded, serene in his knowledge that I would obey him.

"Why do you want to know?" I asked, to tease him.

"I want to know everything!" he said intensely. "I want to explore and examine and investigate everything, I want to find out the secrets of life and death and the earth and nature and everything!" He leapt to his feet and his shapely hands gestured with passion. "I want to understand how the eye sees, and how a bird flies, and how gravity and levity work, and what the nature of force is, and what the sun and moon are made of, and the exact internal structure of a man's body, and the experience of nothingness—"

"I understand!" I held up a hand. "You want to know everything!"

"Except Latin," he said, clenching his fists alongside his head. "I'm not good at that. It's like I know it, but I've forgotten it, and there's some secret gate within me that is closed, and it keeps me from becoming fluent. But everything else, yes, that I want to know!"

"A friend once said to me, 'Anytime you can learn for yourself, experience for yourself, apprehend directly and with no intermediary, you must do so!'" I said.

"Your friend was wise," the boy said seriously. "I have thought about it often, and I believe that although nature begins with reason and ends in experience, we must do the opposite. We must begin with our own experience and from this proceed to investigate the reason!"

"These are weighty thoughts for one so young," I observed sympathetically, because I, too, had been yoked to oppressive thoughts as a child. Perhaps that was why I had avoided them as a man in exile, and why they rushed back in, ready to gore me, when I returned home.

"Am I supposed to wait until I am old to think deeply?" he replied. He narrowed his luminous eyes. "You seem familiar, as if I already know you. . . . Your wise friend, did he speak those words to you when he was dying?"

I nodded, remembering with a sharp, sweet pang Geber

the Cathar alchemist, frail and covered with oozing bubboni in his workshop. Then I willed myself to the simple peace that I had enjoyed over the last sixty years, during which I had traveled the world, practicing my art as a physico, quietly offering the consolamentum to anyone who needed it, trying to heal pain and alleviate suffering while I eluded the Confraternity of the Red Feather. Finally I said, "My friend died a good death. He was alive when he died."

"I know what you mean. Perhaps while we think we're learning how to live, we're actually learning how to die. If we're honest. So tell me honestly about your vision," the boy insisted with a charming smile, and I knew there was no escaping it.

I smiled and sighed at the same time. I gazed out over the mountain with its colorful profusion of wildflowers. An eagle circled overhead. I lay down to look up into the infinite blue sky. My shoulders were tense and my spine was clutched tightly by the long muscles of my back, as if I'd been thrown from a horse and stood immediately, unhurt but internally shocked. What had this unusual boy said to me, that he wanted to understand nothingness? I couldn't conceive of such a desire. My deepest desire had always been to know fullness, the fullness of love and belonging. I had tasted it once in the arms of Rachel Sforno, and now that I was but a few minutes of celestial arc away from Florence, that old desire was suddenly back in full force.

"Signore?" the boy prompted, sitting again beside me.

"My friend was an alchemist. And my teacher. He gave me the philosopher's stone one night when I was upset, cast out of my usual ways of thinking because another friend had died."

"What's the philosopher's stone?" the boy asked, his eyes widened despite the glare of the sun.

"A magical elixir of the self," I said. "An elixir of transformation. It took me inside myself, and I died. And after dying, I saw things. . . ."

"Yes, that's what I want to know, what did you see?" he demanded, and scooted closer until his knees were touching my arm.

I took a deep breath. Even one hundred sixteen years after the events, I feared that to speak of the night of the philosopher's stone would invoke its magic. "I saw the present and the future. I saw kings and artists and weapons that spit fire. I saw machines that fly through the air or swim deep in the water. I saw an arrow that flew to the moon! And I saw wars and plagues and famines, and new nation-states that change the destiny of the world. Little of what I've seen has come to pass, but it will. It takes time for the visions to ripen."

"I want to fly," the boy confessed. "I want to learn how birds and butterflies fly. I love birds. Horses, too, because it feels like flying when a horse canters and I'm perched on his back. I love all animals, but most of all, birds and horses!"

"Perhaps you'll be the man to build the flying machine, then," I murmured, with my eyes still closed.

"That's my ambition!" he cried. "I watch birds, trying to learn the secrets of flight, so that I can one day build a flying machine! Did you see that, in your vision? Did you see me?"

I opened my eyes, jerked as if from a dream by the boy's question. "I did not see you," I admitted, sitting up. I looked closely at his fine-boned face, intelligent eyes, and curly gold hair burnished with auburn. "Not as a boy. What will you look like as an old man . . . ?"

"I will have long flowing hair and a long flowing beard," he answered with great certainty, "and I will still be handsome, but differently. I have visions of the future, too, during my daydreams, and I've seen this. I will be important and respected and everyone will know my name, even after I have died, for a long time. I am Leonardo, son of Ser Piero da Vinci."

"I am Luca Bastardo," I said. "I don't know who my parents were." Though I had looked for them again during this latest exile.

"I'm a bastard, too," he confided, with an impish twinkle. "My mother is Caterina the barmaid, and she's pretty and funny and kind and she wet-nursed me herself and I love her very much. But it doesn't much matter if we're bastards, does it? Everyone has bastard children, priests and Popes and especially kings. It matters more what you make of yourself, don't you think? If you sow virtue, you'll reap honor, and that has nothing to do with your parentage."

"I agree," I said quietly, looking away with uneasy surprise. No one had ever framed bastardy this way for me. This boy too easily evoked the piercing questions I worked so hard to avoid. What had I made of myself in the past hundred years? A wealthy adventurer and a lover of beautiful women. A fine swordsman and a skilled physico. I had been privileged to know men who had shaped the world, visionaries like Giotto and Petrarca and Boccaccio and Cosimo de' Medici, and to learn from men of genius and insight, like Geber the alchemist, the Wanderer, and Moshe Sforno. I was gifted with beauty and unending youth. With the privilege and learning and gifts, what had I made of myself?

It was time I stood firm and commanded my destiny. One of the Gods had picked up the thread of His joke again. At that moment, a wolf cub ran across the mountain not far from us, scrambling up and over the sun-warmed rocks in the scree field. A moment later two large, lean wolves followed it. Some distance below us, my horse Ginori whinnied, smelling the creatures, alerting me. I eased my short sword, the squarcina, from my belt. The wolves seemed intent on their errant son, but I always held the opinion that it was best to be prepared for the unexpected actions of divine signs.

"You can seek your parents," the boy was saying. He looked over his shoulder at the merrily yapping cub with its parents in pursuit. He said, "Maybe they're seeking you, and they'll come to you on some important day in your life, and you'll be gladdened as never before! What was your friend's name? The alchemist who gave you the philosopher's stone."

"A friend once told me that it ruined a great story to confine it to specific names," I said.

"Unfair!" he said indignantly, scrambling to his feet and putting his arms akimbo. "And untrue! A story is better because of the details, like names!"

"His name was Geber." I laughed. "The name he was using then, that is."

"Geber the alchemist who was your teacher," he murmured. He stroked his face, turned to stare inside the cavern, then turned to me with his eyes blazing. "You must be my teacher, Luca Bastardo!" For a moment I stared at him, thinking, *No, you will be my teacher, Leonardo. You will teach me about openness.* Then, despite my earlier ruminations about staying in Florence, I remembered that my very life was in danger as long as I did so. Openness was a secondary consideration when the Confraternity of the Red Feather still wanted to burn me at the stake. Indeed, its power surged during times of the plague, when people wanted a scapegoat. I had no wish to come under its scrutiny. I was not ready to die.

"I'm no teacher," I said firmly, rising to my feet. "You're an intriguing child, Leonardo son of Ser Piero da Vinci, but I have an obligation to keep. After that, I leave Tuscany. My life depends on it." I started to walk away from the cavern, saying "Besides, I don't know what I have to teach you."

"You can complete your obligation while you teach me,"

he said stubbornly. "And you have much to teach me. Teach me alchemy, as Geber taught you."

"I'm a failed alchemist. I never learned how to transmute lead into gold."

"Good, I don't believe in alchemy. You'll teach me other things." He paused beneath a cypress tree at the grassy col below the cavern. "Don't you think teaching and sharing your secrets would be worth the risk to your life? If there really is one? I mean, you don't act like a murderer or a thief——"

"I've been those things and more. I've been dark things you can't imagine."

"——who would have a sentence on his head, and I've never heard of a Luca Bastardo who has been exiled for political reasons. Everyone knows who the Medici's enemies are, they're very open about that," he finished, as if I hadn't spoken. "Stay and teach me!"

"The risk is too great. Someday I will risk my life, I will give it, but that will be for love, for my one great love who will come," I said, unsettled.

"Maybe you're supposed to look in Florence for her while you teach me," he said slyly. Leonardo always had an answer for everything.

I pulled out the dagger I kept sheathed at my thigh and threw it so it landed upright, its point in the ground, at Leonardo's feet. "Here, there are wolves about. You can take it into the cavern with you, too."

Leonardo took the dagger. He marched back toward the cavern, paused at its mouth, and called, "The wolves are here because they are meant to be! As are you, Luca Bastardo. Beneath the surface of everything is a tightly woven fabric of meaning!" He disappeared into the cavern at the same moment that one of the wolves howled mournfully. His lyrical words and the slow, long howl echoed off the rocks in uni-

son and blended together until they were one word tumbling down the mountain. That word bore an uncanny re-
semblance to the word the Wanderer had whispered into my
ear more than a century ago, the night of the philosopher's
stone. Then, the next day, Geber had died after uttering the
same sentence to me that Leonardo had just said. I was
struck with the sense of time coming back around like a
snake on a caduceus to claim me. Perhaps young Leonardo
was right, and I was meant to be his teacher; but first I had to
go to Florence to pay my respects to the aged and ailing
Cosimo de' Medici.

"THEY'RE ALL GONE, Luca," called Cosimo, in quavery
voice. He lay in a magnificent bed, covered with sumptuous
linens embroidered with gold and silver. I stood not in the
Medici palazzo in Florence, but in an exquisite villa in
Careggi, in the hilly countryside north of Florence. Cosimo
was in residence here, avoiding the resurgent plague. As
they'd been doing for over a hundred years when bubboni
appeared, nobles and rich merchants with country estates
fled the city and shut themselves inside their villas; there
was still no cure for the dreaded Black Death.

"I am sorry to see you uncomfortable, Cosimo," I said,
perusing his face sadly. He did not look well, this man who
was famed for going nights without sleep and days without
food. But he'd always been sallow, and now he was gouty
and arthritic. He had high color in his cheeks and a thin
sheen of sweat glistening on his brow, and I could tell by
looking at him that he wasn't passing his urine as he ought.
The physico skills taught me by Moshe Sforno and practiced
in exile came to the fore. I began to think of ways to ease his
suffering.

"I feel better with you here," he said, and a genuine smile

came to his lips. "I'm happy you came. I wanted to see you one last time. We've met many times far from Florence, but I wasn't sure that you'd come home, even for me."

"Always for you, Cosimoletto," I said, and hearing his father's old nickname for him widened his smile. Then a look of sorrow passed over his face.

"They're all gone, Luca," he repeated. "My son Giovanni died last year. My grandson Cosimino two years ago. He wasn't even six yet. I couldn't stay in the palazzo on Via Larga anymore. It was just too large for so small a family as remained."

"It's hard to lose those we love," I replied softly. I felt Cosimo's forehead and noted his fever, and then counted his pulse at his wrist.

"One time, I was meeting with an embassy from Lucca, we were discussing matters of state, you know how fraught it is with Lucca." He paused, looking at me for confirmation. I nodded. "Cosimino came in and asked me to make him a whistle. A whistle!"

"I'll bet you did, right then and there." I smiled.

"You know me too well," he answered, squeezing my hand. "I adjourned the meeting, and we made the whistle together, that boy and me, and only when he was well pleased did I resume the meeting. The Luccan delegates were much put out!" He chuckled softly and I joined him. Then he said, "And I'm so glad I did it, Luca, because I will never have another opportunity to play with him. He'll never again climb into my lap, or interrupt a meeting, or stick a frog in the pocket of my mantello and laugh when I put my hand on it and scream."

"You took advantage of the time you had with your grandson and you loved him well," I said. "You can take comfort in that."

"Yes!" Cosimo cried, his sagging, seamed face lighting

up. "I loved him, and love doesn't end. Love is the only immortality we can have, Luca. I hope you have found it for yourself!"

"I seek it. And there are old friends for whom I have great affection. You're one of them, Cosimo. I hate to see my old friends unwell. We must think of a way to mend you."

"Mend me, bah, I am ready to go," he sniffed.

"Now, that I do not want to hear," I said sternly. "As a physico, I have always found that a man who is ready to die will die."

"And what's so bad about dying, eh, Bastardo? Accepting death isn't so terrible."

"Sometimes it isn't, sometimes it's the end of pain and the beginning of freedom. But still, it should not be allowed one minute earlier than it must be," I said. "Life is too precious to surrender easily to death!"

"It's not surrender when a man grows beyond his fears and sheds this, this"—he picked up his shrunken pale quivering arm with his other hand as if it were a stick—"sheds this box! But don't worry about yourself in the event of my death. I've left instructions about your account; your money will always earn the most favorable interest, and you'll always be able to access it anywhere in the world that you wander, Bastardo," he teased me, and something of the old sparkle came into his eyes.

"Listen to how wise you are, we cannot let the world be deprived of a man of such excellent sense," I returned lightly. I put my hands on the arm that Cosimo had treated so scornfully and felt its frailty, its humanness. Would we not all come to this? Deep down in the bone of his arm, perhaps in its marrow, there was a fading thrum like a song that had played out and was about to end. My heart opened and a delicious warmth ran out of my chest, down my arms, and out my hands into Cosimo. Geber's consolamentum was moving through me, like soft water flowing through the living pipe that was my body. Cosimo sighed.

"Your hands feel so good, Luca mio," he said softly, and his face melted as pain eased out of him. His gray lips parted and some slight color washed into them. I waited until the flow of the consolamentum trickled to a stop, then spoke.

"Tell me about making water, old friend, how is that going?"

"Not well." He shrugged, and turned his large-nosed face away. "I have some wonderful paintings you should see. There are a few panels here by Fra Angelico—"

"The small, saintly friar you told me about, when I met you in Avignon ten years ago?" I said. "The one who prayed before he touched his brush to holy figures?"

"The very one," Cosimo said, delighted that I'd remembered. But of course I did; I never forgot an artist or a work of art. "Fra Angelico wept when he painted Christ on the cross. He was a man of holy simplicity, the easiest artist to work with. Most of them are so difficult, and they commit outrageous actions, like children who never grow up, but they must still be treated with the utmost respect."

"They understand and render beauty, so allowances must be made for them."

"I learned that from another artist, a man of opposite temperament to Fra Angelico: Fra Filippo Lippi. A talented artist, but he was a beast of earthly and sensual desire, couldn't stay away from women. Absconded with a nun, even; cost me a pretty sum to buy him out of the clergy, and even his gratitude to me couldn't induce him to work when lechery took hold of him. I once tried locking him up in his room to get him to finish a painting, but he tore the bedsheets into strips, knotted them together, and escaped down the window!"

"Men always find ways to escape," I observed, which

made me wonder if I'd truly escaped from Bernardo and Nicolo Silvano; wasn't that what Leonardo was asking me to do? Leave behind the prison of my fear and anger and create a life here, at home, anew?

"So they do, eventually." Cosimo sighed. "From whatever they consider their prison. I think Fra Angelico, pious as he was, thought of life on earth as his prison, and painting was his escape. He did a splendid job at San Marco, when I renovated it."

"The old Dominican monastery," I remembered, suddenly eager to return to Florence the city, to enter in through her strong gates and stand within her incomparable churches and busy piazze, her stone walls and her fine palazzi and her grand, imposing public buildings.

"I have financed a great deal of public work, as my father did." Cosimo nodded. "Fra Angelico's *Crucifixion with Saints* fills the whole north wall of the chapter hall. It's an extraordinary painting, three crosses rising into a blue sky, while the saints are spread out in front. It has peace and innocence while showing the tragedy of the Crucifixion. Every artist paints himself; you can see that in Fra Angelico's faces, which are filled with awe. I look forward to being in the presence of the God who could inspire that awe, Luca. Now that you're back in Florence, you must see it! That is, if you're going to stay, Luca mio? To see me through to the end?"

"I hope it's not the end," I said somberly, dodging the question.

"We've been friends too long for us to fool one another," he said. "I can still remember you saving me from criminals, long ago in the year of the plague, when I was a simple boy."

"Cosimo, of all men, you have never been simple."

"That's a big secret!" Cosimo cried, his eyes flashing. "You must pretend you don't know that, and listen kindly to the reminiscences of a sick old man! I remember, back then, how you looked like a saint or an angel as you put me on top of that beastly donkey. Then you drew your dagger and killed those men, just as they deserved."

"Whatever happened to that donkey?" I wondered.

"I was fifteen when a Jew with a wild beard showed up, claiming to be a friend of yours; he asked for the animal, so we gave it to him. I still remember him, a big man with a lot of questions. Isn't it funny what you remember when you get old? Yet here you are, looking exactly the same, not having aged at all. This is some strange gift you've been given. I envy you, Luca."

"Don't," I said shortly. "I would die to know the love, and the family, you've known."

"You'll have it." He smiled, as if he already shared the joke with whichever God was laughing now. "Death, too, because we all get that. But I wonder if you'll ever know the travails of old age. It's not for cowards. There's pain and humiliation. It's not a condition for one who abhors cages."

"I've had my share of pain and humiliation," I said. I gave him a serious look. "What do you hear of the Confraternity of the Red Feather these days?"

"Not much, but then I am not much on the streets of Florence these days. There are still Silvanos about, let's see, a young man named Pietro, looks just like Domenico did. Same distinctive nose and chin. Domenico also had a daughter who married and had sons, but I've forgotten their names. They must be grown men now. But Luca, it's been sixty years. Maybe that's not long for you, but it is a lifetime for the rest of us. Perhaps the old enmity has faded—"

"We're Florentines, enmity never fades!" I laughed. "You know that better than anyone, Cosimo. Hatred, like hell, lasts an eternity!"

"Then are we not all always in hell, because we feel hatred constantly and keenly? And always in heaven with our love?" He shrugged. "I am old enough now, and sick enough, and I've spent enough time in contemplation of late to wish I'd done some things differently in my life, Luca. Perhaps shown some mercy at times."

"One doesn't show mercy to an asp. One cuts off its head."

Cosimo sighed and squeezed my hand again. "Perhaps you need your long life to learn what the rest of us do in sixty years. Tell me of some of your travels, Bastardo. That ancient manuscript you sent to me via your agent, oh, was that only three years ago? You obtained it in Macedonia, yes? Your letter said there was a story attached to it. . . ."

"The *Corpus Hermeticum*," I said. "I found it in a monastery in Macedonia."

"I know the title," Cosimo said slyly. "I didn't know if you did. Would you care to divert a dying man with the story of your finding it?"

Evening was well darkened into night hours later, as I was leaving, and Cosimo's wife Contessina de' Bardi stopped me. She was a fat, fussy, cheerful woman whom I'd met only once before. This was because I had always met Cosimo outside of Florence, and when he traveled, he took with him a Circassian slave girl of whom he'd been inordinately fond. I'd liked her, too, finding her pretty, pleasant, and undemanding. The Circassian had borne Cosimo a son whom he'd named Carlo and brought up with Contessina's sons. Contessina hadn't minded. As Leonardo had pointed out, powerful men often sired bastards. Now Contessina laid her plump old hand on my shoulder.

"He has a special fondness for you," she said, in a low voice.

"And I for him," I said.

"Isn't that convenient," said a nasal, cracking voice. I

turned to see a tall, strong youth of fifteen. He had thick dark hair which fell almost to his shoulders, a long, flattened nose that looked as if it had been broken and badly set, and a heavy, jutting jaw. But the combination of his ugly features was striking, even mesmerizing, and his dark, penetrating eyes flashed with will and intelligence. He gave a cool, tight smile. "Many men profess their love for Nonno now that he is dying, and yet we all know that he has been as ruthless as he has been charitable."

"It's not for me to criticize a great man," I said quietly.

"You were closeted alone with Nonno for hours, and now you speak with the slick tongue of a spy," Lorenzo barked. Fear flickered in his eyes but was quickly masked by his arrogance. "Do you report to that fool Pitti, or to the traitor Agnolo Acciaiuoli, who are dogs tearing at the sides of a grand old lion, trying to bring him down? The Medici do not stand for disloyalty! Nonno and Papa may be ill, but I will soon have authority, and I will wield it with a sure hand!"

"Lorenzo, please," Contessina chided. She turned to me. "Please excuse my precocious grandson; the Medici have many critics, and Lorenzo's very protective of his nonno."

"A laudable quality," I said politely, meeting the young Lorenzo's eyes directly. "I am a friend of your grandfather's, signore. I am Luca Bastardo."

The suspicion dropped from his face and a canny brilliance came into Lorenzo's eyes as his gaze traveled from my scalp to my toes and back again. He stepped toward me with his feet spread apart and his chest thrust out. "I've heard the name. I'm told you have special gifts. Nonno speaks well of you, signore. Many men would be envious of the lavish praise you receive from Cosimo de' Medici. He isn't easily impressed. I myself strive always to excel, just to earn a modicum of the praise he gives so freely to you."

"I try to be worthy of his good opinion," I answered, unable to keep the sarcastic edge from my voice. This young Lorenzo was a warrior, a lion more in the likeness of his grandfather than of his sickly, gouty father Piero. Lorenzo, however, had teeth and claws and wanted to show them, whereas Cosimo was a deeply reserved man who hid his power.

"I'm sure you're worthy of it, as am I. Nonno never makes a mistake," he said, stepping closer, so that the space between us tingled with a complicated interplay of rivalry and grudging acceptance, curiosity and demand. Lorenzo would soon succeed Cosimo; Lorenzo's magnificent energy made his ascent to power inevitable. I wanted his protection from the Confraternity of the Red Feather, as I had received it from Cosimo. I didn't know yet what Lorenzo wanted of me.

"Signore, I stood outside his bedchambers, and I heard my husband talk to you with great liveliness." Contessina stepped between us. "I was happy to hear that. He spends much of his time alone and in silence. I asked him why he did this, and he answered, 'When we are going away, you spend a fortnight preparing for the move. Since I soon have to go from this life to another, don't you understand how much I have to think about?'" Contessina shook her gray head, and her sweet old face drooped. "He dwells too much in the past, in somber thoughts that do not strengthen him. I pray you will come often and distract him!"

I could hear the strains of divine merriment in her plea, which was the question at hand: would I stay in Tuscany? I didn't know whether it was the good God or the evil one who was laughing, but I realized that I had to stop traveling and find out. I had to know, once and for all, which God it was who had His hand on me.

"For Cosimo, whom I love, of course, anything," I answered finally, and my decision to stay was made. Whatever the consequences, I would be beside my old friend Cosimo until he died. I was choosing friendship over fear, and though I did not know it then, it would lead to the great love I'd yearned for all my life, as well as to the greatest sorrow. "I will be staying in Anchiano, tutoring a boy there. It's not far on horseback."

"I have a splendid idea!" Lorenzo snapped his fingers. "We will have a dinner in your honor, Luca Bastardo, a few days hence! It will be a relief from the plague. I will invite some family friends; have you met the philosopher Marsilio Ficino, my teacher and one of Nonno's dearest friends, with whom he still plays chess? Ficino is here every day; he can see this villa from his. My brother, Giuliano, arrives tomorrow, and I will invite some of the younger friends and cousins, also. Everyone's out in the country, anyway, because of the plague. We can have a rousing game of calcio!"

"I'm not much for games," I said.

"If you don't know how to play calcio, I'll teach you; Nonno likes to watch, it'll be good for his spirits. It'll be good for everyone's spirits, with the plague about," Lorenzo said easily. "A man of your talents will pick it up in no time!" He gave me the direct, nearly contemptuous look of a man issuing a challenge. I knew there was no escaping the calcio, and that it would be a game played in deadly earnest. So did Contessina, who sighed heavily and patted my chest.

"Signore Bastardo, there is no gainsaying this stubborn grandson of mine; you must resign yourself to dinner and calcio here. You seem strong enough with all these hard muscles, I'm sure it will be no problem." She gave me a broad smile and angled her eyes like a flirtatious young girl, then pulled her plump hand off my chest.

"I have work to do with my new charge," I said, stalling.

"Bring the boy." Lorenzo smiled. "He should learn calcio."

"You'll stay overnight." Contessina nodded, fixing her full silk sleeves. "It's settled."

IT WAS A TYPICAL JUNE EVENING in the Tuscan countryside, glowworms lighting up the hills, which exhaled the fragrance of vine and leaf and buds closed for the night. I relaxed into the sweet earthy smells as I waited outside under a flickering lamp for my horse to be brought out to me. He was a tall, handsome chestnut stallion I called Ginori, because the red in his coat reminded me of my old friend from my days as a becchino. The stallion had been washed, curried, and brushed while I was closeted with Cosimo. A new and finely wrought saddle had been placed on him, a gift from Cosimo, I guessed. I ran my hands over it, admiring the expensive, well-tooled leather and expertly crafted metal fittings. It was a saddle fit for a king; it was a saddle upon which to ride proudly into my destiny. It felt good to have it, if I was going to risk my life to stay in Florence. I checked the girth and made ready to mount Ginori.

"You have an eye for horseflesh," said a high-pitched, cracking voice.

"I paid a fortune for him, and he's worth every dinari," I said, swinging myself up onto the horse's back. "He's smart, well trained, and has never deserted me in battle."

"A laudable quality," Lorenzo returned. He stepped out of the darkness into the lamplight, so that the flickering yellow flames distorted, dissolved, and re-created his bold, ugly features, making him one moment demonic and the next celestially handsome. "Nonno has an eye like that for friends. I've tried to develop it; I have to live up to him.

Because of my position, I keep friends like your horse about me, friends who've been put to the test and shown their mettle. Friends who will stick."

"Your friends will be kept busy with all the battles you'll have," I said. He lifted one side of his mouth in a lopsided smile. I touched my heel to Ginori's side and the horse flicked his ears forward and moved immediately into a brisk, forward walk.

"Enjoy the saddle. I had it made for myself, but your horse deserved it more than mine!" he called. For a moment I was too surprised to do anything. Then I swung around to thank him, but Lorenzo had melted back into the darkness. Another complicated Medici, I thought, only this one was an unknown quantity. His gift was no gift but a test, and I resolved to bring Lorenzo something to reciprocate when I returned. I also resolved to find out how much power the Confraternity of the Red Feather still possessed. I had to know this, both for my own safety and because Lorenzo would know. He was a man not afraid to exercise power, and my own freedom was too precious to me for me to surrender it willingly to anyone, even a Medici.

Chapter 16

I WOKE THE NEXT MORNING with golden and lavender Tuscan sun touching my face like an old friend for the first time in over half a century. I had stayed overnight at the only inn in Anchiano, a ramshackle, ivy-covered place with a serviceable tavern attached. I was relieved to wake, because a long dream had gripped me: Nicolo Silvano was preaching from a pulpit, pointing his finger at me, laughing maniacally. Then I was stuck in a web, a vast outstretched web of pink and green, with people crawling on it. I flailed and tore through the web, and suddenly I was standing in a room, at a masque. Music played for gorgeously costumed people. A slim feminine form approached, and my heart ached: it was the woman from the vision of the philosopher's stone. She stood in blinding radiance, her face obscured. That gut-level awareness of her that I had felt many times over the last century blossomed into her presence, soft, sweet, smooth. But when I reached for her, she kept receding. My heart beat wildly with longing. Then there were warm fingers on my cheeks, and when I opened my eyes, it was a long beam of light, and not the hand of my beloved.

I felt stripped bare and undefended, but there was no gainsaying the dream. I had known yesterday, when telling the young Leonardo about my vision, that I was invoking it, putting on the noose of its enchantment. I dressed quickly and went downstairs to the tavern for breakfast. Crusty bread, a thick, steaming porridge, chunks of cottardite ham, and a sliced white pear were served to me by a lovely blond woman. I was eager to break the spell of vulnerability that the dream had cast upon me and focused on her to distract myself. She had golden curls worn long down her back in a fashion to make a man's fingers itch to run through them. Her hazel eyes flicked up at mine and she smiled, showing her full pink lips and even white teeth. I took in the large, widely spaced eyes set in her sculpted oval face, and I knew who she was.

"Caterina," I said.

"You have the advantage, signore. I don't know your name," she replied huskily.

"That's Luca Bastardo," sang a musical voice. "He's my teacher now." It was Leonardo wearing an emerald-green lucco whose uneven hem looked as if he'd shortened it himself. He skipped in and sat on the bench beside me.

"Is that so, little man?" Caterina asked, ruffling his hair. "I'll get you some bread and honey, *bambino*." She went off with her shapely rounded hips swaying beneath her sleeveless giornea.

"I don't think you should look at my mother that way," Leonardo said. He placed my dagger on the table beside me and then slid my bowl of porridge over in front of himself. I watched him dig into the food, remembering how I'd always eaten alone at Silvano's. The food there had always been delicious and plentiful, but the company was scant and tainted:

myself. Leonardo had no sense of that kind of poverty of the spirit, or how far one would go to alleviate it. Something else generated his life, something shining and unbounded at his core.

"I didn't say I was going to teach you," I temporized. I gazed away from him. Something about Leonardo's beauty reminded me of the horror to which my own looks had consigned me as a child. After decades of barely recalling the brothel, I now remembered it all too well. Leonardo, so sure of his prerogative, had no notion of that kind of suffering. I would have considered him insolent if he weren't so serenely warm and gracious, if calm didn't stream off him the way halos radiated from angels in paintings.

"You're here, you're going to teach me," he said, between spoonfuls of porridge. "Let's start today. I'm ready to learn, professore."

"Today I am going into Florence to see the Duomo," I said, a little crossly, because I never liked the feeling of being maneuvered, and lately that was happening a lot. There was dried blood on my dagger, and I wiped it on my lucco before sliding it into its holster on my thigh.

"Florence, that's a splendid idea!" he cried. His mother came back with a plate of bread slathered with butter and dripping with honey. "Mama, Luca's taking me into Florence today!"

"Hold your horses—" I started.

"Oh, yes, is that your beautiful horse in the stable? The chestnut stallion?" Leonardo asked eagerly. "I should like to draw him! I'll get started before we leave!"

"Don't you think we should talk to your papa about a new tutor?" Caterina asked. She set the plate down in front of Leonardo and seated herself opposite us. Her full bosom strained against the yellow apron over her plain blue giornea, her collar opened to show her white throat. She smelled of cooked meats and yeasty breads and spilled wine beneath her flowery perfume, and a little slick of honey glistened along her lower lip. I wanted to lick the honey off. She leaned over the table, asking "How much do you propose to charge, signore? Ser Piero is ever mindful of cost."

"I don't know what tutors earn," I said. I took a long draught from my cup of water to conceal the way her charm made my breath accelerate.

"We'll pay him well, I'll talk to Papa," Leonardo said earnestly. "But not so well that Papa gets angry." He took the ham from my plate, beaming first at his mother and then at me. He was irresistible, and he knew it. I had no idea what to teach him, but he did. I would have to follow his lead. This would have dismayed me with any other person, living or dead. Since liberating myself from the brothel, my own freedom had been of primary importance. There had never before been anyone for whom I was willing to compromise it even slightly. Even the great love of my vision had been relegated to a nebulous future. Now—because Leonardo had asked, and because Cosimo was dying, and because my peripatetic heart cared for them both, and because I wouldn't flee from the hand of God anymore, whether that hand was cruel or kind—I willingly settled in a city where I could be imprisoned and killed. The whole situation made me cross.

"I have to make arrangements," I said, rising from the table.

"You'll be back soon?" he called. I nodded to him over my shoulder, found Caterina holding her son's hand to her lips as she stared after me. I sucked in my gut, held my shoulders a little wider and my spine a little straighter. Anchiano was going to be an interesting place.

I RODE TO THE LITTLE VINEYARD I OWNED and introduced myself to my tenants as a descendant of the original Luca Bastardo who owned it. So I became the son of myself, for Leonardo and Cosimo. An older couple with two grown sons tended the place, and they were skeptical at first, but I recited for them the figures from the past ten years, yields of grape harvested and casks sold and which merchants bought the wine for how much and so forth. I was completely accurate because I kept meticulous account of my half-share of the yield. They were soon convinced of my authenticity and fell all over themselves to please me. I explained that I would be staying in Anchiano for an undetermined length of time, and there was some discussion as to where I would live. With the wealth I'd accumulated over many decades, I could have lived anywhere. I did not tell them that because the vineyard suited my requirements. I wanted neither to flaunt my money nor to call attention to myself by setting up a household. The couple and one son lived in the main villa, and the older son, who had a wife and baby, lived in a small cottage on the property. It was agreed that the young family would move back in with his parents and I would take up residence in the cottage. I told them that I expected my horse to be well tended. The younger son, a big, rawboned country lad about Lorenzo's ago, lit up and promised to treat Ginori "better than husbands do their wives."

Having arranged things to my satisfaction, I rode back to the tavern. Leonardo was outside on the lawn in front of the inn, playing a skipping game with rocks arranged in a square. He held a fluttering piece of paper in his hand as he leapt around.

"Luca, your horse, want to see?" he called when I dismounted.

"Where did you get the paper?" I asked, because paper was a costly luxury. Little drawings were scattered all over the sheet, faces and birds and insects and the shape of Monte Albano from a distance. A crude charcoal pencil had been used, but the hand guiding the pencil was extraordinarily fine and perceptive, far too advanced to be that of a twelve-year-old boy. The use of shading to show depth and minute gradations of surface, in particular, was eerily sophisticated. "Who drew these?"

"I drew them, of course. Mama buys paper, whenever she has money. Sometimes I can coax Papa into getting me some," he answered happily, scooping up some round gray stones and dropping them into his pocket. "I like to draw."

"Where's the horse?" I asked, bemused and ogling the miniatures, each one a delicious expression of precocious and emotive draughtsmanship. Leonardo's love for birds showed in every elegant curve of a wing; his delight in people palpitated out from the turn of a cheek or glance of an eye. It would take only minimal training to turn this boy into a master artist. I knew that what I could teach him was limited; he was intended for better teachers, better men, than me.

"Here." He reached up and turned the paper over, and then upside down. Underneath a sketch of a fat baby and a dog, there was a horse. "Do you like it? What's your horse's name? Are we riding him to Florence? When are we leaving? How long will it take? Can we go soon?"

Only the horse's neck, head, withers, and one leg had been finished. There were some vague strokes indicating the other three legs and its rump. "It's beautiful, but it's not finished," I pointed out. Leonardo shrugged. I looked back at the paper and noticed that most of the sketches had been left incomplete. Half of a face would be superbly drawn, but the other half only suggested, or one wing of a bird would be

exquisitely depicted, while the rest of it was implied by a
few spare strokes on the paper. "Do you never finish what
you start?"

"There's so much to see," he said. Impish dimples appeared on both sides of his wide smile, so like his pretty
mama's. "Isn't the eye wonderful, Luca, the way it takes in
images?"

I shook my head. "You must learn to complete things, it's
important." He gave me a beatific smile, and I thought that,
if nothing else, I could at least teach him perseverance,
which was a quality of mine. Much later, I was to laugh at my
own vanity. Whatever he learned from me, I learned well
from Leonardo that teaching is a matter of drawing out from
men what is already in their hearts, and that men learn only
what they want to.

"You can keep that," he said, with a wave of his cherubic
hand. I had always valued gifts, and this one was no different. I went back into the inn. This sheet of boyish drawings
was precious, and I meant to preserve it. I ran up the stairs
to my room and opened my leather bag. This portmanteau
was only a few years old, having been bought at a bazaar in
Constantinople, where goods were cheap since the fall of
that city a decade ago. I pulled from it Petrarca's notebook,
which I kept with me always, just as I did the panel of
Giotto's St. John with the reddish-blond dog at his heels and
Geber's eyeglasses. I opened the leather-bound notebook
carefully to its center.

"What's that? A notebook? Why is it blank?" said a lyrical
voice at my elbow, and, of course, Leonardo the curious had
followed me to my room.

"It's blank because I haven't written in it yet," I said.

"Why not?"

"I don't know."

"You must," he insisted. I sighed.

"I'm waiting for something special to happen. Then I'll write in the book."

"Something special like what?" he pressed me. "Something from your vision of things to come? Like the great love you told me about, by the cave, when I first met you?"

"You are too inquisitive of matters that don't concern you," I said as sternly as I could muster.

"Let me see," he ordered, taking the notebook. He sat on the floor and looked at each fine vellum page as if it was covered with these very words, and he could read them even though they were far in his future. But then, if ever there was a man who could read the book of the future, it was Leonardo. "I'll draw something for you. On the first page, to encourage you to write in this book." He smiled slyly and took a worn and nubby old pencil from his pocket.

"Wait, what will you draw?" I asked.

"Something wonderful, especially for you," he murmured. He stared at me with his head cocked, and then his hand moved rapidly over the page.

"You're left-handed," I observed, sitting on the bed to wait.

"Uhm," he grunted, bending over the notebook. So I sat there, watching the boy sketch. It was a warm day in June, with a single bird warbling outside the window and the fragrance of wildflowers breathing into the room. Light reflected from peaceful hills and bright sunflowers, from the rocks of Monte Albano and from the rippling surfaces of streams, and softened into a golden mist that permeated the room. I was reminded of that long-ago day in Bosa, Sardegna, when the Wanderer had come for me with Rebecca Sforno's letter. As on that day, the flickering shadows that were the rest of my life fell away, and all that was left was the single present moment, complete and heartfelt.

Finally he looked up at me. "This notebook is very fine. I

should like one just like it. Will you buy me one?" He asked
with such a sincere air of entreaty that I found myself saying
yes before I had even considered his request. He smiled ra-
diantly. "Very good. Thank you, Luca professore. You are as
generous as you are beautiful!"

"Uh-huh," I said, with some skepticism. I knew when I was
being played. Leonardo threw back his head and laughed.

"No, truly!" he protested. "But I'm not going to leave my
notebook blank! I'm going to fill it up with magical writing.
Then I will fill another one, and another one after that!"

"Uh-huh," I said again, but with far less skepticism. One
could believe of golden Leonardo that magic was his servant. That being so, I wondered if he was someone I could
trust, eventually, with the seeming magic that haunted my
life: my long youth and longevity. In all my wanderings over
many decades, I had only met one other person who possessed the same longevity: the Wanderer. There might have
been alchemists like Geber who possessed the secret, but
none had admitted to it, at least not in my presence. And I
had inquired. Of Leonardo, I asked, more casually than I
felt, "How are you going to make it magical?"

He hopped up and handed me back the notebook. "I
don't know. I'll write backward, or something." His eyes
widened suddenly and he laughed. He said, "You told me
about your vision of times to come. Sometimes I see something. It's blurry, like a foggy mirror. I just saw men who live
far in the future trying to read my backward handwriting.
They'll be mystified and awed. My writing will look magical
to other people, but the explanation will be simple and natural. Magic can always be explained that way, don't you
think?" I didn't answer but stared at his sketch. It was of a
handsome man in his twenties with symmetrical, fine-boned
features, not delicate but certainly refined. There was something pensive and sad about his eyes and a small, ironic,

almost bitter smile played about his full mouth. The man was lithe and well muscled, and he stood with two pairs of arms outstretched within a circle which was set inside a square, as if he had been moving. He also had a second set of legs that were spread outside the first set.

"He must be a very good swordsman, with that extra set of arms." I smiled. "But how does he get around, trotting like a horse?"

"Silly!" He giggled. "He doesn't have extra arms. I drew him moving from one position to the next."

"And why the circle and square?"

"It shows how perfect forms are in nature, expressed by a man's body, and how geometrical a man's proportions are," he said. "You're well formed, Luca. You have excellent proportions. I've never before seen so clearly this geometry, but I was struck by it the first moment I saw you on Monte Albano. Though you're not very tall. I hope I'm taller when I'm a man."

"Am I so sad?"

"Aren't you?" he asked innocently.

"No."

"Maybe you will be." He shrugged. "Maybe you won't be able to have your great love and you'll feel very sad! Then won't you be glad you tutored me, and if you didn't have your great love, at least you had my friendship?" I gave him a wry look. He waited while I carefully placed his sketch of animals atop the sketch of me standing within the geometrical forms, closed Petrarca's notebook and tied a leather thong around it, and then replaced it in my portmanteau. Then he asked cheerfully, "So are we going to Florence now? What are we going to see? Can I ride in front of you on the horse, or do I have to ride in the back?"

THE DUOMO WAS COMPLETED. I had never seen it thus. The graceful red dome itself was the largest in Christendom and towered over the city, its shadow seeming to sweep over all of Tuscany. It wasn't necessary to stand in front of it, as we were; it was inescapable, looming above the narrow stone streets, breaking majestically into view at every corner and piazza. It was a poignant reminder to me of what I had missed by being away. If Nicolo Silvano hadn't managed to burn me at the stake sixty-four years ago, he had managed to steal from me a lifetime of memories of Florence, my home, the city whose very streets seemed to have gestated me with my inhumanly long youthfulness, whose churches and palazzi were my kinfolk, and whose river Arno had baptized me.

"It was built circle by circle," Leonardo said, interrupting my thoughts, "so that the stress of the forces goes around and around and doesn't break. The circles allow it to soar to new heights, undreamt of before this duomo!"

"It's octagonal."

"But it was built with circles inside it," Leonardo insisted. "The cupola has two shells within which are a series of concentric circular rings, circles that decrease in circumference as they ascend. That's how Capomaestro Brunelleschi built it without scaffolding. He relied on forces converging at the cupola's apex, where the lantern and its weight could absorb the inward force and redirect it outward. He also used an ancient Roman herringbone pattern for the brickwork, interlocking each new course of bricks with the course below it in a way that made the structure self-supporting. So the dome rose because of the integrity of its own design!"

"How do you know so much, bambino?" I asked, ruffling his soft hair as I stared up at the cupola. Few people were about, because of the plague, though it was a fine summer day.

"Everyone talks about the Duomo," he said. "I listen! And

guess what else? Clever Brunelleschi invented a number of machines to help him build it, isn't that wonderful?" Leonardo cried. "I want to invent things, too! He invented a hoist to move and carry the tremendous weights to great heights, a hoist that was driven by oxen. Can you imagine? He hoisted marble, brick, stone, and mortar into the very sky! It was a marvel, this hoist, so huge and powerful, and had a wonderful reversible gear——"

"Enough!" I held up my hand. "I am no architect or mathematician, I know nothing of such technical matters. You need a different teacher, if you want to study those subjects!"

"But aren't you fascinated by them? By these problems of force and movement and weight and geometry?" He gestured toward the Duomo. "If we master them, there is nothing man can't accomplish! We can build the flying machine you saw in your vision, and the swimming machine, and other inventions too wondrous to believe! Don't you see the importance of it?"

I could hardly believe that this was the same child who jingled the rocks he'd placed in his pocket after a hopping game in the grass; he sounded so mature as he spoke of the hoist. I said, "I'm more interested in the question of beauty. Notice how graceful the octagon is, delicate yet strong and massive at the same time, like a sculpture. . . ."

"Sculpture, bah, that's a lesser art than painting," the boy said. "Painting surpasses all human works because it contains so many subtle possibilities. Sculpture lacks many of painting's natural parts, and can't show transparent or luminous or shining bodies, as a painting can."

"Then let's go to the chapels in Santa Croce to look at Giotto's frescoes. That's beauty!"

THREE DAYS LATER Leonardo and I rode over together to
Careggi for the dinner at the Villa Medici. My caretakers'
tall second son Neri rode with us. I'd asked Neri to accompany us, thinking it prudent to have a strong shoulder at my
back during the calcio game, even if it was only an untutored peasant shoulder. My own experience had taught me
that a man's station in life did not decide his value.

It was a brilliant June morning, cloudless, with a breeze
ruffling the lavender in the Tuscan fields. We rode over the
rolling hills, past orderly vineyards and groves of silver-
green olive trees and fragrant cypress stands. We saw men
working, but none called out to us; the plague made everyone fearful of strangers, as it always had. I brought with me
a falcon I'd been given by an old condottiere with whom I'd
fought in a few campaigns. The gruff old soldier was Frankish,
not Florentine, but he'd retired to the Tuscan countryside
after hearing me describe it. When I said I needed a gift worthy of a king, he'd almost refused to take my money. I insisted. He was, after all, retired, and he'd need the funds.
So he'd sold me the finest peregrine falcon from his mews, a
handsome, mannerly largewing who easily let herself be
hooded. Then we were off to present the bird to Lorenzo
de' Medici.

Leonardo rode in front of me, wearing the glove, with
the jess securing the bird to his hand. He was thrilled to have
this task and, between cooing at the bird and praising her, he
urged me to canter the horse. I complied and he shrieked
with delight. Ginori's stride lengthened out and his shoulder
flexed around a turn, and we were flying over the hills toward
the Villa Medici.

We arrived in Careggi and trotted around a massing of
carriages filled with chattering women. We came to a stop in
a throng of horses with plaited manes and tails and men dis-
mounting. A tall, baleful magistrate was checking people for

signs of the plague. He allowed us in with a wave, and a servant appeared to take Ginori and Neri's horse.

"Luca Bastardo, the guest of honor." Lorenzo's high, nasal
voice hailed me. "Welcome!" He strode through a laughing
group of men who parted respectfully for him; at fifteen,
he already had an air of command to which other men de-
ferred. He approached us with his black hair swinging and
his strongly featured face lit with pleasure. Or it seemed
thus, though I suspected that nothing was ever as it seemed
with Lorenzo.

"Signore," I said, with a slight bow. Lorenzo laughed and
embraced me warmly.

"You are an old family friend, Nonno loves you, you can't
think I would let you get away with such a tepid greeting!
And who is this young rascal with the fancy bird on his
gauntlet?" Lorenzo said, stepping back to examine Leonardo.
His face went still at the sight of Leonardo's beauty, a typical
reaction. The fear that glittered briefly in Lorenzo's eyes was
not typical, however. I wondered what the fear was about.

Leonardo smiled serenely at Lorenzo; there was seldom
fear in Leonardo, just calm acceptance. "You're going to be
very important. You will lead the world," Leonardo said.

Lorenzo did a double take. "Has Nonno met you, boy? I
shall bring you in to the family."

"Certainly." Leonardo nodded. "I am Leonardo, son of
Ser Piero da Vinci," he said, with great gravity. "This is a gift
for you from my professore, Luca Bastardo." He held the
bird toward Lorenzo, whose eyes glowed. Lorenzo seemed
to stop breathing as he focused on the bird. He untwisted
the jess and then loosed the falcon's hood with a quick practiced flick of his fingers. Then he took Leonardo's hand in his
and cast off the bird. She soared up into the sky. A hush fell
over the crowd as men turned their faces upward to watch.
She circled high above the hills, a dark speck against the sun,

her form outlined in a thin line of violet radiance. I thought that's what my spirit must have looked like, all those years ago when I traveled to see Giotto's paintings while I was working at Silvano's, though I was not the predator then, but the prey. Suddenly the falcon tucked her wings and dove. Her silhouette grew larger and larger at breathtaking speed, until she slammed into something on the ground on a hill at some distance from the villa. A cheer went up and everyone raced toward the landing site.

"A hare!" cried Lorenzo, who naturally sprinted past everyone else to be in the lead. "A hare! Bravo!" yelled several voices. Leonardo ran to Lorenzo, who took the glove from the boy and retrieved the bird. I joined them, pushing my way through the throng of spectators.

"We need meat for this sweet beauty," Lorenzo crooned. His hair was askew and he was breathing hard. I slipped my dagger out of its holster and held it by its tip to offer to Lorenzo. He laughed and tossed the hare to me. "Cut her a piece, then," he said. "You're not a man who fears blood and guts!" I shrugged and slit open the hare at its belly.

"Now, professore, if you cut delicately, you can see the thin membrane that separates the skin from the innards," Leonardo clucked at me, sounding like an old professore himself. "Don't hack at it. Gently, the insides are a marvel to see, nature's own machine!"

I cast a jaundiced eye on him and asked sotto voce, "Who's the teacher here, boy?" He giggled. I cut out the hare's intestines and tossed a chunk of bloody meat to Lorenzo, who fed it to the peregrine falcon.

"A worthy gift," he said, bowing his head to me. "A gift fit for a king. I accept with pleasure!" But his eyes were as fierce as the falcon's and I knew, even if I had passed the first test of responding to the saddle he'd given me, that he was not done testing me.

"Don't waste the hare. Give it to your servants for a stew," I suggested. He laughed with high good spirits and indicated the Moorish man. I threw the hare to him, and he bowed.

"I have to show this princess to her new palazzo," Lorenzo said. "Then we're ready for a game of calcio!" He strode off with many men following him and congratulating him on the bird's beauty and skill. I turned to Leonardo.

"How do you play calcio?" I said. Leonardo clapped his hand over his mouth, giggling.

"You've never played?"

"Who has time for games when there's money to earn, to stave off starvation and misfortune, ruin, abomination, and death?" I demanded. I'd never liked games since Massimo, my old friend from the street, had sold me to Bernardo Silvano. I knew how seriously people took competition, even when it purported to be for entertainment.

"Easy, easy, professore," Leonardo said, with a quieting motion of his hands. "Calcio is a simple game. There's a leather ball, and you get it over the other team's line; that's a *caccie*. You run with the ball or pass it to someone else to run with. You can kick it, too."

"Sounds simple," I agreed. "What are the rules?"

"What do you mean, rules? You get the ball over the other team's line. But you have to do it skillfully. If you make a bad attempt, that's half a caccie for the other team."

"So how do you get the ball over the other team's line?"

"Any way you can." Leonardo shrugged.

"YOU'RE ON MY TEAM, of course, I must have men of *forza* around me," Lorenzo said cheerfully, tossing me a green lucco. The other team's color was white. "I must see for myself some of that bastard mettle that Nonno praised, and use it as well as he did!" So that was the test. How well I play for him. I didn't like it one bit, not the test, and not the intention behind it. If I proved myself worthy, Lorenzo would press me into service; my freedom of choice would be limited. If I proved unworthy, he'd discard me, rescinding the protection I had long enjoyed from his grandfather. Neither outcome appealed to me.

"Give a lucco verde to my comrade Neri here," I responded, jerking my thumb at the lad. Lorenzo gave Neri one of his lightning-fast scans.

"Reinforcements," he said. "Clever." He threw another green tunic to me. I motioned to Neri, who was sucking on a blade of grass and standing in a patch of sun with Leonardo. Neri gave me a big lazy grin and shambled over. I tossed the lucco and he shucked off his torn and patched farsetto and slipped it on. I, too, doffed my farsetto and pulled on the green lucco.

"You have a real nice camicia. I hope you don't love it as much as you love your horse. You want Ginori kept nice and clean," Neri said earnestly. "Everyone's camicie get ripped up and torn off during calcio."

"Have you played before?" I asked. He brightened.

"Sure, lots of times. I'm real good," he said. "I don't get hurt easy because I'm so big!"

"So what are the rules?"

He scratched his shaggy head. "You have to get the ball over the line for a caccie." He pointed to a chest-high wooden fence that ran the full width at each end of the field, a flat expanse cleared of grass behind the villa.

"I gather that," I said, between clenched teeth. I saw wooden benches being placed around the sides of the field under colorful, beribboned tents. Babbling women in festive dress, whooping children, and jabbering old men were streaming from the house and grounds to take seats. I was surprised to see so many people gather during the plague. A throaty cheer went up and Cosimo was hobbling out. Contessina held one arm and a short man in his thirties held the other. Cosimo raised his hand in greeting. He caught my eye and waved. I asked Neri, "How exactly is a caccie accomplished?"

"There are two teams of twenty-seven men," Lorenzo answered. He gestured for the greens to gather around him. He introduced me only as "Luca" to the other Verdi, many of whom had old noble names. Lorenzo explained, "The object of calcio is to get the ball over the other team's line. You can run with it, throw it, kick it, or pass it to another player. You have to avoid the other team's defensive players, who will try to block you any way they can: by knocking you down, punching you, kicking you, anything."

"Anything?" I asked.

Lorenzo touched his misshapen nose. "How do you think I did this?" He winked. "You're not afraid, are you, Bastardo? After all I've heard about you from Nonno? Or is it that you reserve your courage for him?"

"The only honor is in winning," I answered dryly. The Verdi around me cried, "Bravo!" and clapped me on the back. Lorenzo winked, having caught the irony, but also nodded.

"You're my kind of calcio player," he said. "Tough and determined. Nothing matters to me more than winning. I keep men who help me achieve that close beside me." He leaned his mouth close to my ear, so only I could hear his words. "And those who can't help me win are given away." He looked pointedly at the Bianchi, and I turned to follow his gaze. I saw a lean young man run onto the field to join the game. He was obviously wealthy and well liked by the other nobles, who were teasing him about his late arrival. Then the young man turned around, and my stomach dropped. There was the face that haunted my nightmares: a bladelike nose over a pointed and jutting chin. I whipped back around before he could meet my eyes. I knew in my bones that the Silvano clan would remember me.

"Pietro Silvano," I whispered, with my windpipe closing up.

"I'm glad to hear you understand the stakes," Lorenzo said.

"*FORZA VERDI!*" cried some of the spectators, while others screamed, "*Forza Bianchi!*" Giuliano de' Medici, Lorenzo's handsome and precocious brother, captained the whites. He was a few years Lorenzo's junior and he strutted around, blowing kisses to the women, who giggled. One fat matron stood up and called out something about the skinny shape of his legs in his hose, and Giuliano cupped his crotch at her, which elicited much laughter and hooting. Lorenzo rolled his eyes. He wasn't one to waste time grandstanding, but instead barked out instructions. He assigned me to defense and told Neri to receive passes. Then a drum rolled and a trumpet sounded a fanfare, and an expectant hush fell over the spectators. The players took their places on the field. I stood in back, noting where Pietro Silvano was and resolving to stay away from him. The sport was gone from the game, which no longer felt like a game to me.

A youth in a green lucco carrying a green flag took his place in front of the wooden fence at one end of the field, and a white-lucco-clad, white-flag-carrying youth did the same thing at the other end, marking each team's line. There were sly cries for them to hold their flagpoles higher to make their teams proud, which caused them to blush. The trumpet sounded three quick blasts. A portly referee with a plumed hat tossed the ball into the air, and mayhem broke out.

Lorenzo was taller than Giuliano and, naturally, willing to jump higher and hit harder to get his hands on the ball. He batted it toward a green player, and men exploded in running patterns all over the field. I ran toward Lorenzo, intending to clear Bianchi from his path, as I guessed defensive players were supposed to do. Neri followed, and two Bianchi tackled me. I hit the ground hard and was pummeled without mercy. Fortunately, Neri had seen me go down. The two Bianchi went flying off me, and Neri grinned.

"You're supposed to do that to the Bianchi," he hollered, so I'd hear him over the uproar of players calling to each other and spectators screaming.

"I'll bear that in mind," I yelled, wiping blood off my lip. Neri sprinted off, and I looked around for Lorenzo, Silvano, or the ball. It was a mistake to linger, because the next thing I knew a Bianchi was diving at me from the air. He hit me and we rolled over and over on the ground. This time I didn't let myself get pinned. I brought my knee up between the man's thighs, hard; he squealed and rolled off me. I leapt up and ran in a zigzag pattern. I didn't know exactly where I was going, but it was better to move quickly than to stand around and get tackled again. Silvano ran at me but veered off in another direction. The next thing I knew, the leather ball flew at me. I caught it hard in the stomach. The wind left my body and my eyes felt as if they were going to pop out, but I didn't stop running. I clutched the ball to my chest and looked around for someone to pass it to. Neri was kicking men off somebody. I continued running in an eccentric pattern, and then Lorenzo, lucco torn and blood on his face, hopped up from the ground by Neri. Lorenzo waved. I threw the ball as hard as I could at him. It was heavy, but he

caught it squarely and was running even before he'd brought
it all the way into his solar plexus.

Four whites threw themselves at Lorenzo, but I dove in
to trip them. Lorenzo burst free, closed in on the line, and
threw the ball over. Cheers erupted, and the drum rolled
again as the trumpet and horns blasted another fanfare.

We set up again, and I stayed in back, noting where
Silvano was on the other side of the field. His white lucco
was ripped and he had blood on his face, as most of us did. I
wanted to approach him from behind and knock him out
without him seeing me.

The referee tossed up the ball again. Again mayhem broke
out. This time I knew better than to loiter. Four Bianchi
closed in on me. Now they were mad because I'd aided in a
caccie. I used every trick I'd ever learned as a street urchin
and a condottiere to elude them as well as stay out of
Silvano's line of sight. Still, a Bianchi barreling at me from
behind grabbed my arm and spun me around like a top. I
stumbled into the group of Bianchi, who threw me down,
leapt on me, and flailed away at my face and ribs. It felt like
forever but it was probably only a few moments before
Bianchi were being heaved off me like bags of grain being
tossed off a pile. I hopped to my feet, punching out with my
fist at a Bianchi. I caught him in his nose, which exploded
in a shower of bright scarlet blood. The man went down
clutching a fistful of the ribbons of my tunic. Trusty Neri
was panting as he stood next to Lorenzo.

"You're learning," Lorenzo sang. Then he and Neri were
off again, sprinting out at angles from each other, and I dove
at a Bianchi who'd stumbled to his feet.

Another cheer went up, and this time the Bianchi had
scored a caccie. The trumpet sounded, the referee whipped
his hat off at the Bianchi, and the white-flag bearer ran down
the field with Bianchi players falling in behind him. Most of

the players bore crimson stains on their white lucchi, and many men wore no lucco or camicia at all, as they'd been torn off. Silvano was one of these shirtless men, standing in front, close to Giuliano. He appeared not to have seen or recognized me. I slunk back behind some of the Verdi. Leonardo gestured to Lorenzo. Only magical Leonardo could have commanded him thus, because Lorenzo trotted over and bent close to the boy's golden head to listen. Leonardo gesticulated and Lorenzo nodded, and then Lorenzo ran out to talk to Neri and a few other Verdi. They huddled together, and then the trumpet sounded for us to take up our positions on the field.

The referee tossed up the ball, and Lorenzo crouched instead of jumping, which allowed Giuliano to bat the ball. Young Giuliano didn't expect to lay hands on the ball. He hit it badly. It sputtered to the ground and Lorenzo grabbed it, ran directly into the Bianchi, and then swiveled to throw the ball to Neri, who had burst out alongside him, plowing down Bianchi as a bull might knock over sheep. Neri didn't hold the ball but dropped it in front of himself and kicked it in midair. It was a great feat of strength because the ball was heavy, and it arced into the air and landed in the waiting arms of a fast Verdi who was close to the Bianchi line. The Verdi quickly tossed the ball over the line, and the crowds roared. Another caccie for Verdi, and this one on the very heels of the Bianchi caccie. Lorenzo gave Leonardo a thumbs-up, and the cheeky boy grinned and swept his hand out in an elaborate bow. Even then I knew I was watching the birth of a friendship. I wondered if, instead of taking up my own destiny, I was facilitating the destinies of other men in returning to Florence. What had I let myself in for?

Later—I lost track of time in the brutality of the game and in the necessity of staying out of Pietro Silvano's view— the score was four–four. I was bruised and spattered with blood, mostly from other men. One of my ribs was cracked, but, as always, I'd given as good as I'd got. The man who'd cracked my rib had limped off the field with a broken arm. The Bianchi had just scored a caccie and Lorenzo looked over at Leonardo, who was standing beside the seated Cosimo. Leonardo ran out from under the tent. Lorenzo went to him, and they conversed, with Leonardo pointing at me. Lorenzo waved me over.

"You play offense now," he said tersely.

"What? I don't know how. It was luck that I passed you the ball for the first caccie," I said in dismay. "I'm just trying to keep from getting thrashed every play!"

"Stand up front on my left. I'll send the ball your way."

"In front? Are you joking? The Bianchi will kill me! They're mad about the guy's arm I broke!"

"The guy is Leopetto Rossi, scion of one of the oldest, richest families in Florence, and he's going to marry my sister Maria," Lorenzo said, with a sideways look. Just as the rest of us were, he was nicked and bruised all over. He wore the blood with superb indifference, like a triumphant war horse, and plunged into the heart of the action with every play, eliciting cries of "Bravo, Lorenzo!" from the women and old men. I think he would have been humiliated not to be bloodied and bruised. He might have looked indifferent to his own position. It was what he feared more than anything.

"Yeah, your rich brother-in-law has a lot of friends, and they're all out to get me now," I said grimly. I hoped the enmity I'd engendered during this game wouldn't linger.

"It's not personal"—Lorenzo squeezed my shoulder affectionately—"it's calcio."

"What about Silvano?" I retorted in a low voice, so no one else could hear.

"Don't worry about that letter his family has." Lorenzo

shrugged. I started and Lorenzo smiled crookedly. "Nonno confides in me, too, Bastardo. But victory requires sacrifices, yes? When the referee throws up the ball, run forward and expect it. You'll be a hero for my team!" The trumpet blared, and everyone took their places. I ran up front near Lorenzo, as ordered, and the man whose position I took grinned and ran back. Several Bianchi saw me, including Pietro Silvano, who shared a smile with the others. My heart sank. I was going to get pounded. Worse, I was going to be recognized. If I survived the pounding, I would find myself carted off to be burned at the stake by Pietro Silvano and the Confraternity of the Red Feather. The referee tossed the ball into the air and Lorenzo leapt for it. I charged into the Bianchi line. A dozen of them tackled me. The air was crushed out of my lungs. I fought with no hope of freeing myself from the scrum atop me, and even less chance of laying my hands on the ball. Then, at the bottom of a heaving, punching mass of bodies, I realized that I wasn't supposed to get the ball. That was never the plan. I was supposed to do exactly what I had done: run into the Bianchi line, distract them. I had been used. Worse, I had let myself be used, despite all the times over my long life that I had promised myself that would never happen again. Lorenzo de' Medici did not care for other men's vows to themselves and their Gods. Staying in Florence for Cosimo, I put myself in the position to be a pawn for his ruthless grandson.

The trumpet blazed out a fanfare; Leonardo's plan had worked: the Verdi had scored. Then the trumpet and drums rolled out together, signaling the end of the game. The two Bianchi on the bottom of the pile closest to me kept pinching me, and another Bianchi dug his elbows into my knee. Anger flushed through me. I wrapped my hands around a nearby throat and squeezed. It wasn't Pietro Silvano's throat, but he was close, perhaps in the pile on top of me, which lent vicious strength to my hands. The man writhed but couldn't speak. Bodies shifted off me and then someone grabbed my arms and jerked my hands off the Bianchi's throat. He rolled over and lay on the ground, cursing hoarsely and stroking his bruised windpipe. A number of Bianchi knelt over him, including Silvano, who had his back to me. Neri and Lorenzo stood above me.

"Easy, professore," Lorenzo warned, reaching down to help me to my feet. "This is a friendly game! We're not killing anyone today, especially not Francesco de' Pazzi."

"Then I'll save that for another day," I growled.

Lorenzo's dynamic eyes danced. "Cheer up, you're a hero! The Verdi won!"

"Because I took the front and drew off a dozen Bianchi," I said angrily.

"A cunning sacrifice. You're none the worse for the wear, and you'll have a dozen invitations from the ladies tonight!" exclaimed Lorenzo.

"I would have liked to know I was being used!" I snapped. I looked over at Leonardo, who was cheering from the sidelines, and shook my finger at him. He giggled and clapped his hands and danced around, enchanted by my anger. Cosimo caught my eye and clasped his hands over his head again, calling "Bravo, Luca!"

"We knew you'd figure it out, Leonardo and me. I'm interested in that young man," Lorenzo said, softly but fiercely. "He's quite unusual!" Then the Verdi team swarmed around us, laughing and clapping me on the back. Lorenzo let the men embrace him and enthusiastically joined in the congratulations. I lost track of him when the Bianchi streamed through the grouped Verdi and everyone embraced and kissed. I backed away. I was in no mood for what would have been fake goodwill on my part. I didn't want to risk coming face-to-face with Pietro Silvano.

"Well played, Luca Bastardo." Cosimo laughed. Leonardo, no fool, saw me coming and hid hastily behind Cosimo's chair. Cosimo reached trembling, gray hands out to take mine. "Well done, old friend! A bold, brave move on your part, that final charge into the very heart of the Bianchi that allowed the Verdi to defeat the Bianchi!"

"That was my idea," Leonardo said from behind Cosimo's chair. "Wasn't that an excellent strategy?"

"Indeed, Leonardo, we must have a discussion about the art of strategy," I said grimly.

"You can talk about strategy and art later." Cosimo laughed. "Come, Luca, here is one of my dear friends, the leader of the Platonic Academy—which is the finest philosophical institution in the world—the many-talented scholar, physico, musician: Marsilio Ficino!" A short, slim man a little hunched in his shoulders stepped up and bowed to me.

"Signore Cosimo, you must never stop a man from-from talking about art," Ficino said, with a slight stammer and a smile. He had a ruddy complexion and wavy blond hair that curled high over his forehead. His eyes were effervescent with thought, reminding me of Petrarca's eyes. Ficino said, "Art reminds the immortal soul of its divine origins by creating resemblances to that world. To talk about art is to talk about God, and our divine origins; it reminds us that we have the power to become all things, that man can create the heavens and what is in them if we can obtain the tools and heavenly material. We claim our own dignity in talking about art!"

"If we have the power to become all things and to create the heavens, do you think we can build flying machines?" asked Leonardo, peeking out around Cosimo's chair. I grabbed, but he darted down before my fingers closed on the scruff of his neck. He peeked out from the other side of the chair and stuck out his tongue. I frowned ferociously. He giggled and hid.

"Young Leonardo, I think that since the immortal soul can fly, it will not be long before man invents a way for the body to follow suit. That is the nature of man," Ficino answered.

"There is no discussion with Ficino that does not begin and end with immortality of the soul," Lorenzo said, approaching us from behind me. "Unless it begins and ends with Plato!"

"Lorenzo, my best pupil, at such a young age already an accomplished poet, diplomat, and athlete." Ficino twinkled at the young man, who towered over him. With his rough-hewn face, his bare rolling shoulders covered in blood and sweat, and the blue veins on his arms bulging, Lorenzo looked like some ancient god of war.

"Whatever I accomplish is a tribute to the excellent teachers Nonno has placed around me, and to Nonno himself," Lorenzo said warmly. "But now I must bring our heroic Luca to meet my mother, who is most impressed with him."

"My mother Lucrezia of the Tornabuoni is a remarkable woman," Lorenzo said as he led me toward the field. "Everyone except my grandmother adores her, but that's how it goes in families, the women bicker." He shrugged. His name was being called, so he waved. Then he lowered his voice so only I could hear him. "I like you, Luca Bastardo. You're strong, smart, and willing to do what it takes to win. You must be the son of a dangerous man and a woman with a cool, clear head. I can use such a man."

"Use me for what?"

"Delicate missions, errands that require discretion, overseeing embassies, information gathering, a variety of things for which a leader needs a discreet and loyal man, you know,"

Lorenzo said, shrugging. "And in return, I could offer such a skillful, loyal man my protection."

"What would your protection entail?" I asked softly, wondering how far Lorenzo would go to have me in his service.

"Obtaining a certain letter that might get a man burned at the stake for having parents who were witches, all of which is proved by the witchcraft he uses to stay young," he said sotto voce. "Nonna was frustrated in his efforts to secure the letter, but I don't have the same scruples he does. I'm not afraid to use whatever means necessary to block the Confraternity of the Red Feather, which, as you may have guessed today, may be out of favor, but still lives in secret."

I WAS GLOWERING as I limped up the steps to my room at the inn. I was muttering under my breath, too, invectives in the many languages I'd learned during my travels. The Saracens possessed colorful curses, expressed in satisfying, flowery phrases. I was venting vociferously when I heard my name called. Caterina's curving form was outlined in moonlight below me.

"Luca, are you hurt? Come down, I'll tend you," she said. I didn't need to be asked twice but descended as rapidly as my aching body would allow. "Look at you, is that a split lip?"

"We won," I said in answer.

"That makes it all right, then," she said, with mild sarcasm. "Let me see what I can do about the pain that's making you hobble about like the town cripple." She led me into the tavern, then lit a few lanterns that shed a soft light around her golden curls like the halo of an angel in one of Giotto's frescoes. She stoked the embers in the fireplace. Then her soft hands guided me to a bench. I sat and she placed a lantern near me on the table.

"Leonardo is not with you?" she asked, and gently stripped off the camicia I'd borrowed from Lorenzo.

"He wanted to stay in Careggi," I said.

"My little man always gets what he wants," she said, mirth sparkling in her large hazel eyes. "I suppose he wangled himself an invitation?"

"From Lorenzo de' Medici himself." I nodded, and we exchanged an amused glance. Then her fingers roaming over my bruised shoulder found a sore spot. "Ow!" I grunted. She patted me so solicitously that I groaned again, louder, eliciting another soft stroking. Naturally I then moaned pitifully. It was nice to have her caring for me.

"You're bruised all over," she murmured in sympathy. "It must have been some calcio game!" She caressed my cheek and then bustled off. She returned with a damp rag and a tub of ointment.

"This is a liniment made from an old family recipe," she said. "Herbs in a purified lard. It should do the trick and ease some of your pain." She wiped my shoulders and chest gently with the rag. I didn't say that I probably knew more about herbs and liniments and easing pain than she did, because where would be the fun in that?

"You know, Leonardo is responsible for the worst of the bruises," I said.

"Let me guess." She sighed. "In his clever way, he devised some strategy that had you running directly into the path of most resistance."

"You know your son," I said. I reached out to touch a long blond curl that dangled down between her full bosoms, which strained against the front of her sheer gonna. Her lock of hair was so fine and soft that it felt like silk wrapping around my finger.

"And it probably won the game for you," she said, taking some ointment onto her palm. She held it for a moment, warming it, before massaging it into my shoulders. Where she rubbed, warmth seeped into the muscles. I felt myself relax.

"It was the winning play," I said, and reached up my other hand to comb it through her luxuriant curls. "But it bruised me horribly!" She flicked an amused glance at me and massaged the other shoulder, then moved down to work the ointment into my chest. The night air was grainy and purple and dappled with the yellow lucency of lanterns. The mellow light glowed along Caterina's sculpted cheekbone and saturated her poreless skin. I was deeply aroused by this woman's touch and didn't bother to try to hide it. When she was finished with the liniment, she pulled away from me to wipe her hands with the rag. I grasped her around her waist. Her pink lips quirked upward in a smile, so I pulled her into my lap. I took her head between my hands and kissed her.

"Careful, you'll hurt that fat lip!" She laughed.

"Worth the pain," I said, and kissed her again.

"But, Luca"—she pulled back—"aren't you waiting for some great love from a vision? That's what Leonardo said you told him."

"Waiting, sure, but I don't deny myself in the meantime." I nuzzled her cheek.

"But don't you have to stay true to your vision?"

"I am true to it." I caught her earlobe gently between my teeth and nibbled.

"By not giving your heart away?" she asked softly. I lifted my head and met her gaze.

"My heart is open to you, Caterina," I said in a somber tone, and believed it to be so, in that moment. She looked so piercingly into my eyes that I shivered, and knew from where Leonardo had inherited his unusual powers of observation. I wondered briefly if Caterina was, indeed, the one I'd chased for so long like a distant star, the woman whose love would complete me and fulfill me in all the hidden ways I'd longed for since I was a hungry orphan child.

After a few moments she sighed. "Not the deepest places of your heart."

"I had a friend a long time ago who talked about the places inside us," I said, gathering her a little closer, but leaving my arms loose in case she chose to leave.

"The entrance door to the sanctuary is inside us," she murmured. She leaned close to me and grazed her lips over my bruised mouth. "It's okay, Luca. It is what it is. Each of us has a secret companion musician to dance to, a song we alone know and hear. Yours is a woman from a vision. I can accept that." With that she put her arms around me and eased my pain much more fully than any liniment could.

Chapter 17

COSIMO DE' MEDICI DIED a few months later. It was the first of August and Leonardo had me helping him with a project. His father, Ser Piero, having grudgingly accepted me as a tutor for his precocious son and even more grudgingly consented to pay me a pittance, had given Leonardo a small shield, called a buckler, made from a fig tree, and asked him to paint something on it. In his careful, observant way, Leonardo had examined the buckler and found it clumsy and poorly made. He straightened it himself in the fire and then we gave it to a turner who made it smooth and even. Leonardo applied a coat of gesso and prepared it for painting. Then, with boyish enthusiasm, he decided to paint something utterly terrifying on it, something that would instill such fear that it would turn anyone who viewed it to stone, like the Medusa. To that end we wandered all over Monte Albano seeking lizards, crickets, serpents, butterflies, locusts, bats, and any other strange creature which happened onto our path. We collected the specimens and then took them back to Leonardo's room at his father's house.

Leonardo went freely between his mother's and father's homes, but preferred to work at his father's; with the summer heat, the room at Ser Piero's soon took on the stench of the rotting, decaying carcasses. The servants and Leonardo's stepmother complained and Ser Piero spoke to me in strong language about overindulging his son. I just shrugged, as if anyone could deny Leonardo anything. So the animal carcasses stayed and the women wore scarves around their mouths when they passed near his room. Still, Leonardo wasn't satisfied. He had exacting standards and hadn't yet found the perfect combination of horrifying features for his chimera. We went out crawling through the ripening grapes in my vineyard in Anchiano, looking for rare worms and beetles. It was a typical day of tutoring, which, from the beginning to the end of my years with him, consisted of me following Leonardo around, assisting him in his projects, and making sure he didn't hurt himself in his enthusiasm. I knelt down to examine the leaves of my vines for any sign of rot which would shrink the harvest, and Leonardo threw a small rock at me.

"Professore, you're supposed to be looking for scary creatures," he chided me.

"Rot is a very scary creature to me."

"You know what I mean!" He threw another rock. "Professore, have you heard what Ficino says about friendship and the convivium?"

"Ficino, yes. Plato, Plato, Plato, the soul, music, good manners, more soul, yakety yak."

"Professore!" Leonardo laughed. "Ficino is a great philosopher! You must agree with what he says about art and love. . . ."

"Art, sure, but why love?"

"Because you're waiting for a great love you saw in a vision, aren't you?"

"I'm doing more than merely waiting," I said, smiling with a private thought of Caterina, who filled up my evenings in delicious ways, after Leonardo had gone to bed. She wasn't the woman from my vision, but she was tender and sweet, and my life was richer because of her. I picked off a fuzzy brown spider from a leaf and held it up. Leonardo shook his head no. I said, "Really, I'm looking for her!"

"If you were really looking," Leonardo said slyly, "you wouldn't be here tutoring me."

"Maybe . . . it's just that everyone has a secret companion musician to dance to, a song that we alone hear, and she's mine," I said airily, quoting Caterina's words to him.

"Even Ginori makes smaller piles of manure than that!" Leonardo giggled. "I think you want your love to remain a vision."

"I'll find her," I insisted. "I don't know when. Whenever it amuses either the good God who brings sweetness or the evil God who showers us with cruelty. I'll have my great love when the bitter irony of it comes around, and not one moment before."

"Professore mio, it's not irony that has to come around. It's your heart," Leonardo said. He picked some grapes and ate them, spitting out their skins. "When the heart is ready, the beloved appears! I think you don't want to find her because you've been hurt, because you've had a strange life filled with pain and you aren't ready to meet your great love. But God doesn't control that, you do, with free will. You have to choose love over fear."

"I have always chosen love over fear," I said. "In fact, in my vision, I was given the choice of love and death or long life, and I chose love, even though I will die much younger!"

"You've chosen that in the abstract," Leonardo argued.

"In the world, your heart hasn't chosen it. That's why you have all those women around you."

"We haven't seen this beetle before," I said hastily. I shot Leonardo a covert glance, hoping he hadn't figured out that Caterina was the woman in my life right now. "Have we?"

"You don't want to talk about your secrets," Leonardo said. He took the beetle from me and examined it in the palm of his hand. "I think you are different from other men, Luca. I heard Lorenzo whisper something to his nonno about it."

"You eavesdrop on matters that don't concern you," I growled. "Go back to your bugs."

"Ficino says friendship comes out of the soul," Leonardo said. "We live in a web of relationships which nourishes the soul."

"I have lived in great aloneness most of my life," I admitted.

"But you're not alone anymore, Luca. You have me, Cosimo, and Lorenzo—"

"Cosimo is dying and I'd say that Lorenzo de' Medici has me," I muttered.

"Lorenzo's not a bad man, just calculating. He'll be a great ruler," Leonardo said, tossing the beetle back into the vines.

"What is it you mean to say, Leonardo?" I asked, with some impatience.

"Why do you hold yourself back from people? Why have you split the one God in two and assigned them different tasks? Because of your history? Do you really have no idea at all about your parents, your origins?" Leonardo asked.

I sighed. I couldn't distract him. "I have suspicions about my parents. When I was young I heard tales of a foreign couple, nobles attended by Cathars, who lost a son. Cathars are—"

"I know about the Cathars!" Leonardo exclaimed. "But no one talks about them!"

"How do you know about Cathars, *ragazzo*?"

"My mama's family descended from a Cathar who escaped the Pope's crusade."

"Caterina is of Cathar stock?" I asked, startled. I may have been keeping the deepest places of my heart from Caterina, but she was withholding a few secrets of her own.

"Isn't that what I said? Mama tells me in secret about our beliefs. We don't really believe that the Crucifixion killed Christ, because Christ was purely of the spirit, and spirit can't be killed. We believe in experience and not in faith, because every person can experience God for themselves. It's our purpose on earth to transcend matter and attain union with divine love."

"Leonardo, never speak those words around any but me," I said, placing my hand on the boy's shoulder. "Men have burned for far less! Women, too!"

"Yes, women." Leonardo sighed. "Cathars thought better of them than Roma does. Though Mama told me a poetic story about how Satan created a beautiful woman called Lilith to seduce other angels into fighting with him against God. The angels fought fiercely and broke the heavens, but their bodies were overcome. Their souls fell. Then nine long, heavy days and nights dropped down from the heavens, thicker than blades of grass or drops of rain, until God got angry and decided that women would never again pass through the gates of heaven. I like the way time falls down, like a fabric, creating the world, but the story does seem to contradict the way Cathars treated women, letting them be priests."

"Women priests. That would be one reason for the Pope to call for a crusade."

"The other reason being the Cathar treasures." Leonardo shrugged.

I stared at Leonardo. "What do you know of those treasures?"

"I don't know where they are, but I know they're real. Holy artifacts like the Ark of the Covenant, manuscripts from the Temple in Jerusalem, powerful ancient things still held in secret by Cathars. I wonder what secret about your parents the Cathars were protecting?" Leonardo asked. "Maybe something about a treasure, something like the Ark? Or something else from the Old Testament? What kind of spider is that? Do you see it, Luca, the one with the brown stripes?"

Leonardo crawled off into a tangle of vines, leaving me sitting very still, wondering about the strange coincidences of life that had led me to a uniquely gifted boy descended from Cathar stock. My arms crawled with goose bumps. Then a galloping horse appeared on the crest of a distant hill, distracting me from my reverie.

"A horse, that's what I should make," Leonardo cried, sitting up from under a vine. A cluster of sun-burnished purple grapes had wrapped itself around his ear, and with his golden curls and his hands full of insects and his lucco stripped off because of the heat, he looked for all the world like a Dionysian cherub. "I should make a horse of clay, like Ginori, a small model—"

"Finish the buckler," I said. "Let's please your papa. He's unhappy enough about having to pay me a salary. If you can call it a salary. I'd make more money begging on the streets of Florence, and Florentines aren't generous to their beggars, I assure you!"

"You don't depend on Papa's money for your living," Leonardo said slyly. "You're rich. You own this vineyard and you have a lot of money in the Medici bank, I overheard Signore Cosimo saying that to Signore Ficino."

"You mean you eavesdropped on another conversation that didn't concern you."

Leonardo dimpled. "You're richer than Papa, you don't need the money he gives you."

"It's the principle of the thing," I insisted. "A man should be paid for his hard work."

"I'm hard work?" Leonardo threw his head back and his laughter floated out around us like music. "We spent yesterday swimming in the water hole up on Monte Albano. We spent the day before climbing trees and throwing acorns at people who came to the well!"

"Sure, I'm your nanny." I shrugged. "I should be paid for it!"

"You're not my nanny, you're my professore, and I think, since you're rich, and you're only getting richer, that you should buy me things. Like a notebook. You promised you'd buy me a notebook; when are you going to do that?"

"Soon," I said. "Maybe when you finish the buckler." I gave him a sunny smile and he made a face at me. He held up a garden snake.

"Is this scary?"

"I'm quivering with fear," I said dryly, at which Leonardo tossed the snake at me. I caught it with one hand, and just like that, watching the serpent's green-and-brown body writhe into strange etheric shapes against the yellow sunlight, I knew that death, my old familiar friend, was paying me a visit. "That horseman is coming for me," I said quietly. I tossed the snake back to the boy and stood up and dusted myself off. Leonardo scrambled up out of the vines, picked the grapes from his ear, and pulled on the emerald-green lucco which he'd shortened himself so that it reached only to his waist. We waited as the horse cantered toward us. It was the Moorish servant from the Medici villa at Careggi.

"Come quickly," he said, panting slightly. "Lord Cosimo has died."

By nightfall Leonardo and I arrived at the villa. I dismounted and handed my stalwart horse Ginori to a servant, leaving Leonardo to jump off and trip along after me. I was ushered immediately into Cosimo's chambers, where somber men and women were gathered. Marsilio Ficino rushed over to embrace me.

"Luca, he's been take-taken to-to the Lord," Ficino stammered tearfully. "But he has gone with gr-grace. A few days ago, Cosimo got out of bed, dressed, and made his con-confession to the Prior of San Lorenzo." The tiny man laid his face on my chest and sobbed raggedly. I patted his back gingerly.

"Then Nonno had Mass said," Lorenzo added, approaching us. The boy's craggy face was set in harsh lines, his brilliant eyes reddened and bleary. "Papa told us that he made all the responses as if he were perfectly well."

"There was never such a-a leader! A man so in touch with his divine, immortal soul, whence he drew his power and his wisdom! Cosimo must be-be with his beloved Cosimino and his son Giovanni now," Ficino stammered and sniffled, as I peeled him off me. He smeared at his face with his arm, then lifted his agonized face to me. "Luca, you must speak some comforting words to Contessina, she hasn't stopped weeping."

"Grandmother will keep for a few moments," Lorenzo said grimly. "I must speak with Luca." He led me out into the garden, which nestled behind a high wall. "Nonno's beloved architect Michelozzo couldn't restructure the entire villa to reflect the new principles he loved: orderliness, classical detailing, symmetry, a mass that is"—Lorenzo paused, touching

his incongruously elegant finger to his large flattened nose—
"inconspicuously conspicuous, as the palazzo on Via Larga is.
That is a fitting description of Nonno, yes?"

"Yes." I smiled. "He was always more than his modest ex-
terior suggested."

"He said you were a friend," Lorenzo said. "He told me
things about you which Papa himself doesn't know." We
walked in the dusk under myrtle, poplar, oak, and citrus
trees, alongside full, blooming flowers, wild orchids and
roses and lavender and well-tended lilies.

"There's more to the story of Nonno making his confession," Lorenzo said finally. "He went about asking pardon of
people for wrongs he'd done them." Lorenzo paused, looking at me. I said nothing. Lorenzo snapped, "You know as
well as I do that there are too many people hurt by him for
him to obtain forgiveness from all of them!"

"Your grandfather exalted his friends and crushed his enemies."

"Exactly. Things will be difficult now." Lorenzo pulled a
plum from a tree and took a voracious bite before continuing. "The Medicis' enemies will see weakness and want to
strike at us. There must be plots afoot already. I cannot let
the house of Medici be taken down! I must live up to Nonno
and his legacy, protect what he built!"

"Your father will not retain power for long," I agreed.
"He has not the health nor the stomach for it. He'll be lucky
to survive five years in power."

"Don't say those things!" Lorenzo barked. He tossed the
plum pit, then ran his long fingers through his black hair.
"I love Papa. But it's true. I don't know if he has the strength
to respond decisively when the strike against us comes. We
need our friends more than ever now, Luca Bastardo!" He
laid his hands on my shoulders, swinging me around to look
at him.

"I have been and ever will be a friend to the Medicis," I said, meeting Lorenzo's eyes squarely. Abruptly he released me.

"Good. Here's what I need you to do: wander around Florence and listen for plots against us. Socialize, mingle freely."

"I try to avoid that, given my history."

"I sent Pietro Silvano out of Florence on business, and I'm making arrangements to buy orders in the Church for two of the young men in the family. The Silvanos will be dispersed. It won't be long before I obtain the letter that you fear; I employ some men who are skilled burglars. You will be protected from the Confraternity of the Red Feather, Luca Bastardo."

"I would like to have that letter in my possession," I said grimly.

Lorenzo smiled and looked away, and I guessed that he wasn't about to turn it over to me. The leverage was too important to him. He said, "You and I will meet discreetly. I'll feign some coolness, some distance from you. Nothing overt, but people will think I've some small displeasure with you. It'll make you seem trustworthy to those who plot against us."

"Sending me into the front line again to draw out the opposition, Lorenzo?"

"You won't get clobbered this time." He smiled. "If you do, you're a survivor, you'll be fine. But you'll be even more of a hero!"

"Let's go back in," I said wearily, knowing that I'd let myself in for danger and intrigue by traveling down this road of an alliance with Lorenzo de' Medici. "I'd like to pay my respects to your grandfather's body and offer condolences to your grandmother and father."

We walked in silence back into the villa. When we entered Cosimo's chambers, a sad sweet song greeted our ears.

Someone was playing the lute and singing, with such haunting sorrow communicated in the lyrical timbre of voice that everyone in the room wept. I looked through the milling mourners, and, of course, it was Leonardo. He stood near Cosimo's bed, where the body lay in state. Leonardo held a lyre and sang with his eyes closed, his entire being thrumming with loss and love, which are inseparable, and dog us as long as we live on earth.

Cosimo de' Medici was buried with as little pomp as the city could be persuaded to show him, in accordance with his wishes. He was interred among a huge, solemn assembly of fellow Florentines before the high altar of the church of San Lorenzo, the Medici church. The plain slab over Cosimo's tomb carried his name and the inscription Pater Patriae, father of his country. I remembered him best as a somber boy with big dreams, all of which had come true.

I BEGAN A NEW LIFE IN TUSCANY. It was a sweet life and for a time, the two Gods seemed to maintain a truce, keeping a peace in the battlefield of my life. Caterina gave generously of herself and asked little, which made things even sweeter. Early on I inquired about her Cathar connection. We lay together in the room I kept at the inn for this purpose, which seemed safer from Leonardo's incursions, or Ser Piero's for that matter, than her room. I was running my fingers along her beautifully shaped back, smiling to imagine her as a child playing happily in Anchiano, when I remembered what Leonardo had told me about her ancestry.

"Caterina, is it true that you are descended from Cathars?" I asked.

She lifted her head so that her blond curls swept over the

pillow. "You've been talking to my son." I nodded. She rolled onto her side to face me. "It's a private matter."

"My parents traveled in the company of Cathars, or so the story goes," I said, stroking her white shoulders, which were rounded with muscles from lifting heavy trays at the tavern.

"Really?" she asked, propping her head up on her palm. "What do you know of Cathars?"

"They were mystical Christians from Christ's time who wandered, eventually settling in the Languedoc, where they practiced charity and purity. They were slaughtered by the Pope."

"The siege of Montségur." She sighed. "The Pope's troops burned alive more than two hundred Cathars. But some survived and fled. My ancestor, for one. Those few tried to keep the old knowledge, the old lineage alive, to retain the old tolerance and charity."

"I heard that Jews were among them at one time."

"That's true, although we saw the creation differently," she said. "We believe in a good God who is pure spirit and a lesser God, a blind and deluded God, who created the earth. For us, the Hebrew God Jehovah was a fool, and the Serpent was a benefactor who taught Eve the truth about spirit and matter. Eve was the teacher of her children, of all humanity."

"If there were not two Gods, why would there be suffering, disease, betrayal, murder, and cruelty in the world?" I said. "There must be some truth to the Cathar beliefs."

"This world is full of pain, Luca mio." She nodded. "But I often wonder about two Gods. I think that's too crude an understanding. I think maybe there's the God we all know about from the Bible, who is jealous, who is a master and a king and a creator and a judge, and then there's a deeper understanding of God as the source of all being."

"Most people stop with the first God," I said.

"Yes," she said, laying her beautiful cheekbone down onto her hand. "But perhaps that's just an image of God, not really God."

"The Church would not like your interpretation," I said, stroking her soft hair. "Bishops claim to rule the world in God's place, by means of the same hierarchy through which God rules the earth from heaven. If people stopped accepting God as a king, they would stop accepting the authority of the clergy, who are the king's representatives on earth. They burn those who question their authority, their order."

"I keep my thoughts to myself." She smiled. "I've told no one except my son the tales of my people. But I want the tales preserved. They go back even before Christ. We've always been the keepers of secrets, since the beginning of the world. For us, Christ was the fulfillment not just of the prophecies of the Hebrews, but of all the old secret traditions that spoke of the divine spark. The spark that is lit by that Source that I think is God. Christ came to reawaken man to the knowledge of that spark, like a star, trapped within people since Adam's time. Christ was an incarnation of Eve's son Seth, who fathered a race of people with unusually long life spans."

I sat bolt upright in bed. "Unusually long life spans?"

"Luca mio, have I startled you?" She caressed my thigh. "It's an ancient tradition of my people. We speak of these Sethians who were gifted with lives that last centuries."

"Do they carry the mark of heresy on their chest?" I asked.

"Calm yourself, caro. They don't have any mark on their chest, that's a silly rumor spread by the Church, like the superstition that Jews have horns. The Church spreads ridiculous tales about things it doesn't understand, or that it fears! But perhaps this rumor came about because Melchizedek the priest, who was a Sethian, bore a mark in the shape of a sun on his chest. He also possessed the robes of Adam, and handed them down to Abraham, who paid tithes to him."

"What happened to this Melchizedek?" I exclaimed. "Were there others like him?"

"Peace, Luca." Caterina sat up and moved around behind me to massage my shoulders. "I don't know much more. The old tales are incomplete among my family."

"I'm peaceful! Don't you know anything else about these long-lived people?" I pleaded.

She pressed her warm, soft breasts into my back, embracing me. Her sweet breath moved along my cheek. She said softly, "One other thing, caro. This Melchizedek could travel in special ways. He could move through time and space with his mind to see anything."

I LIVED FOR TWO YEARS IN ANCHIANO. Inspired anew by Caterina's Cathar tales, and reassured by her that Sethians did not bear marks on their chest, I took up again the practice of sending out hired agents to seek information about my parents. I was hopeful that the woman from the marketplace whom Silvano and others had seen was my mother, and perhaps someone still knew something, even from so long ago: a scrap of a family tale, a legend of an unusual babe, an alchemist who'd baptized a child with magic, anything. It seemed logical that my parents and I were related to this Melchizedek, and that my parents shared my longevity and hardiness. My inquiries were vaguely worded but designed to elicit the attention of secret Cathars or people with peculiar longevity. There was no response, as if I had no antecedents but had been germinated on the streets of Florence, the product of its gray stones coupling with the river Arno.

Periodically dreams perturbed my sleep. I never saw the

face of the woman from my vision, but I yearned for her. I could even smell her, a fresh delicate scent of lilacs on a spring morning and lemons and things that were white, like clear light and mild clouds. It was as if I already knew her from choosing her during the vision of the philosopher's stone, and now I missed her. It was a secret lovesickness for a woman I hadn't met yet. It infected me even though I cared deeply for Caterina. I reflected on what Caterina had said about the secret song no one else could hear and on what Leonardo had said about my not being ready for love, which echoed the Wanderer's question to me when I left Bosa decades ago: Was I saving my heart or protecting it? If I was protecting my heart, was that why I hadn't yet met her? How could I ready myself for her? I couldn't answer these questions, so I busied myself, practicing with my sword and racing Ginori for hours all over the Tuscan countryside. Mostly I tutored my young charge, Leonardo, son of Ser Piero.

Leonardo eventually finished the buckler, painting on it a wondrous and horrifying creature emerging from a dark cleft in a rock. It belched forth venom from its open throat and fire from its eyes and poisonous smoke from its nostrils in gruesome fashion. When Leonardo presented it to Ser Piero, on an easel in a shaded part of his room, it looked like the fearsome creature was springing out of the wall. Ser Piero jumped and shrieked. Leonardo was delighted. Ser Piero wiped his brow and praised his son lavishly, going so far as to clap me on the shoulder and tell me that I was doing a good job with the boy.

"I stay out of his way and let him teach himself," I told Ser Piero honestly. "Your son is a great genius who's ready for better teachers than me." Ser Piero's eyes narrowed as he took in what I was saying. He was a tall, stately-looking man, strong and with a quick mind one would call canny or shrewd, rather than intellectual. He grasped the import of my words immediately.

Leonardo saw his father's mind working and ran over to lay his hand on his father's arm. "Not yet, Papa! I like my professore. I have more to explore here!"

"You do have great talent," Ser Piero said, picking up the buckler. He examined it closely, smiling. Ser Piero was, like all good Florentines, mercenary at heart, and I saw numbers being calculated in his head. Whatever his former plans for the buckler were, he now planned to sell it. I decided to send an agent to purchase it from him.

"I can go to Florence when I'm sixteen," Leonardo said hastily. "I'm still learning so much from Luca! Besides, he's much cheaper than any master in Florence will be!"

"Very well, since you want to stay." Ser Piero nodded, pursing his lips. "Besides, I don't want your pretty mama to miss you too much!" He winked at me and I struggled to keep my face straight. It was well known in Anchiano that Ser Piero, with one barren wife after another, had great fondness for lovely Caterina, who'd produced this extraordinary son for him. He still visited her; I'd been forced to clamber out her window on a few occasions, just in the nick of time, with my camicia and shoes tumbling down after me.

So Leonardo continued in Anchiano, under what was laughably called my tutelage, but which was really his own program of discovery into all things natural. He was obsessed with flying, and like Icarus made wings for himself out of different materials: wood, animal bones, wax, parchment, leather pasted over with real feathers. More than once I rescued him from a cliff moments before he was to leap. I bought him a notebook, as promised, and he filled it with drawings and ideas, writing in the small backward script that he claimed was magical. Here, now, in this small cell, awaiting my execution, I can see what halcyon days those were. I lived with Leonardo the boyhood I'd never been allowed to have.

At the same time, I was insinuated into Lorenzo de' Medici's affairs. At only fifteen years old, he was entrusted with daunting responsibilities. He was already building a core group of intimates and advisers he could trust. He was dispatched on diplomatic missions to meet Federigo, the son of King Ferrante of Naples; to Milan, to represent the Medici at the marriage of King Ferrante's elder son to Francesco Sforza's daughter, Ippolita; to Venice to meet with the Doge; to Naples to see the king himself. On most missions, Lorenzo sent me ahead for reconnaissance. I was to take the pulse of the place and to listen to the gossip on the street. I knew how to blend in, to joke with cobblers and beggars and lords, and to flirt with ladies' maids, who always had the best information.

Lorenzo directed me to listen for news in Florence, as well. In 1466, after the death of Francesco Sforza, the ruler of Milan and Cosimo's staunch ally, I brought Lorenzo news of a plot about to simmer over. I'd taken Leonardo into Florence for the day and we had wandered through Santa Maria del Fiore, arguing about paintings and sculpture. We stopped at the left-hand wall of the nave in front of Paolo Uccello's painting of Sir John Hawkwood, the great condottiere who had served Florence well and earned her goodwill. I liked the painting, as I had liked the man, having met him before he died in 1393. Leonardo had another opinion.

"I like the terra verde monochrome, which makes reference to antique equestrian statues and honors the condottiere as the successor to the great Roman commanders," Leonardo said. He was fourteen now, and shooting up in height so rapidly that he stood as tall as me. He was saying "But, look, professore, this fresco has two different systems of perspective: the sarcophagus looks like a tomb projecting from the wall, while horse and rider are portrayed in strict profile with clear contours against the dark background."

"Perspective wasn't well worked out during Uccello's time." I shrugged, enjoying, as always, the give-and-take with the precocious youth.

"It still isn't," Leonardo said, gesturing with his beautiful hands. "I will perfect it. I will be famous for it; people will talk about my work for generations."

"I'm sure you will. And I will still appreciate Uccello."

"You can ogle this mediocre painting, I'm going to look at the clock Uccello painted; time and timekeeping interest me," Leonardo sniffed. He went off and after a while I went to sit in a pew and look up into Brunelleschi's marvelous Duomo. This was my form of prayer, the reverence I had it within me to tender: perusing, admiring, and adoring beautiful art. Creeds and faiths and myths of virgin birth and crucifixion meant little to me, convinced as I was that human life was a joke that brought laughter either to an ill-tempered divine intelligence or to a kind one, according to their engagement in a war no man understood. In beauty, in art, I found peace. I found freedom and redemption.

It was only a few minutes before Leonardo came back. "Luca, Luca," he whispered. His face was puckered with worry. "There are men over there talking, and you should listen. I think they're plotting against Lorenzo's papa! I heard them, and then I had one of those glances into the future that come over me: blood on the road to Florence!"

I went with him toward the front of the church. We moved nonchalantly, and when we stood in front of Uccello's clock with its star-shaped hand and twenty-four-hour cycle of the day, we heard men speaking in low voices. Something about the shape of the cathedral carried their words to us. I stood still, listening. When the voices stopped, I knew what I had to do.

"We're leaving at once for Careggi," I told Leonardo. "I'll take you home first."

"I'm going with you," he insisted. "I always like talking to Signore Ficino."

LEONARDO AND I ARRIVED at the Medici villa in Careggi in the afternoon, our horses soaked in sweat. I didn't like riding Ginori so hard, except for such urgent need. The Moorish servant took the horses, telling me that Lorenzo was in the garden with Ficino and others. I ran around to a side entrance with Leonardo at my heels. Ficino and some visiting Greek scholars sat on benches beneath the poplars with thick afternoon sunlight dappling their shoulders. I greeted them hurriedly and asked for Lorenzo.

"Lorenzo has gone inside," Ficino said. He turned to Leonardo. "Young signore Leonardo, you're taller every time I see you! Tell me, have you returned to finish our discussion about finding the daimon who will lead your life?"

"The daimons are the unnamed spirits who motivate and guide life." Leonardo smiled. "You say that whoever examines himself thoroughly will find his own daimon. I say that I go deep into myself to see how deep is the place from which my life flows. That's how to live a soulful life!"

"I say I have to find Lorenzo de' Medici right now," I growled with great impatience, "or life won't flow well for any of us!"

"Inside. Piero's ill again. He came an hour ago from Florence in a litter." Ficino waved.

I bolted inside toward Cosimo's old chambers, which

were now inhabited by the invalid Piero. When I reached the chambers, Piero was being made comfortable. Lorenzo sat on the edge of the bed, talking to his father, while servants bustled around.

"Excuse me, signori," I called. "I have urgent news for you!"

"Easy, Bastardo, is the house on fire?" Lorenzo smiled at me.

"Would that the Lord would grant me that kind of energy," Piero said. He wasn't a bad-looking man, especially as the Medici went, with his determined chin and well-proportioned features, but the droopy eyelids and swollen glands on his throat made him look sleepy and ill. I knew him to be patient and courteous, and because of my long experience as a physico, I guessed that what others perceived as a certain coolness in his character resulted from prolonged physical discomfort. His lips compressed and I knew that he was in pain again, and my heart sank. Florence needed him to rise to the challenge that was now facing him.

"The Medici house may catch fire," I said, motioning for the servants to leave. "Leonardo and I were at Santa Maria del Fiore and we overheard men discussing the insanity of Sforza's son in Milan. They said that with Piero ill and the Medici's ally Milan in the hands of a lunatic, Florence is alarmed, faith in the Medici is low, and now is the time to strike against the Medici!"

"Nonno made an alliance with Milan the cornerstone of his foreign policy," Lorenzo said, leaping to his feet beside me. "He did not foresee the jeopardy we would be placed in upon Sforza's death! Luca, who did you overhear?"

"Dietisalvi Neroni and Niccolo Soderini. I heard them, I didn't see them," I admitted. "There are others involved, and a request to the republic of Venice and to Borso d'Este, the Duke of Ferrara, for armies to march against you. The Duke of Ferrara agreed."

"The other conspirators would be Agnolo Acciaiuoli and Luca Pitti," Lorenzo said, pounding his fist into his hand. "Papa, we must act!"

"It could be idle chatter." Piero sighed, scooting down beneath the linen sheet. "People talk, it's hot, it's August, armies don't like to march in the heat."

"Papa, Luca Bastardo was well beloved of Nonno, who trusted him! I have found that Luca is a most reliable man. You must listen," Lorenzo urged. "This confirms other rumors with which I did not want to disturb you in your illness!" He gripped his father's arm in his own. Piero blinked his heavy lids a few times, and then let Lorenzo pull him to sitting.

"We will need a ruse, about how I've heard of this," Piero muttered, stroking his sweating brow. "I don't know why, but your nonno always protected Bastardo's identity."

"I have dangerous secrets—" I began, hoping my confession would prod him into action.

"I don't want to know." Piero sighed, waving. "Papa knew, Lorenzo knows, I don't need to know. I just need a ruse."

"Scusi, signori," Leonardo called from the doorway, smiling in that beatific way of his that always got him out of trouble. "I couldn't help but overhear. For a ruse, wouldn't a messenger who's just arrived with a letter serve nicely?"

Lorenzo snapped his fingers and crowed. "Yes! A letter from the ruler of Bologna, who is friendly to the Medici. The messenger says the letter's urgent, there's a plot against you afoot!"

LESS THAN AN HOUR LATER, Lorenzo and I were galloping into Florence. To our happy surprise, Piero roused himself, readied his litter, and sent us ahead to prepare for his arrival. I rode a spirited black stallion, one of Lorenzo's horses, because it would have been unkind to run Ginori again. I knew courageous Ginori would have gone flat out for me until his heart burst, but I didn't want him to endanger himself. Lorenzo rode a leggy bay with a smooth stride, and we flew along the road to Florence. We rose over the crest of a Tuscan hill, and in the thick, slanted light of late afternoon, I saw dark shapes on the road ahead. Something about the sinuous dark silhouettes of the horses against the ocher and gold Tuscan field stirred the hairs on the back of my neck. My keen old sense of the presence of danger kicked in and sent frissons of cold down my spine. Leonardo spoke of blood on the road to Florence. I was willing to trust his prescience because I, too, had gazed into the future.

"Lorenzo," I called, "slow down! Those men are dangerous!" Lorenzo glanced across his horse's withers at me. Once he saw my serious face, he slowed down until we were both trotting. There were six horsemen. We had to get past them. My mind went blank for a moment, and then, like a ghost from the past, a favorite ditty rose up. I sang, loud and raucously, "She loved my MASSIVE tool so she never ever denied me her favors!" Startled, Lorenzo did a double take. But he was ever quick and shrewd. He caught on instantly. He tucked his black hair up into his hat and then slouched down low over his horse. He joined in, affecting a basso unlike his usual high-pitched voice, and I thought it was lucky that I'd taught him the lyrics. Lorenzo had a taste for bawdy songs, lewd jokes, and ribald stories, and that saved him now.

"That Napolitana with the huge juicy melons and the sweet ripe figa," we chorused, riding right into the center of the milling horsemen. I spied among them a nervous Luca Pitta, who was no longer young, and a determined-looking Niccolo Soderini, though neither knew me. They were clearly waiting for someone, either for allies and reinforcements to join them or for the Medici. It would not go well for Lorenzo and Piero if Lorenzo was recognized. I waved sloppily and hiccuped. "She loved my massive tool," I bawled, and then slumped, as if drunk. The milling riders guffawed, except Pitti, whose age put him past those kinds of amorous considerations. Lorenzo and I didn't stop but kept trotting on, and when we'd dropped below the next crest, Lorenzo straightened in his saddle.

"That was Soderini and Pitti, did you see? And their scum friends! I owe you a cask of Chianti for getting me through!"

"Only if it's better than what we were drinking the night I taught you the song," I said. Indignation at the conspirators flushed Lorenzo's young cheeks crimson. The heat of his anger reached me where I sat on the black stallion. Lorenzo's enemies would pay for their disloyalty.

"Go back and warn Papa to take another road," he barked. "I'm on to Florence!"

INSTEAD OF BEING OVERTHROWN, the Medici consolidated their power. They took decisive action over the next month. The first day, upon my warning, Piero found a seldom-used road to take. His unexpected appearance in Florence unnerved the conspirators, and over the following weeks, he summoned his men at arms, sent to Milan for help, and arranged for the election of a pro-Medici Signoria in the forthcoming elections. The handpicked Signoria was duly elected, and the power of the Medici was assured. Soderini, Neroni, and Acciaiuoli were all banished from Florence while Pitti begged forgiveness and swore an oath of fealty.

Later on in the year, Lorenzo brought me to Rome. He was sent to congratulate the recently elected Pope Paul II on his ascension. Of course, though he was still a teenager,

Lorenzo had business to conduct, as well, regarding the valuable alum mines at Tolfa. Alum was essential in dyeing, which was a huge part of the Florentine cloth industry. Until recently, most alum came from the East, particularly Smyrna; in 1460 huge new deposits were discovered at Tolfa near Civitavecchia in the Papal States. The powerful Medici bank smelled revenues and naturally wanted to control and exploit this valuable find. Lorenzo was sent to discuss it personally with the Pope. To my amazement, Lorenzo went so far as to bring me in during a private meeting with the Holy Father.

The Holy Father was a handsome, imposing man who laughed when he heard I didn't know if I'd been baptized.

"I can remedy that," the Pope said, in a jocular tone. He placed his hand on my head and spoke in a sonorous voice. "I baptize you with the Holy Spirit, in the name of the Father, the Son, and the Holy Spirit." I felt a soft flow like a clean wind from his hand into the crown of my head. It reminded me of Geber's consolamentum: it was a true transfer of something spiritual. It wasn't part of my personal faith and I was startled. I sat back on my heels, staring at the Pope.

Paul II grinned. "Bastardo, eh? I'm sure your parents were good Christian folk, Luca; a fine, handsome face like yours would only come from such. You don't have to keep the surname. I can grant you something more honorable that you can leave to your children with pride."

"You are more than generous, Holy Father," I answered, with new respect, "but I think it rests on me to bring honor and pride to my name, not the other way around."

The Pope raised his eyebrows. "You're not one of those pagan humanists, are you?"

"I'm a man who grew up on the streets of Florence and is trying to make something of himself."

The Pope nodded. "There's something noble about you. You have the look of a good Christian soul. I want to encourage your faith as you proceed in your life. Young Lorenzo tells me that you live outside Florence. Do you own a place in the city?"

"No, signore," I said, having long since liquidated my holdings in Florence.

"The Church owns property in Florence. I will see to it that some suitable palazzo is deeded over to you," the Pope said.

"What?" I gasped in disbelief.

Paul laughed. "It's a papal inducement to righteous Christian living. I expect you to take a wife who will bear children that you will have correctly baptized and catechized."

Of course I wanted my future children to be properly raised in Florentine society. "Holy Father, thank you for your generosity!"

"Of course." He smiled. "Be good to young Lorenzo here. Like me, he is going to need friends who protect him. He'll make enemies, though I foresee a long, illustrious career for him." Paul II sighed then, and wiped his hand across his face. "I wish I could say the same for myself," he muttered. Then he bade us farewell.

And so Lorenzo and I rode back to Florence along another turn in the road, and I started yet another phase of my life in the city of my birth in a lovely palazzo given to me by a pope, the head of Christendom and the Vicar of Christ on earth.

Chapter 18

THE TIME CAME FOR LEONARDO to leave my tutelage.
He was sixteen, and Ser Piero, as he often did, brought him
to my palazzo one day when I was in residence in the city. I
first thought it was an ordinary visit, but one look at Ser
Piero's august, withdrawn face told me that something was
afoot and that Leonardo didn't know about it yet.

"Welcome," I said to them. I turned to Leonardo, who
was now taller than I. "Ragazzo mio, your friend Ficino says
there are some new manuscripts in the Medici library. Why
don't you run along and take a look?" Leonardo didn't have
to be told twice. He brightened and waved and was off to
the Medici palazzo on Via Largo, which wasn't far from my
own palazzo, a spacious manor that Pope Paul II had selected
for me.

"My cook made an excellent *ribollita* for lunch," I said to
Ser Piero. He shook his head and sat down heavily on a bench
in my foyer. Now I knew something serious was occurring;

Ser Piero had refused my offer of a meal. I sat down on a bench across from him and waited.

"I've shown the painter Verrocchio some of Leonardo's drawings," Ser Piero said. It was a cool March day, but he mopped the sweat from his brow.

"When does Leonardo start with him?" I asked, affecting a neutral tone that belied my sadness. I'd known this day was coming. I just hadn't expected it to be today. Leonardo was as close to kin as I had. My inquiries about my parentage failed to turn up any more information than that nobles in the company of Cathars had lost a son in the 1320s. I suspected that Lorenzo de' Medici had the old letter about it, but he wouldn't turn it over to me. And the woman from the vision of the philosopher's stone remained frustratingly aloof, as if kept from me by the time that fell like fabric from the sky in Leonardo's Cathar tale. I yearned for her more now that I lived in Florence and never saw Caterina, whom I missed. Leonardo was my family, a kind of son to me. I would miss him.

"Tomorrow, the next day. Verrocchio was amazed. I asked him if it would be beneficial for my son to study with him, and after a moment of looking at the boy's drawings, he was pleading for Leonardo to start his apprenticeship today!" Ser Piero looked at me in proud fashion. I tried to smile but couldn't. He said, "You're not surprised."

"No, signore."

"You're familiar with his astonishing intelligence, of course," Ser Piero muttered, more to himself than to me. Then he looked up at me. "Has he made any progress on the Latin?"

"Not really. Ficino's tried with him, too. There seems to be a gate in his mind that's closed against learning it," I said honestly. "As if he had made some prior decision not to learn the language. I haven't pressed him about it. Leonardo is like a wise old horse that already knows the way up the mountain, so you give him his head and don't interfere."

"I know what you're saying, and he is so good at everything else." Ser Piero gestured.

"Especially mathematics," I remarked. "I taught him everything I knew in a few months, and now he just laughs at my feeble attempts to discuss it with him!"

"You've done great work with him, signore. He's enjoyed your scholarship." Ser Piero heaved himself to his feet and moved toward the door with a rapidity unhindered by his bulk. "I've business to attend to, Luca. You'll tell the boy, yes?"

"You haven't told him? That he's apprenticing with Verrocchio?" I was flummoxed.

"That's your job, don't you think?" he said, scooting out the door before I could argue.

THE MEDICI PALAZZO ROSE, square and impregnable, directly from the street in three immense stories and ten bays to a side. The three stories were graduated in height like those of the Palazzo delle Signoria, emphasizing the Medici connection with the city politic. In every way, Cosimo's favorite architect, Michelozzo, had designed the palazzo to impress. Its huge mass had replaced twenty earlier homes, and it showed a kinship with the imposing fortress-towers which had once dotted Florence, and where long ago, even before my birth, warring nobility had lived. The Medici had thus managed to demonstrate both their dominance and their connection with the old traditions of Florentine aristocracy. I passed through the main portal and smelled citrus trees and the pleasant dampness of shade on stone. Then I entered into a handsome inner courtyard with an open arcade supported by classical columns. Sculpted roundels suggesting the ancient Roman intaglios of the vast Medici collection decorated the frieze above the arcade, and everywhere was the Medici emblem: seven *palle*—balls—on a shield.

The number of palle was fluid, not fixed, and the palle were said to represent either dents on the shield of the original Medici, a knight named Averardo who fought under Charlemagne and received the dents in a heroic fight against a giant terrorizing the peasants in the Tuscan countryside, or the round shape of pills or cupping glasses, as the Medici had originally been apothecaries. Some people said the palle represented coins. I thought the undefined shape was a brilliant ploy by the shrewd Medici. It allowed people to see in the balls what they wanted to see. The Medici knew how to engage the imagination, and thus the hearts, of their countrymen.

On a pedestal in the center of the courtyard stood Donatello's sculpture of David. I admired its technical brilliance and its daring in being the first freestanding nude created since antiquity. However, the sculpture was unnecessarily erotic, with its sinuous, girlish hips and its strutting posture emphasized by teasing high boots. Why should David be so provocatively posed? Only to please those men who loved other men. I remembered all too well, wishing I could forget after so many decades, the patrons at Silvano's. There was no surpassing or understanding the labyrinthine nature of desire.

My own desires lacked complexity. I simply enjoyed women, their soft skin and long silken hair. So I pursued my own simple desires and did not judge other men unnecessarily. My shadowed past and the dark deeds I had committed to survive made that imperative. Moreover, Donatello had been a good friend when he died, the same year that Piero was almost overthrown. Still, because of Silvano's, I had difficulty being comfortable with men who loved other men.

I found the ever-ebullient Leonardo in a sunny corner of the courtyard, chatting with a scrivener who sat on a marble bench, taking advantage of the mellow weather to copy a manuscript outdoors. The Medici employed dozens of scriveners to copy their manuscripts, either to sell them for profit or to present them as gifts to foreign rulers and thus curry favor. It was impossible to visit the Palazzo Medici without tripping over one of these supercilious men.

"Professore!" Leonardo cried. "Isn't this a manuscript you sent to Cosimo?"

"The *Corpus Hermeticum?*" said the scrivener, a narrow, thin-lipped man with ink-stained hands and a high, arched nose. He sniffed. "I don't think so. This manuscript came into the Medici hands in '61. Your professore with the big coarse muscles"—he rolled his eyes, finding it humorous that I would be a teacher—"would have been a young man your age!"

"I'm older than I look," I said.

"And more discerning?" The scrivener smiled, looking down his nose at me, which was a feat, considering that he was seated and I was standing.

"I don't know," I said easily. "But I'm discerning enough to hope you have other skills, signore, than copying manuscripts. I hear there's a new process for printing from movable type that will soon make your skills obsolete."

"My skills will never be obsolete," the man argued shrilly. "That is a vulgar process, practiced among barbarians in some German city. Real collectors like the Medici would be ashamed to own a printed book made by some gross mechanical process!"

"There are printing presses in Napoli and Roma. Soon there'll be one in Florence. They make good sense; they turn out books cheaply and quickly. They'll catch on," I said. "You should learn a new trade, just to be on the safe side. Sheepherding, maybe."

"You have a low and common mind, signore," the scrivener hissed. He gathered his manuscript to his chest and flounced off in a huff. I took his spot and sat down beside Leonardo.

"That was not kind to poor Armando," Leonardo chastened me.

"I don't like pretentious scribes."

"I think you're right about the printing press. You know that when I daydream, I feel as if I catch a glimpse of the future. I've seen things like the world full of books that are inexpensive and abundant, that everyone reads, because of the printing press."

"An interesting world you see."

"As did you; I often think of the vision you told me about, the very first day I met you. But something's amiss. Luca, you have something to say, and you're not happy about it," the young man said suddenly. He wore a yellow and pink lucco that he'd shortened himself, whose flamboyant design he'd probably foisted on the ever-permissive Caterina, and ragged gray hose with holes in them. I knew he owned at least two pairs of fine, unblemished hose, because I myself had taken the grumbling Ser Piero to the tailor to purchase them. But Leonardo eschewed them for these torn old things; he had his own unique sartorial taste.

"You are too perceptive, ragazzo," I said. "You read me like Armando's manuscript."

"Better than that, I hope." Leonardo chuckled. "Armando copies Latin, and I'm terrible at reading Latin! I feel like I used to know it and don't want to be bothered anymore."

"Your father has apprenticed you to Verrocchio," I said baldly, not to delay it more.

"But I do read you," Leonardo murmured, as if I hadn't

spoken. "Sometimes it's like a light pours forth from people, and I can just barely make it out. Your lights are like veils with torn places for the light to shine through, almost un- willingly. The holes in your lights aren't empty, they're full. Full of secrets. You harbor secrets, Luca Bastardo. Secret gifts, secret fears. And the hand of fate is upon you."

"All men have secrets."

"Not like you." He shook his golden head. I looked into his finely sculpted face and noted that auburn stubble dark- ened his cheek and chin. His beard was coming in. I'd have to take him to a barber to be shaved and instruct him in car- ing for the beard. I should have done so before now. I had been remiss. I was turning him over to Verrocchio unfin- ished, like one of Leonardo's own sketches. Part of me had known that Leonardo was entrusted to me for only a short time, but another part of me thought our time would con- tinue without an end, as my own life seemed to. Despite the great spans I was unaccountably allotted, I did not under- stand time. There were things I had meant to teach my young charge, to say to him, and now I wouldn't have the opportunity. I tore my eyes away and found my gaze resting on the David.

"You don't like Donatello's sculpture," observed Leonardo.

"I liked the artist."

"Why don't you like it?" he asked.

"It's not that I don't like it," I replied. I closed my eyes, seeking a greater honesty with him, now that we were part- ing. "Something from my childhood. It makes me uncom- fortable to remember it." I opened my eyes and the young man was gazing steadily at me.

"Your childhood. That was long ago, wasn't it, Luca Bastardo? There's an old panel that the nuns at San Giorgio own. There's a boy in it, an onlooker, he has your face. I've studied it many times, to be sure. The coloring, the features, it could only be you, professore. I know this. What you said to the scrivener is true: you are much older than you look."

I let my breath out slowly, nodded, turned my eyes up to the sky, remembered Giotto's beautiful panel of St. John's ascension, the infinite blue sky into which the saint so gracefully rose. I whispered, "Giotto painted that panel. He showed it to me without telling me he'd put my face in it, and then when I recognized myself, he laughed and told me that a man who knew himself would go far in life." It was a relief to admit this to someone I could trust, someone who wouldn't use my past as leverage against me. After more than a century of protecting my secret, of hiding the inescapable and alienating fact of my great age from other people, it gave me chills to speak it now, openly and without fear.

"Ficino says things like that," Leonardo said in a neutral tone of voice. "Ficino likes to get his friends together at banquets and have discussions, and he talks about the immortal soul. What is the soul? Can it be known? Is it even a thing? Is it essence? Is it the same as spirit, incorporeal and invisible? I think soul is a quality or an amplitude, that it has to do with imagination and love and nature. I'm not much interested in talking about it when there's so much to explore in nature that isn't nebulous.

"Ficino says the essence of each person originates as a star in the heavens. But what is a star, that's the better question. What is the sun, what is the earth? By what rules do they operate? Any intelligent man who studies the night sky realizes that it is the earth that moves around the sun, not the other way around! Stars are natural objects; can they really determine human destiny? Ficino would refer you to a horoscope to understand your unusual longevity. He's a brilliant man, but his astrology, so like necromancy, is supreme foolishness." The boy shook his head. "Could a star

grant you a life that stretches past a hundred years, professore mio?"

"There are men who say my long life and youth arise out
of necromancy and enchantment," I admitted.

"That's the point," Leonardo said, with some satisfaction.
"Necromancy and enchantment don't exist except in the
minds of fools! There must be some natural reason for your
long life span. Internal to your body, perhaps." He perused
me up and down, examining me as if I were some specimen
on a table, as I used to see in Geber's laboratory. "Too bad we
can't examine your parents to see if you inherited your gifts
from them, as one inherits hair color or a particular shape of
the nose, or if your longevity is yours alone. I remember you
told me when we first met that your parents were attended
by Cathars. Perhaps this longevity is the great secret which
brought them together with Cathars, who are keepers of secrets."

"I've looked for my parents. There are one or two small,
insignificant questions I'd ask them," I said, with humor and
regret and a trace of the old longing.

"I know you looked for them." Leonardo smiled. "You
used to quiz me and my mother about the Cathars, and then
the next day your agents would come to your cottage at the
vineyard. I'd hide outside and eavesdrop on your instructions to them."

"So naughty, poking into other people's business!"

"You wouldn't have it any other way." He flashed his dimples at me in his old, boyish way, treating me to that smile
like the sun coming out from behind the clouds. "There's another Cathar legend. After Satan created the world through
rebellion, God sent to earth an angel who had remained loyal.
That angel was Adam, the direct ancestor of my mother's
people, the Cathars. But Adam was captured by Satan and
forced to take human form. Since Adam lived in this form

against his will, he was saved, with all his descendants. And Adam was the father of Seth, who in turn fathered a race of long-lived people. Perhaps you're one of those sons of Seth."

"Caterina told me about Seth, and I've always wondered about that," I admitted. "But I don't know for sure that the nobles who lost a son were my parents. I simply don't know how to solve the riddle of my years. Perhaps my soul is too earthbound to free itself," I offered, with both irony and whimsy. If I didn't know my origins, at least I knew myself. I knew that I was not particularly soulful, in the way Giotto and Petrarca had been, and Leonardo and Ficino were, and even the magnificent, manipulative Lorenzo was, with his poetry and statesmanship and athleticism. I was literal, dogged, not particularly creative, though I revered creativity in other men. I could not paint, sculpt, or write in verse. My gift was something I could not claim credit for. I could only shrug it off as a rich joke for whichever God wanted the diversion.

"The *Corpus Hermeticum* would imply that you have an abundance of the fifth essence beyond the four physical elements; it would say that there's something particular about your arcanum, that your arcanum is a larger receptacle of the celestial effluvia that pours down in a torrent through the souls of all species and all individuals. But I don't think so." Leonardo raised his golden-brown brows. "I think your longevity results from something that can be measured and examined in nature. Something about your organs renewing themselves, perhaps, or the structure of your organs, or the amount and healthfulness of your physical fluids. It's an interesting question. I wish I knew more about organs; someday I shall make a great study of the mechanical structure of man, to reveal the inner mysteries. Then I will know about you, Luca. I believe that Ficino's mystical soul will come back to merge with the body in some way. I don't wish to be considered heretical, but I think"—he paused, his eyes alight—"that the soul resides in the seat of judgment, and the judgment resides in the place where all the senses meet, which is called the common sense; and the senses of hearing and vision and smell and touch pass through the body, the body is the vehicle. . . ."

"You're to start with Verrocchio soon. Maybe tomorrow. He was most impressed by your sketches and begged your father to let you start even today," I said. "You will have a great career as an artist, ragazzo mio. The world will know of your genius. Fortune and fame are yours!"

"I will get old before you do, Bastardo," Leonardo answered, with some sadness. He stared into me, as if he saw clearly the starlike essence that other men sensed but couldn't quite perceive. In a musing voice, he said, "I don't know if I will die before you, though. . . . I think you have other secrets, dangerous secrets that Lorenzo de' Medici knows and uses to keep you tied to him. I see the way you look at him, with distrust and anger and respect."

"I will always be your friend," I said softly. He wasn't going to discuss his apprenticeship and our parting. It was too close to his heart; he had, after all, chosen me as his teacher. I rose and stood in front of Leonardo.

"It will be a few years before I see you again, ragazzo. Apprentices work day and night to learn their craft. They are always at the beck and call of their master. Verrocchio will keep you busy, as he should." I put my hand on Leonardo's shoulder and was surprised to feel the consolamentum start, the soft lyrical flow of something, a transfer of spirit or whatever natural thing Leonardo would want to call it. It originated in the warm lucent percussion of my heart and moved into the young man seated on the marble bench in front of me. His face softened and he smiled, closed his eyes, and drank in the flow. The radiance around him which always made him seem more vital than other people seemed to expand and brighten. I waited until the flow of the consolamentum slowed, then I took my hand from Leonardo and placed it on my heart. "It has been my joy and my honor to spend time with you. You have enriched my life."

Leonardo's eyes were damp and he blinked rapidly and looked away. He could not answer and I finally walked out of the courtyard. "I will discover your secrets, professore," he called after me. "And I will find a way to help you with them!"

SO LEONARDO PROGRESSED to a better teacher than me. It left more of my time available for Lorenzo's use, and he took advantage of that. When he was nineteen, his mother, Lucrezia, chose the Roman aristocrat Clarice Orsini as a bride for him, which scandalized Florence. For him to marry outside Tuscany was tantamount to a betrayal, especially when Tuscan women were the most beautiful and intelligent in Christendom! But canny Lorenzo preferred to scandalize all of Florence rather than to anger particular families by choosing one Tuscan bride over another. He also liked the advantages of the alliance with a wealthy family of old nobility that had important ties to both Roma and Napoli.

In June 1469, the match was made.

A few months later, early in December, Piero the gouty died. Two days after Piero's death, a solemn delegation from the city asked Lorenzo to assume its guidance. He accepted, though he was only twenty, and as vigorous and lusty as any newlywed twenty-year-old man. But Lorenzo immediately showed his perspicacity and his fitness for the position he'd inherited more from his grandfather Cosimo than from his sickly father, by appointing a council of seasoned men, myself included, to advise him. I remained in the background, though.

The Silvano clan was dispersed from Florence, but that might be temporary. And they had friends. The Confraternity of the Red Feather awaited a resurgence of the Inquisition and other instruments of the Church's intolerance. Besides, other men might notice that I didn't age as they did. Circumspection behooved me. So Lorenzo kept me busy with private errands, sensitive diplomatic missions, the carrying of secret messages to foreign ambassadors and princes, and the like. Sometimes I arranged for a woman to meet him; Lorenzo had an unquenchable appetite for the fairer sex, as I did, though I planned to be faithful when I married. I did not judge him for his adultery. I had committed too many dark acts to sit in judgment of other men, and besides, Florentine men of wealth deemed it their right to keep mistresses. Lorenzo considered himself first among Florentine men, with all accompanying privileges. He was on course to lead the city to greater glory, both for itself and for the Medici, when the path of history turned. Generous Pope Paul II, a good friend to Lorenzo, died in 1471, and the Franciscan Francesco della Rovere ascended to the papacy as Sixtus IV.

One fine summer day in June of 1472, Lorenzo summoned me. I thought it was to discuss another of the carnivals and pageants with which he entertained Florence, and which endeared him to pleasure-loving Florentines. I was strolling in the Mercato Vecchio with Sandro Filipepi, who inexplicably called himself by the name Botticelli, which was his brother's nickname. We meandered through stalls of pink strawberries and red raspberries and cured ham and silver fish brought in from the sea and tables set with fresh game like grouse and deer. We joked and negotiated the price for a tondo of a Madonna and child that I wanted. It wasn't for devotional reasons, or perhaps it was, considering how I felt about art. Sandro painted in a graceful style, depicting bodies that were at once ethereal and voluptuous;

his female figures were celebrations of beauty and femininity, light and receptivity. I was intent on acquiring one of his works to place in my personal collection and accord the reverence it deserved.

"It doesn't matter how much I pay you; you'll piss it away immediately," I said.

"Then you should pay me a huge amount so I can piss like a stallion!" Sandro said, laughing. He was a good-humored, intelligent man who was also kindly and appealing, with deep-set eyes and long, flowing locks of which he seemed inordinately proud, a large nose, and a prominent cleft chin.

"Fifty florins is a huge amount of money."

"One hundred florins is twice as huge." He made a hand sign that referred to a man's parts. "I'll make a much bigger puddle!" I had thrown up my hands and was laughing when Lorenzo's Moorish servant hailed me. Sandro patted me on the shoulder. "You're off at the beckoning of our magnificent Lorenzo, who wouldn't quibble with me over fifty florins, but I'll see you in Careggi a few days hence, for Ficino's dinner, yes?"

"I'll be at Careggi. Sixty florins," I called, walking toward the Moorish servant. After all, someday I would make a gift of Botticelli's painting to my wife. I felt that I was ready for her, and prophetic Leonardo, whose companionship I missed, had told me that when the heart was ready, the beloved would appear.

"Seventy-five!"

"Done!" I agreed. Sandro laughed and clasped his hands overhead in a victory sign.

"I'd have done it for fifty, I like the subject matter!" he said.

"I like your work, I'd have paid a hundred!"

"Maybe you still will," he yelled back good-naturedly. I

would have answered him, but the Moorish servant touched my sleeve.

"Signore Lorenzo requires your presence. Will you take my horse?" he offered, and gestured to the outskirts of the mercato, where horses were tied up.

I shook my head as I dug out a coin for some of the fleshy orange apricots, which the vendor passed me with alacrity. I bit into the sweet, juicy fruit, chewed, and then answered, "It's a fine day to walk, and it won't take me long. Tell your master I'll be there shortly."

TOMMASO SODERINI AND FEDERIGO DE MONTRE-felto, the Duke of Urbino, were already there when I arrived at the Palazzo Medici and went into Lorenzo's opulent chamber, with its marble floor and coffered ceiling. The men stood by one of Paolo Uccello's three paintings of the battle of San Romano, paintings of the sort which were usually hung in government buildings to commemorate state military victories. The placement of the paintings in Lorenzo's private chamber gave the room the air of a prince's hall or public council chamber. Yet the grandeur of the room could not distract me from a sense that something serious was transpiring.

"Kind of you to join us, Bastardo," Lorenzo said coolly, and I knew he was displeased that I'd arrived at my leisure. "We were just discussing the new Pope, Sixtus."

"He's been polite, and he renewed the Medici management of papal finances," I said cautiously, coming to stand beside Soderini, who wore a gloomy face.

"Polite but cool," said Soderini, an older man who was devoted to Lorenzo. He'd been horrified at the attempted coup against the Medici, and had since become one of

Lorenzo's closest friends and staunchest supporters. Some men thought Soderini was the only man in Florence who could disagree with Lorenzo; in fact, Soderini and Lorenzo worked together in harmony, their friendly antagonism maintained for show only, so that Florentines could maintain their cherished illusion of a republic. Now Soderini turned to me. "Our old rivals, the Pazzi, are making overtures to him. He finds their blandishments congenial."

"The Medici have been the papal bankers since early in Cosimo's career," I said. "Would Sixtus disrupt this time-honored arrangement? It's been lucrative for everyone."

"Besides, Sixtus is consumed with foreign interests," said Federigo. He was a fifty-year-old noble, renowned both as a master of warfare and a patron of the arts and of learning. His palace in Urbino was said to be the fairest in Italy, and his library rivaled the Medici library. He was built as I was, lean with hard muscles rolling on his frame, and he was handsome enough on the left side of his face, though the right side lacked an eyeball and bore scars from a tournament injury in his youth. I knew him to be honorable, a man who kept his word, but I had never quite trusted him. In his quest to win every battle, he laid siege to cities and left the weaker inhabitants, that is, children and women, dead. Whatever men wanted to do should be done to consenting equals, and not forced on those who were smaller and weaker. I believed this with every fiber of my being. Federigo went on, "The Pope promotes his crusade against the Turks and the Church's authority in France, where Louis XI insists on the French church's independence. He also wants the re-unification of the Russian church with Roma."

"You've left out the most important promotion: his nephews' interests," said Lorenzo tensely. "He wants to put Florence under their control, and they're incompetent fools."

"What's the immediate problem?" I asked, knowing that there must be one, or Lorenzo wouldn't have sent for me. I clasped my hands behind my back and waited.

"Volterra is rebelling," said Soderini. "We have to send troops."

"Alum mines are the problem," Lorenzo said, in his nasal, measured tone, "money and alum mines. The Medici bank furnished the capital to those who were given the concession to develop the mines when the mines were discovered a few years ago. In return, the contract for mining the alum went to a consortium consisting of three Florentines, three Sienese, and two Volterrans. The Florentines were my men, of course. Now the mines have proved lucrative. And the Volterrans, with the town behind them, are demanding a bigger cut of the profit."

"It always comes back to bribes," Soderini said, pacing around us. "The contractors are bringing the matter before the Signoria. I know from talking to them that the Signoria will vote that the profits should go to the general treasury of the whole Florentine republic."

"It's natural that Volterrans want the money for Volterra," I commented.

"That's what we're counting on. They'll revolt, and I'll march immediately on them to quell the rebellion," said Federigo blithely. He came from an illustrious family of soldiers, all of them leaders of great mercenary armies of condottieri, and he made his fortune from conflict. "The effect of victory is enhanced by its swiftness, and my army is ready to move!"

"Wait, you mean the Volterrans haven't revolted yet?" I asked, astonished.

"They will," Lorenzo said. He and Federigo exchanged a pregnant glance. "They're notoriously turbulent. They've been looking for an excuse to assert their independence. They think I'm too young to act decisively, that I'll placate them because I'm weak."

"In the Signoria, I'll suggest that a show of force is unnecessary and provocative," Soderini said, nodding. "I'll recommend conciliatory measures; I'll remind the Signoria of the ancient proverb, 'Better a lean peace than a fat victory.' It'll emphasize Lorenzo's boldness. His resolution and foresight will be publicly demonstrated."

"The Volterrans will serve as a fine example of what happens when my authority is countermanded," Lorenzo said with satisfaction. "They'll be a lesson for all the towns under the sway of the Florentine republic. I won't have Florence losing territories that my nonno worked so hard to annex! I'll prove myself worthy of his legacy by strengthening the Florentine borders! Moreover, Sixtus will see that I don't falter, that I'm willing and able to raise an army to defend my interests. It'll send him a message, as well."

"You're sending troops against a town that hasn't rebelled yet, hoping it does so you can crush it? Will you even wait for the revolt? How many civilian Volterrans will die to prove your point?" I asked angrily.

"As few as necessary." Lorenzo shrugged.

"But some will, and they will be women and children!" I snapped.

"Sacrifices to the general good." He waved. "You'll ride with Federigo, Bastardo."

"I don't fight innocent people," I growled. "I've seen too many innocents die. No good comes of it! It creates hate, and hate makes more destruction! Lives are ruined! Generations carry the blight!"

"I could ruin your life with documents in my possession!" Lorenzo barked. I gave him a stony look and he softened. "I'm not asking you to fight, Luca mio. I want you to do what you do so well: take the pulse of the people, keep your ear to the street. Tell me what's going on. You're my eyes and ears in Volterra. Are they getting the lesson? I'll pull back as soon as they submit. You can help minimize casualties."

I could hear the sound of a battle rumbling on the horizon, but it wasn't Lorenzo's lesson to his territories. It was the old antagonism between the good God and the evil God. There was no evading it; there never was. I could only commit myself to the side of kindness, as best I knew it. If I obeyed Lorenzo, there was a chance I could save lives and help the Volterrans. "You'll listen if I get word to you that conflict is unnecessary?" I asked, uneasy.

"I always listen to you, Luca. I trust you," Lorenzo promised. "You get the word to me, and my army moves out! The fighting's over!"

"I myself won't fight the Volterrans," I said. "As long as you understand that."

"Of course not, Luca, you're there to observe and to moderate," Lorenzo said. "I don't want innocent people hurt, you know that."

IT WAS A JUNE MORNING ruffled through with a clean sea breeze, and the hills around us undulated green and gold with olive groves, cypress valleys, and vineyards. But the wild Volterran landscape wasn't entirely domesticated. It had raw vistas of stark, forbidding ravines, clay-walled chasms, high cliffs, dark woodlands, and a long view down to the Tyrrhenian Sea. The profile of the city was visible on the highest sandstone hill, at the junction of the Bra and Cecina rivers. Gray stone walls hundreds or even thousands of years old snaked around the town, which was situated southwest of Florence. I rode Ginori at the front of Federigo's army, but off to the side of the main phalanx of troops, at a distance to shield me from their filth and clamor.

Armies are loud, dirty, uncouth beasts. Even at the distance at which I rode, I couldn't escape the cacophony: horse hooves striking the ground and men's feet stamping, armor clanking and shields creaking and the ends of pikes dragging sibilantly in the dirt, the heavy large wheels of Federigo's massive iron cannons thumping along the ground, supply carts rattling in the rear, and drumming and trumpeting from musicians practicing during the march. Over it all was the babble of voices, shouting, laughing, singing, as if death, destruction, and dismemberment were something to celebrate. The air was thick with stirred-up dust. It was also rank with the smells of sweaty bodies and with the foul scents of human and animal urine, excrement, and sputum that any army on the march produced. Behind the ranks of soldiers were the auxiliary personnel necessary to any moving army: priests, physichi and barber-surgeons, blacksmiths, farriers, armorers, leather-workers to maintain saddles, grooms for the horses, and so forth. At least there were no women trailing Federigo's army. As a serious professional condottiere captain, he eschewed the usual practice of bringing along a contingent of prostitutes for the soldiers. I was looking again at the high green mountain on which Volterra perched, when Federigo trotted over from the main corps to ride beside me.

"It's beautiful," he called.

"And very well defended," I observed. "It's only approachable from one side, near the church of San Alessandro. The other sides are heavily fortified. What's your strategy?"

"We're going to ride right up the accessible side and ask them nicely to open the gates," he said, smiling with the good half of his mouth.

"You'll say 'pretty please'?" I responded, with some skepticism.

"That would be a nice touch, don't you think?"

"And just like that, they open the gates for you?"

"Surely I make a good argument for it." He winked at me with his one good eye, which seemed an act of courage, considering that he was a one-eyed man sitting astride a monstrous beast of a gray stallion that was trotting along at a good pace. But then, no one could accuse Federigo Montrefelto, Duke of Urbino, of cowardice.

I turned in my saddle to look at the ten thousand footmen and the two thousand cavalry troops. "You make twelve thousand good arguments," I said.

"Nope. I make one thousand good arguments," he said. "But we'll pause first. I want Mass said for the troops. It's good to focus the soldiers' minds on our Lord. In case we have to fight." He kicked his horse and steered back toward his army.

"Why one thousand?" I called.

"That's the number of condottieri the Volterrans have hired to defend themselves!" he called, before galloping back to disappear into the rank and file of his soldiers.

EXACTLY AS FEDERIGO HAD PREDICTED, the Volterrans opened the gates to him. He assembled his vast, expert army in front of the approachable side. The usual taunts and insults were flung back and forth over the Volterran walls. Then Federigo sent in a messenger to invite the Volterran leaders to talk. I wasn't at the conference, but I heard later that Federigo pointed out to the Volterrans that their condottieri were overawed by his army, and that they were likely to turn on the Volterrans and do violence to them. Mercenary soldiers other than his own were not to be trusted, they were little more than organized bands of brigands, out for profit, apt to change sides to protect their own hides. He must have been compelling, because the Volterran leaders scampered back into the city and opened the gates without firing a single arrow or drawing a single blade. And that was when death struck that town. It was completely undeserved and even more vicious because of the Volterrans' capitulation.

I rode into the city alongside the middle body of troops, and I was unprepared for the devastation before my eyes. It shocked me to my core. Red, orange, and blue flames leapt out of homes and shops. The hilly, uneven streets were littered with ransacked belongings: hacked-up furniture, shards of dishes, torn clothes, casks of wine and jars of olive oil toppled over and draining onto the stone. Animals had been loosed and horses, pigs, sheep, goats, cows, and chickens wandered through the streets, crying out. Condottieri from both the Volterran and the Florentine armies ran amok, breaking down doors, stabbing unarmed men, chasing women, carrying valuables out of buildings. Soldiers surged through the streets of the town, using pikes and swords to shatter windows from the outside, or heaving furniture out from the inside. They howled like animals over the hissing of fire and the moans of women and the shrieks of the elderly and the high-pitched, terrified screaming of children. I saw three condottieri chase a young girl down an alley and I leapt off Ginori to pursue them. The alley ended in a twisted maze of smaller alleys, and I saw one of the condottieri drop back and grab a cowering woman by the hair, so I grabbed my sword and plunged it through the back of his neck. He went down without a sound and the woman grabbed my knees and babbled. "Hide!" I told her, which was all I could do for her, and then I turned to find the girl. I had to protect her.

I ran down one alley, it twisted around and came to a dead end, so I turned, swearing, and sprinted down the next alley, and then the next. Finally, abutting the stone wall of some palazzo, I saw the two remaining condottieri. I was too late. One brute was hauling up his hose amidst a fit of guffaws, while the other, hose pulled down around his ankles, knelt, hairy thighs exposed, with one of the girl's legs stretched out underneath him. He cackled and waved a bloody dagger. He was finished despoiling her. Now he was amusing himself by carving into her skin. I charged him, pivoting through my hips as I swung my sword. All the unnatural strength at my disposal surged through me, and his head was sliced from his neck with a single long fast sweep. The head went rolling into a gutter and crimson blood spurted from the headless body, which toppled over onto the girl. The other condottiere was shouting and fumbling for his weapon, and I ran my sword through him, gutting him like a fish.

I turned to the girl. She wasn't making a sound and I feared she was dead, but when I pulled the body off her, she sat up. Her gonna was shredded, with the skirt torn off at her waist. She was covered with blood and other substances, and the condottiere had cut a deep crosslike mark into her thigh. She turned her agonized, tearstained face to me, and I could see that she was only about twelve or thirteen, in that middling age between childhood and youth, though her face already showed the breathtaking woman she would become. It was heart-shaped and delicately sculpted, with high cheekbones, large golden-flecked eyes bright with terror, and a wide pink-lipped mouth open in a silent scream. She seized the dagger from the hand of the headless soldier. I knew she meant to hurt herself. I grabbed it from her.

"Let me die," she whimpered, and the anguish in her voice couldn't hide its husky melody.

"No, no!" I told her. "You have to live. You will live. It seems like the end of everything, but it's not. You'll survive."

"I'm not worthy of living. I'm nothing now," she wept.

"Stop it," I said sternly. "You're alive, and plenty of people won't be after today. Your town will need you. Your family will need you. You have to help them." I looked around for the remains of her skirt, found it, and tore some long strips out of the fabric. "Your wound is deep, but not dangerously so. I'll bind it. Watch for infection over the next few days."

"How can there be days after today?" she cried.

"There just will be; time goes on," I said. I looked at her carefully. "You go hide. I've got to see if there are other children I can help."

"Aren't you one of the condottieri?" she whispered. I shook my head. She said, "Other children, you're right, they'll need help, I'll go with you to help them. . . ."

"No! Hide! You can't help anyone right now, and if you don't hide, you'll get hurt again. Hide in an alley or gutter, not in a building that can be torched." I was done tearing strips of cloth and I took a deep breath and made my hands very gentle as I laid them on her leg. I closed my eyes and felt myself soften, hoping to invoke it, letting myself surrender to my pity for this child, and it started: the consolamentum, the sweet warm flow like clean water through my heart and out my arms. The girl quieted, stopped crying. When the consolamentum ended, I wrapped her leg. "This may hurt, but it'll stop the bleeding."

"They killed my father," she said softly. "They were laughing. He was lying on the floor with his eyes so empty. I have no other family. There's no one to give me a dowry, so I'll never marry, and what man would want me now anyway? I'm damaged, soiled. I'm nothing now."

"You can't think that way," I said hoarsely, tightening one

of the cloth strips. I was sickened again by the cruelty with which grown men could treat a child.

"My life doesn't mean anything, with no parents, and now like this, and it hurt so bad, what they did to me!" She scrunched her narrow shoulders together and cradled her head in her arms. She had a thick mass of soft dark hair, but as she turned her head and sunlight caught her hair, I saw that it wasn't black at all. Her hair was a variegated chestnut color, tousled through with rich red, umber, black, and even gold strands. I'd never seen anything like it.

"Your life can mean anything you want it to," I said fiercely. "You are not what has been done to you, you're more than that! There'll be work here in Volterra, rebuilding the city. Helping other children and women. Concentrate on that, on helping them. That will get you through!" She nodded, but her face was so waxy and bruised with pain that I didn't know if she heard me. I was done wrapping the wound and I leaned back. "Hide somewhere safe—you know the good hiding places, children always do—don't come out for any reason until you hear the condottieri marching out of Volterra!" She scrabbled up onto her hands and knees and then up onto her feet. She swayed, looked down, and covered her nudity with her hands. I stripped off my blue lucco and gave it to her, and she slipped the tunic on over her head.

"Go," I said, picking up my sword. She ran and I made my way onto the street. Looting and despoiling greeted my eyes. I stuck my sword into the shoulder of a condottiere who ran past, chasing a woman with an infant at her breast. He went down with a scream which I silenced with a quick slit across his throat. "Hide," I called to the woman, who disappeared into an alley.

"Hide" was a word I repeated a thousand times. It was the only help I could offer. I was one man fighting through an army of twelve thousand, each of whom seemed intent on committing the most horrifying atrocities. I lost track of how many I killed, I just kept following screams. The condottieri were lewd and wild, intoxicated with their own brutality. They acted like stampeding animals, without discipline or thought.

I had just sent a condottiere into the afterlife to share the evil God's ribaldry when, out of the corner of my eye, I saw a familiar blue lucco fluttering. There was the girl, carrying a baby and leading four children across the cobblestone street from a burning wooden cottage toward a stone palazzo. The smaller children followed her in a line like ducklings behind their mother. People were still screaming and running in all directions, and I thought the children would make it to wherever the girl was leading them. Then shouts were raised. Three condottieri trotted laughing toward the children. The lead soldier broke into a run with his sword outstretched, the bloodied tip pointing directly into the round belly of the smallest child toddling at the end. I knew he meant to spit the child on his sword. I was faster than he was. The condottiere met my sword, instead of the plump tiny body of the toddler. His two comrades screamed and converged on me. But I had been wielding a sword for a hundred years, and even together, they could not hope to equal my skill and experience. They both lunged at me at the same time. I saw it coming with the first twitch of their thigh muscles and leapt out of the way. Then it was a lightning-fast parry, slash, back slash, and both men were dead on the street.

The girl kept moving across the street with the other children. I darted after them.

"I told you to hide," I said grimly, when I caught up with her.

"Pick up those two." She pointed at the toddler who had nearly been killed and another child in front of him who was only slightly larger. I grabbed one up in each arm and followed the girl toward the stone palazzo. She made her way to the back of the palazzo and went into a small pantry structure. "There's a cellar down here," she called. I followed her and she grunted and scooted away a flagstone on the ground. "I'm not the only one," she said, pointing. I looked down into a dugout crawl space. Several pairs of eyes looked up out of the dark hole; other women and children were already tightly packed in.

"Make room," I said, handing down the toddler. Silently the women shifted for the other children to climb in. The girl went in last. I touched her head gently. "Stay hidden now!"

"Condottieri dragged off their mother, and I couldn't let them burn to death," she said, eyes bright, and I knew she'd survive the day with her heart intact. It would take a terrible toll on her, but she'd survive. I pulled the flagstone back to cover the entrance, feeling sorrow for these people, but also relief that this one young girl would not let her essential self be destroyed.

For the rest of that long terrible day of the sack of Volterra, I stayed on that nameless street, near the cellar. I shut down my senses and went into some terrible place inside myself, a relentless, lunatic place where even the Gods' laughter couldn't penetrate. I slaughtered any condottiere who came close to the hiding hole where the girl was. They weren't men, they were dark moving shapes begging for the kiss of my sword. I wasn't Luca Bastardo anymore. Or, rather, I was the Luca Bastardo who had killed seven patrons and the proprietor of a brothel as a boy.

A sound beat against my ears. I was covered in sweat and blood and I was as tireless and obdurate as stone. A man was shouting. The man I was fighting was shouting. He was a skilled fighter, formidable, a challenge. He was trying to tell me something. I leapt back, sword ready. "What!" I demanded. There was a red mist before my eyes, and then dim gray streaks of light from the overcast sky unfolded. My hearing cleared with my vision.

"Holy Mary, Mother of God, how many of my men have you killed, Bastardo?" said Federigo. He was looking at me with horror writ on the good half of his face.

"How many women and children have your men raped?" I demanded. "How many old men have been cut down as they tried to defend their grandchildren?"

"I know, I know, it's bad," he muttered. With no warning, the sky spat down fat raindrops which a split second later crystallized into solid sheets of water. Federigo wiped the rain from his face with the hand that wasn't holding his sword.

"How could you let this happen? Wholesale rape and murder—I'll report it to Lorenzo!"

"Who do you think ordered it?" Federigo retorted. For a moment, the whole world stood still, as if some condottiere's axe had cleaved me in two. Of course, Lorenzo was capable of this, and he had lied to me when he said he didn't want innocents killed. "I don't like it, either," Federigo said, his one good eye turning away. "But don't you see the necessity? The Pope intends to control Florence, the territories plan to break free, everyone thinks Lorenzo is too young to hold the republic firm—everything is teetering on the brink. Lorenzo has to make a stand! He must show the world that he will lead and safeguard Florence as only a Medici can. My God, man, do you not know what will happen if the Pope puts his dimwit nephews in charge of Florence? They will ruin our city, and everything that the Medici have done, as patrons of art and learning and establishing the Platonic Academy, this will all come to an end!"

"And that's worth ruining lives for?" I asked bitterly. "Ficino's right to ramble on about the soul is important enough for little girls to be raped after watching their fathers killed?"

"We're talking about civilization," Federigo said with passion. "This is the price for it. Lorenzo de' Medici is a great leader who doesn't flinch from paying. We're lucky he has this strength, and future generations will thank him for it!"

"I don't see how civilization depends on the slaughter of innocents!"

"It depends on Lorenzo discouraging those who would seize his power and dismantle Tuscany," Federigo returned. "Florence is at the very center of everything, all the advances in art and philosophy. We have to protect her! Lorenzo's not happy about this. He's going to make reparations. He's coming here later to claim he didn't know this would happen."

"Reparations? To mutilated children? To women who will bear bastard children that no one will want to look at in nine months? People are dead, lives are ruined! For civilization? You can justify horror on this scale like that?"

"I've explained it to you, you can choose to understand or not," Federigo snarled. "Lorenzo needed an ugly job done and he chose me to execute it! I was paid for it and I did it!"

"That's why they call it whoring," I said softly. Federigo lifted his sword and I thought he was going to strike and I made ready to take him down. I would enjoy it, too.

He swore, then turned away with a contemptuous curl of his lip. He sheathed his sword and then hurried off to take shelter under the eaves of a nearby palazzo. I followed him and saw him take something out of his mantello and fumble with it. He bent over it anxiously, murmuring "I don't want the rain to ruin this, it's a rare polyglot Bible. . . ."

"You took a Bible?"

"I collect manuscripts, I have a library, and this Bible is beautiful and rare. . . ."

"You looted some Volterran's library and stole a religious

article? Is this more of that civilization that you're willing to defend at any price? What use is your civilization if it doesn't keep you from inflicting suffering on people?" I was repulsed, and under my gaze Federigo's jaw jutted out. I spat, "You're no better than the animals you lead!"

"This is war, Bastardo, it's not supposed to be pretty!" he snapped.

I felt the cool clean grip of my sword in my hand, and I wanted to kill him. But that wouldn't solve anything. It would only bring Lorenzo's wrath upon me. He'd want to punish me, but he wouldn't even do it himself. He'd simply recall the Silvanos whom he'd sent out of the city on various pretexts. "How much longer is the sack supposed to last?"

"Until sundown. I'm pulling the men back now. The rain will calm them, too, and put out the fires."

"Get your men off this street," I said bitterly. "Keep them away. Anyone who sets foot here is a dead man."

Chapter 19

MY LIFE CHANGED AGAIN after the sack of Volterra. That evening, the rains poured with such force that they set off a mudslide, further devastating the city. Federigo's troops marched out at sundown, and when the gates closed behind them, I pushed open the flagstone and let out the women and children who'd hidden in the cellar. One blue-veined, parchment-skinned elderly woman had died during the wait. I lifted her out and gave her to the other women to bury. I worked through the night to help the Volterrans tend to the injured. Men had lost limbs and women had been raped and sliced into, with that particular inhumanity that war engenders in the crazed minds of soldiers. The evil God seemed to have emerged from this battle victorious.

The rains stopped the next morning, though the sky remained overcast. I had once been told that a tea of cohosh root would prevent pregnancy, and I repeated that to many women, apologizing that I didn't remember how to prepare the tea. I reunited children with their mothers and I helped wives find their husbands and fathers and sons, whether dead or wounded.

By midmorning the next day I was hungry and tired, and I sat down against the rough stones of the city wall to rest. Everything hurt: my arms and shoulders and back from swinging my sword, my thighs from lunging, my throat from screaming, my jaw from grinding my teeth in anger at the destruction I'd witnessed. I was covered in mud and blood and I couldn't remember when I'd eaten last. I closed my eyes and banged my head back, gently, but with enough force to feel the ragged edges of the stones against my head. Then something grazed my fingers, and, wearily, I opened my eyes. A plate of food was thrust into my hands.

"You have to eat." It was the girl whom I'd been too late to save from the condottieri. She was now clean, her long hair plaited back away from her exquisite heart-shaped face, and she was wearing a nice gonna with a pale pink giornea over it, an incongruous color amidst the devastation.

"Come on, it's good, ham and hard cheese and bread with olive oil," she said softly. She was right, I had to eat, though my stomach still churned with fire at the wanton brutality I'd witnessed. Slowly I took a bite of ham. She watched me with her intelligent large eyes, which were pale brown with flecks of green and gold and even black against very white sclera. *Her eyes are as variegated as her hair,* I thought, though I did not know then that those eyes would haunt me for the rest of my life. Even now, I can still see them in all their hundred moods: narrowed and sparkling with laughter, or dancing with quick thought, or widened in playful mischief, or black pupils swollen with love and desire. She was like quicksilver, no one had more expressions and humors than she did. But back then, she was just a pretty young girl watching me eat, and I was almost re-

pulsed by my attraction to her. I had long since vowed, by
Giotto's art and by everything else I held holy, never to direct my lust at a child. I pretended to ignore her and ate with
more gusto. She gave me a tentative smile which I did not
acknowledge and moved away.

When I was done eating, I leaned my head back and slept
for an hour. I woke because someone was gently tonguing
my ear. In my somnolent state I thought it was the pretty
girl, which made me smile and roll my head around with
drowsy interest. Then I remembered how young she was
and I leapt to my feet with a startled exclamation. But the
lascivious friend was none other than my trusty steed Ginori.

"Ginori!" I hugged him unabashedly. He whinnied and
stamped, wanting to go home. "We can't leave now, there's
work to do," I told him. He rubbed his nose on me, understanding.

"I knew that was a friend of yours," said the girl, coming
up from his other side. "I saw him trotting around, sniffing
the air, and I just knew he was following your strong smell!"

"Anyone would smell strongly after fighting the way I
have."

"That's not what I meant!" She blushed. "I meant that
you're strong, strong and brave the way you helped me and
so many others, so you must have a strong and brave smell!"

"No matter how I smelled, Ginori would find me anywhere. This is one of the great horses of the world," I said,
laughing and scratching his neck. He was covered in muck
and blood, but as I ran my hands over him, I found no in-
juries.

"I'll wash him and brush him for you," she offered shyly.
She was clasping her hands behind her back and rocking on
her clogs, looking unbearably lovely.

"You have other work to do, ragazza," I said sternly, refusing to be charmed by her. "Volterra needs you now. Ginori is a grand old man and he's been in many battles. He knows how to be patient."

"Do you want more food? Or some wine? How about fresh clothes? You're wet and dirty, I can get you fresh things!" Her words tumbled over each other.

"I've been wet and dirty and worse, many times before."

"You don't have to be now. I've told people how you helped me. Volterrans are very grateful. They'll give you anything you need."

"I can take care of myself. If I need anything I'll scrounge it up." I shrugged. At this she sniffed and flounced off with her skirts twitching around her rump in a way that would be trouble in a few years. I turned back to Ginori, who nuzzled me, looking for food. "Big trouble in a few years," I told him. He nickered back. I led him out into the street to find food. When he'd eaten his fill, I meant to get back to helping the Volterrans reconstruct their lives.

LORENZO RODE INTO VOLTERRA in the late afternoon. With much fanfare, he arrived on one of his magnificent black stallions, surrounded by a chattering coterie of friends, advisers, and hangers-on. They were a group of about thirty men, looking clean and well fed and wearing the chatty, blank faces of those unscathed by tragedy. Lorenzo dismounted at the city gate and walked in, exclaiming in loud dismay at the sights before him. I was setting the broken arm of a young blond woman who'd been raped and beaten and left in an alley for dead. But people are always more resilient than they ever imagine they can be, and she'd crawled out of the alley to the makeshift staging area where I and the town physico and some midwives were tending the injured. We heard Lorenzo and his party enter the city and she lifted her bruised face up to me. I shrugged and she pursed her swollen lips over the gaps in her mouth where teeth had been punched out. I felt her arm bone with my fingers and it seemed straight, so I wrapped it with strips of cloth so it could mend. The pretty girl came over with a pitcher of wine and some cups tucked in a bag on her shoulder, and she poured the blond woman a cup.

"Isabella, your hair is messy, why don't I comb it for you?" the girl crooned, patting the woman's head softly as she swallowed the wine.

"I'm done," I said, tying the last strip. "I don't think you're bleeding inside. I can't be sure. Rest for a few days. Don't work yet. See how you feel in three days' time."

"Do you hear that, Isabella?" the girl asked. "You're going to be fine after some rest. Come, I'll wash your face and comb your hair." The blond Isabella stood, teetering. I reached a hand out to steady her but she flinched. It would be a while before Isabella could tolerate a man's touch, even one like me who was trying to help her. The girl braced her slim shoulder under Isabella's good arm and they struggled off. The girl gave me a serious look over her shoulder.

"These outrages are horrible, insupportable," said a voice behind me.

"Wasn't that the point, signore?" I said softly, staring into Lorenzo de' Medici's brilliant black eyes. Something flashed across his face and was quickly concealed. An expression of deep compassion spread over him and he nodded his head in the direction of Isabella and the girl, who were hobbling together into a palazzo where the injured were resting.

"This is appalling. I had no idea this would happen! The troops went berserk!"

"You had every idea this would happen."

"How can you say such a thing? I am horrified! Every Florentine citizen is horrified!"

"Yes, I imagine they are. As are all the other Florentine territories and Sixtus."

"Bastardo, what are you saying?" Lorenzo shouted. He strode away to where a ragged, wizened elderly man sat on a bench. The old man was curled into himself and Lorenzo, with a show of gentleness, picked up his arm to look at the sword cuts crisscrossing it. Fortunately for the old gentleman, the cuts were superficial. I knew they were painful, though, and he'd been waiting patiently for me to look at him. Lorenzo took the man's bloodied hand in his own and clutched it to his chest. Then Lorenzo turned to the growing crowd of Volterrans.

"My fellow Florentines and I are shocked! We profoundly regret this; words cannot say how horrible these outrages to Volterra are! I have come to make reparations!" He nodded to Tommaso Soderini, who scurried over to stand beside Lorenzo. Attending Soderini were two brawny Moorish servants straining to carry a heavy chest. Lorenzo nodded again, and Soderini opened the chest. Lorenzo brought out a gold florin. He held it up, but there was no sun to catch it, so it was just a dull yellow disk in his oddly refined hands. He looked out over the people, but they didn't make a sound.

"I am making restitution! I am distributing money to all who have suffered losses!" he proclaimed loudly. There wasn't a sound among the few dozen elderly people, women, and children who stood watching him. Each one was dirty and bedraggled; most wore bloodstained clothes; many were bandaged; there were no adult men among them. Lorenzo's black-haired head swung around as he looked into the crowd, seeking a response, but they simply surveyed him in stony silence. He tossed the florin to Soderini, who went into the crowd and handed it eagerly to a dark-haired woman with a bandage across her head. I knew what Lorenzo didn't, that she'd lost an ear when the condottiere who wanted to rape her couldn't get an erection and had bit it off. She was one of the lucky ones, though; her husband had survived. He had a stab wound through his thigh and it hurt him, but he'd live. As long as infection didn't set in, he'd live. Unsmiling, unspeaking, the woman took the coin from Soderini, then looked away. Soderini motioned hurriedly to the Moorish servants. They carried over the chest and Soderini dug into it, shoved more coins at the woman, then handed out coins to everyone assembled around him. No one said a word. Lorenzo watched the scene from a distance. I went to Ginori and took off his saddle. It was the very saddle Lorenzo had given me eight years ago, expertly crafted of supple, sturdy leather and well-worked metal fittings and the finest stirrups, worth a king's ransom, and like all beautiful things I'd ever been given, I'd taken excellent care of it.

"Your coins won't buy back their wholeness," I said. I tossed the saddle onto the muddy street in front of Lorenzo. "Nor will it purchase my services." He gazed at the saddle and then angled his face to one side, as if he were Federigo and had only one good eye to see with.

"I heard you killed over fifty of Montrefelto's good men," Lorenzo said in a tone that was half envy, half reproof. His eyes went to the sword at my side in a calculating fashion. I knew he was wondering if he'd have scored as high.

"How good can they be if they'd do this," I sneered, with a gesture that indicated the ruined town and damaged people around me, "even if they were under orders?"

Lorenzo nodded slowly. "You realize, my long-lived friend, I can't protect you if you won't place yourself under my protection."

"I'd rather have the devil's protection."

"That's what the Silvanos think, no? Soon they'll have a

letter in their possession to prove it." He smiled contemptu-
ously, and I knew I'd just made a bitter enemy. I didn't care.
I placed my hand on his shoulder, spoke in a low confident
tone so that only he could hear me.

"My dear friend Cosimo de' Medici would not have done
this," I said. "He would never have stooped so low. He
wouldn't have needed to." Lorenzo recoiled as if I'd stabbed
him, which, of course, I had. Lorenzo had grown up in the
looming shadow of a man who was worth two of him, a man
whose genius and accomplishment Lorenzo could hope only
to equal and not to better, and he knew it.

IT WAS NIGHT and long plum shadows fell in lattices of
fog around sodden, bloodstained Volterra. I was folding and
refolding the saddle pad, figuring out how best to protect
my testicles while I galloped a saddleless Ginori back to
Florence. Bouncing around unprotected on the withers of a
horse was hard on a man. I'd heard of gypsies and men from
the Far East who rode bareback all the time; perhaps if one
was born and suckled in a saddle as they were, it was an easy
feat.

"Maddalena," said a husky, lyrical voice behind me.

"What?" I turned and the curving white light from torches
held in brass fittings on the stone walls illuminated the face
of the young girl whose unusual beauty had captivated me.

"That's me, Maddalena." She smiled and held up a large
saddle with a quaint old-fashioned shape. I stared at the saddle in bemusement. She thrust it at me. "It's heavy!"

"This is for me?" I asked, clutching the saddle and feeling
foolish.

"They said you gave your saddle to Signore Medici. I
thought you'd need one. This was Papa's saddle. He won't

need it anymore." She sighed. I gave her a sharp look, saw that she was sad but not distraught. I was glad to see it; I have always approved of people who could bear their suffering with grace. It's an important skill in this world where the cruel God snickers at pain that the good God allows. I placed the saddle on Ginori, scooted it into position, and hooked the girth.

"Why did you give your saddle to the great lord?" asked Maddalena.

"For reasons of my own," I said vaguely.

"You're not very trusting, are you?"

"I trust that people will be who they are."

"Do they have a choice? How come you didn't tell me your name? That's what you're supposed to do when someone introduces herself to you!" She sounded indignant and I couldn't help but smile at her, though I knew I should discourage her interest. I knew that I must seem like a hero to this young girl whom I'd saved from a soldier's blade.

"I'm—"

"Luca Bastardo," she said. "There'll be a lot of bastards running around Volterra next year. Maybe they'll all call themselves 'Bastardo' and you'll have a big family!" A lilt quickened her voice and she fluttered her lashes; she was teasing me.

"Just what I always wanted," I responded, rolling my eyes. Then I sobered. "Perhaps the midwives can prevent unnecessary births."

"I hope so. I don't think they can help me. I'm too young to bear a child, but a woman told me I might not be able to have one at all after what happened." Her voice was neutral, but there was an undertone of anxiety in it. "I always wanted to have children, and I'm not so far from being old enough for a husband, some girls get married at fourteen and that's only in one year for me! Well, no man would marry me now, but if one did . . ."

I swung myself up into the saddle. "You'll find a husband. You'll have children."

She gave me an intent look. "How do you know that?"

"I've always found that the inner mind determines what happens to the body," I said, reining in Ginori, who pranced with desire to return home. "Someone who is ready to die, will. Someone who intends to live, will. Someone who intends to live fully, will. It's not complex."

"I hope you're right," she said shyly. Then she giggled. "I know I'll get a husband because I took a bunch of gold florins from Signore Medici and I'm going to save them for my dowry!" She covered her mouth with her small, fine-boned hand as if she'd said something naughty, reminding me again of how young she was. Young but practical; it was clever of her to save for her dowry. Marriage was everything for a woman. She stroked Ginori's neck and looked up. "Will you come back to Volterra, Luca Bastardo?" She stretched the syllables of my name out into a song, seductively, the way a grown woman would if she wanted a man. I swallowed, Maddalena saw my response, and she added flirtatiously, "I would like it if you did!"

"That's Signore Bastardo to you, ragazza," I said, struggling not to be seduced by her too-youthful charm. But I was drawn in by her, I couldn't help it, and as I steered Ginori away from her and toward the town gate, I smiled back at the lovely Maddalena. "Save your dowry for ten years, I just might come back!"

AS I APPROACHED THE WALLS OF FLORENCE by the milky first light, I spied a figure moving down the road among the farmers' carts headed for city markets. The figure was flame-shaped, indigo and orange in the wan light of dawn. Yet there was something bulky and familiar about it, about the man leading a gray donkey that kept stopping to graze. I touched my heels to Ginori's flanks and cantered up beside the man. The donkey bared its yellow teeth and brayed at us.

"I can't believe that beast's not dead, Wanderer," I called down.

"Why should he be?" said the Wanderer, his white teeth carving a smile in the thicket of his beard. "You think we're the only creatures lucky enough to stave off the inevitable?"

"My question is, is it our good luck or our bad luck?" I teased, overjoyed to see him, and at this very moment, when I was heartsick about Volterra.

"Isn't that the eternal question?" he hollered. I dismounted and we hugged, laughing and pounding each other on the back. He stepped back and looked at me. "The wolf is becoming a man. You're finally showing some years, Bastardo. There are a few good lines under your eyes."

"It's not the years, it's the struggle." I grimaced. I took Ginori's lead rope and walked alongside him. I could smell the donkey all the way over on the other side of the Wanderer; I'd forgotten how the animal stank. I shook my head. "What brings you back to Florence?"

"The question is, what brings you back? What are you going to do now that you've pissed off your protector?" he said, running his gnarled fingers through his bushy beard.

"How do you always know what's going on? Where do you get your information?"

"The whole world is brimming with information, if you're willing to listen," he said with a twinkle in his eyes. "I told you this before: 'In the beginning, when the King's will began to take effect, He engraved signs into the heavenly sphere.' There are no secrets, just men not willing to pay attention to the signs around them!"

"Let me guess, you have a few ideas about what I should be doing," I said wearily.

"Are you satisfied with your education? You never pursued what you started with my old friend Geber," he said. "Now he's transmigrated into the soul of your artistic young friend—"

"I don't believe in that, I told you once before!" I said, with some impatience.

The Wanderer shrugged. "How else do you explain so many things?"

"Jokes for some laughing God!"

"You and God's laughter." He shook his head. "One day you'll become reconciled to God, and find not laughter, but a heart of living song. . . . It's simple fact that the soul's presence in the body means it hasn't completed its work, and that it must transmigrate until the work is finished, until all is repaired, until it has wound through every branch of the tree of life. The work of creation is slowly refining the mirror of existence into a higher and more subtle state in order to reflect in every man a more lucid image of God. Then the soul can return to its source."

"You and Marsilio Ficino with your talk about souls emanating out of the Godhead," I said. "What use is it? Does it make our lives better? Does it prevent war, rape, looting, murder, the death of innocents? Ficino just gets depressed and has to listen to music to come out of it!"

"I like the sound of this Ficino." The Wanderer smiled. "He has potential."

"You should meet him, definitely."

"That sounds like an invitation; I accept. You have a big house in Florence, yes? But no wife yet. Donkey and I will keep you company. We'll help you set up a workshop like

Geber's, so you can get back into your circles of instruction." The Wanderer winked.

"Just what I wanted, guests," I grumbled, but I wasn't displeased. I had to fill my time some way, now that I had quit Lorenzo de' Medici's service. I thought of sharp-tongued Geber, and the months I'd spent with him as he slowly succumbed to the plague. He'd died without teaching me what I really wanted to know: how to transmute lead into gold. That would be a worthy skill, especially now, with Lorenzo angry at me. There was no telling if my money, saved so carefully over so many years, would be safe at the Medici bank, or if Lorenzo would find a way to confiscate it as punishment. Lorenzo was vindictive; Volterra had proven that. I said thoughtfully, "Alchemy might hold some interest for me now."

"The transformation I am talking about is not one of simple matter," said the Wanderer, straightening his torn gray lucco. "Though what is base can be transformed when work and worship are one. It all starts with the heart, with learning to submit the heart."

"I don't like submission, but I understand work."

"Start where you are." He shrugged. "That's where the doors will open."

SO I RETURNED TO MY PALAZZO in Florence and began a new phase of my life with two houseguests, the Wanderer and his donkey, though the latter lived in the stable. The Wanderer helped me turn a spare room into a workshop like Geber's. He would disappear after breakfast and return for dinner with items he'd discovered in a pawnshop or in the garbage behind an apothecary: beakers, a still, an alembic, flasks, a rare ebony mortar one day and a good alabaster pestle the next. I scoured the markets and met with merchants and purveyors of rare goods for other items: parchment, vials of dye and ink, clay, various powders and elixirs, waxes and pigments and oils, salts and minerals, the desiccated bodies of animals and insects, feathers, seashells, and eggs from a wide variety of species of birds and lizards. I accumulated samples of sulfur, mercury, and vitriol, indeed, of all seven of the alchemical metals: lead, iron, tin, quicksilver, copper, silver, and gold. I also looked for useful books. I didn't start experimenting with how to turn lead into gold, but I made everything ready for the quest.

A few months into my preparations, I came home from the market with a vial of frankincense. I was pleased to have obtained this rare and precious substance, and eager to show it to the Wanderer. I ran up to the workshop, and there was the Wanderer beside a tall, bearded, auburn-haired youth, both of them perusing a book spread out on the table.

"I didn't know you had company," I said, and both men looked up. I looked into the face of the bearded young man, and then I cried, "Leonardo!"

He seemed to leap over the table to embrace me, and I couldn't believe how he'd matured. He was truly a man now, at twenty. He laughed. "Professore mio, it took you long enough to recognize me! And here I have your face in my mind always!"

"How are you? What are you doing here? How is your mother?" I stepped back from him but held on to his arm through his sleeve, I was so delighted to see him. He wore a luxurious lucco of fine orange silk with silver embroidering, and he had attached well-puffed-up sleeves with black and yellow stripes. I noted that his lucco was much shorter and tighter than fashion allowed and figured that he was still up to his old tricks, coaxing Caterina into tailoring for him and then cutting the hemlines.

"Mama is well, she sends her love. And I've been admitted to the Company of St. Luke, the guild of apothecaries, physicians, and artists," he said. "I've more freedom now. I thought I'd come see you. I heard your name mentioned the other day, in a way I didn't like, by our old friend Lorenzo de' Medici."

"That man is no friend of mine."

"That explains it," Leonardo said, gazing into my eyes. "I was at Verrocchio's and Lorenzo came in. I was working on an angel for one of Verrocchio's paintings. He talked to Soderini, who was with him. They must have known I could hear them." He paused, arching a golden-brown eyebrow at me to see if I took in the implications, and I nodded. He went on, "Lorenzo spoke of recalling someone to Florence. Someone who didn't like you."

So that's how it would play out, exactly as I'd thought. Lorenzo wouldn't do anything to me himself; he'd call back the Silvano clan, and they'd take care of matters for him. I affected a neutral voice and asked Leonardo, "How did the angel come out?"

"Fine." He smiled and looked away, as if he were pleased and trying not to crow. He had grown not only tall, but well muscled, with wide shoulders and arms that looked power-ful even in the extravagant sleeves he favored. He walked back over to the table and stood next to the Wanderer.

"I heard the angel was ravishing. Verrocchio swore he'd never paint again, when he saw the angel," said the Wanderer, gesturing in the air with his thick fingers.

"He's just being dramatic." Leonardo waved away the Wanderer's words. "Luca, I brought you a gift. And when I arrived, your friend was here." He indicated the Wanderer, who waggled his bushy black-and-white eyebrows. Leonardo laughed. "I feel like I've met him somewhere; did you intro-duce us when you were my teacher?"

"Yes, you and I are old friends," said the Wanderer, with

his broad grin bisecting his wild beard. I shook my head, hoping to forestall a conversation about the transmigration of the soul.

"It wasn't necessary for you to bring anything, your presence is gift enough for me!"

"I thought you'd like it, the *Corpus Hermeticum,* Ficino's translation." Leonardo indicated the book on the table. "A nice copy done by hand, though I'm sure you like those new printed books! We talked about it once. . . . I see you've set yourself up a rather nice workshop, professore. Why? Are you going into the apothecary business, or the manufacture of paints?"

"I'll leave paints to you. I'd like to fulfill some old alchemical aspirations."

Leonardo shook his head. "Alchemy, ugh, such nonsense, you know what I think about that, but I am intrigued by some of the animals you've got here. Like this, what is it, a wildcat? Or a dog?" He indicated one of my recent purchases, procured from a merchant who made forays to the Far East and brought back novelties. In truth, neither the merchant nor I had known what the animal was. I liked the mystery of it and bought it for my workshop.

"I don't know what it is, Leonardo. Why?"

"Mmm, curious," he said, bending over it. "Would you mind if I cut into it, to look at its innards?" But he was already looking around on the table for a knife to cut with.

"I guess you'll be staying for dinner," I said.

"Probably longer," he muttered, turning the dead animal over and examining its spine.

"I'll have the maid set up a room for you. Put on an apron so you don't ruin your lucco."

"Look at these claws, and the teeth! How odd!" he said, as if he hadn't heard me. He glanced up. "I'll work as quickly as I can, but it'll take me all night to work my way through all its tissues and organs. You know it's going to start smelling."

"Take as long as you need, I don't mind the odor." I beamed, happy to have him around.

"You won't say that tomorrow when the smell wafts through the whole house." He laughed. "Smudge pots help, if you set some up with pine or cypress in them."

"I hope you like company," the Wanderer said. "I think you'll have a lot of it now."

And, for the next few years, I did have.

Chapter 20

"SODOMY, LEONARDO?" I snapped. I was striding away from the austere Palazzo della Signoria with its stone bell tower pointing up like an angry, admonishing finger. Leonardo walked beside me, having been released by my intervention with a committee that oversaw public morality. If this charge were ever proven, he faced imprisonment.

"What do you want me to say, professore mio?" he asked quietly, his melodious voice hoarse with emotion. "I am embarrassed enough without your disapproval. This is a shocking indignity. Why should I be singled out for public accusation when there are so many men who engage in congress with other men? Many men are open about their affairs!"

"You and your friends were going to pay some, some b-boy?" I stuttered, so incensed that I couldn't look at Leonardo. My stomach twanged like the broken string of a lyre, roiling with sick, unnatural sounds. "Do you know what it's like for a boy to submit to that? Do you realize that boy will forever see himself as a piece of shit because of his dealings with you?"

"Not a boy, Luca. A man."

"Still! A man! Sodomy!"

"I am a grown man with passions and needs!"

"For the love of a man?"

"Luca, can you not have known?" he said in a taut voice. "All these years we've been friends, all the time we've spent together—I am twenty-four next week, you've been my teacher since I was twelve—you didn't realize what I am?" He laid his hand on my shoulder and I shrugged it off.

"It's insupportable. That you could be . . . this."

"I don't force my will on anyone, nor does anyone do that to me. This is not about men who desire children. It's about men who desire other men, equals."

"I don't judge other men often."

"Nor should you. You have a different woman every month. You dallied with my mother when my father still bedded her!" His gaze was steady and guileless. I looked away. "I am leaving Verrocchio's," he said, pulling his peach and green wool mantello with the ermine lining closer around himself. It was April, overcast and threatening to rain, and a cool wind tunneled through the gray stone streets of Florence. I took a turn toward the Arno, quickened my pace along the flagstones. Leonardo matched his steps to mine and said, "It's time for me to have my own studio. I'm accepting commissions so that I can afford the rent."

"You know if you need money I'll lend it to you," I said miserably, sensing the distant strains of divine laughter. Part of me wanted to shun Leonardo; the larger part of me loved him unconditionally. We arrived at the Ponte alla Grazie, which was built entirely of stone and was seven archways long, crossing at the widest part of the river. We passed the little church built on one of its piers and the few little shops on it and then stood and looked out at the Arno, which was bleak and choppy, with peaks that punched up into the air as if to hurt it.

"No, Luca mio, you would not lend money, you would give it." He smiled. "I cannot allow that. I'm a man now. I'll earn my way." He walked across the bridge toward the Oltrarno. I groaned and followed him. On the other side was a small market. There were stalls with large brown eggs and crusty, fresh-baked breads, dried fruits and salt cod, pickled vegetables and country cheeses and chunks of churned butter wrapped in wax cloth. Leonardo leapt forward and ran to a stand with a dove in a cage. He reached in his pocket and took out a coin, looked at it, and then handed it to the old woman tending the stand.

"Do you have other money now, or is that the last of it?" I asked with reproach.

"Look at her face, she would make a marvelous subject, she's practically deformed with old age!" he whispered. I glanced sharply and it did seem as if time, which had abandoned me, had warped her. It had dragged down her nose and pulled her spotted skin like soft dough into pleats. Leonardo always noticed those kinds of human details. He'd probably show up later to follow her around until he had her physiognomy fixed in his mind. Then he'd go home and sketch her. The old woman had palmed the coin eagerly. She gave him a toothless smile, then shoved the cage at him. Leonardo pulled out the dove. He held it with both hands and brought it to his cheek, so that his beard rested against its wing. He seemed to sing in a voice too low for me to hear. After a moment he closed his eyes and reverently pressed his lips to the bird's gray head. Then he threw the bird into the air, crying out as it took wing. His beautiful face was alight with joy and yearning, his whole body strained to follow the dove as it soared.

"Do you remember when you took me to the Medici villa at Careggi for the first time, and we stopped and bought a falcon as a gift for Lorenzo?" Leonardo's large eyes glowed. "And you let me hold that beautiful bird as we galloped on your red stallion Ginori? With the horse and the bird, it was like flying! Do you remember, Luca Bastardo?"

I was about to respond when a young voice piped up, "Bastardo, that's a strange name!" I turned with a smile to the little boy at my elbow. But then my heart froze, and my throat closed up. The pointy, insistent chin and sharp-edged nose: this runty little boy of about six was the exact image of Nicolo Silvano when he had been the same age. The boy looked back at me with a frank, curious gaze. My history with his sinister clan reverberated like wasps singing in the air between us, and he tilted his head as if he felt it, too. "Gerardo, where are you?" called a woman. The boy glanced back over his shoulder.

I said nothing but turned on my heel and stalked off. Leonardo chased me.

"Luca, what's wrong?" he asked, concerned. I gave him an incredulous look. Leonardo drew up short. "My predilections you will have to make peace with, and learn to love me for the man that I am, and not the man you wish I were. But why did you run from the child?"

"He looks like someone I used to know," I muttered.

"Your past is coming around like a little dog to haunt you today," he said softly. "Be careful that it does not one day bite you. Since you are entertaining old wounds, I should tell you something. I've made new friends of late—"

"Uh-huh."

"Don't!" he said, coloring. Then he went on in a voice of total equanimity. "I've heard things. Whispers, really, of a plot against Lorenzo de' Medici. The Pazzi are instigating it."

"The Pazzi are happy, they took management of papal finances away from the Medici."

"Yes, but Lorenzo retaliated by sponsoring a law that disinherited daughters who have no brothers but who do have male cousins. So Giovanni de' Pazzi's wife did not receive her father's huge inheritance, which they'd counted on. The Pazzi are plotting. The Pope supports the plot, he wants to put Florence under the control of his nephew. And the King of Napoli backs the plot. Many would benefit from Lorenzo's death. This conspiracy is incomplete, mostly rumors and gossip. But it may bear fruit in a few years. You may want to say something to him."

"I haven't spoken to Lorenzo in four years, since the sack of Volterra. I have no plans to start now," I growled. "He isn't well disposed toward me. I'll be lucky if he doesn't finagle to have me burned at the stake. What do I care if the Pazzi or the Pope want to depose him?"

"He's the grandson of a close friend of yours; he could yet do you a good turn, perhaps save you from the stake, if you save him. And I have a feeling that his young son Giovanni will one day be Pope. It would be helpful for you to cultivate friends in high places," Leonardo said.

"The boy is a year old, he could be anything," I said, shaking my head.

Leonardo shrugged his powerful shoulders. "It's a feeling I have about the child, from one of my glimpses into the time to come. Listen, I'll invite you to my studio for a meal, when it's set up properly to receive visitors. You'll come, won't you, Luca? If you can spare some time away from your all-consuming work of changing lead into gold . . ." And his voice trailed off uncertainly, with his years falling away until

he sounded very young, like the boy I had met at the mouth
of a dark cave. That boy had changed my life. He had appointed me his teacher and then had taught me the most
important lessons: what it meant to be close to someone,
how to share thoughts and secrets in total safety. There
were people along the way for whom I had cared and whom
I had partly trusted, men like Giotto and Petrarca and
Cosimo de' Medici. There was no one, before Leonardo,
whom I had trusted fully. I had to accept him with his
predilections, despite my bone-deep distaste for them. I
didn't know how to reconcile them with my love for this
man who was like a son to me. Somehow I would have to
find a way.

"Of course I'll come for a meal at your studio," I said.
And it broke my heart but it stretched it, too. Nothing
Leonardo did, no matter how repulsive to me, would keep
me from being his friend. And, in retrospect, looking over
the long years of my life, I see now how choosing love over
fear, choosing my love for Leonardo over my fear of men's
desires, finally won for me the approval of the good God,
who is love. Thus it made me worthy of Maddalena.

I CAME FACE-TO-FACE with the grown Maddalena for
the first time on a Sunday in April 1478. Leonardo showed
up at my palazzo and interrupted my work with the reconstruction of Zosimos's still. "Come to Mass with me, Luca
mio," he called from the door to my workshop.

"Mass? I don't do that." I dismissed it. "Besides, I'm making progress today, with the sublimation process, and it will
lead to better things."

"You're making progress with the sublimation process,
and that's all," he said, laughing.

"No, ragazzo, today may be the day I succeed in turning

lead into gold! Then I'll never have to worry about money again!"

"You don't have to worry about money, professore, you're rich as Croesus," Leonardo said. He eyed the still with which I was fiddling. "You've set the flame too high," he noted. He paced around restlessly, poking at various objects on the coarse-grained tables I'd bought because they reminded me of Geber's old workshop. I hadn't managed to replicate that magical place entirely, though. I couldn't get colored smoke to crawl about like curious fingers or the beakers to rattle antiphonally as if they were speaking to one another. But I had time; I would get it right eventually. Leonardo sighed. "I hope you don't expect anything more out of your alchemy than entertainment. It's like astrology. Silly, a waste of men's time."

"You only say that because you have Mars in the sign of the Water Bearer," I said smugly. "It gives you a rebellious, contradictory nature."

"Not astrology, too!" Leonardo groaned.

"Ficino gives me lessons and books," I admitted. The flame on the still flared up orange and blue, overboiling the liquid so that the whole apparatus shook, and then the flame, making a sound like a breath exhaling, fanned out. I exclaimed in dismay.

"Now you have no excuse," Leonardo sang. "Come with me to Mass. It will be interesting today. Really, I think you should come!"

"You're not bringing along any of those pretty men who swarm around you?" I said.

"It's just you and me," he promised, so I went with him. It was always a pleasure to spend time with Leonardo. Just to be in his company and be privy to his thoughts was a treat— even if that meant going to Mass.

We weren't far from Santa Maria del Fiore with its vast

duomo and we walked at a leisurely pace on Via Larga, the street of the Medici palazzo. "I don't think either God cares one whit whether or not men go to Mass," I started darkly, but Leonardo sang a low mournful hymn in his sweet, enchanting tenor before I could fulminate with any satisfaction. We came to the church and spied a gathering of gorgeously attired men.

"The Cardinal of San Giorgio, Lorenzo de' Medici, the Archbishop of Pisa, the Count of Montesecco, the Pazzi and Salviati," Leonardo said softly, interrupting his song. He gave me an inscrutable sideways look. "You know that my first loyalty is to you, professore mio? Since that day that I chose you as my teacher." His voice was fierce and low, almost a whisper. "If someone was your enemy, even if he was my friend, I wouldn't serve him!"

"That's gratifying to hear, ragazzo. I've never doubted your loyalty to me," I said, wondering what he was up to. With Leonardo, there was never any telling. He squeezed my arm, then led me into the church.

"Giuliano de' Medici isn't with them," he murmured, sounding puzzled. We took seats on pews and after a short time, the Mass started. As I stared up into Brunelleschi's dome, the Latin words led me off into a daydream about my alchemical inquiries. Transforming base metal into gold had something to do with the proportion of sulfur to mercury, I thought, and then Leonardo poked me in the ribs. "Giuliano's here!"

"*Ite missa est,*" proclaimed the priest. It was followed by a faint cry of "Here, traitor!" Suddenly there was screaming. Leonardo leapt up to stand on the pew so he could see; he yanked on my sleeve until I did the same. Giuliano de' Medici was stumbling, spurting blood from a puncture in his chest. A number of men with drawn swords closed on him. "The dome is falling!" someone screamed, which was taken up as a chorus. People erupted in screeches and thousands of feet slammed against the marble floor. The vast cathedral was filled with congregants in an uproar, and men, women, and children ran in all directions, bolting from the church. Leonardo pointed at the southern side of the church by the old sacristy, where Lorenzo, short sword drawn and blood spattering his neck, jumped over the low wooden rail into the octagonal choir. A number of men shielded him as he ran in front of the high altar, where the Cardinal of San Giorgio, who looked to be only about seventeen years old, knelt in prayer. One of the Pazzi screamed crazed apologies, while others with bloody daggers ran after Lorenzo.

"Let's get out of here," Leonardo said. He hopped down, pulling me after him. We bolted, joining the screaming throngs of people who poured out of the great cathedral into the piazza. His hand fell from my arm and he was lost in the crowd. After being pushed and shoved, I came to rest against the Baptistery. I flattened myself back against it to get out of the mob's way. A woman stumbled out of the crowd and I caught her sleeves to prevent her from falling. I was stunned by the scent that emanated from her: lilacs, lemons, clear light, and every good thing I had ever seen, heard, smelled, touched, or imagined in one hundred fifty years. Then she looked up at me and her variegated eyes met mine. In that single instant, I knew her. All of her, her essence, her vital nature, spirit, soul, whatever name there is for the infinite point of light each person is at the center of his or her being. It was catastrophic and miraculous. It was a lightning bolt that seared through me into the deepest, most hidden places of my own essence. It set up a musical resonance like a silent song between us. It was far more intimate than sexual relations and took place without our flesh touching.

"Maddalena," I breathed. She was about nineteen years

old now, petite but lithe and strong, and that heart-shaped face that I remembered from Volterra had matured to a marvelous beauty. I clutched her to my chest and felt the vibrance of life like a bubbling stream strumming through her body, which was wrapped in a cottardita of the best pink silk, with large white sleeves, a brocade of gold threads, and lustrous pink-toned pearls sewn along her collar.

"Signore Bastardo," she said, flushing. She struggled in my arms, so I pushed her beside me with her back against the Baptistery, then shielded her with my arm. Fear washed through me—I didn't want her hurt, now that I had found her. I knew with certainty that, in this moment, my life had changed. The promise of the night of the philosopher's stone was suddenly, when I least expected it, fulfilled. Love and death awaited me, and staring into Maddalena's eyes, I knew that I had made the right choice all those decades ago.

"Let's go in!" she suggested, wriggling from my arm and pushing open the door that the goldsmith Lorenzo Ghiberti had sculpted, having won the commission in a contest that young Cosimo had suggested to his father. She darted into the building with me following. The place was empty and quiet and she sat down on a bench, breathing hard.

"Giuliano de' Medici is dead, he was covered with gore," she said. "But Lorenzo was running, so he must still live. He'll rally the Milanese and drum up support. The Medici will stay in power despite today's deeds."

"That's likely," I agreed breathlessly, unable to take my eyes off her, even to look at the gorgeous mosaic of the Last Judgment encrusting the ceiling or the intricate geometric designs of the tessellated floor. For once there was a woman more compelling than the art of a Master! I stood and Maddalena sat, knitting her small slender hands together in her lap. Her head was poised at a thoughtful angle on her long neck, and I could see the blue vein pulsing at her throat. Outside the whole world could have been ending in fire and earthquake and thunder and the horsemen of the Apocalypse raining down death, but it wouldn't have mattered. For me there was only this moment in Maddalena's presence. It was the holiest moment of my life. Something wondrous that had gestated for over a century was born. It was fitting that it should occur in the Baptistery. My flesh tingled, and the air between us palpitated, filled with unseen brilliance and a thousand dreams waking into real life.

"It's incredible! So frightening and unreal, a nightmare! Blood spilt at High Mass, a desecration of the great cathedral! Florence will never be the same. I wonder who could have instigated this, and to what end," she said, her husky voice starting with terror and finishing with a speculative note.

"The Pazzi, the Pope, the King of Naples. For money, power, vengeance. The Medici have many enemies. Lorenzo has not ruled our city with Cosimo's talent for keeping friends close and enemies closer," I answered without thinking. I couldn't believe we were discussing politics when all I wanted to do was sit down beside her and touch her beautiful skin.

"Volterra must be included among his enemies, though my hometown would never dare to attack, after the sacking he gave us." She nodded, then smiled shyly at me, and my heart skittered up into my throat and my knees buckled. "We seem to meet when there is blood about, signore. Fortunately, this time, it's not mine. And I'm dressed. I'm happy to see you looking well, also. You haven't changed at all in the years since you rescued me from the condottiere!"

"What are you doing in Florence?" I asked.

"I moved here six months ago," she said, looking away. Then Ghiberti's door was flung open.

"Maddalena? Carissima, I was worried about you when

I lost you in the crowd," cried a well-dressed older man who scooted into the pew and wrapped his arms around Maddalena, kissing her forehead. He had white hair and a neat gray beard. She rested her head against him for a moment, then laid a gentle hand on the man's chest, and I would have given every soldi in my bank account and ten decades of my life to be the fabric of that man's farsetto and have her hand caressing me.

"Rinaldo, this gentleman is an old acquaintance of mine, Signore Luca Bastardo. He saved me just now when I fell. I would have been trampled to death. Signore, this is Rinaldo Rucellai, my husband." She smiled at him, and I had never felt so shocked in my whole preternaturally long life. I'd finally found her, The One from my vision—there was no denying the thunderbolt that had shattered my soul—and she was married to someone else. She was the culmination of every yearning I'd ever felt. How could she have a husband? Had the good God offered me a choice between love and death that the evil God would never let come to fruition because of the inner sense of alienation I could never quite escape?

"Signore Bastardo, I owe you a debt of gratitude for saving my wife!" Rucellai cried, springing up to pump my hand with both of his. "You must come for dinner! I insist, signore, that I repay you for your kindness toward my wife!"

"That would be lovely." Maddalena stood beside her husband, who encircled her waist with his arm. I felt an army of agonies in the security she showed, belonging to someone else.

"Are you hurt, signore?" asked Maddalena, with concern in her voice.

"*Scusi?*" I grunted.

"You wear a terrible expression of pain, have you been hurt in the fray?" asked Rucellai. I shook my head, and Rucellai gripped my shoulder. "There will be terrible consequences from this dirty business today, and I must now offer my services to Lorenzo de' Medici. But you will come for dinner, perhaps in two weeks' time?"

They took their leave. I sat down in the Baptistery. Bells throughout the city gonged, and the pealing was picked up by bells on the outskirts and even far into the contado: Florence was at arms. I heard the commotion through the walls of the Baptistery, people stamping and crying out in terror, troops marching, mounted condottieri trotting through the streets. After a while, I heard two different shouts thrown back and forth in the streets: "People and liberty!" which was the traditional cry to overthrow a despot, and "Palle! Palle!" which referred to the Medici insignia, and was a cry of support for the Medici. It meant nothing to me. I was fixed on two preeminent facts: I had found Maddalena; she had a husband.

I went home, finally, bent over against the gusting wind, chilled to the bone in the gray light of a sun obscured by ominous gray clouds inflating to fill the sky. I avoided the men running through the streets with drawn swords. Some of the men carried bloody, dripping heads on the ends of lances and swords; Perugian soldiers had been found and killed in the Palazzo della Signoria. I made it home unmolested and stormed upstairs to my workshop. Unhinged, I grabbed an empty vial and threw it against the plastered wall. The tinkling sound and glittery fall of shards felt good to me, so I picked up a jar with sea salt in it and heaved it. It shattered with a deep, satisfying crunch and spray of crystals. I howled. I moved around the workshop, picking up objects of glass or pottery and throwing them as hard as I could against the wall. There was a flask of purple wine that made a stain like blood on the floor. Finally I stopped, panting, in the middle of the room, an island amidst a sea of jagged pieces.

"It will cost you many florins to replace everything," said Leonardo, who stood at the door with his arms crossed over his chest. I had no idea how long he'd been watching me.

"Screw the money!"

"Now, there are words I never thought to hear you say," commented Leonardo. "I'm fine, thank you for asking. I made my way to safety after we were separated in the crowd. Yes, I had heard rumors that something drastic was planned for today. No, I didn't warn Lorenzo de' Medici. He hasn't been kind to you of late."

I didn't want to hear about Florence's politics or Leonardo's choices. I had a bigger problem. "A woman." I pounded my fist against my forehead. "I met a woman today! Met her again. I met her as a girl."

"A woman, eh? You see why I stick with men. Women are bad for your health." Leonardo stroked his beard and smiled. I bared my teeth and growled. His auburn eyebrows climbed up his forehead as he made a placating motion with his hands. "Easy, easy, professore! Come and drink some nice wine with me, we'll send a servant in here to clean the mess."

"Wine won't make me feel better!" I cried, faced with two conflicting certainties: that I had been irretrievably struck to the heart by Maddalena, and that it was impossible to be with her. She would not betray her husband. I knew that she was loyal, because I had felt her essence in the moment that I'd held her upright at the Baptistery. I'd perceived her loyalty then as I'd perceived her intelligence, her courage, her sweetness, her humor, her kindness. I knew her utterly when I looked into her eyes. No woman had ever seemed so beautiful to me. It burned me and froze me and tore me apart and condensed me around my desire, simultaneously.

"You'll have her." He shrugged. "You're the handsomest man in Florence, after me. You have any woman you want.

You succeeded with my mother, and she wouldn't do anything to anger Papa, who had no intention of letting her go despite his string of wives."

"She's married."

"So?"

"She's not the kind to betray her husband!" I said in despair.

"That does complicate matters," Leonardo agreed. He put his strong arm around my shoulders, firmly, so he could direct my steps. "Come, Luca mio, let me pour you some wine. You'll do yourself harm if you stay in here. Come with me upstairs to the open loggia, we'll sit in the night and listen to men fighting for control of Florence. You'll tell me about this remarkable woman. I can listen as long as you wish; I'll stay here, in the room you keep for me. I don't want to be out on the streets on this bloody night. Tell me, what's her name?"

"Maddalena Rucellai," I answered, letting myself be led out of the workshop.

Leonardo made a tsking sound. "You have a fine eye. I know the lady. She is astonishingly lovely. She's a Volterran, the new bride of Rinaldo Rucellai. He's a cousin to the father of the man who married Lorenzo de' Medici's sister Nannina. Rinaldo's first wife died a few years ago. I heard he saw Maddalena on a visit to Volterra on Lorenzo's business and was instantly smitten, had to have her. It's a good match for her; he's quite wealthy and has no children, comes from a respected old family. Many of the Volterran girls haven't been able to find husbands, either because they were despoiled or because their fathers were killed or their families were impoverished in the sacking and there's no money for a dowry."

"Maybe Rucellai won't survive the night," I said coolly. "Maybe I can hasten him on his journey to meet his first wife in heaven. Where's my short sword?"

"Luca, I won't allow you to do anything stupid," Leonardo said firmly. "But I can tell you where she lives."

THE NEXT MORNING I waited outside of Rinaldo Rucellai's palazzo for Maddalena to come out. Florence seethed with turmoil over the murder of Giuliano de' Medici and the attempt on Lorenzo's life. Every man was embroiled one way or another. Lorenzo would be furious and implacable, doling out death for months. I didn't care. I only wanted to see Maddalena.

After an hour she came out attended by a maidservant. I smiled; a small thing like rioting and murder in the streets wouldn't keep her indoors. After all, when she was a child who was still bleeding from being raped, she had left safety to rescue other children. She had courage. Her husband's palazzo was located close to the Mercato Vecchio, and she set off in that direction. I followed from far enough back that she and her maid wouldn't know I was there.

On the outskirts of the market a street urchin ran up to her with his hand outstretched. He knew her, because he cried, "Maddalena! Maddalena!" The round maid gave her a purse, and Maddalena dug for a coin. She handed it to the ragged boy, who called out thanks and ran off. I watched as the scene was repeated a few more times. Maddalena finally stepped into the rectangular square of the market, and her plump maid paused and knelt to fix her shoe. This was my opportunity. I hastened to the woman's side.

"Signore Rucellai has urgent need for you at the palazzo," I told her. "Immediately!"

"But the signora." She gestured after Maddalena.

"I'll tell her you've been sent for by her husband," I said. She looked dubious. I shrugged. "If you'd prefer to explain to Signore Rucellai why you disobeyed him . . ." She shook her head and waddled back in the direction in which she'd come. I strode after Maddalena. The market was thronged today, people coming not to buy goods so much as to gossip. When I caught up with her, she was giving a coin to yet another urchin. I stood quietly beside her, watching. My heart flopped like a hooked fish on the riverbank. I didn't know if I could speak with the dryness in my mouth. She patted the dirt-stained boy on his head.

"You're very generous, Maddalena," I said, only a little hoarsely.

"Signore Bastardo, I didn't see you," she said. She looked down at the blue brocade purse that was lumpy with coins, and then blushed and laughed. "Florentines are so practical with money, you must think me silly. These are just dinari, but I like to have coins on hand for the beggars, especially the children. After all, that could have been me. If it weren't for the restitution monies and some kind neighbors, I could have been a beggar on the street, with my father dead and my home destroyed. I've been lucky. So I feel that I should help these unfortunate souls. My husband is very kind and indulges me by keeping this purse filled for when I go out to the market."

I asked, "Is Signore Rucellai with you?"

"Oh, no, he's gone to the aid of Lorenzo de' Medici," she said, looking around. In a puzzled tone, she added, "My maid was with me, but she's disappeared."

"The crowds here are thick today, maybe she's lost sight of you," I said. "It could be dangerous after yesterday's events. Why don't I accompany you?"

"I couldn't impose on you," she said, blushing faintly and looking away.

"It's no trouble," I said firmly, gesturing for her to walk on.

"I suppose it's better not to be alone today," she said, stealing a glance at me. She moved forward and I took the opportunity to lean in toward her hair and smell her lilac scent. We walked through the hordes of chattering people, passed by a row of vendors with bright spring flowers from the contado. Today the vendors were less interested in selling their wares than in jabbering together: what would happen to Florence? Maddalena turned to me.

"So, Signore Bastardo——"

"Call me Luca," I said, knowing it wasn't appropriate and not caring. She half-smiled and her thick lashes dropped to hide her eyes. Today she wore an indigo velvet cottardita embroidered with silver threads and encrusted with a design of pearls along the bodice. Over it she'd thrown on a white wool mantello. The effect was rich and striking with her fair skin, her variegated hair with its lush mix of brown, red, gold, plum, and black tones, and her eyes that were as complicated as agates.

"I suppose we are old friends. You saw me at my worst! So, then, Luca, you look very well, exactly as I remember you. It's wonderful to see my memories of you weren't childish fantasies, after all." She laughed shortly, her cheeks coloring again.

"What kind of fantasies did you have of me? Good ones?" I gave her a suggestive smile.

"That's not what I meant!" She reddened from the perfectly shaped widow's peak on her scalp to her delicate collarbones.

"I know what you meant. I just wanted to see what other meanings there could be."

"Suggestion is the bastard child of wicked intentions."

"Relatives, both," I said, punning on my surname.

"Please, signore, I am not like your sophisticated Florentine women. I find this conversation unbecoming!" She took a deep breath. "I, ah, I never asked you back then, what do you do in Florence? That night in Volterra, you fought like a

condottiere, but you were so skilled at treating injured people, I assumed you were a physico of some kind."

"I've been a doctor and a soldier. Now I'm pursuing the
art of alchemy."

"Alchemy, how interesting." She brightened. "We were at
dinner at the Medici palazzo just two weeks ago and I listened to Marsilio Ficino speak on that topic. He's a fascinat-
ing man, so learned and mystical. I want to learn alchemy.
Astrology, too. I'm not as educated as your clever Florentine
women, and I'm eager to catch up. I find I enjoy learning. I
have a hearty appetite for it. My husband has been so kind as
to offer to hire a tutor for me."

You deserve kindness, I thought, and was torn between feeling grateful to Rucellai for his generosity and envious that
he was the one able to show it to her. Aloud, I said, "Even in
Florence, few women study alchemy or astrology."

"I would like to," she said, giving me a thoughtful look.
"Perhaps you could teach me."

I was almost overwhelmed by my longing to touch her
and didn't trust myself to say something reasonable about
teaching her. Instead, I asked, "What are you shopping for? If
you don't know who to buy from, I can show you the best
purveyors."

"My husband has been most solicitous in taking me around
Florence and introducing me to shopkeepers." She made a
gesture with her fine-boned hand. "Besides, I really came today to hear what people are saying. The Rucellai are deeply
involved in the political life of Florence. I like to keep abreast
of events so I'll have something to say to my new relatives
over dinner."

"I'm sure your husband appreciates your diligence," I said,
and couldn't keep the sharpness from my tone. Maddalena's
head snapped up as she looked at me. Her brows knitted.

"Have I offended you?" she asked, a look of concern spreading over her lovely face.

I shook my head. Then, because I couldn't help myself, I said, "I thought you were going to wait until I came back to Volterra for you."

"Wait?" She looked startled. "You mean that last conversation we had, as you were mounting your horse—what was his name, Ginori—and leaving Volterra?"

"You asked me to come back for you. I said I would."

She colored, laughed once, and placed her hand on her throat. "Signore, I could not take to heart your kind words to a wounded young girl!"

"But you should have," I said mordantly, and she looked away.

"Maddalena, Maddalena! What are you doing out?" cried a familiar voice. Rushing toward us with his sword drawn was Rinaldo Rucellai, flanked by two other sword-carrying men whom I recognized as friends of Lorenzo's, another Rucellai cousin and a Donati.

"Carissima, you should not be outdoors when people are rioting," Rucellai said anxiously, after kissing his wife's forehead. He went on breathlessly, "There is a Volterran implicated in the conspiracy; the man who nicked Lorenzo in the neck is a Volterran. You should stay inside lest people associate you with him and take vengeance! I don't want you killed in the streets of Florence. I would go mad with sorrow at the loss of you!"

"The market is calm, people are gathered only to exchange news, I'll be safe here," Maddalena objected with a gesture that took in the swarms of people babbling with excitement.

"Your life is my responsibility now, Maddalena mia," Rucellai said, with an air of lordly determination that became him, with his height and his closely cropped gray beard and his white hair.

"I'll escort the signora home," I offered.

"I would be most grateful," Rinaldo Rucellai said, gripping my arm in thanks. "And again indebted to you. I must attend to Lorenzo's business, but you will join us for dinner soon, Signore Bastardo? To let us show our appreciation?"

"Surely," I said. Maddalena and I watched the three men scurry off. "Come, signora, let's obey your lord and master." Her mouth tightened for a moment, then relaxed. "I would not rule my wife with so heavy a hand," I said blandly. "A man should allow his wife to govern herself."

"Then your wife might be hurt when there are riots in the streets," she said lightly, with a flutter of her thick black lashes. "My husband's love for me makes him protective."

"Love doesn't include incarceration," I said stiffly.

"Signore Bastardo, it's not incarceration for me, it's my pleasure to do my husband's will. His wisdom is apparent, these are uncertain times!"

It's not wisdom because he has white hair, I thought, and then was ashamed of my jealousy. I was glad that Rucellai took good care of Maddalena. It's just that I longed to do that myself. But I said nothing. I didn't show it, but I trembled inside as I took hold of her elbow to escort her. It was small and fine, a delicate birdlike notching together of bones, a delight in my hand. If I couldn't touch her anywhere else, at least I knew what her elbow felt like, through her sleeve.

"I WROTE A PLAY FOR MY CHILDREN," Lorenzo was saying, as dessert dishes were cleared by servants, "entitled *San Giovanni and San Paolo.* They each have a part in it, as do I. It's great fun to enact with them! We put on costumes and

make their mother watch and laugh through the whole thing.
I miss them terribly. A good wife and many children are the
greatest blessing life and God can offer." He took a draught
of his wine and then gave me a long sardonic look across the
table with his black eyes glittering over the rim of his silver
goblet. "You must be getting ready to choose a wife, Luca.
You're wealthy, allied with the most excellent families." He
indicated Rinaldo Rucellai, who was pleased at Lorenzo's
attention and bowed his head in response. Lorenzo continued, "Isn't it long past time for you to think of starting a
family? You look young for your years, but a man must settle
down and produce children eventually."

"I've considered it of late," I allowed.

"A man as handsome you, and as virile as you're said to
be, must want a wife," Lorenzo continued, playing his familiar game of cat and mouse with me. "Is it true, as rumor has
it, that you sometimes visit several ladies in a night? What
marvelous stamina you have! I'm envious!" Maddalena, who
sat next to her husband at the head of the table, knocked
down her wineglass. A servant bustled over to mop up the
garnet liquid.

"Virility is common among Florentine men, who take
their cue from their leaders," I answered, with a level gaze at
Lorenzo. "I don't give any credence to rumors."

"Perhaps he intends to reproduce his name," cracked
Sandro Filipepi. "Florence will be overrun with bastards!
Luca, you must be the son of a vigorous man and an insa-
tiable woman!"

"There are a few bastards around," Leonardo replied.
"But there is only one Luca." It was late in the evening and
we were a dozen guests in the dining salon at Rinaldo
Rucellai's richly appointed palazzo. The meal was over, and
successful, having left us mellow and convivial with good
wine. Since the dinner party was nominally in my honor, I sat

near the head of the table, next to Maddalena, who was on Rucellai's left. I was close enough to her that I'd been inhaling her lemon and lilac scent all evening, which eroded the edges of my reason into rags. Lorenzo sat at Rucellai's right hand, across from me. It was the first time Lorenzo and I had been in the same room together, the first time we'd spoken, since the sack of Volterra six years ago. I was uneasy. Lorenzo with his cunning like a street rat could sense it.

"How about it, Luca, are there marriage plans in the offing?" Lorenzo pressed me.

"Eventually," I said.

"Any prospective brides in particular?" Rucellai asked. Matchmaking, with large amounts of money changing hands via dowries, was a topic of supreme interest in Florence.

"Perhaps," I answered.

"I could introduce you to the mothers of some of the young women I've met in Florence, if you can be dragged away from your ladies," Maddalena offered. Her long lashes were lowered, making her protean eyes unreadable. I struggled to keep my face from showing my revulsion at her words. Crafty Lorenzo saw something that made him sit up straighter.

"I think caro Luca is far too busy endeavoring to turn lead into gold to worry about marriage right now," Leonardo said easily, diverting the other guests' attention.

"I would love to study alchemy!" said Maddalena.

"Luca would be the man to teach you," Leonardo said, as if confiding in her alone. "He studies and works in his workshop until late every day. He reads and rereads Ficino's translation of the *Corpus Hermeticum*. He has other alchemical works spread about his workshop. He is a man possessed with discovering the great secret of alchemy!"

"I thought the great secret of alchemy was immortality,"

said Lorenzo, smiling at me while playing with the stem of his wine goblet.

"Your grandfather once told me that the only immortality we could hope for was in the love we felt for other people," I replied, knowing how my reference to Cosimo would affect Lorenzo. He pushed the silver goblet back with a spastic motion.

"I like to think my paintings will enjoy some sort of immortality, like the timelessness of nature," Leonardo said serenely, again rescuing me from unwanted attention. "Since painting embraces within itself all the universal forms of nature. This is why it's so important to paint from nature, to learn from nature. To this purpose I have hired a young peasant woman and her baby as models for recent sketches of the Madonna and Child. The peasant woman is physically beautiful, and I would like to capture the essence of her beauty so that it ravishes the viewer. And not just the beauty, but the mystery of femininity and grace!"

"What is immortal is the soul, inclined toward God and propelled by love," commented Sandro. "That's grace, that propelling. Ficino says the soul is so responsive to beauty that earthly beauty becomes a way to access divine beauty, which is universal goodness and harmony."

"If anyone can paint universal beauty, it would be you, Signore Leonardo," said Maddalena warmly, and I loved her even more for championing Leonardo.

"So I shall account myself a second-rate draughtsman who is denied nature's favors as a husband is turned away by a wife who locks her knees together!" exclaimed Sandro.

"No, Signore Filipepi, that's not what I meant; your works are full of grace," Maddalena cried. "I love your *Adoration of the Magi* in Santa Maria Novella, with the radiance of the star pointing at the sweet haloed head of the Christ Child, held so lovingly in his mother's lap, and the way you captured the emotional face of Cosimo de' Medici as the wise man, and Signore Lorenzo here, and young Pico della Mirandola with whom Ficino is so taken—"

"Signora, pay Sandro no heed, he is a great trickster and is playing upon your tender sympathies," Leonardo said graciously, smiling at Maddalena.

"Well, don't spoil the joke for me," grumbled Sandro, but he lifted his wineglass with good humor in a salute to Maddalena.

"You know what a husband should do with a wife who locks her knees," Lorenzo said, with a serious mien. "He should roll her over onto her belly!" Sandro burst into guffaws, Leonardo choked on his wine as he tried to contain a laugh, and Rinaldo Rucellai with his neat gray beard colored and grinned. To her credit, Maddalena didn't flinch.

"Poor Clarice, I will offer her my sympathy if I see her limping," she said in a deadpan tone of voice. Her comment elicited hoots and cheers around the table, and it was only when at the other end of the table the wives of Donati and Tommaso Soderini clapped and called, "Brava! Bravissima!" that she blushed and cast her eyes down. I couldn't believe how adorable she was in that instant. It was all I could do to restrain myself from reaching out to touch her.

"A toast to your wife, Rucellai, she is as good-humored as she is beautiful!" applauded Sandro.

"She is a treasure," Rucellai agreed, reaching his hand out to squeeze hers. "I would love to have Maddalena's portrait, Sandro; perhaps we could discuss it."

It took away my breath to think of Maddalena painted by Sandro Botticelli, and I resolved at once that I must own that portrait. Thereafter I was absorbed in figuring out how to obtain it and didn't listen to the dinner conversation. But I did watch Maddalena. Her expressive face reflected a dozen emotions and ideas over the course of a few minutes, like notes rippling off the strings of a lyre. Her fine hands were animated, too, illustrating her words, touching her husband's arm, gesticulating for servants to refill wine goblets. I didn't want to stare but couldn't help it. I only managed to drop my eyes when Leonardo tread on my foot, warning me. After that I managed to confine her mostly to my peripheral vision. Mostly.

LEONARDO AND I WERE THE LAST TO LEAVE. We stood at the large carved doors to the Rucellai palazzo and said thanks and good-bye to our host and hostess.

"Signore Luca, I've spoken to my husband about studying with you. He's amenable, if you have the time," Maddalena said. She stood next to her husband in the doorway, with the melting yellow candlelight from the foyer dissolving around the curves of her form.

"I'll pay you for your time," Rucellai said. I opened my mouth to tell him that I didn't want money, I wanted his wife, but Leonardo grabbed me bodily and shoved me down the street.

"It's something to consider," Leonardo said. "Thank you again!" They called their good-byes. I was still looking backward when the great door closed, leaving me on the outside and Maddalena on the inside with that man, her husband. I almost couldn't bear thinking of her with him, even though I knew he was a good match for her, and that he adored her.

"Stop it!" Leonardo said sharply. "Luca, you're pathetic!" He grabbed my farsetto by the shoulder and shook me once as we walked down the street in the moonlight. "You are completely unmanned by that woman's beauty."

"Do you think anyone else noticed?" I wondered.

Leonardo laughed shortly, then shook his head. "Perhaps Lorenzo. He misses nothing."

"I'll never have her," I said sadly. How could I come so close to love and have it denied me? Was this the cruelest divine joke of all, and, if so, which God was laughing? I looked up at the sky, which was deep and indigo and spattered with milky stars.

"No, you won't! Is it so, what's the word you used, Luca mio, 'insupportable,' that you'll never have her?" asked Leonardo. He stopped short and I turned toward him. He reached his hand out and took mine in his, raised our hands together so that I was clasping his in the crisp night air. Moonlight silvered over his golden-red hair and gave him a fuzzy halo, like a saint. He was staring at me with an intense, rapt look on his sculpted face.

"Leonardo?" I said uncertainly. He dropped my hand.

"Do you not know how I feel about you?" he asked softly, staring down at me from his greater height. "How I've felt since the day I saw you, more beautiful than an angel, walk up over the crest of Monte Albano to where I stood by the cave? All these years I have loved you. Only you, Luca. Can you not imagine how it could be between us?" He was breathing hard and I felt his male presence, his erotic core. He was aroused and also tender; he brimmed over with the strength and vulnerability of a man who was offering himself as a man to me. After what I had endured at Silvano's as a child, I would have thought that a moment such as this would nauseate me, enrage me, drive me to draw the dagger I kept strapped to my thigh. But this was Leonardo, whom I loved. Nothing he did could disgust me. I was moved by his honesty, which I valued, and his willingness to reveal himself, a willingness I almost never duplicated in my own life.

"No, ragazzo mio, that is not who I am," I said softly. I

didn't back away from him. I just stood there, feeling my own erotic core. That core was filled with Maddalena, as perhaps it had been since the first time I saw her. I understood her, and I realized that all along, these many decades, I had been waiting for someone who could understand me, too. Only a woman who had experienced similar atrocities, and survived them, could do that.

"You are not like me," he cried raggedly. "I love you and it is impossible because you are not like me, not at all!" His voice was full of raw pain. I nodded. He recoiled as if from a serpent. Then he straightened and set his noble head high on his neck. "It's a waste of time. I have much work, painting, observation, the study of anatomy; sensuality would only hamper my efforts. Intellectual passion drives out sensuality." His eyes were remote and detached.

"Leonardo, you will love again," I said quietly, feeling compassion for him.

"I'll leave Florence, anyway, in a few years. Perhaps for Milano, or Venezia. I've ideas for new weapons," he said as if speaking to himself. He quickened his pace and I had to hurry to keep up. "Ideas for inventions. I'll write a letter, seek new employment. But not right away."

"Leonardo, we will always be friends," I said. I stopped for the turn down my street. He glanced back over his shoulder, saw that I was at the junction of my street, and paused.

"Will you, Luca? Will you? Love again. Since you can't have Maddalena," he said with a bitterness that was never before, and never after, in his deep, melodious voice. I didn't answer, because it was obvious to me. There was only Maddalena. From now on, if I couldn't have her, there was no one. Leonardo nodded. "That's what I thought! There's one love, and it's forever!"

Chapter 21

A FEW WEEKS LATER, Maddalena confronted me as I was entering an apothecary shop near Santa Maria Novella, whose facade had been redone some twenty years ago by Alberti. The renovation was financed by Giovanni Rucellai, cousin to Rinaldo. With his renovation, Alberti had achieved the aims of the humanists, and perhaps the rest of us, too: he had fully integrated the past with the present. He had pulled the rose window, intricate marquetry, and arched recesses of the church's origins into a handsome classical design that was completely current.

This particular apothecary shop, in the western part of town near the massive city walls, offered a selection of flasks and beakers, and I was still replacing the ones I'd broken in my tantrum. I turned to enter the shop.

"Luca," called a husky, beguiling voice. I closed my eyes and didn't respond so she'd repeat my name and I could have the pleasure of hearing it again on her lips. "Luca Bastardo!"

"Maddalena," I said. She walked swiftly across the piazza.

Today she wore a pale green brocade cottardita with yellow-and-blue silk sleeves and crimson embroidery; her thick woolen mantello was bright purple and lined with white fur. She crackled with color and texture, as did her being; her garb suited her.

"Let us speak," she said, stopping at the edge of the piazza. I went to her, unable to master my ragged breathing. I stopped at a distance because I didn't trust myself to stand close to her. I might seize her and cover her face and throat with kisses and pleas and promises. She swallowed, then said, "I know how you feel about me, signore."

"You do?"

"It mustn't be spoken aloud. But it concerns me. I wish to study alchemy with you. My husband has agreed to it. He's a good man, and I won't dishonor him." Her eyes were serious, and I saw slivers of gray in them today, the gray-green of the Arno when it surges out of its shores and washes away bridges. "He deserves my loyalty—no matter what. I owe him a tremendous debt of gratitude for marrying me under circumstances which would have put off any other man."

"Not every man," I interjected. "I wouldn't have been put off."

She blushed but went on as if I hadn't said anything. "I had no family and little money for a dowry. I had only myself to offer. Yet every day Rinaldo makes me feel as if he is the fortunate one. I am grateful to him and always will be. I hope to bear him many children and make him proud and happy."

But, Maddalena, I wanted to say, *Rucellai is the fortunate one. In offering yourself, you've given him everything.* An ache gnawed at my heart, but I pushed it away. "What do you want from me?"

"I want you to teach me and to strictly observe the proprieties. No more sending away my maid! I have a voracious hunger for learning; I want to be as worthy as all the Florentine women with their illustrious families and good

education. I want you to teach me everything you know!"
Impassioned, she took a step toward me with her lips parted.
I could see the rosy soft tip of her tongue. I wondered what
it would feel like in my mouth.

"Education doesn't make people worthy. People are born
worthy, and they live their lives either to enhance that worth
or not," I said. It was the one essential thing I'd learned in my
long life, and it was a gift I gave now to Maddalena, whether
or not she received it.

"I have something to prove to myself," she answered.

I shrugged. "I'm a failed alchemist."

"I have great respect for Leonardo; he's an extraordinary
man. He says you are the best alchemist around, barring
Ficino, who's too busy and too important to teach me."

"I'm not important." I smiled wryly, looking off at the
green-and-white facade of Santa Maria Novella, because it
was something other than her to focus on, and maybe it
would keep her from seeing the naked hunger in my eyes.

"That's not what I meant!" she cried. "I'm sure you're
very important. When I talk about you and ask people
about you—"

"Why do you ask people about me, Maddalena? What do
you want to know? I'll tell you anything about myself. Anything. Just ask."

"Please, signore, let me explain myself!" Maddalena
shook her head, blushing furiously. "Ficino runs the Platonic
Academy. People say you keep to yourself, other than to be
with a few friends, that you stay out of politics, that's what I
meant about important."

"I know what you meant."

"The thing I want to know is, can you teach me, as a friend
and only as a friend, remembering always that I am married
and faithful to my husband?"

No, my body and soul and mind and every dram of my being screamed. "Yes," I said aloud. I retrained my eyes on her and vowed, in that moment, to always say yes to her. If I could not give her the love I wanted to, I could at least give her the spaciousness of knowing her desires would always be fulfilled by me. Whatever desires she brought to me, that is.

Her beautiful face glowed and she laid her hand on my chest eagerly. Then she saw what she was doing and removed it with alacrity. "Thank you, signore! Can we start tomorrow? I'll arrive after breakfast at your home. Is there anything I should bring with me? My husband has told me to purchase whatever I need for my studies!"

"Bring yourself. That's everything," I said. Her wide, mobile mouth turned up in a smile. She skipped off like a little girl, but then, nineteen wasn't so old, even if any Florentine girl whose family could afford her dowry was married by then. Just then a group of children ran by chasing a wooden wheel. They were well fed and well dressed in good wool and all were laughing. As they raced past, one little girl turned toward me with her plaited blond hair flying out around her and her eyes alight with giggles.

"It's too funny!" she said, pointing, but at what I couldn't see. Then I realized that it didn't matter what she was pointing at. Her words were a sign; one of the Gods wanted me to know that the joke was in play. As usual, I was the butt of it. It didn't matter if I prayed. Beneath the surface of everything lay a tightly woven fabric of meaning. That was the ultimate joke.

FOR A FEW YEARS, Maddalena and I met once a week when she was in Florence. I didn't see her when she went with her husband to his villa in the contado, a lonely time which could stretch to as long as a month. I started our work together with exercises in Latin, because most of the alchemical texts, including Ficino's translation of the *Corpus Hermeticum,* were in Latin. Maddalena had a quick mind and within a year was better at the language than I was. If I fumbled with a declension, she teased me mercilessly. Of course, she had her rich old husband buying her manuscripts in Latin to supplement whatever I taught her, which was her secret weapon.

It was the same when I began to teach her about the zodiac, which I did even before Ficino completed my instruction. She grasped the metaphor of the signs, houses, and seven planets much more deeply than I did, literal as I was. We had a discussion about it one day while I showed her pictures of the constellations in an old bestiary Leonardo had given me as a gift.

"That's Leo, the gorgeous lordly animal, it shows kingship," I said, pointing. Maddalena stood at my elbow, leaning over my arm so I could stare at the soft white column of her slender neck. I was mesmerized by it, as I was by every curve and line of her flesh, and by the sweet eroticism which she wore as unthinkingly as a comfortable mantello.

"It shows the arena of life where the soul is magnificent," she said. "You must think of what each sign and planet represents, Luca. The Archer shows where the soul is on a quest."

"The Archer is a centaur with a good strong bow in his hands," I said. "Mars, here, is the harbinger of war and destruction."

"Mars is the principle of action," she said, "whether that's to build or to wreak havoc." She tilted her head to look up at me out of the corner of her eyes.

"Venus is the goddess of love and beauty," I said, trying not to sigh, because Maddalena herself embodied Venus for me. I grew erect and twisted my hips to hide it. I'd not been with a woman since Maddalena had reappeared. It wasn't easy for a man used to frequent amorous interludes to find himself celibate, even if he chose that state. It was, after all, an unnatural state. Unlike the alchemist Geber, I believed that the flesh was to be enjoyed, with kindness and respect certainly, but also with appreciation. The earth was a feast full of delights, great paintings and beautiful women and succulent foods, and not to cherish those delights amounted to a great sin. After all, tragedy and suffering lurked around every corner, demanding their due.

"Venus speaks to the capacity for love and an appreciation of beauty," said Maddalena.

"Too abstract," I argued. "With that interpretation, you lose sight of the practical use of astrology: timing specific events! Venus strongly placed can show a love match occurring."

"Luca, specific events are the least of what astrology signifies!" she said, straightening. Her silk dress sluiced over her like a sheet of water, skimming her lovely curves in a way that left me breathless. "The material world is under the rule of the stars, I mean astrological law, insofar as people are always seeking revelation, insight into the divine, and salvation!"

"If you want insight into the divine, go watch a boy tear the wings off a fly. If you want to know when specific events will occur, use astrology," I said. "Astrology is significant insofar as it reads like a clock on a bell tower. The earth and heavens are woven together in a vast fabric, so it is below as it is above. But this is an impersonal phenomenon. Salvation for the individual is a big hoax with which one of the Gods teases us when He wants some amusement. If we're lucky, it's the kind God, and there is some gift for us amidst the suffering. If we're unlucky, it's the evil God, and only horrors follow."

"No, Luca, you cannot believe that God is split this way, and mostly cold and uncaring!" Maddalena cried.

"How could I not?" I asked. "If there were one good God, how could He permit suffering and evil?" I moved to the other side of the table. Her fresh water and lilac scent aroused me almost to madness, and the desire would burn in me for hours, unabated. It was something I simply had to endure; only Maddalena could meet my need. I said, "How could you believe in one good God after what happened to you in Volterra?"

Somberly, she said, "I can't fathom why events happen that ruin lives. I'm not that wise. But I know that this earth is impregnated with the divine in every instant. The earth lives and moves with God's life, the stars are God's living creatures, the sun burns with God's power, and there's no part of nature which is not good because all are parts of God."

"Were you thinking that while the condottieri were raping you?" I asked, crudely and cruelly. I was ashamed of myself the moment the words had left my mouth.

Maddalena didn't flinch. "Of course not," she said. "I was a little girl hoping they wouldn't kill me when they were done brutalizing me." She stood out from the table and jerked her skirts up to her waist. She wasn't wearing stockings and her slim thigh was bare. Her maid leapt up and shrieked in consternation. "Hush, he was there when it happened, he bound the wound!" Maddalena waved her to silence, then turned to me.

"I still have the mark from that day, where the condottiere carved into me as if I were a roast fowl, when he was finished using me." She pointed and I stared at the thin, cruciform scar high up on her leg. Her beautiful leg. It saddened me again to remember little Maddalena cut into by the brutes who did Lorenzo de' Medici's bidding. I wanted to hold her and touch the scar with love and tell her how beautiful she was, how much I admired her for her honesty in revealing herself. My tenderness threatened to overwhelm my restraint, so I lowered my eyes. She dropped her skirts. She said, "I thought this mark diminished me."

"It doesn't. It couldn't," I said grimly. I understood what it was to feel demeaned.

"That's what Rinaldo says, too," she said softly. "I showed him this when he asked me to marry him. Tears came to his eyes and he said it only made me more beautiful to him, and that he loved me more because of what I'd endured."

"Rucellai isn't a stupid man," I conceded.

Maddalena smiled. "He's a good man, and this scar gave me further proof of it. So something good came out of my having it. I think of that, how good comes out of evil, and how God is in all things, when I'm praying, and when I'm remembering that awful day. Sometimes when I'm praying I can feel something, something that doesn't have words or maybe can't be said in words, about God's perfection in every moment, even those moments that wear cruel faces. Grace is acceptance of the love of God within a world of seeming hate and fear." She looked down at the bestiary and traced the lion's golden mane with one delicate finger. A sad smile curved her lips. "When the worst happens, as it does in many lives—someone is raped, a parent is killed, a child dies, everything that matters is taken away—that's when we need our faith the most."

"That's when the cruel God is laughing."

"God isn't cruel, Luca mio, and there aren't two powers at work in the universe, good and evil. There's only one great goodness always at work. It's the task of an open heart to affirm that goodness; that's what we can do for God. After all, if Volterra hadn't been sacked and I wasn't hurt by those soldiers, would I have met you?"

I was almost unhinged by the heartrending sweetness of

her question and didn't trust myself to answer. If I spoke of our meeting, I would declare my love for her, and she had made it clear that she didn't want that. She was loyal to her husband. Perhaps he even deserved her loyalty. My silence didn't matter because she turned the page in the bestiary and inquired about the condition of the moon, in dignity or in its fall. She would soon become a far superior astrologer to me. I had taken up the study of astrology because I thought the stars would tell me which day I would succeed in turning lead into gold. Maddalena used it as, perhaps, it was meant to be used—as a map for the soul.

Finally, after studying Latin and some Greek and astrology, I planned to turn to the great texts of alchemy: the *Corpus Hermeticum,* which Ficino called *Pimander;* Lactantius's *Sermo Perfectus;* Raymond Lully's *Ars Magna.* I brought them out one day before she arrived. When she came in with her maid, I said nothing. I stood on one side of my reconstruction of Zosimos's keratokis and waited. Maddalena looked at me expectantly, and still I waited. Finally she said, "I see the manuscripts; what are they?"

"Alchemy is the search for what not yet is, the art of change, the quest for the divine powers hidden in things," I said in a solemn voice.

"What does that have to do with those manuscripts?" she demanded, her face shuttering in annoyance. I stepped away, hastily, in case she threw something at me. She'd done that once when I'd corrected her Greek conjugations in a way she didn't like. She said, "I hope that's Ficino's work; I'm ready for it, after two years of Latin and astrology!"

"Tell him to give you this book," boomed a familiar voice which I had not heard in a while, and I smiled. "Why is it taking so long to get to the good stuff? Have you asked him that?" said the Wanderer, his broad-shouldered body standing in the threshold. He trudged in and heaved himself down on the stool next to Maddalena. She scrutinized him thoroughly, and he met her gaze directly. After a few moments she reached out to touch his wild gray beard. He laughed and leaned back, avoiding her hand.

"How long did it take you to grow that?" she asked, unoffended.

"How long does any great work take?"

"That depends on the work," she answered, her dark brows puckering. "It could be a few days, or hundreds of years. It could take a moment or a millennium!"

"Exactly!" he responded, straightening his patched gray tunic.

"So how long have you had?" Maddalena persisted, smiling at him with great charm.

The Wanderer grinned. "How long do you want me to have had?"

"Millennia, of course! Aren't there legends about men who live almost forever, wandering the earth until the Messiah returns?"

"Until the Messiah comes," the Wanderer answered slyly. "But your legends concern a shoemaker who offended the great rabbi Jesus on his way to his crucifixion, and thus the rabbi cursed him to walk the earth alone until the world ends."

"I thought it came from the beloved disciple to whom Jesus said, 'There are some standing here, which shall not taste of death, till they see the Son of Man coming in his kingdom,'" said Maddalena. "Which do you think it is?"

"That depends on whether you think the millennia are a curse or a blessing," the Wanderer responded.

"Did you stable your beastly donkey, Wanderer?" I asked, changing the subject. I had not decided for myself if longevity was a blessing or a curse, and I had no stomach to hear the topic debated between the woman I loved and the mysterious, maddening Wanderer, who probably knew my origins but would only answer my questions with more questions.

"What, would I insult him that way? He's downstairs in the foyer!" said the Wanderer. I didn't know if he was joking, anything was possible with the Wanderer, so I made a frantic motion for the maid to run downstairs and check. The Wanderer grinned voraciously and handed me a thick, leather-bound book with shiny gilt edges.

"*Summa Perfectionis,*" I read. Then I yelped, realizing what I was holding. "Geber's manuscript, his life work. You published it!"

"What's important is that I brought it to you, to remind you of the goal of alchemy, and it's not the creation of gold! Have you attended to yourself, are you ready to rectify the world?"

"What is this manuscript?" Maddalena asked. "How do you know about it?"

"Il Bastardo here knows many things. Have you told her about the consolamentum?" asked the Wanderer.

"The consolamentum? What's that?" cried Maddalena. "Tell me, Luca!"

"It's a transfer of soul or spirit, something like that," I said, sighing. "It comes through the hands. I've given it to sick people to good effect."

"When your hands grow warm and tingly and everything looks bright and soft," Maddalena cried. "You gave me the consolamentum that day in Volterra, that terrible day! It made me feel better. Maybe it even saved my life." She gave me a tender look, almost reluctantly, as if she couldn't stop herself. I melted.

"There's a donkey in the foyer!" screamed the maid from the stairwell. The Wanderer burst out laughing, leaning back on the stool with his black eyes dancing and his huge beard wagging like a furry animal on the run. Maddalena, who was like Leonardo in her eternal curiosity, leapt off her stool to go see.

I CHERISHED, in particular, one night that was a great victory for me, even though it also exposed me to the danger that ever dogged my steps. It occurred during a festival that Lorenzo sponsored to rebuild Florentine morale during the years following the Pazzi conspiracy. The revelry began in the morning, but I went at sundown, when the light turned crystalline and the sky purpled and grew fragrant like lilacs. Like everyone else, I wore a costume. I was dressed in the leathers of a condottiere. I had been invited to a few parties, at least one of which would surely have devolved into an orgy, but I preferred to be alone with my thoughts of Maddalena.

I bought a skin bag of wine from a vendor and walked along the banks of the pearlescent Arno, listening to lyres playing, flutes piping, trumpets blaring, drums beating, and squeals of laughter echoing off the stones. Bands of young nobles paraded the streets, singing ballads bawdy enough to embarrass a Neapolitan sailor. A pageant with horse-drawn tableaux designed by Leonardo processed along the Via Larga; some of the lath and plaster tableaux with living actors were a re-creation of the story of the Three Magi and the Christ Child. This referred to the Medici, who saw themselves as the Magi of Florence.

I felt no urgency to watch the pageant, having discussed it exhaustively with Leonardo. He'd shown me his sketches for the tableaux from their inception. I'd even watched them being constructed to his exacting standards. So I walked in a leisurely way along the Ponte Santa Trinita, sipping my wine, wishing I were with Maddalena, feeling doubly lonely because I was not only a freak with a dubious past,

I was also alone, unable to have the great love I'd been promised. Suddenly a woman in a gorgeously feathered, befurred, and bejeweled cottardita thrust herself in front of me. She had been running and she was out of breath.

"Hello, stranger!" She laughed. Her face was obscured by a fantastically plumed, and probably expensive, mask, and her hair was hidden under an outrageous hat that was the head of a wildcat. But I would have recognized the small, curving form anywhere. She giggled and I wondered how much she'd had to drink. "Aren't you going to say hello?"

"Oh, yes," I said. I wrapped my arms around her and pulled her to me and kissed her thoroughly, despite her mask. Her lips parted and I pushed my tongue in, savored the grapey wine taste of her soft wet mouth. Every part of my being had yearned for a moment like this, and I took full advantage of it. She melted into me, her thighs embracing mine, and I nearly made love to her there, on the bridge. Finally I released her. Her scent of lilacs and lemons and crisp spring morning lay on my arms and chest like a magical mantello.

"That's not what I meant." She sighed.

"I know what you meant."

"Do it again!" she said tipsily, stepping toward me. I was about to oblige her when a laughing group of people, all dressed as animals, surrounded us.

"Look, a soldier!" shouted Rinaldo Rucellai, who wore a lion's-head hat and a lucco of golden-brown fur. I stepped away from his wife. "Have you killed anyone today, soldier?" he asked with drunken hilarity.

"Not yet," I said. "But I'm thinking about it." That provoked gales of laughter, and the group, with Maddalena in their midst, moved away toward another bridge.

We never spoke of the moment during our lessons, because such feathery things as transpired during *carnevale* were not meant to be addressed. And Maddalena wasn't the only person I saw wearing feathers during that fantastical night. On another bridge, later, when the stars tumbled out of an indigo sky as if they'd been shaken from a blanket, after I had imbibed too much crude wine, I came face-to-face with a boy. I had seen him once before. His sharp nose and thrusting chin were instantly recognizable. He was about ten years old now, a little older than I had been when his ancestor had made me a captive in his brothel. He wore red feathers sewn onto his camicia, and he recognized me, too. He looked back at me with open contempt.

"Luca Bastardo," he said, and saluted me.

"Gerardo Silvano," I said.

"Until soon." He nodded, fingering one of the red feathers, and stepped away. My blood ran cold, but I could never bring myself to regret going out that night, because the few minutes of holding Maddalena would make death itself worthwhile.

ALL THINGS END, even me, and endings are also beginnings. Here in my cell, awaiting my execution, I don't know what beginning I will have after they burn me, but I know there will be one. My precious time as Maddalena's teacher came to an end, also. Not long after the carnevale, there was a pounding at my door. It was late and I was dressed only in a camicia, which hung open. The servants weren't around, so I descended the stairs, cracked open the door, and peeked out. It was Maddalena, alone, wearing only a plain pink gonna. I'd never before seen her so intimately dressed. Sweat beaded up on my back and forehead. I shivered. I saw the outlines of her breasts and the lush dark points of her nipples through the gonna's sheer fabric. *She's come to be with me,* I thought, suffused with joy. A lightness I'd never before experienced spread through me, dizzying me. I had never known happiness until that very moment, I realized. I threw open the door, heedless of my undress and the erection springing forth to greet her. My arms spread wide to pull her inside the palazzo and sweep her close to me.

"Luca, come quickly. Rinaldo is sick, he is going to die! You must give him the consolamentum and save him!" Maddalena cried, as her scent ravished me.

No, I thought, dropping my arms. Everything inside me went cold. *Let Rinaldo die.*

"Please, Luca." She grabbed my arm. Her long soft hair flowed down around her face and neck, and even in the candlelight, it glimmered with red and purple and gold. She cried, "The doctors can't do anything. But you can! Don't let him die. He's been good to me!"

No. Don't ask this of me.

"You're my only hope, Luca, my last hope! You're my friend. Please, come with me to save my husband!" she begged. Tears like polished crystal enlarged her limpid eyes, those amazing eyes that stayed with me long after she left my workshop and the lessons in alchemy. She pleaded, "Get dressed, and come on! Hurry! Won't you come?"

"Yes," I said. I had promised myself that I would always say yes to her, and a man is only as good as the promises to himself that he keeps.

RINALDO RUCELLAI WAS IN A BAD WAY. He was pale and sweaty as he lay in his bed, the bed he shared with Maddalena. His white hair was unkempt, his gray-bearded face slack. I took his pulse, which was thready and erratic. I watched how shallowly he breathed, and I knew he was at the end. Rucellai was dying. I would finally have Maddalena.

These two years of teaching her, of staying at the distance her loyalty demanded and the proximity her friendship allowed, had been purgatory. Now, at last, I was climbing into heaven. I'd earned it. I'd waited for the woman promised me in my vision. She was mine by divine right, I felt that as surely as I knew that the evil God laughed cruelly and the good One enjoyed His reflection in Giotto's frescoes.

But Maddalena wanted me to save him. I sat down heavily on the edge of the bed, rested my head in my hands. Everything inside me, organs and bones and blood, was quaking, dissolving. Maddalena had asked me to help her husband live.

"Be good to her," whispered Rucellai.

"What?" I jerked up my head. He looked at me out of dark, compassionate eyes set in a linen-white face. His breath came even more shallowly. He smiled slightly, knowingly.

He knew how I felt about his wife and he was giving his blessing. Maddalena could come to me happily, with a clear conscience, her loyalty appeased. But she wanted me to save him. I looked at Rucellai, thought of all the people whose deaths I had witnessed: Marco, Bella, Bernardo Silvano, Geber. I was no stranger to death, even if Death and his brother Decrepitude had left me alone for a hundred sixty-some years. I was not afraid to watch Rinaldo Rucellai die.

But Maddalena wanted her husband to live. A blue-and-gold Venetian vase on the chest at the end of the bed held a dozen blossoms, red, pink, yellow, and white roses. It looked like a bouquet Maddalena might have set there to brighten the room for her husband. It bore her signature: the profusion of colors both strong and delicate, but not fragile; petals in all states of maturity, from closed in the bud to drooping with senescence; the sweet scent; the thorns.

What was love, if not surrendering the self for the

beloved? I felt how deeply I wanted to take her, to let my desires rule over hers. I knew how selfish I was. My life was still a battleground between the good God and the evil one. I could only hope to effect a truce by committing to love and surrender.

I laid my hands on Rucellai's chest. I didn't know if I could save him; he was far gone. And I had never completely mastered the consolamentum. It streamed forth from me when it chose, not when I did. But I would try. What had Geber said? "It's about surrender, fool, when will you understand that?" I closed my eyes and surrendered. I gave up my own desires. I allowed myself to melt. I felt despair at losing Maddalena again—it felt like another loss—and my heart throbbed with pain, with longing, with love. I swelled with those immortal twin guardians of human life, love and loss, and almost couldn't contain myself.

A gate within me banged open. The consolamentum gushed out with such force that my whole body shook. I would have to tell Leonardo about this; he was always interested in questions concerning force. It was a deluge that poured through me and out of my hands into Rucellai's chest. He gasped, arched his belly high up into the air to make a bridge with his spine, and then dropped back down onto the bed. He gasped again. Color washed over his face. He gave a third gasp, and this time, he inhaled deeply into his abdomen. He exhaled and it was the sound of waves breaking as the living river coursed past.

Rucellai would live. The consolamentum surged through the desperate vessel of my body until it slowed to a stop, like a tide flattening. I removed my hands and rose, a hollowed man, and stumbled out into the hall where Maddalena waited. I nodded. She understood. She threw her arms around me, murmuring words of thanks. It was agony to have her body pressed into mine and I pulled her arms off me, pushed her away before I could be provoked to madness.

"I can't see you anymore," I said harshly, not looking into her eyes. Because I was mortal, I was only a man, and there was a limit to what I could bear. All of my years weighed down upon me as if I stood at the bottom of a well with stones pressing upon me. "Find another teacher."

I went back into the streets and my face was wet with tears. Never in my life, not even at Silvano's brothel, had I felt as alone as I did on that midnight walk back to my palazzo. Always before I had dreams to comfort me. Now they were gone, my dreams of love and the promise of it from the night of the philosopher's stone, all the deep treasures of the heart that I had clung to with stubborn hope, now blown away like chaff in a strong Tuscan wind. It was a damp spring and too cold and foggy even to see the stars.

I let myself into my palazzo and went upstairs. I intended to retire immediately but stopped at the door to my workshop in amazement, because a finger of green smoke stretched out of the open door and tapped along the ceiling. I pushed open the door and saw everything in my workshop rattling with animation: stills dancing, flames licking up from candlewicks, hunks of metal glowing, salt chafing in its pot, and liquids gurgling with laughter and bubbling as if molten, as if filled with swimming creatures. Curious and bemused, I crossed over to my latest round of experiments with sulfur and mercury. I cupped the flask with my hands, which still tingled from giving the consolamentum. A swirling mist appeared in the middle of the flask. I stared into it. A black light flashed out, making the dark objects in my workshop appear like forms of milky light while the candlelit empty space in the room thickened into solid darkness. A sharp crack like lightning split the room, and then the light reverted. In the center of the flask was a shining nugget of gold.

I GREW USED TO LIVING WITHOUT MADDALENA. It wasn't easy. Despite the many decades that had been my portion, I'd never before noticed how empty my life was. For months I was inconsolable. Then I was angry. Then I was listless. I dragged myself around the city with no appetite for my old pursuits. In my mind's eye, I kept seeing her fine-boned face alight with love of learning, or radiant with laughter, or focused on some knotty problem of linguistics. In the market I heard a laugh like hers, but it turned out to belong to some other woman. I looked in the windows of carriages that rolled past for her face, I peered inside botte-gas and restaurants, hoping to spy her small, slim form. I flagellated myself for remembering her. Nothing else mat-tered. Even turning lead into gold had lost its allure. I went out to my vineyard in Anchiano and moped there for several months until I couldn't stand myself anymore. *Basta,* I told myself; it is enough. I rode Ginori back into Florence.

It was the spring of 1482 and Florence enjoyed an uneasy peace, if not a prosperous one, after the war with Calabria that had followed the Pazzi conspiracy. Lorenzo had paid a huge indemnity to the Duke of Calabria to thwart Pope Sixtus's ambition for his nephews to rule Tuscany. The city was quiet but brisk with business. Shops were open, wool factories were operating, smithies clanked and hammered, markets bustled. Horses trotted through the stone streets pulling carriages and everywhere there were carts with goods from the contado. I was pleased to be back. My palazzo was shuttered because I hadn't sent word ahead for the servants to open it, but I didn't mind. I settled Ginori in the stable and went inside. I opened windows and lit lamps, then climbed the stairs to my workshop, which I hadn't set foot in since the night I had succeeded in turning lead into gold. The room was quiet, cold, and still, as my heart was, I thought wryly. Surfaces were sueded with dust, because I never let servants clean in there.

"I saw the lamps glowing and let myself in," said Leonardo. "I thought you'd be back sooner." There was curiosity in his mellifluous voice. He came to stand beside me. "I expected you a month ago. You didn't come, so I planned to ride out to Anchiano to see you this week."

"Ragazzo mio, how are you?" I said, embracing him happily.

"Well." He nodded. "I'm leaving Florence. I've been welcomed to the court of Milano, and Lorenzo is eager that I should go and cement Florence's relations with Lodovico Sforza."

"Everyone works for Lorenzo's ends," I commented dryly.

"It suits me." Leonardo shrugged. "I'll be playing the lute. And Sforza has written of giving me a commission for a bronze horse; it's an intriguing project." He gave me a cool smile. "I thought I'd use my old sketches of Ginori. There's no more nobly built steed!"

"His heart is still noble, but he's getting a bit long in the tooth," I commented.

"Aren't we all? Everyone except you. You're eternally young and beautiful. But I won't be. I'm turning thirty. I'm no longer a ragazzo, professore, not even for you. Time consumes all things." He walked to the nearest table, dragged his finger across the surface to leave a thick line in the dust, then twiddled with the beakers on Zosimos's still, aligning them. "I sometimes think about the Cathar legends we used to discuss, how my mother's people believed that our souls are divine sparks that have been entrapped in a tunic of flesh. Do you remember, Luca?"

"Angelic souls captured by Satan, the *Rex Mundi,* King of the World." I smiled. "As if Satan could be anything other than God's favorite jester!"

Leonardo was in a rare melancholy mood and didn't smile back. "Perhaps the Cathars' view held some truth. Perhaps we must perfect ourselves to free the angel within. Lately I've come to think that if we don't curb lustful desires, we're on the level of the beasts. Mine has been curbed by the unavailability of my beloved, so I hope for some reward."

"You will find love, Leonardo."

"So I have, thanks to the impossibility of being with you: I love nature and her laws. I will pursue her with single-minded determination for the rest of my life. And she will surrender her secrets as a whore does his sweet round rump!" Leonardo grinned now, but I winced. Surprised understanding spread over his face. He was always perceptive. He spoke with his customary kindness. "Luca mio, have I unwittingly hit on one of the secrets of your dark past?"

I walked to the other side of the room and looked out a window. "I was imprisoned within a brothel for many years as a child."

"That explains so many things," he murmured. "I'm so sorry, Luca—"

"How long will you be in Milano?" I asked brusquely.

"I don't know. I think in the long run Sforza will be a better patron than Lorenzo. People say Lorenzo's fortune is disappearing."

"Never underestimate a Medici," I said. "Lorenzo may yet increase his fortune tenfold."

"He's a wily statesman, but when it comes to money, he's no Cosimo," Leonardo said.

"Then cultivate Sforza. I'll come to Milano to visit, it's

not far," I said, with my heart aching again. Long ago, it was Rachel; then it was Maddalena; now Leonardo; I was destined to lose those I loved most.

"Won't you be busy here?" he asked, sounding puzzled.

"I don't know, I'm not much interested in alchemy anymore." I laughed. I sat down on a stool, stretched my legs out in front of me. "I'll stay in Florence until the summer heat gets unbearable, then maybe I'll go to Sardegna. There's a fishing village called Bosa . . ."

"A fishing village? Maddalena wants to go to a fishing village in Sardegna?"

"Maddalena? What does she have to do with anything?" I asked, confused.

"I just thought she'd be with you. . . ." His voice trailed off uncertainly. Then he laughed. "Oh, you haven't heard! Isn't that funny? I thought you were waiting out in the country to allow a decent interval of time to pass, so people wouldn't gossip!"

I leapt to my feet. "Heard what?"

"Rinaldo Rucellai died peacefully in his sleep a month ago. Maddalena is a widow now."

SHE SAT WITH HER MAID in her parlor when I arrived. She was holding a book. She wore a black damascene cottardita of watered silk that emphasized her creamy skin and the protean depths of color in her eyes and hair. She looked up, startled at my arrival. "Signore——"

"Go," I barked at the maid, who took one look at my thunderous face and dropped her embroidery. She scampered out of the room as fast as her short, rotund legs allowed. I stayed where I was because I didn't trust myself. I didn't know what would happen if I got too close to her. I was capable of violence, not toward Maddalena but toward this palazzo, because she hadn't sent for me as soon as her husband had died.

"I thought you'd forgotten me," she said breathlessly.

"As if that's possible? Do I look like my memory fails me?"

"No, I meant because you couldn't be with me—"

"I know what you meant. Marry me."

"Luca—" Maddalena said, coloring. She looked very young and vulnerable.

"Marry me *now*," I demanded. "I don't want to be away from you for one more minute!"

A slow smile spread over her face. "When you didn't come, I thought I was just a passing fancy. That you were spending your time with other women."

"There hasn't been another woman since I saw you on the day they tried to kill Lorenzo," I said. "I haven't touched another woman in four years!"

"I don't know if I can keep the inheritance from Rinaldo's estate," she said. "We never had children, and he had male cousins. I don't know what kind of dowry I can bring to you."

"I don't need a dowry. I'm rich, richer than Rucellai. You'll have a beautiful palazzo. I'll build you one bigger than this one, as big as the Duomo. I'll give you everything and anything."

"I'd marry you if you were poor," she said softly. "I'd live on the streets with you!"

"I'd die before I let us get that poor," I said. I covered the distance between us as if I had wings. I crushed her into me, reveling in her warmth and the hum of life twanging in her like the well-tuned string of a lyre. When she took my face in her hands and touched her soft lips to mine, it was worth it. It was worth the long wait. It was worth the surrender. It was worth everything.

But now I couldn't wait any longer, and she led me upstairs. Evening was beginning, with violet and green shadows outlining the edges of things and dissolving them from the inside out. Maddalena led me into a different bedchamber than the one in which I had given Rucellai the consolamentum. I knew at once that it was her private room. Texture and color were everywhere. Curtains that alternated sheer emerald panels with strips of heavy crimson velvet fluttered at the side of the windows, and several of Botticelli's pretty paintings hung on the walls, as did a worn old tapestry showing St. Francis with the birds. She pulled my head down so my lips met hers, and I kicked backward to knock the door closed.

"You are so beautiful. I've thought of this for so long," she whispered.

"I thought I was the only one!" I took the pins from her hair. I didn't hurry because I wanted to anticipate watching her thick hair fall down around her beautiful shoulders.

"I couldn't let you know how I felt. I was married! And Rinaldo was a good man!" She reached to pull my lucco off over my head. I let her and then I went back to her hair, which was supple and heavy in my hands like the finest satin. Her hand trembled as she unfastened my farsetto, and I shrugged it off to fall on the floor. I finished with her hairpins, and her hair slid down in a brown-red-black sheet, wafting out the scent of lilacs and lemons and dew and every good thing that God or man had ever created. I was happy and I was intoxicated. My knees buckled, my tongue went dry, and the room spun around me.

"It's too much," I said hoarsely. "You're too much."

"You want to stop?"

"No! I didn't mean that, I meant because you're so beautiful!" I cried.

"I know what you meant." She smiled, which nearly undid me.

"God must be kind if I am touching you, I can almost believe that now," I murmured, reaching for the buttons on her cottardita. "One God, a kind God."

"Believe it," she answered, helping me pull off her silk gonna. Finally she stood before me, tiny and luminous, as I'd imagined for the last four years. The scar on her thigh stood out, white on white, her past writ on her flesh in the way of frail humans, made in God's likeness to embody all of time at once. I carried her to the bed. Her skin was inconceivably soft and fragrant. I ran my tongue over her curving shoulder. She smiled. "I always told myself that if we ever came together, if I was ever blessed to hold you, I would always say yes to you. I would never hold back anything from you, never deny you anything. So I'll say it, yes, Luca Bastardo!"

She said yes again eleven months later, when we were married. And she always said yes during the happy years of our marriage, the happiest years I ever knew.

Chapter 22

TIME FLOWED as sinuously as the Arno itself for Maddalena and me as the brilliance and strength of Florence under Lorenzo de' Medici came to an end. Our marriage was celebrated at the crest of Florence's power and influence, and then we lived together in ignorant delight as everything around us unwound. I didn't apprehend the Laughing God's signs until it was too late. Tragedy struck, and everything I held dear was lost. Now my own life will soon be forfeit; such are the costs of ignoring the strains of divine laughter. Perhaps I was always meant only to look and pass on. Perhaps I was not meant to be embedded in the textures of human life the way other people are. I was, after all, a freak, seemingly generated by the gray stones of Florence and her cruel river, the inscrutable Arno. Perhaps the gift of my longevity was simply about observing for a little while longer than other people.

Maddalena gave me what I had always wanted most: a family of my own. In early 1487, she bore me a fine daughter.

We didn't know why it had taken so long, five years, for her to conceive; we theorized that the rape in Volterra had hurt her generative faculty. We were thrilled to find her pregnant at last. Because I was a physico, I was present in the room when the midwife delivered our beautiful, squalling baby girl. We called her Simonetta. She had my peach complexion and reddish-gold hair but had her mother's marvelous variegated eyes. I wondered if she would have my long life span, which I had not discussed with Maddalena. We were too happy for me to cast a shadow by dwelling on that freakish quirk of my nature. Nor did I want to precipitate loss by delving into unsolvable riddles. So I kept silent about important matters which I should have discussed with my wife, who had the right to know everything about me.

I was confronted by my secrets as I went out into a carnevale one spring night under a full moon whose silver light cast mysterious shapes on the cobblestone streets. There seemed to be more and more of these wild, licentious nights as Lorenzo de' Medici stoked Florence's lust for revelry. It was a few months after Simonetta was born, and I was walking with jovial Sandro Filipepi, who had dropped by our home and insisted that I come out and enjoy the festivities.

"You can't allow your beautiful wife to tie you to the bedpost every night and give you a good figa whipping," he was teasing me. "You have to spend some time with men!"

"Go on, you're always poking fun at me." I laughed.

"You're besotted with your wife, it's a good joke on a man," he returned.

"A joke I bear willingly."

"Eagerly, I would say." Sandro chuckled. "With a filly that gorgeous, who wouldn't? Might as well ride her while she's young and sleek. Their looks don't last, you know. Neither does a man's horsemanship. Nothing lasts forever."

"Change is the only constant," I murmured. The bright

sweetness of life couldn't last. I was uneasily reminded of the imminence of the other half, the cruel half, of the choice I had made that night of the philosopher's stone: that I would lose Maddalena. That would be losing everything.

"Life doesn't change you," Sandro said. He took a draught from the jug of wine he carried and then elbowed me in the rib cage. "Is there any truth to those whispered rumors, that you don't age like the rest of us?"

"Only little girls believe gossip," I grumbled. A crowd of screaming, laughing youths raced by, drunk and intent on mischief. Tomorrow there would be graffiti and litter everywhere in the city, stolen horses and broken shop windows, some despoiled young women with blighted marriage prospects, and headaches for both hungover revelers and the city fathers, who would have to clean up Lorenzo's mess.

But Sandro was fixed on another topic. "You better hope you age, Luca, if you wish to keep your wife."

I turned on him so sharply, jabbing my finger into his chest, that he jumped back. "Why do you say that?"

"Easy, easy, man. I don't care about rumors. I know you. You're Luca Bastardo, a purchaser of art who doesn't haggle too much with an honest painter, a good physico, a great drinking buddy, a man crazy in love with his wife. It's just that I also know women, how they are all imbued with the vanity of Venus, though we wish they had the virtue of the Madonna."

"What about women?" I said, turning on my heel and resuming my pace. We passed a band of musicians who were haggling with a group of prostitutes. The former wanted their fun for free, and even during carnevale, money must be made.

"A beautiful woman fears age more than death," Sandro said, combing his long hair back off his shoulders. "And your Maddalena is very, very beautiful."

"Maddalena will be beautiful to me with white hair and a dowager's hump!" I said.

"I believe that's true." Sandro grinned. "But she won't be beautiful to herself."

"I don't believe you," I said with some asperity. But it was true, Maddalena had discovered a wrinkle under her eyes. She didn't like it one bit. She had gone in search of creams and paints which I assured her that she didn't need. With her quick mind, she would soon wonder why she was aging and I wasn't. I should have had this conversation with her long before now. But there was too much joy in the present for me to excavate the past and ruminate on the future. The discussion could wait. Anxiety rose up in me and I tried to quell it with denial. "You speak nonsense, Sandro. My Maddalena is a practical woman."

"You'll see," Sandro said with an air of smugness. We had reached the Ponte alle Grazie, which glowed with silver as if the bridge's stones had absorbed the moon's light and were radiating it back out, multiplied. The Arno gleamed and swirled like a river of white gold beneath the bridge, and the fragrant air from the contado breezed through the streets. Sandro inhaled mightily and said, "Such a beautiful night for a carnevale! Better than the one last month. Tell me, how is your baby? Doing well?"

Instantly I was all smiles. Simonetta was the incarnation of my joy with Maddalena. "She's so amazing," I gushed. "She smiles now. She's ten weeks, so intelligent and beautiful!"

"First children always are," he sang. "By the third, parents are a little less impressed with their own offspring. Are you planning more babes? Have you set to work getting them?"

"A husband has to wait awhile after childbirth before he returns to his wife's embraces," I said with more severity than I intended.

"Really? You've been deprived for a few weeks? How do you manage?" Sandro teased. "Are you visiting every courtesan in Florence?"

"I'm faithful to my wife," I protested. "There's no woman for me but Maddalena!"

"Well, tonight is carnevale, the ordinary rules don't apply! And the more of these Lorenzo holds, the freer people are! You can indulge yourself, there are no consequences. Even decent women lose themselves during carnevale. Like that woman over there, coming up on the bridge, she must look pretty good to you right now. . . ."

I sputtered about my loyalty to my wife, but I couldn't help looking over to where Sandro pointed. A group of boisterous costumed people paused before me, obstructing my view. When they left, I saw one of the goddesses Sandro painted, haloed with the brilliant moonlight. She was small and curvy, and her breasts were so voluptuous that they strained against her sheer gonna, which was clearly visible under her wispy silken mantello. Then I looked at her long thick hair, in which were tied many small ribbons, streaming down her shoulders and back. Black, chestnut, red, gold, all shimmering together in the platinum light of the full moon. Sandro laughed. "I believe your wait is over, friend. And how I envy you!"

Sandro drifted away and the woman floated toward me. Her fragrance reached me first: lilacs, lemons, vanilla, white foam on the sea, and something else, something muskier. The scent of a woman who wants her man. I reached for her but she paused just beyond my fingertips.

"Maddalena, there are things I must tell you," I said, stifling a groan of desire. But it wasn't just desire I felt. I loved this woman completely, with all of my soul. "I don't want to keep secrets from you. I don't want to hold anything back from you, ever! It's time for me to tell you some dark things about myself."

"I think the time for talking is later, after carnevale," she said, her husky voice full of laughter. "Come, let's enjoy the evening! Don't you remember that carnevale night when I was still married to Rinaldo, and you kissed me? I so wanted to be with you! Now I can be!"

"But wait," I said. "You must know . . . I have traits that differentiate me from other men, and they say I am a sorcerer! The people I believe were my parents kept the company of Cathars, a sect the Church eradicated for heresy. There is a letter about it that was in the Silvanos' possession, and then Lorenzo de' Medici acquired it, and I think he's given it back to them. . . ."

"Lover, this is not a time for conversation about secrets and letters," she murmured. Slowly, provocatively, she slipped off her mantello and let it flutter to the ground. I shivered. She moved closer, letting me caress her heavy rich hair. I was filled with heat. Then she sort of skipped up into my arms, and I caught her with my hands under her round bottom and lifted her. She wrapped her legs around me and her skirt rose up around her waist; she wasn't wearing anything beneath the gonna. I cried out, urgently.

"Are you well enough?" I asked hoarsely.

In response, she pulled my head down and kissed me. Her tongue was on me, on my lips and tongue. One of her small clever hands stroked my face, the other held my shoulder. She arched so that her breasts thrust toward my face, and all reason left me. I turned and shoved my wife against the wall of the bridge, tore down my hose, and made love to her where I stood. We weren't the only ones doing this, of course. This scene was played out all over Florence tonight.

We didn't see the cloaked figure standing in the shadows

until after I had set her down and reached a hand out to smooth her luscious hair, which was tousled, its many colors shining riotously in the moonlight.

"They'll arrest us for public lewdness, but it was worth it." I sighed.

"You should be arrested!" the figure cried then, emerging from the shadows.

Maddalena grabbed up her mantello and struggled to cover herself. I faced the man. It was a monk, a Dominican, thin and ugly with a hook nose and overly bright eyes. He looked shocked and inflamed. His eyes were glued to Maddalena's face with the same greed I had seen at Silvano's. I had the bizarre thought that the monk wanted her, that he would never forget her.

"This is my wife, Friar," I said coolly.

"And you treat her like a common whore, rutting out here in the open on this bridge?" He shook his head, still glaring at Maddalena. "I come to this city in which I once preached, wanting to see for myself one of these wild carnevales of which people everywhere are whispering, and what do I find? Immorality and indecency. Whores, ribaldry, debauchery, evil of every stripe and texture; God will smite this place with terrible scourgings!"

"It is carnevale, Friar!"

"It is Satan's folly!" he screamed. "Lorenzo de' Medici has gone too far!"

"We will return to our home immediately, you need not be concerned," I snapped.

"All of Florence is my concern, the tainted soul of the body politic is my concern," he hissed, approaching. Maddalena shrank into me. I put my arm around her. The priest speared me with his eyes. "You were about to confess to some dark things, sinner. Confess properly, to me, and I will give you harsh penances so that God might forgive you your evil!"

"The dark things in my life are between me and God," I said.

"What of this letter I heard you mention? What is the connection between your parents and Cathars? Were your parents Cathars, a galling and heretic people who deserved to be burned? Are you such a blasphemer as well as a . . . a fornicator?" He stepped closer, too close, and I put my hand on his chest to stop him. He wasn't deterred but kept talking, almost rabidly. "I have been told by young Gerardo Silvano, who will go far as a cleric, of an abomination living in Florence. Are you that one? Has God arranged divine justice for you through me?"

"We will be on our way, Friar, you may forget you ever saw us," I said tightly.

"I command that you confess to me!" the man shouted, spitting in my face with his fury. I took Maddalena's hand to pull her around him. The monk blocked my way, shouting about Cathars and the scourge of sorcery and fornication. I kept trying to move around him. He kept thrusting himself in my face. Then he turned to Maddalena. "Whore, Satan's mistress, you fornicate with a sorcerer!" He ripped her mantello through to her gonna, exposing her breasts.

"Enough!" I roared, shaking with anger. I slapped the man with my open palm so hard that he dropped to the ground. "Do not lay hands on my wife!" I drew my sword.

"You have unholy strength," the monk panted. "You practice a sorcery that would undermine all that is good and orderly about this world!"

"There's not much that's good and orderly about this world, monk," I replied. "My wife is the best thing about it!"

"Your wife is a whore, rutting in public, and married to a satanist!" he spat. I held the sword to his throat. I thought about using it. I wanted to kill him. I could have easily in that moment. I would get away with it. Lorenzo's carnevales increasingly left some dead in their wake; this act would not even be questioned. But even if the monk's faith was spiteful, I did not want to be like the Confraternity of the Red Feather, hurting people who differed from me. I had become reconciled to a good God in the last few years. Killing a monk would surely undermine the delicate balance of my truce with heaven, would surely provoke the kind of divine snickering that I no longer heard, and never wanted to again, especially now that I had Maddalena and Simonetta. I withdrew the sword. I have often wondered since then what would have happened if I had used the sword instead. Would my wife and child still be with me? Would Florence still be the greatest city on earth? Or was the wheel already set in motion, would it still have turned through some agency other than this virulent monk?

"Hold your tongue or lose it, monk," I said. "We're leaving now." I carried the sword unsheathed and clasped Maddalena's hand in my free hand. The monk's gleaming eyes were glued to her face. She held her head high though her cheeks were flushed, and we walked with dignity to the other bank. We felt his eyes on our back the whole way.

"God will punish you!" the monk screamed, unable to contain himself. "Your sorcery will bring you to destruction! There is no escape for satanists and fornicators like you!"

We didn't answer but turned down a side street that was thronged with merrymakers. We threaded our way through them, and when we finally stepped free, we took off at a sprint.

Back home we were seized with a fit of laughter which continued unabated until we crawled into bed, where I tried to put the fiery-eyed monk from my head. My intention to reveal the secrets of my long life to Maddalena was dissolved, shattered by the monk's threats, which I wanted to

forget. So I just held my wife with gratitude and let my secrets remain hidden.

WHEN SIMONETTA WAS FIVE, I was summoned to the
Medici villa in Careggi. I saddled a new horse named Marco.
Stalwart Ginori, whose red coat was stippled through with
white, still lived but was hampered with arthritis and age,
illnesses I would never know. I only knew that I was happy:
happy with the incomparable Maddalena, the wife of my
life; happy with Simonetta, my sweet-natured daughter;
happy with my small circle of friends, with my palazzo and
my vast bank account. I rode through the stony streets with
a whistle on my lips. Florence was my home, the greatest
city in the world, and I was finally at home in her.

It was April 1492, a warm spring that had seen many
storms. I wore a light woolen mantello and enjoyed the ride
into the country. A servant let me into the villa and led me
to Lorenzo's bedchamber. He was still young, in his forties,
but he was gravely ill. He burned with a fever that attacked
not only his arteries and veins but also his nerves, bones, and
marrow. His eyesight was failing and his extremities were
swollen with gout. Little was left of *il Magnifico,* who was a
master at everything a man could master: fortune, family,
statesmanship, riding horses, composing music, writing poetry, collecting art, winning allies, championing artists and
philosophers, falconry, calcio, seducing women.

"I didn't know if you'd come," he whispered.

"I'll leave if we're playing cat and mouse," I said. That
made him laugh.

"We've had a grand game of it, haven't we, Bastardo?"
Lorenzo said.

"I don't much like games."

"That's true, you've always been a bit humorless." He

sighed. He rolled his swollen, distorted, pale face away, then looked back at me. "Do you remember when we first met?"

"Here, your grandfather was ill." I sat down on the edge of the bed.

"Yes. I've thought of that day often," Lorenzo said. "You showed up looking like a young god, exactly as you do now, and my grandfather was thrilled to see you. I was so jealous."

"You were his grandson. I may have amused him, but you were the light of his heart."

"You did more than amuse Cosimo de' Medici. He was devoted to you. Is it true you were with him in Venice when he was exiled there as a young man?" Lorenzo asked, his ugly face twisted with pain and illness. I nodded. He said, as if with afterthought, "You'll never forgive me, will you?" I shook my head.

"I've done wrong by you, Luca Bastardo. But you'll have the last word. You know I'm dying, don't you? I won't recover from this illness. There are omens. Two of Florence's lions died in a fight in their cage. She-wolves howl in the night. Strange colored lights flicker in the sky. A woman in Santa Maria Novella was seized by a divine madness and ran around during Mass, screaming about a bull with flaming horns that was tearing down the church. Worst of all"—he wiped his hand across his face—"one of the marble palle, one of the balls, from the lantern on the Duomo fell toward my house. The palle fell, the Medici palle. It's a sign."

"Signs are what you read in them. Mostly they're God's jokes."

Lorenzo laughed, but more weakly. His face was ravaged with pain. "You worship comedy, and here I've always considered you humorless."

"What do you want from me, Lorenzo?" I asked, but not unkindly.

"Just before he died, Nonno told me that you had a

marvelous power in your hands. You touched him, and it soothed his heart. It helped him. He said it gave him extra days to live!"

"It's not power. It's the opposite. It's what happens when you relinquish power."

"Can you touch me thus?" he whispered. I stared at his ugly face with its fierce, glittering black eyes. Despite the suffering there, I could not imagine letting my heart open for him, as the consolamentum required. The sack of Volterra, the years of controlling me through my fear of the Silvano clan, the way he used people like pawns for his own goals . . . I did not trust him. I went to look out the window at the leafy poplar trees Cosimo had planted.

"What did you do with the letter you obtained from the Silvanos, about my origins?"

"I kept it. I made a copy which I gave back to the Silvanos a few years ago."

"There's a monk who's heard about it," I said grimly. "It doesn't bode well for me or my family. And you want me to give you the consolamentum?"

Lorenzo laughed wheezily. "I understand, Bastardo, it's impossible for you. That letter is just the latest round in those games you don't like, starting with that calcio game a few weeks before Nonno died. At least we won. We've had our victories, even if death wins ultimately."

"I could try to give you the consolamentum," I said, grudgingly. Lorenzo was Cosimo's grandson, and Cosimo had been a true friend.

"But would you be trying for my sake or for his?" Lorenzo whispered, reading my mind in his canny way. "I don't want Cosimo's leftovers! I never have!"

"Then what can I do for you?"

"You can bear witness," he said, licking his dry lips. "Remember the glory of what I've done. Your youth seems to have no end. Perhaps your life won't, either. You're like one of the ancient patriarchs of whom the Bible speaks, who lived for hundreds of years. Perhaps your father and mother were such people, and that's why those mysterious Cathars attended them. Ficino translated a document which seems to indicate this."

"Lorenzo, what document? And how do you know so much about my parents? Only from that letter?"

"I had to know everything about you. I tracked your movements, paid your agents to reveal to me what they did for you, and what they discovered. I was jealous, jealous of Nonno's affection for you and of your service to him. I wanted you to love me as you loved him."

"You cannot manipulate affection from people. It must be freely given."

"I have been trusted with the governance of the greatest city on earth. I had no time to waste worrying about other men's freedom when the security of Florence demanded everything!" he barked, then panted from the exertion. "I answer to history, not to individuals! That's why Volterra had to be sacrificed. If I did not act with ruthless authority, everything my grandfather and his father had worked to create here in Florence, all the art and letters, all the learning from the Platonic Academy, everything noble we've achieved, it would all have been uprooted and denied to future generations! What is freedom when compared to that?"

"Freedom is everything, it's what created the art and letters and learning you're so proud of. Individual lives matter." I turned away, feeling nauseated. "I would have liked to have had that letter. And I'd like to read Ficino's document. You've interfered with the destinies of other men, Lorenzo. How can you expect love to be given you when you do that?"

"I have been more concerned with allegiance than with love," he admitted. "But it has been my gift to guide the destinies of other men! It has been my gift to create history, to shape the future. Your gift is longevity. Since you can't give me the consolamentum, I want you to use your gift in witness to my gifts. My gifts to Florence."

"You may have a reversal of your illness and be back on your feet in the Signoria, commanding the city," I said. "The consolamentum may be unnecessary."

"Don't tell me what I want to hear; you've never done that, and it doesn't suit you!"

"Because I didn't tell you what you wanted to hear about Volterra, you recalled the Silvanos sworn to kill me!" I snapped.

"You're the one who left my service over Volterra!" Lorenzo replied. "Why are you still so angry? Isn't that where you first met your lovely Maddalena? I heard rumors to that effect! Would you have met her and come to love her if it weren't for the sack of Volterra?"

"Innocent people were hurt! Innocent people died!"

"There are no innocent people!" he flung back at me. "Being born into this life sets us all up for suffering! And we don't ever know what joy will come out of suffering!"

"And that's what makes God laugh," I said with more ferocity than any other living man would have dared direct at Lorenzo de' Medici.

"If God laughs, it's at me, who am dying! You've been given God's embrace: Cosimo's respect and love, unending youth, and the beauty of Apollo!" Lorenzo spat back. We regarded each other with fury which slowly softened to pain. We each had suffered. Each saw it in the other. No words were said, but we came to an understanding. I still would not give him the consolamentum because of what he'd done to me and Volterra, but I no longer hated him. I have wondered since then, in light of all that's happened, how time and events would have passed if I had just placed my hands on him, without thought or judgment, in that moment of understanding. Would the consolamentum have poured forth and saved him, as it had resurrected Rinaldo Rucellai? If the consolamentum had healed him, could I have averted the tragedies, personal and civic, that came to pass after Lorenzo the Magnificent died? Was I partly responsible for the events that have rendered me willing to die, not just because I chose love and death in a vision, but also because I did not alter the course of history when I had the chance, by killing Nicolo Silvano and Savonarola or by saving Lorenzo de' Medici? Could I have changed fate if I had chosen love over anger, over fear, as Lorenzo de' Medici, the flawed protector of Florence and all things Florentine, lay dying? Or was the wheel just turning?

"Listen then, Luca Bastardo who pins his hopes of salvation on God's laughter. Listen to what I have accomplished. I have guided Florence to glory in commerce, in letters, and in the arts. I have sat with Popes and I have been excommunicated. Most important, I maintained a balance among the states," Lorenzo recounted in a dreamy voice.

"This was my greatest feat. I kept Milano and Napoli from war, kept the balance with Venezia and Roma. My peace kept the peninsula of Italia strong. This strength allowed Tuscan culture to flourish. It gave our nobles and merchants money to sponsor art, so that artists could paint and sculpt and create. It allowed educated men to promote education, the study of the past, philosophy, and science. The fruits of this period of peace will feed mankind for a thousand generations! Don't you see that, Luca?"

I was quiet for a moment. Then I nodded. "There's truth to what you say."

His old pleasure in victory flashed over Lorenzo. It was quickly followed by an expression of sorrow. "But the strength and peace of Italia won't outlive me. The Frankish monarch will march into our land. The Italian states lack strength of unity, and he's united the Frankish states under him. There's one France, but not one Italia. He'll march through the peninsula. One city-state after another will fall to his armies. Even if all of the peninsula doesn't surrender, he'll siphon away the might of Florence. You'll see. I love my son Piero, but he will not maintain the balance. Perhaps, if I could live ten more years, he'd mature into something worthy of the Medici name. But now he's too young. Foolish and fearful. Weak."

"You were young when your father left the guidance of Florence to you," I pointed out, sitting again on the edge of his bed, where I'd sat to speak with the ailing Cosimo so long ago.

"Too young." Lorenzo sighed. "Strong enough. But I've made mistakes."

"I never thought I'd hear you confess that!"

"There are people I've invited back to Florence who should not be here."

"The Silvanos."

He laughed weakly, closing his eyes against pain. "Others, too. But I am sorry about the return of that family, Luca Bastardo. Truly. I was happy for you when you and Maddalena were married. I knew you loved her when I saw you sitting next to her at dinner that night at Rucellai's. Did you receive the wedding gift I sent?"

"Several casks of fine wine," I said, raising my eyebrows. "I had them all tested for poison."

Lorenzo laughed again, this time until he coughed. His high-pitched, nasal voice sounded almost cheerful when he spoke next. "So I was right in my judgment of you, after all, Luca Bastardo. It consoles me. You are humorless. Killing you would have ruined the game, ended it too quickly. Don't you understand yet?"

"It's more diverting to watch me squirm."

Lorenzo nodded slowly. "It's not the Silvano family I would worry most about, if I were you. You've avoided them successfully for a long time . . . a hundred fifty years? More?" He paused, gazing at me, but I didn't answer. He sighed deeply. "Two years ago I invited back to Florence someone I shouldn't have. He'll cause trouble. A Dominican preacher born in Ferrara."

"My wife likes the eloquent Augustinian monk Fra Mariano."

"So do all the upper classes, but the *popolo minuto,* the little people, have different tastes," said Lorenzo. "They like to hear about wickedness. They like to hear the vanity of the upper classes denounced. They can't afford vanity, the very vanity that has fueled Florence to greatness, so they want to hear it condemned."

I narrowed my eyes, considering. "You're speaking of the idiot monk who preaches against good art and Plato's philosophy and threatens everyone with the world ending if we don't reform our ways instantly? I've never seen him, just heard about him."

"He's not an idiot, though he's even uglier than I am. He claims that God speaks through him, and his sermons have become so popular that San Marco can't hold his congregants. He's moved to Santa Maria del Fiore. The friar criticizes us Medici continually. He wants Florence to frame a new constitution, based on the Venetian constitution, without the office of the Doge!"

I shrugged. "I'm not worried. We Florentines are who we are: pleasure-and-money-and food-loving folk who produce great artists, thinkers, and bankers. No monk, no matter how fiery, can reform the basic nature of Florence and her people."

"Not in the long run," Lorenzo whispered. "But he's fired

the imagination of the people, so he'll wreak havoc for a few years, watch and see. I know how people are. I know what people want. He'll seize on the Frankish advance to remake Florence in his own mold. He'll cast out the Medici. His sermons will reach into the Church to shake it; he's already called the Church a prostitute; he'll bring the wrath of Roma onto Florence. He wants reform, in the Church and in our city. Between him and the Frankish, Florence will lose her power. She'll never again be the fifth element, the greatest city on earth. If I were to live, I would exile this monk, or, better yet, have him murdered in his sleep. Watch him and beware, Luca. You possess a singular gift, and when a Silvano calls his attention to it, Savonarola will suspect you of demonism. Fear him, Luca. If I were you, I would fear for you and yours."

"I already know about fearing people who call me a witch," I said dryly.

Lorenzo lifted his head up. "It's not demonism, though, Luca. I know that. You asked me before how I know about your family and I told you about a document that Ficino translated. It's called the *Last Apocalypse of Seth,* and it's a forbidden gospel, a Cathar holy book. It speaks of a secret race of men fathered by Adam's son Seth. These people have lives of fantastic longevity, but not because they're evil. It's because they hid themselves and kept their blood pure."

"Pure blood won't endear anyone to the Church," I said.

"No, it won't." Lorenzo shook his head. "The story is that these pure-blooded people have been persecuted and killed throughout history, especially by the Pope's armies. They're living proof of a history the Church doesn't want revealed. But, Luca, the real threat to the Church is greater than you, and this is my gift to you." He paused and I watched him carefully, wondering what he was going to reveal. He smiled. "You're not the only one of these people left. There was a recent note written on the manuscript that Ficino translated. It says a large group of them have a community hidden in distant mountains. They're waiting until their numbers grow strong, then they'll reveal themselves. Your family will come for you, Luca. Avoid trouble if you can, and you'll be reunited with your own kind."

Chapter 23

LORENZO DIED A WEEK LATER. I did not attend the funeral, though I did send a letter expressing my condolences and asking for a copy of Ficino's translation of the *Last Apocalypse of Seth*. I received a curt response that Lorenzo had left explicit instructions that the only thing to be given to me upon his death was an old saddle, which was duly delivered to my home. It was, of course, the same saddle he had given me decades earlier, which I had returned to him after the sack of Volterra. I was left with the uneasy knowledge that Lorenzo had known more about my origins than I did, which did not bode well for me, and that he was still playing games with me from whatever purgatory had received him.

And Lorenzo's words to me from his deathbed ripened into fact. After Lorenzo's death, Savonarola's sermons grew more intense and apocalyptic. The friar was determined to stamp out the immorality and corruption in Florence that he claimed was encouraged by the Medici. He prophesied

doom and the scourge of war. In 1492, Savonarola predicted
that Lorenzo and Pope Innocent VIII would die, and when
they did, he was emboldened. He thundered from the pulpit
of the Duomo: Florence would be cleansed at the hands of
the Frankish army. As he predicted, and as Lorenzo had told
me would happen, in 1494, King Charles led a vast Frankish
army into the peninsula. The army crossed the Alps bearing
white silk banners that read *Voluntas Dei*. Lodovico Sforza,
the ruler of Milano, saw a means to realize his own ambitions and welcomed them, despite Milano's alliance with
Florence.

The army marched south and Piero de' Medici, Lorenzo's
son, tried to make peace with Charles by handing him Pisa
and some other fortresses on the Tyrrhenian coast. Florence,
which prided itself on its dominion over Pisa, was outraged
by this craven behavior. Lorenzo de' Medici would never
have permitted such a thing. The Signoria closed the doors
on Piero and expelled the Medici. Mobs broke into the fab-
ulously appointed Medici palazzo on Via Larga and looted it.
Savonarola used his influence with the masses to form a
new republic. He outlawed gambling, horse racing, obscene
songs, profanity, excessive finery, and vice of any kind. He
instituted severe penalties: tongue-piercing for blasphemers,
castration for sodomites. The monk then welcomed the
Frankish army as liberators. On Florence's behalf, he pleaded
with King Charles to stay outside of the city's strong stone
walls. But on November 17, 1494, Savonarola's persuasion
proved unconvincing; King Charles marched twelve thousand troops into Florence.

Maddalena and I stood together on the balcony of our
palazzo, watching. Stamping hooves and footsteps reverberated through the city as a vast army entered into its narrow
winding stone streets. King Charles rode at the head.

"Look at him in his steel armor, a tiny little man astride a war horse so big it makes him look like a girlchild's doll," I commented. I put my arm around Maddalena and discovered that she was shivering. "Carissima mia, are you cold?" I pulled my mantello off and wrapped it around her, tucking it up around her pretty chin to protect her from the wind and chill.

"Not cold," she whispered. "I don't like the sight of an army marching into a city."

"Maddalena, it's not like Volterra," I said, pulling her close to my chest.

"You must think me silly to be afraid." She laughed, but her voice trembled.

"Never," I said, kissing the top of her head. Her vulnerability made me love her more. Maddalena turned in my embrace and looked into my eyes with candor, letting me see directly into the heart of the scared little girl who still lived inside her. That little girl was so achingly real and vibrant that it brought my youthful self to the fore, also. Luca as an abandoned, betrayed, brutalized child was present with her young, hurt, terrified Maddalena. My pain and her pain, and my joy and her joy, my love and her love, my fear and her fear, all existed together like wave peaks on the same bittersweet river, and there were no barriers between us. We didn't speak for a long time. An army tramped into the city and shouts rang out everywhere, but we were streaming into a deep communion of selves. Then Simonetta ran out with her reddish-blond plaits flying around her head. She wriggled herself in between us until Maddalena and I laughed and linked arms around her.

"What pretty costumes they wear, Papa," Simonetta observed. She was seven and had an endless supply of questions, and now she scrunched her nose and tilted her head. "Do soldiers stay so pretty when they fight?"

"No, darling, in a real fight, their costumes won't stay fancy," I answered.

Maddalena winced. She whispered over our daughter's head, "I know what soldiers do to children!"

"I would fight an army for you two," I responded with vigor.

"You would win!" Simonetta said. She gave me an adoring look that made me melt all over again. Something about the way a daughter loves her father made me determined to protect my wife and child at whatever cost to myself. My life meant nothing except as it served their lives.

Simonetta asked, "Will you have to fight, Papa?"

"I don't think so," I said, tugging her braid. "The army won't stay long. Florence let in the Frankish army, but Florentines won't consent to be treated like a captured city. Charles will threaten and the Florentine delegates will call his bluff; Charles won't want to fight in this city. The streets are so narrow that his army can't get a purchase to unfold itself in strength. Florentines who know the city have the advantage. Charles risks having his army stopped on the banks of the Arno. He won't let that happen. He'll take money and be on his way."

"I hope you're right," Maddalena said in an anxious tone. It was an uneasy time for all of Florence, with Savonarola assuming power and then the Frankish army occupying the city. Even after the Frankish marched back out ten days later, Florence was unsettled. Her taverns and brothels were closed, her young men sang hymns instead of ribald ditties, and unruly gangs of children who called themselves "Weepers" roamed the city, enforcing Savonarola's harsh laws. Trade suffered, crops failed—and Florence, the city of bankers and merchants, went broke.

Somehow the tensions of those days did not affect

Maddalena and me. We lived simply and quietly to avoid attracting attention. We were encapsulated in our love for each other and in our pride in our beloved daughter, which shielded us. Maddalena submitted easily to Savonarola's strict dress codes though she did not attend his sermons. Privately we both thought his severity was unbalanced, and we stayed away from him and his entourage. Then, one day in February 1497, Maddalena came home and asked Simonetta and me to attend one of Savonarola's carnevales of sobriety and abnegation.

When she arrived, Simonetta and I were engaged in the study of Latin. I declined to hire a tutor, preferring to spend the time myself with my daughter. I was a worthy teacher. I had taught this intelligent child's mother. I had been professore to no less a personage than Leonardo, about whose work in Milano we heard great things. He'd sent me a letter and a sketch describing a fresco, the *Last Supper,* on the wall of the refectory of Santa Maria delle Grazie. I planned to go to Milano to see it. Sandro Botticelli had seen it, and he'd wept as he described it, an overwhelming and masterful expression of a single dramatic moment, the moment after Christ has said "One of you shall betray me." Each of the different disciples was completely revealed in his expression, from Andrew's astonishment in his open mouth, to Peter's pugnacious, knife-gripping eagerness to declare his innocence, to the swarthy, staring Judas leaning away from Christ in guilt and isolation. Leonardo himself had written me, "The painter has two objectives, man and the intention of his soul. The first is easy, the latter hard, because he has to represent it by the movement of the limbs."

But Leonardo had depicted every soul perfectly in his fresco, including a Christ whose serenity and beauty were deeply moving. Leonardo had added to his virtuoso portrayals a sublime composition of hidden triangles and a ravishing tension among the ordinary, yet transfigured, items of this last meal and first Holy Communion: the wineglasses, forks, bread loaves, and pewter dishes. The bread of life foreshadowed death. But immanent in the *Last Supper* was the sanctity of Communion, an ongoing blessing for believers. And thus is death implicit in life, and the most common moment holds both redemption and tragedy.

One of those common moments found Simonetta and me upstairs, in the workshop that had been converted to a playroom for Simonetta's use. We were working on a translation of Cicero. It was heavy going for a ten-year-old girl, but bright Simonetta was managing. There was a bustle at the door and we ran downstairs to see who it was.

"Mama! I'm so happy to see you!" Simonetta laughed, leaping to embrace her mother.

"Simonetta mia." Maddalena hugged the little girl. "How are your lessons?"

"The hour we spent over Latin was torturous for the ragazza," I said. I leaned over the young blond head to kiss Maddalena, to inhale her lilac and lemon scent and run my hand over her soft cheek. I never missed an opportunity to touch my wife, which comforted me later.

She said gaily, "Luca, Fra Savonarola is holding another carnevale."

"Carnevale, is that what he's calling these dreary events? Carnevale is when a beautiful woman in a costume kisses a man on a bridge and makes him feel like the only man alive!"

Maddalena laughed. "This one is worth seeing; the whole city is outside today, listening to his sermon and taking part in the procession. Why don't we all go?"

I had avoided the monk ever since shrewd Lorenzo had warned me about him, but I had long ago promised myself to say yes to Maddalena. So I agreed, put on my dullest, soberest lucco and mantello, and the three of us went out.

Fury scorched the streets of Florence, the fury of purity, of perfection, of unthinking obedience to a madman, the self-appointed voice of God. I should have known that this kind of insistence on purity must inevitably lead to tragedy, death, and grief. Masses of people dressed in drab clothing surged toward the Piazza della Signoria. A gang of the young thugs who were Savonarola's enforcers ran up to us just as we turned onto the Via Larga.

"Give us a vanity!" a black-haired boy of about twelve demanded. "Some material possession which keeps your heart from righteousness!" A dozen children, all dressed in white, clamored and pressed in on us, causing Simonetta, who was ten, to eye them with curiosity. The boy threatened, "We won't leave until you surrender a vanity, we are collecting them for holy Savonarola himself!"

"Here." Maddalena laughed. She shrugged off her mantello and detached and then pulled off her sleeves, which were emerald green and made of the finest silk. She had put them on thinking her mantello would hide them. The children cheered and grabbed at the sleeves. I smiled at Maddalena's fine slim white arms, which elicited within me warm licentious thoughts of which the pious Savonarola would never approve.

"You'll have your reward in heaven!" the boy cried, and the children ran off.

"You are too generous, Maddalena," I said dryly, helping her put back on her gray mantello.

"Mama is always wonderful, but I don't think she had a choice just now," Simonetta said in her piquant way. "Those children were very determined! Do you think if they were reading Cicero they would have better manners?" Of course her words made us laugh and hug her, and the three of us clung together as we moved on toward the piazza.

Even the outskirts of the piazza were tightly packed with

people. The murmuring throngs had a sinister air of purpose which made my chest tighten with anxiety. I knew from experience that large groups of people too easily whiplash into cruelty. I remembered the crowds who would have burned me for being a sorcerer and the mob that stoned Moshe Sforno and little Rebecca during the first outbreak of the plague. I thought of the army that plundered Volterra. Something in man's nature allowed wanton destruction to flourish unchecked when enough people were present. I thought of turning around to go home, but the swarm of people was too thick and importunate. Maddalena, Simonetta, and I were pressed forward by crowds behind us. I held Simonetta's hand tightly on one side, and Maddalena clung to her other hand.

In the center of the piazza, we beheld a horrifying sight: a vast pyramid of jumbled objects reaching ten stories into the sky. As we were slowly pushed forward to the edge of the pyramid, the objects resolved into their specific forms as the beautiful products which made Florence so rich and full and hungry: books, wigs, paintings, carnevale masks from Lorenzo's time, mirrors, powder puffs, cards and dice, pots of rouge, vials of perfume, velvet caps, chessboards, lyres, and countless other items. Some were silly trinkets, others were precious. In the heap I saw paintings by Botticelli, some by Filippino Lippi, another by Ghirlandaio, and one that was definitely an early work of Leonardo's, which made my heart clutch inward in my chest. I saw rich cottardite and fur-lined mantelli, painted chests, gold bracelets, silver chalices, and even jeweled crucifixes. The masses were throwing more items into the pile, dispensing with the precious, artful vanities the desire for which had made Florence the shining queen of the cities on the Italian peninsula. If Lorenzo de' Medici had lived, he would have rallied the Florentine army against Savonarola and this mob to prevent such a desecration of Florence and all things Florentine. I wondered to what extent I had a hand in this obscenity because I hadn't given Lorenzo the consolamentum, which might have extended his life.

"Down, down with all gold and decorations, down where the body is food for the worms!" cried a voice, and I realized it was Savonarola himself. I had never seen him, had never been interested in attending his sermons, had wanted nothing to do with him, and neither had Maddalena, but now I angled myself to get a view of his face. After all, this friar was turning Florence inside out. His speech created an uproar that almost drowned out his next words: "Repent, O Florence! Clothe thyself in the white garments of purification! Wait no longer, for there may be no further time for repentance! The Lord drives me forward to tell you, Repent!"

I finally caught a glimpse of his face. Instantly I recognized him. He was the thin, fiery-eyed monk who had watched Maddalena and me make love on the Ponte alle Grazie years ago, who had torn her dress and denounced us. All of my old instincts for danger screamed: I still remembered the way that he'd looked at her. I remembered his threats to us. I should have killed him when I could. The flesh on the backs of my arms and neck prickled and my stomach roiled. "Maddalena, we have to leave!" I said urgently. "Right now!"

She couldn't hear me. A ruckus was erupting to our left, as someone with a Venetian accent screamed out offers of twenty thousand *scudi* for all the artwork in the pile. An intelligent man among beasts, I thought, but an ugly roar of disapproval spewed forth from the crazed crowd. The Venetian's voice was abruptly silenced. I hollered again for Maddalena, to no avail. Trumpets blew, bells rang, and drowned out my words. I leaned over, but Simonetta dropped my hand. She pointed at something and ran, pulling Maddalena along behind her. I tried to follow but got caught behind a raging group of people who had laid hands on the Venetian, stolen his coat, and were mocking up a broomstick and straw effigy of him. I kicked and punched, but I couldn't get clear of the group for several minutes, until the effigy of the Venetian had been thrown onto the pile. By that time, there was no sign of Simonetta and Maddalena.

I looked around in a panic and shouted their names, but guards were pouring into the piazza to surround the bonfire, and I couldn't even hear myself over the din of the crowd and the ringing of all the bells in the city. All one hundred thousand people living in Florence at the time seemed to be in the piazza and the streets surrounding it. I kept pushing through people, frantically searching faces. I called out for my wife and daughter until my throat was hoarse. The guards set fire to the pyramid of vanities with the hapless Signoria watching from their balcony. I climbed walls and gates and peered into the crowd from above, to no avail. After a few hours I headed home, knowing that Maddalena and Simonetta would return there, if they hadn't already.

I wended my way against the flood tide of people heading toward Savonarola's bonfire, which blazed orange and red, a funeral pyre for Florence, illuminating the heavens. When I finally reached my palazzo, Sandro Filipepi waited in front of my door. I knew something was wrong the moment I laid eyes on him. Sandro, that good-humored man, was weeping.

"Don't go in," Sandro said brokenly, embracing me. His face was wet against my cheek.

"What happened?" I cried. "Where are Maddalena and Simonetta?"

"Prepare yourself, Luca," Sandro sobbed, gripping me by both arms. "I thought Savonarola would cure the Church of her excesses, that he offered some kind of resolution for us, but now this!"

I ran in through my open door into my foyer, where

there stood a small circle of silent people, my servants, Maddalena's fat maid, two of Maddalena's friends, and a few strangers. They were all weeping. I wailed with dread and knowing. They cleared a path for me. Spread out on the floor lay Maddalena and Simonetta. They were waterlogged, their dark dresses fanning out around their pale incandescent bodies like inky spills from a black river. A glance told me they were dead, but still I checked them for a pulse. I knelt first beside Simonetta, because Maddalena would have wanted that. Our daughter's blondish-orange hair, the same color as mine, was soaked, as was the plain brown cottardita mandated by Savonarola. Her mantello was missing and I moved a thick lock of hair from her face before my trembling fingers could alight on her neck. Nothing. Nothing at her wrist, either. The same for Maddalena. I went back to Simonetta, picked up her small, sweet head and tilted it back and blew air into her. I don't know how many times I breathed into her, willing her to wake up, before Sandro pulled me off her.

"Basta, enough! They're gone, Luca," he cried, his face wet with tears. "But I will paint your daughter's pretty hair and your wife's sweet face until the Lord calls me to Him, so they will live forever that way!"

"How did this happen?" I asked numbly. There were torches blazing in the sconces, but it was hard to see. Everything was melting in front of me, the people and the walls bleeding into each other, a heavy kaleidoscope of color collapsing down like a stone wall to press on top of me. I could barely focus. My body was airless, breathless, locked in.

"I saw it, by chance," whispered Maddalena's maid tearfully. "Savonarola himself pointed at her through the crowd. Some men lifted her up on their shoulders so the monk could see her, and he denounced the book that she was holding, a book she had tried to save from the bonfire. It must have been a book about astrology, because he was screaming 'Whore! Astrologer! Heretic's wife!' She fell off the men's shoulders and a crazed mob chased Maddalena into the Arno. They were screaming at her about being a whore and about the blasphemy of astrology and how she had to be cleansed. Simonetta was chasing them and she ran into the water to help her mother, and a giant swell came over the surface of the water and they both went down! A little while later, they washed up."

"The little girl kept up, even though Maddalena kept trying to get her to fall away and save herself," Sandro added sadly. "Simonetta was determined and wouldn't listen."

"She would be determined," I said hoarsely. "She was devoted to her mother and me." Stricken faces ringed me, and I waved for them to leave. I sent them out, even Maddalena's maid, who howled with pain and had to be led away by the other servants.

When I was alone, I lay down on the floor between Simonetta and Maddalena. The heavy, wet fabric of their clothes made squishy sounds around me as I scooted in. I took each of them by the hand. The river water had made a puddle on the floor that seeped into my clothes, into my skin and bones, as if to dissolve what was left of me after my love had been taken away: my empty, useless physical body. I lay in silence, waiting for death, praying for it. I prayed as I had done only two other times: standing in front of Giotto's frescoes of St. John the Evangelist in Santa Croce, and after burying the burly, red-haired Ginori in the hills of Fiesole. I envied Ginori for dying soon after his family had died, and that's what I prayed for. I prayed to die. I prayed to join my wife and daughter, wherever they were. I begged God, pleaded, promised Him anything, if only He would bring the joke to its end.

My prayers weren't answered. It became clear that I

wouldn't die that night, so I talked to Maddalena and
Simonetta. I told them how much I loved them. I told them
how much they meant to me, how important they were,
how I was infinitely grateful for the chance to love them.
I had told them those things many times before, there
was some comfort in that. And then I told them my secrets.
The secrets that I should have told my beloved Maddalena
when I had the chance, but had failed to, because of the fear
within me.

"My name is Luca, and I am something like immortal," I
said to them. "I am over one hundred seventy-five years old.
I do not age as other men do. I knew Giotto, and I was sold
into a brothel by my best friend, Massimo. I have killed
many people." As my voice spun shadows on the torchlight-
stained walls, they seemed to sit up beside me, and to listen.

When Sandro came for me the next morning, I was
quite mad.

I WAS NOT SANE for the burials of my wife and daughter.
Sandro dressed me and held me still for the funeral service,
so that I did not run naked and howling through the nave of
the church. Then I abandoned my palazzo for the streets.
Wealth and plentiful food and a beautiful home meant nothing to me anymore. As I had done as a child, I slept in piazze
and alongside churches, under the four bridges across the
Arno and beside the great stone walls of the city. I ate whatever I found or what was given to me. I was a beggar again,
with ragged clothes and long, dirty hair and a wild matted
beard.

There was a brief lucid moment when a funeral pyre
pushed back the veils in my mind into something more
diaphanous. Fire lit up the Piazza della Signoria. In the
place where Savonarola had held the bonfire of the vanities,

a scaffold surrounded by tinder was erected. The body of
Savonarola was burned with those of two other monks, after
they'd been hung by Inquisitors. I was almost myself as
flames licked up into the sky. In a state that bordered on
both madness and reason, I could clearly see how the monk
had erred. Savonarola had not perceived one essential fact.
While it is true that things of the other world give meaning
to this life, it is also true that things of this world give meaning to the other. The fundamental truth of the human heart
is that, while we are gods, as Ficino believed, we are also dust
and mud, the rich red-brown mud of hillsides and green for-
est underbrush and black fields furrowed for crops. We are
creatures of both heaven and earth. It is not our purity that
will save us, it is our richness.

In a few hours the three monks were burned, and blackened legs and arms gradually dropped off. Parts of their
bodies remained hanging from the chains that had bound
them to the scaffold, and people in the crowd threw stones
to make them fall. Then the hangman and his helpers hacked
down the scaffold and burned it on the ground, bringing in
heaps of brushwood and stirring up the fire over the dead
bodies so that the very last piece of their bodies was consumed. Carts took away the dust to the Arno near the Ponte
Vecchio so that no remains could be found and cherished by
the fools of Florence who had brought their destructor to
power.

TIME WAS LOOPED UP into a meaningless knot for me, so
I don't know how long it was before the priest came for me.
I spent my days down by the Arno, staring into its depths,
which embodied the cosmos. The beautiful faces of my wife
and daughter were spread out like the film of dissolved pigments, iridescent rainbows on the surface of the water.

Sometimes, if I squinted my eyes, I could even see Marco. Marco my old friend who had given me candy and good advice. I remembered his long eyelashes and elegant gait. I spied other people in the waves, too: Massimo and his mis-shapen body and clever mind; Ingrid with her blond hair and bruised stare; Bella whose fingers had been cut off to punish me for trying to leave the brothel; Giotto who crackled with warm kindness and lively intelligence; the physico Moshe Sforno and his daughters, especially Rachel, who had taught me and teased me and loved me; Cosimo and Lorenzo de' Medici; Geber and the Wanderer and Leonardo. Always there was Maddalena with her haunting eyes and the thick, lush multicolored hair that I never tired of touching and kissing. Sometimes when I saw her looking back at me from the water, I could smell her, too: that scent of lilacs in the clear light with its lemony undertone. I woke on the muddy ground with her scent in my nose and on my tongue, as if I'd been loving her in my sleep. I did not want to wake. And I could not elude my sweet little Simonetta, for whom I cherished so many dreams. She was going to be a scholar and philosopher like Ficino and a painter like Leonardo or Botticelli and marry a king; with her beauty and charm and the huge dowry I could provide, there was no limit to her possibilities. And she would be young forever, as I was.

A WOMAN APPROACHED ME on a warm spring day. She brought bread and I said, "Thank you, signora. But I'm not hungry." I thrust it back at her, but she wouldn't take it.

"I don't like to see people starve," she said. "Please, eat."

"I'm not hungry now." I smiled. "Almost two centuries ago, I was a boy who was always hungry."

"Two centuries?" she said, her voice startled. "Do you know what you're saying? Or are you mad?"

"Maybe. It doesn't matter. I had a beautiful daughter with hair the color of mine, and a wife I chose in a vision, and God took them away. Nothing matters now."

"You must come with me!" she cried, suddenly distraught. Her bright violet eyes lit up, confusing me.

"No," I said. "I must stay close to the river, Maddalena is here, they are all here, everything!" The woman insisted and grabbed my arm, but I shook her off and ran away. The bread fell on the ground and a dog got it, but that's the way of life: necessary things are lost.

The next day the priest came. "It's time, Luca Bastardo," he said. He smiled in satisfaction. He was a man of about thirty, and there was something familiar about his face, but I couldn't place it. The only faces I could interpret were those of Maddalena, my wife, and Simonetta, my daughter, who sang to me from the all-encompassing river.

The priest smiled even more broadly. "It's time." I did not understand and he was little more than a shimmer above a hot flagstone on a broiling summer day, but I went with him willingly. Dimly I was aware that he led me to his refectory. A servant washed me, shaved me, dressed me in clean clothes. The servant took me to where the priest sat at a great desk, and I began to understand that he was important. I looked around and realized that I was at the monastery of San Marco, to which the Medici had contributed so much money. There was an exquisite altarpiece here by Fra Angelico, that reverent painter who wept before touching his brush to the holy figure of Christ. The altarpiece showed the Madonna and Child on a golden throne, with clarity of composition and a background of Tuscan cypresses and cedars.

The mists in my head thinned to admit some light. I turned back to the priest, and carefully I perused his features: the dark hair, narrow face, jutting chin, and bladelike nose. I knew who he was: a Silvano. The welter of confused images and memories in which I had been living suddenly snapped like a tree struck by lightning, and everything came into focus for me. Sanity seized my core, and with it, the agony of loss. I cried out and dropped to my knees.

"Yes, that's right." The priest looked pleased. "You know who I am, don't you?"

"Silvano," I mumbled breathlessly, because the deaths of my wife and child were tearing a hole in my midriff. I couldn't breathe and I was doubled over on the floor, retching.

"Gerardo Silvano." He nodded. "I am the grandson, many times removed, of Bernardo Silvano, of Nicolo Silvano. I have seen your face in a painting by Giotto, and I have been schooled since I was a child in the importance of your destruction. My family has waited a long time to wreak our vengeance on you. You are a freak, a blasphemous creature, a sorcerer of unholy long years, a murderer! The deaths of your wife and child have weakened your demonic powers and made you ready. I will now bring you to justice and fulfill the curse placed on you by my forefathers. And I will use you to this end. You will attract to yourself your doom. A cardinal who is marked to be Pope will pass by you, and you will declare yourself to him."

"I'm ready," I said.

"Do you understand what is required? What will happen?"

"Yes," I said. "I will declare my name and the length of my years, and the cardinal will have me executed for being a witch." My worthless life without Maddalena would come to an end. I would be spared the agony of the loss of my wife and daughter. A vast relief flooded through me; I would finally be with them. It was beautiful to me, a joke worthy of Divine Providence, that a Silvano would be the agent of my deliverance. I looked upon Gerardo Silvano with reverence and gratitude. Hearing now with greater clarity the divine peals that had accompanied me for almost two hundred years, I realized finally, at long last, what my strange life had been trying to teach me: God laughs not with cruelty, but with love. In even the worst of situations, God's grace is complete. It may not be easily articulated in the language of man, or apparent from the outside. It certainly isn't logical. But it can be felt, sensed, understood, in that larger, word-less part of the human soul that belongs to Him anyway. God is one, God is good, God is love, only love.

I STOOD IN THE PIAZZA DEL DUOMO with the shadow of Brunelleschi's incomparable dome falling over me. There was a red feather tied under my lucco. Gerardo had carefully instructed me in what I was to do, and I understood. I was eager, even. Lorenzo's son Giovanni, who was an impor-tant cardinal, was visiting Florence with members of the Inquisition. They would emerge from Santa Maria del Fiore after Mass. When they did, I would accost them.

The day was warm and breezy, one of those delightful Tuscan days when the sky soars up in endless spiraling scrims of azure and white and the contado around Florence bursts into the bright hues of spring flowers. I stood on a small wooden box, trembling with eagerness. I was clean and well fed and I wore a good silk lucco. My heart beat freely in an open chest, and I felt a delirious happiness. Soon I would join Maddalena. Soon my love would merge me with her and sweet Simonetta in the great river of love's beingness that was God. Congregants emerged from the immense cathedral, women in silk and velvet cottardite with their girlchildren clinging to their skirts, shopkeepers and wool-workers, a handful of mercenary soldiers, notaries and bankers and goldsmiths and blacksmiths and armorers and merchants and a few street urchins who sat in the back pews and then begged for coins at the end of the service, hoping Christian charity had been inspired by the Mass.

The gorgeously attired Giovanni, son of Lorenzo de' Medici, walked out of the cathedral. Prescient Leonardo had once told me that Giovanni would be Pope. All I saw was a tall, heavyset man with a pasty face, snub nose, and near-sighted squint. He looked like his Roman mother, Clarice. He moved slowly, surrounded by plainly dressed priests with serious faces who I knew were Inquisitors. Gerardo Silvano was among them, and I regarded him with affection.

"I am Luca Bastardo!" I yelled. People stopped and turned to face me, including the somber group with the cardinal. I cried, "I have lived over one hundred eighty years! I worship the Laughing God, and Him only! I am Luca Bastardo!"

EXCEPT THAT I MADE A SPECIFIC CHOICE, long ago during a night of alchemy and transformation, the story of my incarceration and torture is the same as that of any of thousands of other victims of the Inquisition. I was taken to a cell and questioned. Pope Innocent VIII had issued a papal bull against witchcraft in 1484, and the Dominicans main-tained a set of procedures for handling witches which they followed with precision and seriousness of purpose. I was stripped and shaved and examined for the marks of the devil. Nothing was found on my body, so two priests jabbed me all over with needles, looking for insensitive spots that would prove sorcerous invulnerability. There was some dis-cussion about whether to use the rack, which would have me tied across a board by wrists and ankles and then stretched until every one of my joints dislocated, or the *strappado,* which consisted of tying my arms together behind my back and securing the rope to a scaffold, then throwing me down off the scaffold repeatedly until my arms came out of their sockets and my shoulders dislocated. Gerardo Silvano favored using the *turcas* to tear out my fingernails, and then poking the quicks of my nails with heated needles. Giovanni, who came to watch for a while, grew impatient and had me horsewhipped: two hundred lashes. He didn't have the stomach for more and left when pincers glowed red in the fire and were deemed hot enough to burn me.

The end of the first day came, which was really the end of the second day, because I had been questioned through the night. Finally the Inquisitors tired of their sport and desisted. I wasn't much fun for them, anyway. I readily admitted to whatever they asked. Yes, I was a witch and a sorcerer; yes, I worshipped the devil; yes, I practiced necromancy; surely I drank the blood of Christian infants in a satanic ceremony that mocked the Holy Communion. I was thrown into a small cell, bleeding from the whip-welts all over my body, pus oozing from the burns. My left toes had been broken in a thumbscrew, my left ankle had been shattered by a hammer until the bone was mush and the skin was in tatters. I lay on the floor breathing hard, not caring about the tears dripping from my eyes. In fact, I felt lucky to still have my eyes. Gerardo had wanted them put out with a hot iron.

Time passed, a day, maybe two, while I was ignored. Water and moldy bread crusts were shoved through the bars of my door. Then I heard an urgent voice calling my name. "Luca, Luca mio!" Even through my pain I recognized Leonardo's musical voice. I pulled myself up painfully to sit with my back against the stone wall of my cell.

"Ragazzo mio, how are you?" I croaked.

"Better than you are," Leonardo said. He reached his arm through the bars of my cell to touch my head gently. His beautiful eyes filled with tears, his noble face twisted with grief. "I will do my best for you, caro. I will have Sforza send word to the Pope begging for your life, I will have rich noblemen intervene, anything!"

"How is it you're here?" I asked, blinking from the intensity of the pain, which came in vast palpitating waves.

"Filipepi sent a messenger to Milano when you were arrested. It took a few days for the messenger to find me. I came immediately. I bribed the jailer and priests to get in to see you. Oh, Luca, how could this have happened?" he murmured brokenly.

"I don't care." I sighed. "I don't want to live without Maddalena and Simonetta."

"Why didn't you send for me when they died?" he cried, agonized. "I would have been there to comfort you! I found out months after, and, by then, you had disappeared!"

"I went mad," I said softly, reaching to take his hand. "I've been waiting to be free so I could join them. I cursed my long life that kept me away from them."

"Life is no curse," he said, weeping. "And you're no witch, Luca. We must save you!"

"Why shouldn't I be a witch?" I asked. "I'm marked by this damned youthfulness that I've tried for so long to hide. Maybe the Dominicans are right, some evil sorcery keeps me unnaturally young, some evil magic that endangers the world."

"No! There's an explanation in nature for your life! Your organs and fluids regenerate, something! I don't know what it is now, but in the future, men of science would study you and discover how your anatomy functions!"

"Who knows, nature is capricious, maybe it took pleasure in creating someone like me." I shrugged. "Someone who lived longer than he ought, who lived too long. And 'too long' arrives for a man when his wife and child die."

He studied me for a moment, then nodded. "Maybe the Cathars were right, and your spirit has been imprisoned in your physical body. And nature wanted to watch it struggle with its longing to return to its Source."

"Now my spirit will be free." I smiled despite the pain. "They're burning me at the stake tomorrow."

THROUGH BRIBERY AND CAJOLERY, Leonardo received dispensation to bring me fresh clothes. He left and returned with clothes, with Petrarca's notebook, Geber's eyeglasses, and Giotto's panel, the latter two of which I bequeathed to him. He was distraught and didn't want to take them, but I pleaded. Finally he left, and as much as I love him, I was relieved to see him go. His sorrow weighed on me.

I set to work chronicling my life, not one moment of which I regret, despite my suffering now. I do not even regret the horrors I endured at Silvano's brothel because they made me yearn for love, to love. And I have loved Maddalena, so that is everything. That she loved me back was the grace of God. Some people go without such a love, and they seek the world over for a longevity like mine or for a wealth like the one I accumulated. They do not realize that the greatest treasure is that of the heart.

I have been writing through the night on the fine vellum pages of Petrarca's notebook. It is almost dawn of the day I will be led to the stake. I am sitting with my excoriated back against the stone walls of this cell. A pool of my own blood congeals around me.

There is a shuffling at the bars to my cell, and a brute of a guard looks in. "They've paid well to see you, witch, I hope you're worth it!" He spits at me and then stomps away. My eyes close as I wonder who could have come to see me during my penultimate indignity.

"Luca!" calls a brisk female voice. I look up, and a beautiful young woman with dark hair and intelligent violet-blue eyes stands at the bars. I stare at her, and then I recognize her as the woman who brought me bread as I sat by the river. At her side are a mature man and woman who look to be in their forties. They are fine-boned and handsome, well dressed in clothes that are not Florentine, and there are tears in their eyes. The woman has hair the color of mine, with some gray; the man's features are shaped like mine. I know who they are even before they speak, and I put my hands against the rough stone surface of the wall and struggle to my feet. I am weeping, but not from the terrible pain, which is much worse than anything I could have imagined, even when I lived at the brothel. I plead with myself, will myself, to stay conscious. Soon enough, the pain, and everything else, will be gone.

The older woman sobs as she reaches her hand through the bars. I lurch toward her on my broken and burned legs, fall most of the way, land on my knees, and cannot rise. "I'm sorry," I whisper.

"Please!" she says, and there is a soft accent in her voice. She kneels down, running her hand down along the bars, stretches mightily, and finally grasps my hand. "I am your mother."

"I am your father," says the man, with a catch in his throat. He kneels next to my mother, stretches his arm through, and grips my shoulder. Their touch is soft, kind, full of the tenderness I had always longed for and given up on ever knowing. I peruse them, and it gives me an incongruous happiness to see the similarities between us. God is kind to bring my origins to me when I am soon to come to my end.

"I have to know from your own lips," I croak. "I was stolen as a babe, wasn't I? You didn't cast me out into the street. And are you as different from other people as I am?"

Over the next hour, as the light brightens from indigo through lavender into gold, they tell me my story.

"We are the sons of Seth," my father says. His voice is grave and he doesn't take his strong, warm hands from my shoulder. "We trace our lineage directly back to Seth's descendants who did not perish in the Deluge. There are other families like ours. For a long time we lived side by side with ordinary mortals. Then they began to fear and threaten us, so we scattered and hid ourselves. Over the last few centuries we've come together again, and we've been gathering our strength, so that one day we can live openly again."

"Better days are coming," I say, knowing I won't live to see them.

My father nods. "It's been hard for us, though we've been protected for millennia by the Cathars, who conceal our secret."

"I heard stories about foreign nobles who had lost a son and who traveled in the company of Cathars," I say. "There was a letter about them."

"That was us, that foreign couple!" my mother cries. "You heard of us!"

"The original Cathars were cousins to Seth's sons, and have served us since the beginning times, which were far different from what history records," my father says. "Man's history on earth is unimaginably long and strange. People aren't yet ready to know the true history, how Gods came from the stars and mixed their seed with the primitive beings on earth to create the first humans. The first such man was Adam, and he had three sons. Seth's seed was mixed again with that of the Gods from the stars, creating our race. Other men fear us because of our gifts."

"We were all created by Gods from the stars," I say with wonder.

"We Sethians have been entrusted with secrets from those Gods, because we are most like them," my father continues. "At various points they return and we are in contact with them. Man's true history is full of these encounters, which kings and Popes have concealed, or passed off as visitations by angels. They did not want ordinary humans to know about man's true origins and the existence of a secret race of men. They feared this knowledge would destroy their authority, that it would destroy civic order and law, which, because of man's immaturity, depends on seeing God as a vengeful judge who lives outside them."

"I used to wonder about God's vengefulness," I remark. "Now I see that God is love, inside everything, within each of us."

"The Cathars know this, too, and tried to keep this knowledge alive in the world during times of ignorance and barbarism," my father answers.

"People say the Cathars have treasures that are coveted by those in power," I say.

"Treasures which we entrusted to them." My father nods. "For instance, the creators from the stars told us how to make the Ark of the Covenant, which we gave to the Cathars for safekeeping just before the sack of the Temple in Jerusalem. Then it was our turn to help them after the crusades. We hid them and helped them find hiding places for all the artifacts, relics, and documents that chronicle the true history. One day, in a few more centuries, we will reveal all of this, when we take our rightful place as guides and advisers to mankind."

"So where have you been before now?" I ask.

"We have been living in mountains far to the east of here. I am more than five hundred years old," my father says, gripping me more tightly.

"We were traveling. Your parents were in Avignon and I was in Florence, when I saw you by the river," says the young woman, my cousin Demetria. "What you said about being hungry two hundred years ago, your hair color, your features; I rode at once to get your parents!"

"You were stolen from your crib when you were not even three years old," my mother adds, anguished. Her hands stroke my arm, which lessens the agony in my body, as if she were giving me a consolamentum. It is not the consolamentum, but it is a soothing and maternal caress, and I feel lucky to know it now, when I need it most, and when the impact of meeting my mother is so great that it distracts me from the pain. She says, "I dismissed a nursemaid who wanted vengeance. We were living far from here, in a village near the Nile River. I searched everywhere, even here in Florence, I should have found you then! I have never stopped looking for you!"

"If not for an angry nursemaid, I would have had family and home," I say softly. A pang of sadness and regret and anger slices through me, and then the whole situation strikes me as funny. A common nursemaid, thwarting people gifted with the life span and hardiness of gods! I laugh, but only briefly, because even laughing hurts. "But I wouldn't change anything, because in living this life, I got to love Maddalena. That makes everything worthwhile."

"I would have liked to know your wife," my mother sobs. "And my granddaughter! I should have tried harder, searched different cities. There must have been something else, something more, I could have done to find you."

"I looked for you," I say softly. "I made inquiries and sent out agents."

"We hide ourselves very well," my father says. "We have to, else we are hunted and killed." He groans and pounds his forehead. "We never thought that you'd be looking for us!"

"I don't know how we can get him out," Demetria says. She is tall and slim and beautiful, with quick hands and an alert expression always on her face. She paces around the cell.

"It's too far gone," I say. "This is my fate. I'm going to join Maddalena. I'm ready."

My mother utters a sound like a bone breaking and huddles into Demetria.

"I can pay the executioner to snap your neck before the flames reach you, you don't have to suffer," says my father. His face is raw, his voice thick, and I know what it cost him to say that, because I, too, had a child. Perhaps it was easier for me because I didn't have to watch her die, as he will watch me. He grips my shoulder tightly, fiercely, as if he could pour himself into me and take my place at the stake. I wonder what it would have been like to have grown up knowing him, loved by him, sheltered by him. But I would not have met and loved Maddalena under those different, more fortunate circumstances. And she is all the meaning my soul has ever wanted, so I would not change anything about my life. Not the streets, not Silvano's brothel. Changing any step would alter the whole journey. At least I know in these final hours the closeness and warmth of a family— my family, who are like me, to whom I belong. I am no longer a freak, no longer an alien thing listening to God's spiteful giggles. I am a son, I belong, I am loved by my family and by God.

"Don't pay the executioner. I want to be alive when I die," I say with joy in my heart. "Then it will be a good death."

I am bound and gagged and led through scornful crowds to the Piazza della Signoria. There is a stake and a pile of kindling awaiting me, as there always has been. People beat on me, punch me, spit on me, even cut me with swords and throw slop on me, but I don't care. I can feel Maddalena nearby. I can smell her, sweet lilacs and lemons, as if she is walking next to me, and it makes me smile. I am tied to the stake, with the priest Gerardo Silvano hovering nearby, checking the chains around my feet and ankles. In the crowd I see Leonardo son of Ser Piero da Vinci, and he is weeping. He stands near Demetria, who has one of her lithe arms around each of my parents. They are weeping, too. I am sorry to see them so sad, though I know there is no sparing them. They don't yet behold God's perfection in every moment, even the ones, as Maddalena once told me, that wear cruel faces.

Then, through the crowd, a man makes his way. He is large and barrel-chested, with a thick wild beard and a shaggy mane of black-and-white hair. His eyes are fathomless wells of sorrow and emptiness, and something about them drains away my pain, which is a great relief to me. I nod my thanks to the Wanderer, and he nods back. He gestures and I see that with one of his gnarled hands he holds Maddalena's hand, and with the other, he holds Simonetta's. Maddalena's beautiful head is tilted back, her lovely face is serious and filled with grief. She does not like to see me suffer. In a tight group behind them stand Geber, Marco, Massimo, Giotto, Ginori, Ingrid, Moshe Sforno and beautiful Rachel, Petrarca, Cosimo de' Medici, all of the people I have loved, all of them present, all of them waiting. I shout aloud with joy and freedom, praising God. The executioner's fire leaps up to irradiate my body. I am standing in the heart of the sun. Everywhere there is light.

Acknowledgments

I would like to thank my wonderful editor at Bantam Dell, Caitlin Alexander, who is directly responsible for many of the strengths of this book. Her insightful editorial advice, which was so often brilliant, has shaped and guided this novel from the beginning.

I would like to thank Martha Millard for her hard work and enthusiasm for this work.

I would like to thank Matt Bialer for his support and good advice.

There are many people to whom I must express my love and gratitude for encouragement, support, and good advice along the way, including, but not limited to: Dani Antman, Thomas Ayers, Barbara, Stephen, Ali, Matt, and Tim Baldwin, Lynn Bell, Bill Benton, Adrienne Brodeur, Paul Brodeur, Kim Bunton, Felicia and Jeffrey Campbell, Silver Cho, Johanna Furus, Stuart Gartner, Dr. Henry Grayson, Dan Halpern, Rita and Myron Hendel, Harrison Howard, Geoffrey Knauth, Drew Lawrence, Rachel Leheny, Jennifer Weis Monsky, Matthew and Miyoko Olszewski, Chris Schelling, Ken

Skidmore, Komilla Sutton, Gerda Swearengen, Vincent Vichit-Vadakan, and Arthur Wooten. Thanks to Ronnie Smith, Barbara Pieroni, and the dedicated staff at Writer's Relief, Inc. I send love and gratitude to the splendid folk on the BBSH healers listserve. Lorine "Granny Bee" Adkerson and Judy Poff are always in my heart.

Professors Michael McVaugh and James Beck kindly answered questions. They are not responsible for any mistakes herein. Frederic Morton and Judy Sarafini Sauli helped with research materials; Wendy Brandes Kassan read a draft and offered comments. Thank you all!

I would like to thank my mother, Jo Slatton, who raised a reader, and who supports me with encouragement and the sage advice, "Writers write."

Without Jessica Hendel, this book would not exist. She read the first two chapters and said, "Write the rest, Mom. I have to know what happens to Luca!"

Naomi Hendel and Julia Howard have been tireless in their encouragement of my work. Madeleine Howard is a constant source of inspiration. And thank you to my husband, Sabin Howard, who owns every book imaginable on the Renaissance and who shares "Yes!" with me. Sabin is an extraordinary friend and support, and read every word of this novel at least five times.

Finally, I must acknowledge, with respect, Mr. Jon Hendel, who can rightly say "I called it first."

About the Author

TRACI L. SLATTON is a graduate of Yale and Columbia, and she also attended the Barbara Brennan School of Healing. She lives in Manhattan with her husband, sculptor Sabin Howard, whose classical figures and love for Renaissance Italy inspired her to write a novel set during that time period. *Immortal* is her first novel.